*Forthcoming in hardcover from DAW Books

http://www.cherryh.com/

C.J. CHERRYH
THE DREAMING TREE

BOOK ONE
THE DREAMSTONE

BOOK TWO
THE TREE OF SWORDS AND JEWELS

DAW BOOKS, INC.

DONALD A. WOLLHEIM, FOUNDER

375 Hudson Street, New York, NY 10014

ELIZABETH R. WOLLHEIM
SHEILA E. GILBERT
PUBLISHERS

CONTENTS

BOOK TWO

THE TREE OF SWORDS AND JEWELS

BOOK ONE

THE DREAMSTONE

ONE

OF FISH AND FIRE

Things there are in the world which have never loved Men, which have been in the world far longer than humankind, so that once when Men were newer on the earth and the woods were greater, there had been places a Man might walk where he might feel the age of the world on his shoulders. Forests grew in which the stillness was so great he could hear stirrings of a life no part of his own. There were brooks from which the magic had not gone, mountains which sang with voices, and sometimes a wind touched the back of his neck and lifted the hairs with the shiver of a presence at which a Man must never turn and stare.

But the noise of Men grew more and more insistent. Their trespasses became more bold. Death had come with them, and the knowledge of good and evil, and this was a power they had, both to be virtuous and to be blind.

Axes rang. Men built houses, and holds, rooted up stone, felled trees, made fields where forests had stood from the foundation of the world; and they brought bleating flocks to guard with dogs that had forgotten they were wolves. Men changed whatever they set hand to. They wrought their magic on beasts, to make them dull and patient. They brought fire and the reek of smoke to the dales. They brought lines and order to the curve of the hills. Most of all they brought the chill of iron, to sweep away the ancient shadows.

But they took the brightness too. It was inevitable, because that brightness was measured against that dark. Men piled stone on stone and made warm homes, and tamed some humbler, quieter things, but the darkest burrowed deep and the brightest went away, heartbroken.

Save one, whose patience or whose pride was more than all the rest.

So one place, one untouched place in all the world remained, a rather smallish forest near the sea and near humankind, keeping a time different than elsewhere.

Somewhen this forest had ceased to be a lovely place. Thorns choked it, beyond its fringe of bracken. Dead trees lay unhewn by any woodman, for none would venture there. It was a perilous place by day. By night it felt far worse, and a man did well not to build a fire too near the aged trees. Things whispered here, and the trees muttered with the wind and perhaps with other things. Men knew the place was old, old as the world, and they never made peace with it.

But on a certain night a man was weary, and he had seen very much of horror and of the world's hard places, so that a little fire to cook by seemed a very small hazard against others he had run this day, the matter of a few twigs to cook a bit to eat.

He had come and gone a great deal on the banks of the river Caerbourne and in the fringes of this forest, for five whole years. If there were outlaws hereabouts he knew them all by name. And if there were other dangers he had never met them, so they failed to frighten him, this night, and on other nights when he had come this far beneath the aged boughs and heard the rustlings and the whisperings of the leaves. He made his little fire and cooked his fish and ate it, which seemed to him like a feast after his famine of recent days. He felt home again; he felt safe; he looked forward to a bed among the leaves where no two-legged enemy would be likely to come on him.

But Arafel had noticed him.

She had little interest in the doings of Men in general. Her time and her living were very much different from the years of humankind, but she had seen this Man before as he slipped about the margins of her wood. He was deft about it and did no harm, and he was wary and hard for harm to come to: such a Man never quite disturbed her peace.

But this night he took a fish from the Caerbourne's stream and built a fire to cook it, beneath an ancient oak. And this was far too great a familiarity.

So she came. She stood watching for a while unnoticed in her gray hooded cloak, in the shadows among the oaks. The Man had had his fish, leaving only the naked bones in the fire, and now knelt, cherishing the warmth of the tiny flame and heap of ash, cupping his hands close above it. He was rough-looking, with a weathered countenance and gray-streaked hair—a lean and weary Man with the taint of iron about his person, for a sword lay close beside his knee. She had been apt to anger when she came, but he sat so small and quiet for so tall a Man, clinging to so small a warmth in the great dark of the wood, that she wondered at him, how he had come, or why, presuming so much for so little comfort. She was not the first to come. The shadows moved beyond his little fire and hissed in indignation. He never seemed to notice, deaf to them and blinded by the light he clung to.

"You should take more care," she said.

He snatched at his great sword and came to one knee all in one motion.

"No," she said quietly, moving forward. "No, I am quite alone coming here. I saw your fire."

The sword stayed half-drawn across his knee. He had heard nothing, seen nothing until now. A gray-mantled figure showed like a trick of moonlight in the thicket, so dim even the tiny fire might have blinded his eyes, but he had no excuse at all for his ears. "Who are you?" he asked. "Of An Beag, would you be?"

"No. Of this place. I rarely stir out of it. Put the sword away."

He was off his balance and not accustomed to that. Why he was sitting still at all instead of standing sword in hand was not quite clear to him, only that there had never seemed a moment of clear decision since the stranger started speaking. The voice was smooth and fair. He could not get the timbre of it in his mind, whether it was young or old or what it was even when it was just dying in the air, no more than he could make out the figure in the dark, but he found he had slid the sword back into its sheath, not having clearly decided to put it back at all. His hands were cold. "Share if you like," he said, with a motion toward the fire. "The warmth, at least. If it's food you want, catch your own. I've eaten all I had."

"I have no need." The stranger came nearer, so silently no leaf whispered, and settled at the side of the tiny clearing on the dead log that fended the wind from his fire. "What would your name be?"

"Give me yours," he said.

"I have many."

Little by little the chill of the ground had come creeping up to him, and now the fire between them seemed all too dim and small. "And what would one of them be?" he asked, because he was always a man to want answers even when they were ill.

"I have marked your coming and going hereabouts." The answer came so still and soft the rustle of a leaf might have overcome it. "Other things have seen you, do you not know? Your step was always soft and quick until tonight; but now you settle in to stay—is that your hope? No, I think not. I do think not. You are wiser than that."

She saw the hardness of his face as he stared at her. It was a face which might well have been fair once, but years and scars had marred it; and sun and wind had weathered it, so that it was fit for the rest of him, with ragged hair and ragged clothes and dark, hopeless eyes. As for him, there was no knowing what he saw of her: Men saw what they pleased to see, often as not. Perhaps to him she was some outlaw like himself or some great mail-clad warrior from over the river. His hand never let go the sword.

"Why do you come?" she asked him last.

"For shelter."

"What, in *my* wood?"

"Then I will leave your wood, as quickly as I may."

"There is harm outside this circle—No, it would not

be well to look just now. As for the fish and the fire, both are costly. And what will you offer me for them?"

He gave no answer. If there was any wealth he had besides the sword itself she could not tell it. And that he did not offer.

"What," she said, "nothing?"

"What will you have?" he asked.

"Truth. For the fish and the fire tell me truly what you do in my woods."

"I live."

"No more than that? It seems to be a hard living. There's a sorrow about you, Man. Is there ever joy?"

This was baiting. The Man felt it, and felt his weariness hovering over him like urging sleep. There was peril in that sleep, and that he also knew. He set the cap of his sheathed sword on the ground and leaned heavily on it, looking at the stranger, trying to look more closely, but his sight seemed to dim whenever he looked hardest, and some fold of the cloak was always casting a shifting shadow just where he looked, so that he could see nothing that was beneath it. He knew beyond a doubt that he had met one of the fair folk, and he knew it though the moment was moonbeams and shadows and something his eyes refused to see. He had never expected such a meeting in his life, being occupied with his own business, but he knew it when it was on him and understood his danger, that the fair folk were fell and deadly with trespassers, and given to dark mischief. But perhaps it was part of the binding on him that he felt no reticence at all with this stranger, as if it were the last night of the world and the last friend had come to listen. "I have come here," he said, "sometimes. It seemed safe. I brought no enemy here. An Beag would never follow."

"Why do they hunt you?"

"I am a King's man."

"And they have some quarrel with this King?"

The voice seemed innocent, fair as a child's. The years went reeling back and back for him and he leaned the more heavily on the hilt of his sword, aching in all his bones, and laughed. "Quarrel, aye. They killed the King at Aescford, burned Dun na h-Eoin—now there is no king at all. Five years gone—" He grew hoarse in telling it. It was incredible to him that all the world was not shaken by that fall, but the figure before him stayed unmoved.

"Wars of Men. They are nothing to me. The fish matters. That touches my boundaries."

A chill wandered up his back, but dimly through his remembered grief. "So, but I gave you the truth for it."

"That was the price I named. Now I give you good advice: Do not come again." The shadow rose, graying into dark. "This once I will guide you to the river, but only once."

He leaned on the sword and levered himself to his feet as if it were the last strength he had; and perhaps it was. His shoulders were bowed. His head was down for the moment, but then it lifted, and he pointed another way with a straightening of his shoulders. "Give me leave to go along the shore. A mile or so down the river I can slip my enemies and I will go as quickly as I can."

"No. You must go as you came, and now."

"So," he said, and bent and patiently covered up his fire, then took up his sword, half drawing it although in his eyes was no hope at all. "But my enemies are waiting there, and whatever you are, I will make a beginning here if I have no choice. I ask you again—let me pass along the shore. I was always a good neighbor to this wood. I never set axe to it. I beg your courtesy this once. It is so small a thing."

She considered him, so soft-spoken, so set upon his way. Almost she went fading back again and leaving this Man to the dark and the night. But there was no dark anger in him, only the sadness of something brave that once had been. So the old stag died, among the wolves; or the eagle fell; or the wolf himself went down. She thought a moment and, thinking on such a heart, remembered a place, a small place, the only warmth she knew among humankind.

"I shall tell you a way to go," she said gently, "and help you come to it if perhaps you can, a place deep in the hills and not so perilous as my lands. But you must come with me now step for step and never stray: Death has been very near to you tonight. He is very skillful at stalking, more than any Man. No, never look. Come now, come, put away the sword and follow. Follow me."

A second time he slid the sword back into its sheath and never felt the doing of it; he walked as once he had walked after bloody Aescford, out of the hills, aware first of fending branches from his face and then that he had come some distance never remembering any of it; and lastly that he was lost. He was well-schooled in woodcraft and no man could have eluded him so close at hand, but the gray cloak melted through the thickets before him as if the branches had no substance, and though he went as quickly as he could, he could never come near his guide. He was panting, and his heart labored with a beating he could hear, so loud it dimmed all other sounds. Branches raked his face and arms. Leaves whipped past with a soft and clinging touch.

But at last the stranger waited for him on the river bank, standing against a very aged tree, so that the gray cloak might have been part of the bark in the moonlight. They had come to the widest part of the Caerbourne, where it flowed most shallowly: he knew every stone along the shore.

And his guide pointed him the way across.

"This is the ford," he objected. "And they will be watching it."

"They are not. Not this while. Perhaps not again for several nights—trust me that I know. Yonder you see the hills, and atop the first hill is a cairn; and beneath the second as you follow the river course from the narrows below the cairn, there go up the dale and up the farther hill. The place I send you, you will never see it, except you come up the dell and over against the shoulder of the Raven's Hill . . . do they call it that, these days?"

"That is still the name." He looked toward the shadowy line of hills beyond the river, beyond the trees. The river water danced with a light that broke beside him. He turned his head in alarm toward his companion. There was no one there, as if there had never been, only the fading memory of a voice of a high, fair tone, as he had never heard it, and the recollection of a light he had almost seen.

The world seemed dark then, and cold, and the shadows full of menace.

"Are you there?" he asked the dark, but nothing answered.

He shivered then, and slinging his sword at his back, waded the Caerbourne's chill flood up to his waist, constantly expecting arrows from out of the dark trees on the other side, ambush and after all, the chill laughter of the fair folk at his back. There was no luck in faery-gifts. He doubted all his safety now, forever.

But nothing started on that shore except a small splash that swam away into the reeds, and he climbed out again on the side of the river his enemies held, finding no one watching, and no harm near him. He began at once to run to keep the warmth in his legs, dodging along among the few young trees which grew on the naked borders of An Beag and its villages.

He was Niall, lately called Dubhlachan and formerly other names, who had been a lord in years gone by; but the King he served now was a helpless babe hidden somewhere in the hills—so loyal hearts believed. And the loyal men lived and harried the traitors' fields in Caerbourne vale and elsewhere as they could, which was all they could do till the young King should live to be a man.

Five years Niall had lived in the forest edges, under stone and hidden in thickets, and men had followed him, but most were dead and the rest now scattered.

So he ran, ran at last because the sun was coming, and ran because a dream in the dark wood had promised safety. He was not young any longer. He had lost all his faith in kings to come. It was only a fireside he wanted, and bread to eat, and no more hunt at his heels.

The sun came up on him and still he ran by turns, coming up into the Brown Hills. Men called them haunted, like the wood. But he had long had the habit of such places, where no comfortable men would go. The rumor only gave him hope, more and more as he came among the hills. Weariness left him, so that he ran more lightly than he had run before, through the rough stones and the desolation. The sun was on him. The sweat ran. He heard his steps fall and jar the stones together, but nothing more in all the world, as if some veil lay on his senses and the world had stopped being what it was. If the forest had been dark, this was bright, and the sun danced here, and the stones shone in the light.

He reached the Raven's Hill and climbed. A strangeness glistened under the nooning sun, under the shoulder of the opposing hill. And so he ran, ran, ran, with a great expectation in his heart, and if he began to die in that running, still he drove himself with the hope of something, some barrier to cross, some place one only got to by chance or luck or the last hope in all the world.

It was a homely place, of fields and fences, stone and golden thatch and a crooked chimney, and the smell of bread baking, and the sun shining on the barley round about and on the dust.

"Come see, come see!" he heard someone call as he fell to his knees and full length on the ground. "O come! here's a man come fallen in the yard!"

TWO

BEORC'S STEADING

The sweat ran in rivulets on Niall's back, and it was a good feeling, swinging a mallet and not a sword, driving the pegs in just so, to mend the grain-bin before the new harvest came in, the fields standing golden white in the sun.

A dour-faced boy brought him water; he dipped up enough to drink and poured the rest over his head, blinking in the stream, and the boy Scaga took the dipper back and sulked off about his rounds, but that was ever Scaga's manner and no one minded. Birds lighted on the fencepost when the boy had gone, cocked wise eyes at Niall, darted down to peck a bit of grain from the dust as he turned back to work again. Dinner was foremost in his mind, one of Aelfraeda's fine hearty dinners set beneath the evening sky as they ate in summertime, beneath the spreading oak that shaded the Steading; some would sing and some would listen, and so the stars would light them to bed until the sun waked them out of it.

That was the way of the days at Beorc's Steading, and Beorc himself ordered matters in all this wide farm so that no days were idle and everything was done in its season, like the mending before the harvest. There were full two score hands to work, men and women and children. The fields were wide, and the orchards likewise, and the sheep grazed the hill by the spring while the cattle and the pony pastured down by the tiny brook it made. There gnarled willows shaded time-rounded stones and a child could wade most of it. Closer, where the brook came nearest the barn, lived a herd of fat pigs and a flock of geese as fat as the pigs and noisier, who bullied their way about the farm. But also about the hillside there was a wolf, a well-fed and lazy cub who liked ear-scratching; and a fawn who strayed in and nosed her way everywhere. A badger had his hole in the hollow next to the turnip field; and a host of birds lived round about, from the heron who lived on the brook to the family of owls who lived in the barn. They were all lostlings. They had all come like the cub and the fawn and fallen under the peace Aelfraeda maintained. There was such a spell on them they never preyed on each other, except the heron fished the brook and the owls had the barn mice who minded no laws at all.

This extended to the two-footed kind—for they all had come, excepting Beorc and Aelfraeda themselves, as lostlings themselves, both old and young, and none were kin at all. There was old grandfather Sgeulaiche, as wizened and withered as last winter's apple, whose hands and clever blade turned out the most marvelous things of wood, who sat on the porch in a pool of sweet smelling curls of wood and told stories to whatever girl or boy who was set to work the churn or card the wool—for there were children here, half a dozen of them, no one's and everyone's, like the fawn. There was of course half-grown Scaga, who pilfered food at every chance and hid it, though Aelfraeda would have given him both hands full of anything he asked—he fears being hungry, Aelfraeda said; so, let him hide all he will, and eat all he can—someday he will smile. There was Haesel hardly six and Holen more than twelve; and Siobrach and Eadwulf and Cinhil in between. Of adults there was Siolta, who was lame and in middle years, who baked and made wonderful cheeses, and there was Lonn who had a great swordcut running from brow to chin and many others beside, but his hands were sure and good with the cattle; Siolta and Lonn were man and wife, though never they had known each other before this place. There was Conmhaighe and Carraig and Cinnfhail and Flann; and Diomasach, Diarmaid and the other Diarmaid; and Ruadh; and Fitheach and the other men and women, so that there were never workers lacking for the hardest

tasks inside the house or out, besides Beorc and Aelfraeda themselves, who were wherever work wanted
doing, cheerful and foremost in any task.

In all, the weather blessed the place and the grain
grew tall and the green apples grew round and fine; and
the brook never failed in summer. There was a haze of
light about the hills by daylight, so that it made the eyes
sting to try to look into the distance of the Brown Hills;
and the mountain shoulder lay between the Steading and
the river away to the south, and between it and the
harrying of An Beag and other names which seemed a
dream here.

"Do you not set a guard?" Niall had asked of Beorc
early, while they had tended him in the house and fed
him until he was less gaunt than before. "Do you not
have men to watch the way to this place? I would do
that. Weapons are what I know."

But, "No," Beorc had said, and his face, broad and
plain and ruddy, had creased with laughter. "No. You
had luck to come here. Few are lucky, and them I welcome. So there is a great deal of luck on this valley of
mine. If you will stay, stay; if you will go, I will show
you a way to go, but if you turned around again after,
I do not think your luck would find the place a second
time."

Then Niall said nothing more of boundaries and borders, perceiving some force in Beorc that kept its own
limits and expected everything about him to do likewise.
He is, Niall had thought then with a queer kind of shiver,
more like a king than not. And king did not fit Beorc
either, with his wispy nimbus of gray-red hair, his cheeks
wind-burned above a beard as wild and lawless as his
mane. Like a fire he was, a gust of wind, a great broad
man who laughed much and kept his own counsels; and
Aelfraeda was like him and unlike, a woman of strong
hands and ample girth and beautiful golden braids coiled
crownlike about her head, who carried her own milk-
pails, thank you, and wove and spun and fed strays both
two and four-footed, having the law in her house and
for her scepter a wooden spoon.

It was a place that luck smiled on, and in which more
than a usual share of amazing things happened: for
weeds that happened into the crops turned up in the

morning wilted and limp beside the rows, so that hardly ever did one have to take a hoe to the vegetables; and if some few vegetables vanished in the same night, no one spoke of it. Tools one would have sworn were lost turned up found in the morning on the porch, fit to set a shiver up a less complacent spine. Likewise the panni-kin of milk and the buttered cakes Aelfraeda faithfully set out each night on the bench on the porch turned up missing, each and every crumb, which might have been the wolf cub's doing or the fawn's, or the geese, but Niall never spied the cakes vanishing and had no wish to go out of nights to see.

And most peculiar, there was the brown man, or so Niall called him, skulking here and there in the orchards, or among the rocks, fit to account for a great deal that was odd hereabouts. "He is very old," said Beorc when Niall reported it. "Never trouble him."

Old he might be, Niall suspected, old as stone and hills and all, for there was something uncanny about him and bespelled. Nothing could move so quickly, coming into the tail of the eye and out again, and skipping away among the rocks. There he sat now, a small brown lump by the barn, barefoot, knees tucked up in arms, and watching, watching the mending of the bin. He was wrin-kled as an old man and agile as any child; and his brown hair fell down about his hairy arms and his beard sprayed about his bare and well-thatched chest. His oversized hands and feet were furred just the same. Brown as a nut and no taller than a half-grown boy, with hair wellshot with gray and usually flecked with wisps of straw, he hung about the barn and nipped apples from the barrel and sometimes sat on the pony's back in the stall, feeding him with good apples too.

And this brown man had a way about him of being there one moment and elsewhere in the next, so that when Niall cast him a second look round the corner of the shed he was gone.

On that same instant something prickled his bare back and he spun about with an oath and almost a sweep of the hammer. As quickly as he spun a shadow dived in the corner of his eye and he kept spinning, following it as it nabbed a fistful of grain from the bin; but it was gone, quick as he could turn, and round the corner of the shed. "Hey!" he cried, and hurled himself round the corner, but it was gone a second time, a wisp of brown headed around the corner.

Once he had followed it: he knew better now. It had led him over fences and stones and over the brook and back again. Now he dived back again around the corner and caught it coming round behind him. He flung the mallet, not to hit it, but to scare it.

It screamed and tucked down instead of running. It kept tucked down, its face in its hairy hands, and peered out quickly to see if another mallet was coming.

"Here now," Niall said. "Here." He was suddenly in the wrong and hoping no one had seen.

It ventured another eye above its hands, then spat and scampered off on its short legs.

"Perish it," Niall muttered to himself, and then wished he had not said that either. Nothing went well this day. He left his pegs and his mallet and followed it to the barn and inside.

Straw showered down his neck. "Plague on you," he cried, but it went scampering through the rafters disturbing the owls in a flapping of wings. "Come back!"

But it was gone and out the door.

"Do not try."

It was Beorc who had come in behind him, and shame flooded Niall's face. He was not accustomed to be made sport of or to be caught in the wrong either. "I would not have hit him."

"No, but you hurt his pride."

A moment Niall was silent. "What will mend it?"

"Be kind," said Beorc. "Only be kind."

"Call him back," said Niall in sudden despair.

"That I cannot. He is the Gruagach and no one has the calling of him: he will never tell his name."

Niall shivered then, for his luck seemed to have left him. It will end now, he thought, for frightening one of the fair folk; he remembered how he had come to the Steading, and how it needed luck to find the place and needed luck to stay.

That night he had no appetite, and set his dinner on the porch beside the platter Aelfraeda set out; but in the morning Aelfraeda's gift was taken and his was left.

Yet there was no certain turning in his luck, except that now and again he had straw dumped on his head when he went into the barn and now and again his tools vanished when his back was turned, to appear on their pegs in the barn when he came hunting others.

All this he bore with patience unlike himself, even setting an especially fine apple out where the theft was returned—which gift vanished: but so, daily, did his tools. All the same he taught himself to smile about it, concealing his misfortune and making little of it, no matter how long the walk.

So great a patience did he achieve that it even extended to the boy Scaga's thefts, so that one day when he came on the boy pilfering his lunch in the field, he only stood there, and Scaga looked up with his eyes all round with startlement.

Niall had a mallet in his hand this day too, but he kept it in his hand. "Will you not leave a morsel?" he asked. "I've been hard at my work."

The boy looked at him, down on his haunches as he was and ill-set for running. And he set the basket down.

"Will you have half?" Niall asked the boy. "I'd like the company."

"There's not much," the red-haired rascal said, looking doubtfully under the napkin.

"There's always enough to give half of," Niall said, and did.

It was a silent lunch. Scaga stole from others after, but never from him. And sometimes his tools came back on Scaga's quick legs before he missed them.

One day about that time the Gruagach came and sat and watched him, and he spied it looking round the corner of the barn at him.

"Here," he said, his heart lifting at this approach. He offered a handful from the bin. "Here's grain. I've a bit of bread about me if you like. Good cheese." The head vanished before the words had left his mouth. But it lurked about and looked at him and stole his tools only now and again, just to remind him.

His luck lasted, and the days rolled on, from summer heat to harvest: the fawn grew gangling and the wolf cub yelped at the moon of nights; and the sickles turned up sharpened on their *beorc* each harvest morning.

But one nooning a man came stumbling up the valley from the south, off the shoulder of Raven's Hill, startling the geese.

Niall came as all the house came running. The man had fallen trying to cross the fence, a bony huddle of limbs and weapons, for he carried a bow and an empty quiver, a sword at his side. Lonn had caught him up and held him, and so Niall came, and stopped and fell to his knees in dismay, because he knew this man. "His name is Caoimhin," Niall said. A fear had come on him as if all his safety wavered. For the briefest moment he looked beyond the fences, where the folding hills trapped his sight, half-expecting to see pursuit coming hard on Caoimh's heels. But then he felt a hand close on his and looked down in shame.

"Lord," Caoimhin said, and his hand trembled in its grip on his, Caoimhin, best of bowmen they had had. "O my lord, we heard that you were dead."

"No," said Niall, "hush, be still, lean on me: I'll help you walk."

Caoimhin let him lift him up, trusting only him, clinging most to him and leaning on him, so with Beorc and Lonn and Flann and Carraig and all the troop they brought him into the yard, and so into the house and Aelfraeda's care, than which there was none better.

It was broth that day and bread and butter, but Caoimhin limped as far as the porch in the evening, and then to the yard where the table groaned with food beneath the oak, and the harvesters came singing home. Having gotten that far he only stared with that far lost look of a man too hard for tears, but Niall came to rescue him and Beorc clapped him heartily on the shoulder and called for a cup of ale for him, and another plate at table.

"Here," Niall bade Caoimhin quickly, and gave up his own seat until everyone rearranged themselves and Si-olta brought a dish and cup for him. "He is Caoimhin," Beorc said, lifting his cup to him. So they all did, and fell to one of Aelfraeda's grand good meals.

Caoimhin tried, a bit of this and that, but his hands shook and at last he sat there with the tears running down his face and a bit of bread in his hand. But Niall put his arm about him and held him in his place, he was so weak, and if the company grew quiet a moment, they understood and the merriment picked up again. "What is this place?" Caoimhin asked when he had had a sip of ale.

"Refuge," said Niall. "And safety. A place where ill has never been. And never shall."

"Are we dead then?"

"No," Niall laughed. "Never dead."

But a niggling fear was on him. He even wished Caoimhin had never come, because this man reminded him what he had been, and brought the stink of death about him. More, he was afraid for the peace of all this place, as if it had taken some great danger to its heart.

Caoimhin lay about the house the next few days, or rested on the porch in the sunlight and the breeze, and slept much and drank and ate wholesome food when he waked, so that his face looked less haggard and less desperate.

In those first days he wanted at least his sword by him and kept it by him even napping in the sun. And ever and again his hand would stray to find it in his sleep, and his fingers curl about the sheath or hilt, so his face would lose its moment's trouble and he would rest again. But on the third day he let it go; and the fourth he walked out of the house and left it behind, beside the hearth with his bow and his empty quiver. So he sat with old Sgeulaiche on the porch and finally strolled about the yard and out to the threshing.

There Niall saw him and wiped the sweat and the dust from his brow and came over to him.

"What," Niall said lightly, "does Aelfraeda know you've strayed?"

"By your leave—"

Niall's brows drew down. "No. Not mine. Not here."

"My lord—"

"No lord, I say. No longer—Caoimhin." He clapped him gently on the shoulder. "Come aside with me."

Caoimhin walked with him, as far as the barn and into the shadow inside, and there Niall stopped. "There is no lord in the Steading," Niall said at once, "if not Beorc himself; no lady if not Aelfraeda. And that is well enough with me. Forget my name."

"I have rested. I am well enough to go back again—I will bring you word again. There are men of ours in the hills—"

"No. No. If you leave this place I do not think you will find it again."

The eagerness died in Caoimhin's lean face. From toe to crown Caoimhin looked at him and seemed to doubt what he saw as if it were his first clear look. "You have got calluses on your hands and not from the sword, my lord. There is straw in your hair. You do a farmer's work."

"I do it well. And I have more joy of it than anything ever I did. And I will tell you there is more good in it than ever I have hoped to do. Caoimhin, Caoimhin, you will see. You will see what this place is."

"It has cast a spell on you, that much I see. The King—"

"The King." A shudder came over Niall and he turned away. "My King is dead; the other—who knows? Who knows if he even exists? I saw my King dead. The other I never saw. A babe smuggled away at night—and who knows whose babe? Some serving maid's? Some beggar's child? Or any child at all."

"I have seen him!"

"So you have seen him. And what proof is that? Any child, I say."

"A boy—a fair blond boy. Laochailan son of Ruaidhrigh, like him as a boy could be. He has five years now. Taithleach keeps him safe—would you doubt *his* word?—always on the move through the hills, so that the traitors will never find him, and they need you now—They need you, Niall Cearbhallain."

"A boy." Niall sat down on the grain bin and looked up at Caoimhin with the taste of ashes in his mouth. "And what am I, Caoimhin? I was forty and two when I began to serve this hope of a king to come; and my joints ache, Caoimhin, with five years' sleeping under tree and stone. And if this boy ever comes to take Dun na h-Eoin—look at me. Twenty years it will need to make a boy a man; and how many more to make that man a king? Am I likely to see it done?"

"So, well—and who of the men dead on Aescford field will ever see him king? Or shall I? Or shall I? I do not know. But I do what I can as we always did. Where is your heart, Cearbhallain?"

"Broken. Long ago. I will hear no more of it. *No more.* You'll go or you'll stay as you wish, when you can. But stay for now. Rest. Only a little time. And see what things are here. O Caoimhin—leave me my peace."

A long time Caoimhin was silent, looking desolate and lost.

"Peace," Niall repeated. "Our war is done. There is the harvest; the apples are ripening; there'll be the long wintertime. And no need of swords and no help at all we can be. It's all for younger men. If there's to be a king, he will be theirs, not ours. If we have begun, others will finish. And is that not the way of things?"

"Lord," Caoimhin whispered softly; and then a sudden alarm came into his eyes at a quiet scurrying, a shadow by the door. Caoimhin sprang and hit the door and hurled the listener in the dust. "Here are spies," Caoimhin cried, and nabbed the brown man by the hair and hauled him back struggling and gasping as he was and slammed the door.

"Let it go," Niall said at once, "let it go."

Caoimhin had a look at it and flung his right hand back with an oath and an outcry, for it bit him and scratched and clawed, but he held it with the left. "This is no man, this—"

"Gruagach is his name," Niall said, and took Caoimhin's hand from the brown man. The creature hugged Niall's arm and danced behind him and fled, peering out again from the refuge of a pile of hay, with straw and dust clinging all over its hair.

"Wicked, wicked," it said, a voice as slight as itself, that lifted the hairs on a man's neck.

"He will never hurt you," Niall promised it. Never had he heard it speak, though others said it could. "Open the door, Caoimhin—open it! Let it go!"

Carefully Caoimhin pushed at the door and light flooded in. The Gruagach stirred himself and sidled that way, closer than ever Niall had seen him clearly, face seamed and brown and bearded, eyes lightless as deep water peering out from under matted hair. It looked up at him and bobbed as if it bowed on its thick legs. And then it fled, scuttling out as quick as the breeze, and was gone.

Then Niall looked toward Caoimhin, and saw the dread there, and all the surmise. "There is no harm in it."

"Is there none?" Caoimhin leaned against the door. "Now I know where the cakes go at night, and what the luck is in this place. Come away, Cearbhallain, come *now*."

"I will never go. No. You do not know—the way of this place. Come, a bargain with me—only a little time. You would always take my word. Stay. You can always leave—but you will never find the way back again. Was it ill luck brought you here? Tell me that. Or tell me whether you would be breathing the air this morning or eating a good breakfast and looking forward to dinner. There's no dishonor in being alive. It's not our war any longer. It was our luck that brought us here; it was— perhaps something won. I think so. Think on it, Caoimhin. And stay."

A long time Caoimhin reflected on it, and at last looked at the ground and at last looked at him. "There's autumn ahead," Caoimhin said, weakening.

"And winter. There is winter, Caoimhin."

"Till the spring," Caoimhin said. "In the spring I'll go."

The apples went into the bins; the sausages went to smoke; the oak tree shed his leaves and deep snow drifted down. The Gruagach sat on the roof by the chimney and left prints by the step where the cakes and mulled ale disappeared; and of nights he kept the pony and the oxen company.

"Tell us tales," young Scaga said, as all the household sat about the fire. Marvelous to say, Scaga had taken to making the pony's mash this winter without being asked; and never a thing had been missed about the house since summer. He had, from being last and least, become a thoughtful if sober lad, and attached himself to Niall's side and by adoption, to Caoimhin's as well.

So Caoimhin told of a winter on the Daur and a storm that had cracked old trees; and Sgeulaiche recalled being

lost in such a storm. And after, when the whole house
curled up to sleep each in their warm nooks, and Beorc
and Aelfraeda in their great close-bed in the loft: "It is
a young man's winter," Caoimhin said to Niall whose
pallet was near his.

"A young man's war," said Niall.

"They have taken your lands," Caoimhin said, "and
mine."

A long time Niall was silent. "I have no heir. Nor ever
shall, most likely."

"As for that—" Now the silence was on Caoimhin's
side, a very long time. "As for that, well, that is for
young men too. Like the winter. Like the war."

And after that Caoimhin said nothing. But in the
morning a lightness was on him, as if some weight had
passed.

He will stay, Niall thought, taking in his breath. At
least one man of all that followed me. And then he put
that prideful thought away, along with *my lord* and *Cearbhallain* and bundled himself into warm clothes, for
there was winter's work to do, the beasts to care for.
The children fought snowball battles; Caoimhin joined
in, stalking with Scaga round the barn. Niall saw the
stealth, the skill that Caoimhin taught the boy. A moment the chill got through: but they were only snowballs,
and the squeals and shouts were only children's laughter.

The Gruagach perched on the roof, and let fall a double armful and laughed and ran.

"Ha," it cried, going over the rooftree. "Ha! Wicked!"

"Wither it!" cried Caoimhin, but the ambush was
sprung and the battle lost in pelting snowballs.

A moment Niall watched, and turned away, hearing
still the squeals and hearing something else. He turned
and looked back to prove to his ears and eyes what it
was he heard, and succeeded, and went his way.

THREE

THE HARPER

The harvest had come again. The scythes went back and forth and left stubble in their wake. By morning the sheaves appeared all in rows, neatly tied; so the Gruagach slept a mighty sleep by day, and ate and ate. A pair of fawns had come this year, a fledgling falcon, a bittern, a trio of fox kits and a starved and arrow-shot piebald mare: such were the fugitives the Steading gathered. Now the falcon was flown, and the bittern too; the fox kits instead of tumbling about the porch were beginning to stray toward the margins of the Steading, going the way of the wolf; and the mare had become fast friends with the Steading's own pony, grown fat and sleek on sweet grass and grain. The children were delighted with her and hung garlands about her neck which she contrived to slip and eat often as not: she ate and ate, and began to frisk about at daybreak as if it were the morning of the world and no war had ever been.

So here is another fled from the madness, Niall thought to himself, and loved the mare for her courage in living. He rode at times bareback and reinless when he had leisure, letting her go where she would through the pastures and the hills. He loved the feeling of riding again, and the mare swished her tail and cantered at times for the joy of it, going where she pleased, from rich pasture to cool brook to hillsides in the sunlight, or home again to stable and grain. Banain, he called her, his fair darling. She would bear him of her own will, or any of the children, or the Gruagach who whispered to

her in a way that horses understood. Sometimes she was
willing to be bridled and Caoimhin rode when the mood
came on him, and others did, but rarely and not so well
and not so far, for, as Caoimhin said, she has one love
and none of us can win her.

So this year had been even kinder than the first to
him. But the year was not done with arrivals.

This last one came singing, blithe as brazen, down the
dusty margin of the fields, along the track the cattle took
to pasture, a youth, a vagabond with a sack on his back
and a staff in his hand and no weapon but a dagger. His
hair was blond to whiteness, and blew about his shoulders to the time of his walking and the whim of the
breeze.

> *Hey,* he sang, *the winds do blow,*
> *And ho, the leaves are dying,*
> *And season doth to season go*
> *The summer swiftly flying.*

Niall was one that saw this apparition. He was mending fences, and Beorc was near him, with Caoimhin and
Lonn and Scaga. "Look," said Caoimhin, and look they
did, and looked at Beorc. Beorc stopped his work and
with hands on hips watched the lad coming so merrily
down the far hillside, Beorc seeming less perplexed
than solemn.

"Here's one come walking where he knows not," Niall
said. In a furtive smallness of his heart it disturbed him
that anyone could come less desperate than himself, than
Caoimhin wounded, than half-starved Banain or the
grounded falcon. It upset all his world that this place
could be gained so casually, by simple accident. And
then he thought again on the meanness of that; and a
third time that it was less than likely.

"It be one of the fair folk," said Lonn uneasily.

"No," said Beorc. "That he is not. He has a harp on
his shoulder, and his singing is uncommon fine but he is
none of the fair folk."

"Do you know him then?" Niall asked, wishing some
surety in this meeting.

"No," Beorc said. "Not I." There was no man living

had sharper eyes or ears than Beorc. He spoke while the boy was well off in the distance and the voice was still unclear. But the song came clearer as they listened, bright and fair, and the boy came walking up to them in no great hurry: there was indeed a harp on his shoulder. It rang as he walked and as he stopped.

"Is there welcome here?" the boy asked.

"Always," said Beorc. "For all that find the way. Have you walked far?"

For a moment there seemed a confusion in the boy's eyes. He half turned as if seeking the way that he had come. "I came on the path. It seemed a short way through the hills."

"Well," said Beorc. "Well, shorter and longer than some. The hills are not safe these days."

"There were riders," said the harper vaguely, pointing at the hills. "But they went off their way and I went mine, and I sing as I walk so they will not mistake me— there is still some respect for a harper, is there not, in the lands about Caer Donn?"

"Ah, if you were seeking Caer Donn you are somewhat off your path."

Now the boy looked afraid—not greatly so, but uneasy all the same. "I had come from Donn. Is this then An Beag's land? I had not thought it reached within the hills."

"Freeheld, this is," said Beorc and laughed, waving an arm at all the Steading, the house set on the side of the great hill, the golden-stubbled fields, the orchards, the whole wide valley. "And Aelfraeda, my wife, will give a harper a cup of ale and a place by the fire for the asking. If you've a taste for cakes and honey, that we always have—Scaga, show the lad the way."

"Sir," said the harper, quite courteous in his recovery, and made a bow as respectful as for a lord. He shouldered the strap of his harpcase and went off up the hill with Scaga's leading, not without a troubled glance or two the way he had come, but after a few paces his step was light again and quick.

"You have misgivings," Niall said to Beorc at the harper's back, when he was out of hearing. "You never wondered at me or at Caoimhin. Who is he? Or what?"

Beorc continued to stare after the boy a moment,

leaning on the rail, and his face had no laughter in it, none. "Something strayed. Caer Donn, he says. Yet his heart is hidden."

"Does he lie?" asked Caoimhin.

"No," said Beorc. "Do you think a harper could?"

"A harper is a man," said Caoimhin. "And men have been known to lie upon a time."

Beorc turned on Caoimhin one of his searching looks, his beard like so much fire in the wind and his hair blowing likewise. "The world has gotten to be an ill place if that is so. But this one does not. I do not fear that."

"And what when he goes singing songs of us in An Beag?" asked Caoimhin.

"They may search as they will," said Beorc, and shrugged and took up the rail again. "But we shall have songs for it. Perhaps a whole winter's songs, perhaps not."

And Beorc fell to singing himself, which he would when he wished not to discuss a thing.

"Master Beorc," said Caoimhin, annoyed, but Niall took up the other end of the rail and held it in place in silence, so Caoimhin, scowling still, knelt to set the pole.

That evening there were indeed songs at the table in the yard, beneath the stars. The harper played for them on his plain and battered harp, delighting the children with merry songs made just for them. But there were great songs too. He had made one of the great battle at Aesclinn; he sang of the King and Niall Cearbhallain, while Niall himself looked only at the cup in his hands, wishing the song done. There were tears in many eyes as the harper sang; but Beorc and Aelfraeda sat hand in hand, listening and still, keeping their thoughts to themselves; and Niall sat dry-eyed and miserable until the last chord was struck. Then Caoimhin cleared his throat loudly and offered the harper ale.

"Thank you," the boy said—Fionn, he called himself, and that was all. He drank a sip and struck a thoughtful chord, and let the strings ripple a moment. "Ah," he said, and after a moment let the music die and took up the ale again. He drank and looked up at them with the sweat cooling on his brow, and then gave his attention to the harp again.

> *"The fires are low*
> *The breezes blow*
> *And stone lies not on stone.*
> *The stars do wane*
> *And hope be vain*
> *Till he comes to his own."*

Then a chill came on Niall Cearbhallain, and he clenched tight the cup in his hand, for it meant the boy King.

"That song," said Caoimhin, "is dangerous."

"So," said the harper. "But I am wary where I sing it. And a harper is sacred—is he not?"

"He is not," said Niall harshly and set his cup down. "They hanged Coinneach the king's bard in the court of Dun na h-Eoin, before they pulled the walls down." He stood up to leave the table, and then recalled that it was Beorc's table and Aelfraeda's, and not his to be leaving in any quarrel. "It is the ale," he said then lamely, and sank back into his place. "Sing something less grim, master harper. Sing something for the children."

"Aye," said the harper after a moment of looking at him, and blinked and seemed a moment lost. "I will sing for them."

So the harper did, a lilting, merry song, but it struck differently on Niall's heart. Niall looked toward Aelfraeda and Beorc, a pleading look and, receiving nothing of offense, gathered himself from his bench and went away into the dark , down by the barn, where the music was far away and thin and eerie in the night, and the laughter far.

There he leaned against the rail of the pen and felt the night colder than it had been.

"Singing," piped a voice.

It startled him, thin and strange as it was, coming from the haystack, even if he knew the source of it.

"Mind your business," he said.

"Niall Cearbhallain."

A chill ran through him, that it had somehow gotten

his name. "You've been lurking under more haystacks than this," he said. "I'd be ashamed."

"Niall Cearbhallain."

The chill grew deeper. "Let me be."

"Be what, Niall Cearbhallain?"

He shrugged aside, shivering, ready to go off anywhere to be rid of this badgering.

"Feasts at the house," said the Gruagach. "And what for me?"

"I'll see a plate set out for you."

"With ale."

"The largest cup."

The Gruagach rustled out of the haystack and hopped up onto the rail, his shagginess all shot through with bits of straw in the dark. "This harper does not see," said the Gruagach. "He sits and harps and sometimes it comes clear to him and most times not. Your luck has brought him here, Niall Cearbhallain. He came to you first. He is fey. He is your luck and none of his own."

"What made you so wise?" Niall snapped, dismayed.

"What made you so blind, Man? You came here once yourself with the smell of the Sidhe about you."

He had started to turn away. He stopped and stared, cold to the heart. But the Gruagach bounded off the rail and ran.

"Come back!" he called. "Come back here!"

But the Gruagach never would. He was lost into the dark and gone at least until he came for his cakes and ale.

There was a quieter gathering very late that night, in the hall by the fireside where the harper sat half-drowsing with ale, the harp clasped in his arms and the firelight bathing his face with a kindly glow. Beorc and Aelfraeda, Lonn and Sgeulaiche and Diarmaid, a scattering about the room; and Caoimhin was there when Niall came straying in, thinking the hall at rest.

"Sir," said the harper, who rose and bowed, "I hope there was no distress I gave you."

"None," said Niall, constrained by the courtesy. He bowed, and addressed himself to Aelfraeda. "The matter of the cakes—may I see to it?"

Aelfraeda gathered herself up and everyone was

dislodged. "The harper's tired," she said. "To bed, to bed all." She clapped her hands. Beorc moved and the rest did, and the drowsing harper blinked and settled the more comfortably into his corner.

Niall filled the cup himself and took the plate of cakes out on the porch. "Gruagach," he called softly, but heard and saw nothing. He went inside, as all the house was settling to their rest; and Scaga who had made himself inconspicuous in the corner came out of his hiding.

"Enough," said Niall. "To bed. —*Now*." So Scaga fled.

But over Caoimhin he had no such power. Caoimhin remained, watching him, and the harper's eyes were on him.

"Cearbhallain," said the harper quietly.

"And has *he* told you? And how many know?"

"I knew at the table. I have heard the manner of your face."

"What, that it is foul? That it is graceless?"

"I have heard it said you are a hard man, lord. Among the best that served the King. I saw you once—I was a boy. I saw you stand at table tonight and for a moment you *were* Cearbhallain."

"You are still a boy to my years," Niall snapped. "And songs are very well in their moment. In hall. You were not at Aescford or Aesclinn. It stank and it was long and loud. That was the battle, and we lost."

"But did great good."

"Did we?" Niall turned his side to him, taking the warmth of the dying fire on his face, and a great weariness came on him. "Be that so. But I am for bed now, master harper. For bed and rest."

"You gather men here. To ride out to Caer Wiell. Is that your purpose?"

It startled him. He laughed without mirth. "Boy, you dream. Ride with what? A haying fork and hoe?"

The harper reached beside him at the bricks of the fireplace, pulled forward an old sheath and sword.

"Dusty, is it not?" said Niall. "Aelfraeda must have missed it."

"If you would take me with you—lord, I can use a bow."

"You are mistaken. You are gravely mistaken. The

sword is old, the metal brittle. It is no good any more. And I have settled here to stay."

A pain came over the harper's face. "I am no spy, but a King's man."

"Well for you. Forget Caer Wiell."

"Your cousin—the traitor—"

"Give me no news of him."

"—holds your lands. The lady Meara is prisoned there, his wife by force. The King's own cousin. And you have *settled* here?"

Niall's hand lifted and he turned. The harper had set himself for the blow. He let his hand fall.

"Lord," Caoimhin said.

"If I were the Cearbhallain," said Niall, "would I be patient? He was never patient. As for taking Caer Wiell—what would you, harper? Strike a blow? An untimely blow. Look you, look you, lad—Think like a soldier, only once. Say that the blow fell true. Say that I took Caer Wiell and dealt all that was due there. And how long should I hold it?"

"Men would come to you."

"Aye, oh aye, the King's faithful men would come— to one hold, to the Cearbhallain's name. And begin battle for an infant king—for a power before its time. But An Beag would rise; and Caer Damh—no gentle enemies. Donn is fey and strange and no trust is in them if there is no strong king. Luel's heart is good but Donn lies between, and Caer Damh—No. This is not the year. In ten, perhaps; in two score there may be a man to crown. Maybe you will see that day. But it is not this day. And my day is past. I have learned patience. That is all I have."

For a moment all was silence. An ember snapped within the hearth. "I am Coinneach the king's bard's son," the harper said. "And I saw you at Dun na h-Eoin once, in the court where my father died."

"Coinneach's son." Niall looked at him, and the cold seemed greater still. "I had not thought you lived."

"I was with the young King—King he is, lord—until I took to the roads. And I have lodged under hedges and among old stones and now and again in Luel and Donn, aye, and An Beag's steadings too, so never name me coward, lord. Two years I have come and gone and not all in safety."

"Stay," Niall said. "Lad, *stay here*. There is no safety else."

"Not I. Not I, lord. This place is asleep. I have felt it more and more, and I have slept places round about Donn that I would never cross again. Leave this place with me."

"No," Niall said. "Neither Caoimhin nor I. You will not listen. Then never think to come back again. Or to live if you once pass the gates of Caer Wiell. Have you thought how much you could betray?"

"Nothing and no one. I have taken care to know nothing. Two years on the road, lord. Do you think I have not thought? Aye, since Dun na h-Eoin I have thought and come on this journey."

"Then farewell, friends' son," Niall said. "Take my sword if it would serve you. Its owner cannot go."

"It is a courteous offer," the harper said, "but I've no skill with swords. My harp is all I need."

"Take or leave it as you will," Niall said. "It will rust here." He turned away and went toward his own nook back along the halls. He did not hear Caoimhin follow. He looked back. "Caoimhin," he said. "The lad has a long way to travel. Go to bed."

"Aye," said Caoimhin, and left him.

The harper left before the dawn—quietly, and taking nothing with him that was not his—"Not a bit to eat," Siolta mourned, "nor anything to drink. We should have set it out for him, and him giving us songs till his voice was gone." But Aelfraeda said nothing, only shook her head in silence and put the kettle on.

And all that morning there was a heavy silence, as if merriment had left them, as if the singing had exhausted them. Scaga moped about his tasks. Beorc went down to the barn in silence and took Lonn and others with him. Sgeulaiche sat and carved on something Sgeulaiche understood, an inchoate thing, but the children were out of sorts from late hours and sulked and complained about their tasks. And Caoimhin who had gone down with Beorc never came to his work.

So Niall found him, sitting on the bench at the side

of the barn where he should have gathered his tools. "Come," said Niall, "the fence is yet to do."

"I cannot stay," said Caoimhin, so all that he had feared in searching for Caoimhin came tumbling in on him; but he laughed all the same.

"Work is a cure for melancholy, man. Come on. You'll think better of it by noontime."

"I cannot stay any longer." Caoimhin gathered himself to his feet and met his eyes. "I shall be taking my sword and bow."

"To what use? To defend a harper? What will he be saying to An Beag along the way?—Pray you never notice that great armed man: he set it on himself to follow me? A fine pair you would be along the road."

"So I shall follow. A winter I said I would stay. But you have stolen a year from me. The boy was right: this place is full of sleep. Leave it, Cearbhallain, leave it and come do some good in the world before we end. No more of this waking sleep, no more of this place."

"Think of it when you are starved again and cold, or when you lie in some ditch and none to hear you—o Caoimhin! Listen to me."

"No," said Caoimhin and flung his arms about him briefly. "O my lord, one of us should go to serve the King, even if neither sees his day."

Then Caoimhin went striding off toward the house, never looking back.

"Then take Banain," Niall cried after him. "And if you have need then give her her head: she might bring you home."

Caoimhin stopped, his shoulders fallen. "You love her too much. Give me your blessing, lord. Give me that instead."

"My blessing then," said Cearbhallain, and watched him go toward the house, which was as much as he cared to see. He turned. He ran, ran as he had run that day long ago, across the fields, as a child would run from something or to something, or simply because his heart was breaking and he wanted no sight of anyone, least of all of Caoimhin going away to die.

He fell down at last high upon the hillside among the weeds, and his side ached almost as much as his heart.

He had no tears—saw himself, a grim, lean man the years had worn as they wore the rocks; and about him was the peace the hillside gave; and below him when he looked down was the orchard ripe with apples, the broad meadow pastures, the house with the barn and the old oak. And above him was the sky. And beyond the shoulder of the hill the way grew strange like the glare of rocks in summer noon, the sheen of sun on grass stems, so that his eyes hurt and he looked away and rose, walking along the hill.

Then a doubt came gnawing at him, so that he passed along the ridge looking for some sight of Caoimhin, like a man worrying at a wound. But when he had come on the valley way he saw no one, and knew himself too late.

"Death," said a thin small voice above him on the hill.

Niall looked up in rage at the shaggy creature on the rock. "What would you know, you croaking lump of straw? Starve from now on! Steal all I have, creeping thief, and starve!"

"Evil words for evil, but only one is true."

"A plague on your prophecy."

"Ill and ill."

"Leave me."

The Gruagach hopped down from the rock and came nearer still. "Not I."

"Will he die then?"

"Perhaps."

"Then be clear." Hope had started up in him, a guilty desperate thing, and he seized the Gruagach by its shaggy arms and held it. "If you have the Sight, then See. Tell me—tell me—was there truth in the harper? Is there hope at all? If there was hope—will there be a King again? Is it on me to serve this King?"

"Let go!" it cried. "Let go!"

"Be plain with me," Niall said and shook it hard, for a terror made him cruel, and the creature's eyes were wild. "Is there hope in this King?"

"He is dark," hissed the Gruagach with a wild shake of its shaggy head, and its eyes rolled aside and fixed again on his. "O dark."

"Who? What meaning, dark? Name me names. Will this young King live?"

The Gruagach gave a moan and suddenly bit him

fiercely, so that he jerked his hand back and lost the Gruagach from his grip, holding the wounded hand to his lips. But the creature stopped and hugged itself and rocked to and fro, wild eyed, and spoke in a thin, wailing voice:

> *Dark the blight and dark the path*
> *and strong the chains that bind them*
> *Fell the day that on them dawns,*
> *for doom comes swift behind them.*

"What sense is that?" Niall cried. "Who are *they*? Do you mean myself?"

"No, no, never Cearbhallain. O Man, the Gruagach weeps for you."

"Shall I die then?"

"All men die."

"A plague on you!" He sucked at his wounded hand. "What chains and where? Is it Caer Wiell you mean?"

"Stay," it said, and fled.

He almost had the will to go. He stood on the hillside and looked down at the dale that led away toward the outgoing of the hills. But that *Stay* rang in his ears, and his bones ached with his running, and Caoimhin was nowhere in sight.

He sank down there, and watched till sundown, but the courage for the road grew colder and colder, and his belief in it less and less.

At last a boy came running, jogging along by turns and running as if his side hurt, down in the place between the hills.

"Scaga!" Niall called, rising to his feet.

The boy stopped as if struck, and looked up, and began to run toward him, stumbling as he ran; but Niall came down to him and caught him in his arms.

"I thought you had gone," the boy said, and never Scaga wept, but his lip quivered.

"Caoimhin is gone," Niall said, "not I. Is supper ready?"

For a moment Scaga fought for breath. "I think so."

So he came back with Scaga, and the snare was fast.

FOUR

THE HUNTING

Arafel dreamed. It was only a moment of a dream, a slipping elsewhere into memory, which she did much, into a brightness much different from the dim nights and blinding days and mortal Eald. But her time being never what the time of Men was, she had hardly time to sink to sleep again when a sound had waked her, a plaintive sound and strange.

He has come back again, she thought drowsily, no little annoyed; and then she sought and found something quite different—a fell thing had gotten in, or came close, and something bright fled ringing through her memory.

She gathered herself. The dream scattered in pieces beyond recall, but she never heeded. The wind blew a sound to her and all of Eald quivered like a spider web. She took a sword and flung her cloak about her, though she could have done more. It was carelessness and habit; it was fey ill luck, perhaps. But no one challenged Arafel; so she followed what she heard.

There was a path through Eald, up from the Caerbourne ford. It was the darkest of all ways to be taking out of Caerdale, and since she had barred it few had traveled it: brigands like the outlaw—this kind of Man might try it, the sort with eyes so dull and dead they were numb to ordinary fear and sense. Sometimes they were even fortunate and won through, if they came by day, if they moved quickly and never tarried or hunted the beasts of Eald. If they sped quickly enough then evening might see them safe away into the New Forest in the hills, or out of Eald again to cross the river.

But a runner entering by night, and this one young and wild-eyed and carrying no sword or bow, but only a dagger and a harp—this was a far rarer venturer in Eald, and all the deeper shadows chuckled and whispered in their startlement.

It was the harp she had heard, this unlikely thing which jangled on his shoulder and betrayed him to all with ears to hear, in this world and the other. She marked his flight by that sound and walked straight into the way to meet him, out of the soft cool light of the elvish sun and into the colder white of his moonlight. Unhooded she came, the cloak carelessly flung back; and shadows which had grown quite bold in the Ealdwood of latter earth suddenly felt the warm breath of spring and drew aside, slinking into dark places where neither moon nor sun cast light.

"Boy," she whispered.

He started in mid-step like a wounded deer, hesitated, searching out the voice in the brambles. She stepped full into his light and felt the dank wind of mortal Eald on her face. The boy seemed more solid then, ragged and torn by thorns in his headlong flight through the wood. His clothes were better suited to some sheltered hall— they were fine wool and embroidered linen, soiled now and rent; and the harp at his shoulders had a broidered case.

She had taken little with her out of otherwhere, and yet did take: it was always in the eye which saw her. She had come as plainly as ever she had ventured into the mortal world, and leaned against the rotting trunk of a dying tree and folded her arms without a hint of threat, laying no hand now to the silver sword she wore. More, she propped one foot against a projecting root and offered him her thinnest smile, much out of the habit of smiling at all. The boy looked at her with no less apprehension for that effort, seeing, perhaps, a ragged vagabond in outlaw's habit—or perhaps seeing more and having more reason to fear, because he did not look to be as blind as some. His hand touched a talisman at his breast and she, smiling still, touched that pale green stone which hung at her own throat, a talisman which had power to answer his.

"Now where would you be going," she asked him, "so recklessly through the Ealdwood? To some misdeed? Some mischief?"

"Misfortune, most like." He was out of breath. He still stared at her as if he thought her no more than moonbeams, which amused her in a distant, dreaming way. She took in all of him, the fine ruined clothes, the harp on his shoulder, so very strange a traveler on any path in all the world. She was intrigued by him as no doings of Men had yet interested her; she longed—But suddenly and far away the wind carried a baying of hounds. The boy cried out and fled away from her, breaking branches in his flight.

His quickness amazed her out of her long indolence, catching her quite by surprise, which nothing had done in long ages. "Stay!" she cried, and stepped into his path a second time, shadow-shifting through the dark and the undergrowth like some trick of moonlight. She had felt that other, darker presence; she had not forgotten, far from forgotten it, but she was light with that threat, having far more interest in this visitor than any other. He touched something forgotten in her, brought something of brightness in himself, amid the dark. "I do doubt," she said quite casually to calm him, the while he stared at her as if his reason had fled him, "I do much doubt they'll come this far. What is your name, boy?"

He was instantly wary of that question, staring at her with that trapped deer's look, surely knowing the power of names to bind.

"Come," she said reasonably. "You disturb the peace here, you trespass my forest—What name do you give me for it?"

Perhaps he would not have given his true one and perhaps he would not have stayed at all, but that she fixed him sternly with her eyes and he stammered out: "Fionn."

"Fionn." *Fair* was apt, for he was very fair for humankind, with tangled pale hair and the first down of beard. It was a true name, holding much of him, and his heart was in his eyes. "Fionn." She spoke it a third time softly, like a charm. "Fionn. Are you hunted, then?"

"Aye," he said.

"By Men, is it?"

"Aye," he said still softer.

"To what purpose do they hunt you?"

He said nothing, but she reckoned well enough for herself.

"Come then," she said, "come, walk with me. I think I should be seeing to this intrusion before others do.— Come, come, have no dread of me."

She parted the brambles for him. A last moment he delayed, then did as she asked and walked after her, carefully and much loath, retracing the path on which he had fled, held by nothing but his name.

She stayed by that track for a little distance, taking mortal time for his sake, not walking the quicker ways through her own Eald. But soon she left that easiest path, finding others. The thicket which degenerated from the dark heart of Eald was an unlovely place, for the Ealdwood had once been better than it was, and there was still a ruined fairness about that wood; but these young trees they began to meet had never been other than desolate. They twisted and tangled their roots among the bones of the crumbling hills, making deceiving and thorny barriers. It was unlikely that any Man could ever have seen the ways she found, let alone track her through the night against her will—but she patiently made a way for the boy who followed her, and now and again waited, holding branches parted for him. So she took time to look about her as she went, amazed by the changes the years had wrought in this place she once had known. She saw the slow work of root and branch and ice and sun, labored hard-breathing, mortal-wise, and scratched with thorns, but strangely gloried in it, alive to the world this unexpected night, waking more and more. Ever and again she turned when she sensed faltering behind her: the boy each time caught that look of hers and came on with a fresh effort, pale and fearful as he seemed, past clinging thickets and over stones; doggedly, as if he had lost all will or hope of doing otherwise.

"I shall not leave you alone," she said. "Take your time."

But he never answered, not one word.

*   *   *

At last the woods gave them a little clear space, at
the veriest edge of the New Forest. She knew very well
where she was. The baying of hounds came echoing up
to her out of Caerdale, from the deep valley the river
cut below the heights, and below was the land of Men,
with all their doings, good and ill. She thought a moment
of her outlaw, of a night he sped away; a moment her
thoughts ranged far and darted over all the land; and
back again to this place, this time, the boy.

She stepped up onto the shelf of rock at the head of
that last slope, while at her feet stretched all the great
vale of the Caerbourne, a dark, tree-filled void beneath
the moon. A towered heap of stones had lately risen
across the vale on the hill. Men called it Caer Wiell, but
that was not its true name. Men forgot, and threw down
old stones and raised new. So much did the years do
with the world.

And only a moment ago a man had sped—or how
many years.

Behind her the boy arrived, panting and struggling
through the undergrowth, and dropped down to sit on
the edge of that slanting stone, the harp on his shoulders
echoing. His head sank on his folded arms and he wiped
the sweat and the tangled pale hair from his brow. The
baying, which had been still a moment, began again
much nearer, and he lifted frightened eyes and clenched
his hands on the rock.

Now, now he would run, having come as far as her
light wish could bring him. Fear shattered the spell. He
started to his feet. She leapt down and stayed him yet
again with a touch of light fingers on his sweating arm.

"Here's the limit of my woods," she said, "and in it
hounds do hunt that you could never shake from your
heels, no. You'd do well to stay here by me, Fionn, indeed you would. Is it yours, that harp?"

He nodded, distracted by the hounds. His eyes turned
away from her, toward that dark gulf of trees.

"Will you play for me?" she asked. She had desired
this from the beginning, from the first she had felt the
ringing of the harp; and the desire of it burned far more
keenly than did any curiosity about Men and dogs—but
one would serve the other. It was elvish curiosity; it was

simplicity; it was, elvish-wise, the truest thing, and mattered most.

The boy looked back into her steady gaze as though he thought her mad; but perhaps he had given over fear, or hope, or reason. Something of all three left his eyes, and he sat down on the edge of the stone again, took the harp from his shoulders and stripped off the case.

Dark wood starred and banded with gold, it was very, very fine: there was more than mortal skill in that workmanship, and more than beauty in its tone. It sounded like a living voice when he took it into his arms. He held it close to him like something protected, and lifted a pale, still sullen face.

Then he bowed his head and played as she had bidden him, soft touches at the strings that quickly grew bolder, that waked echoes out of the depths of Caerdale and set the hounds in the distance to baying madly. The music drowned the voices, filled the air, filled her heart, and now she felt no faltering or tremor of his hands. She listened, and almost forgot which moon shone down on them, for it had been long, so very long, since the last song had been heard in the Ealdwood, and that was sung soft and elsewhere.

He surely sensed a glamor on him, in which the wind blew warmer and the trees sighed with listening. The fear passed from his eyes, and while the sweat stood on his face like jewels, it was clear, brave music that he made.

Then suddenly, with a bright ripple of the strings, the music became a defiant song, strange to her ears.

Discord crept in, the hounds' fell voices which took the music and warped it out of tune. Arafel rose as that sound grew near. The harper's hands fell abruptly still. There was the rush and clatter of horses in the thicket below.

Fionn himself sprang to his feet, the harp laid aside. He snatched at once at the small dagger at his belt, and Arafel flinched at the drawing of that blade, the swift, bitter taint of iron. "No," she wished him, wished him very strongly, and stayed his hand. Unwillingly he slid the weapon back into its sheath.

Then the hounds and the riders came pouring up at

them out of the darkness of the trees, a flood of dogs
black and slavering and two great horses clattering
among them, bearing Men with the smell of iron about
them, Men glittering terribly in the moonlight. The
hounds surged up the slope baying and bugling and as
suddenly fell back again, making a wide circle, alter-
nately whining and cringing and lifting their hackles at
what they saw. The riders whipped them, but their
horses shied and screamed under the spurs and neither
horses nor hounds could be driven farther.

Arafel stood, one foot braced against the rock, and
regarded this chaos of Men and beasts with cold curiosity. She found them strange, harder and wilder than the
outlaws she knew; and strange too was the device on
them, a wolf's grinning head. She did not recall that
emblem—or care for the manner of these visitors, less
even than the outlaws.

A third rider came rattling up the slope, a large man
who gave a great shout and whipped his unwilling horse
farther than the other two, all the way to the crest of
the hill facing the rock, and halfway up that slope advanced more Men who had followed him, no few of
them with bows. The rider reined aside, out of the way.
His arm lifted. The bows bent, at the harper and at her.

"Hold," said Arafel.

The Man's arm did not fall: it slowly lowered. He
glared at her, and she stepped lightly up onto the rock
so that she need not look up so far, to this Man on his
tall black horse. The beast suddenly shied under him
and he spurred it and curbed it cruelly; but he gave no
order to his men, as if the cowering hounds and
trembling horses had finally made him see what he faced.

"Away from there!" he shouted at her, a voice fit to
make the earth quake. "Away! or I daresay you need a
lesson too." And he drew his great sword and held it
toward her, curbing the protesting horse.

"Me, lessons?" Arafel stepped lightly to the ground
and set her hand on the harper's arm. "Is it on his account you set foot here and raise this noise?"

"My harper," the lord said, "and a *thief.* Witch, step
aside. Fire and iron can answer the likes of you."

Now in truth she had no liking for the sword the Man

wielded or for the iron-headed arrows yonder which could come speeding their way at this Man's lightest word. She kept her hand on Fionn's arm nonetheless, seeing well enough how he would fare with them alone. "But he's mine, lord-of-Men. I should say that the harper's no joy to you, or you'd not come chasing him from your land. And great joy he is to me, for long and long it is since I've met so pleasant a companion in the Eald-wood—Gather the harp, lad, do, and walk away now. Let me talk to this rash Man."

"Stay!" the lord shouted; but Fionn snatched the harp into his arms and edged away.

An arrow hissed: the boy flung himself aside with a terrible clangor of the harp, and lost the harp on the slope. He might have fled, but he scrambled back for it and that was his undoing. Of a sudden there was a half-ring of arrows drawn ready and aimed at them both.

"Do not," said Arafel plainly to the lord.

"What's mine is *mine*." The lord held his horse still, his sword outstretched before his archers, bating the signal. "Harp and harper are *mine*. And you'll rue it if you think any words of yours weigh with me. I'll have him and *you* for your impudence."

It seemed wisest then to walk away, and Arafel did so. But she turned back again in the next instant, at distance, at Fionn's side, and only half under his moon. "I ask your Name, lord-of-Men, if you aren't fearful of my curse."

So she mocked him, to make him afraid before his men. "Evald of Caer Wiell," he said back in spite of what he had seen, no hesitating, with all contempt for her. "And yours, witch?"

"Call me what you like, lord." Never in human ages had she showed herself for what she was, but her anger rose. "And take warning, that these woods are not for human hunting and your harper is not yours anymore. Go away and be grateful. Men have Caerdale. If it does not please you, shape it until it does. The Ealdwood's not for trespass."

The lord gnawed at his mustaches and gripped his sword the tighter, but about him the drawn bows had begun to sag and the loosened arrows to aim at the dirt. Fear was in the bowmen's eyes, and the riders who had come first and farthest up the slope hung back, free men and less constrained than the archers.

"You have what's mine," the lord insisted, though his horse fought to be away.

"And so I do. Go on, Fionn. Do go, quietly."

"You've what's *mine*," the valley lord shouted. "Are you thief then, as well as witch? You owe me a price for it."

She drew in a sharp breath and yet did not waver in or out of the shadow. It was so, if his claim was true. "Then do not name too high lord-of-Men. I may hear you, if that will quit us. And likewise I will warn you: things of Eald are always in Eald. Wisest of all if what you ask is my leave to go."

His eyes roved harshly about her, full of hate and yet a weariness as well. Arafel felt cold at that look, especially where it centered, above her heart, and her hand stole to that moon-green stone which hung uncloaked at her throat.

"I take leave of no witch," said the lord. "This land is mine—and for my leave to go—the stone will be enough," he said. *"That."*

"I have told you," she said. "You are not wise."

The Man showed no sign of yielding. So she drew it off, and still held it dangling on its chain, insubstantial as she was at present—for she had the measure of them and it was small. "Go, Fionn," she bade the harper; and when he lingered yet: *"Go!"* she shouted. At the last he ran, fled, raced away like a mad thing, clutching the harp to him.

And when the woods all about were still again, hushed but for the shifting and stamp of the horses on the stones and the whining complaint of the hounds, she let fall the stone. "Be paid," she said, and walked away.

She heard the hooves racing at her back and turned to face treachery, fading even then, felt Evald's insubstantial sword like a stab of ice into her heart. She recoiled elsewhere, bowed with the pain of it that took her breath away.

In time she could stand again, and had taken from the iron no lasting hurt. Yet it had been close: she had stepped otherwhere only narrowly in time, and the feeling of cold lingered even in the warm winds. She cast about her, found the clearing empty of Men and beasts, only trampled bracken marking the place. So he had gone with his prize.

And the boy—She went striding through the shades and shadows in greatest anxiety until she had found him, where he huddled hurt and lost in a thicket deep in Eald.

"Are you well?" she asked lightly, concealing all concern. She dropped to her heels beside him. For a moment she feared he might be hurt more than the scratches she saw, so tightly he was bowed over the harp; but he lifted his pale face to her in shock, seeing her so noiselessly by him. "You will stay while you wish," she said, out of a solitude so long it spanned the age of the trees about them, of a stillness so deep the leaves of them never moved. "You will harp for me." And when he still looked at her in fear: "You'd not like the New Forest. They've no ear for harpers there."

Perhaps she was too sudden with him. Perhaps it wanted time. Perhaps Men had truly forgotten what she was. But his look achieved a perilous sanity, a will to trust.

"Perhaps not," he said.

"Then you will stay here, and be welcome. It is a rare offer. Believe me that it is."

"What is your name, lady?"

"What do you see of me? Am I fair?"

Fionn looked swiftly at the ground, so that she reckoned he could not say the truth without offending her. And she mustered a laugh at that in the darkness.

"Then call me Feochadan," she said. "*Thistle* is one of my names and has its truth—for rough I am, and have my sting. I'm afraid it's very much the truth you see of me.—But you'll stay. You'll harp for me." This last she spoke full of earnestness.

"Yes." He hugged the harp closer. "But I'll not go with you, understand, any farther than this. Please don't ask. I've no wish to find the years passed in a night and all the world grown old."

"Ah." She leaned back, crouching near him with her arms about her knees. "Then you *do* know me—but what harm could it do you for years to pass? What do you care for this age of yours? The times hardly seem kind to you. I should think you would be glad to see them pass."

"I am a Man," he said ever so quietly. "I serve my King. And it's *my* age, isn't it?"

It was so. She could never force him. One entered otherwhere only by wishing it. He did not wish, and that was the end of it. More, she sensed about him and in his heart a deep bitterness, the taint of iron.

She might still have fled away, deserting him in his stubbornness. She had given a price beyond all counting and yet there was retreat and some recovery, even if she spent human years in waiting. In the harper she sensed disaster. He offended her hopes. She sensed mortality and dread and all too much of humanness.

But she settled in the sinking moonlight, and watched beside him, choosing instead to stay. He leaned against the side of an aged tree, gazed at her and watched her watching him, eyes darting to the least movement in the leaves, and back again to her, who was the focus of all ancientness in the wood, or dangers to more than life. And at last for all his caution his eyes began to dim, and the whispers had power over him, the sibilance of leaves and the warmth of dreaming Eald.

FIVE

THE HUNTER

Fionn slept, and waked at last by sunrise, blinking and looking about him in plain fear that trees might have grown and died of old age while he slept. His eyes fixed on Arafel last of all and she laughed in elvish humor, which was gentle if sometimes cruel. She knew her own look by daylight, which was indeed as rough as the weed she had named herself. She seemed tanned and thin and hard-handed, her gray-and-green all cobweb patchwork, and only the sword stayed true. She sat plaiting her hair in a single silver braid and smiling sidelong at the harper, who gave her back a sidelong and anxious glance.

All the earth had grown warm in that morning. The sun did come here, unclouded on this day. Fionn rubbed the sleep from his eyes and opening his wallet, began looking for his breakfast.

There seemed very little in it: he shook out a bit of jerky, looked at it ruefully, then split off a bit of it with his knife and offered half his breakfast to her—so small a morsel that, halved, was not enough for a Man, and a haggard and hungry one at that.

"No." she said. She had been offended at once by the smell of it, having no appetite for man-taint, or the flesh of any poor forest creature. But the offering of it, the desperate courtesy, had thawed her heart. She brought out food of her own store, a gift of trees and bees and whatsoever things felt no hurt at sharing. She gave him a share, and he took it with a desperate dread and hunger.

"It's good," he pronounced quickly and laughed a little, and finished it all. He licked the very last from his fingers, and now there was relief in his eyes, of hunger, of fear, of so many burdens. He gave a great sigh and she smiled a warmer smile than she was wont, remembrance of a brighter world.

"Play for me," she wished him.

He played for her then, idly and softly, heart-healing songs, and slept again, for bright day in Ealdwood counseled sleep, when the sun burned its warmth through the tangled branches and brambles and the air hung still, nothing breathing, least of all the wind. Arafel drowsed too, at peace in mortal Eald for the first time since many a tree had grown. The touch of the mortal sun did that kindness for her, a benison she had all but forgotten.

But as she slept she dreamed, and there were halls in that vision, of cold gray stone.

In that dark dream she had a Man's body, heavy and reeking of wine and ugly memories, such a dark fierceness she would gladly have fled it running if she might. She felt the hate, she felt the weight of human frame, the reeling unsteadiness of strong drink.

He had had an unwilling wife, had Evald of Caer Wiell—Meara of Dun na h-Eoin was her name; he had a small son who huddled afraid and away from him in the upstairs of this great stone keep, the while Evald drank with his sullen kinsmen and cursed the day. Evald brooded and he hated, and looked oftentimes at the empty pegs on his wall where the harp had hung. The song gnawed at him, bitter as the song—for that harp came from Dun na h-Eoin, as Meara came.

Treason, it had sung once, and the murder of kings and bards. Keeping it was his victory.

So Evald sat and drank his ale and heard the echoes of that harping. And in her dream Arafel's hand sought the moonstone on its chain and found it at his throat.

She had laid a virtue on it in giving it, that he could neither lose it nor destroy it. Now she offered him better dreams and more kindly as he nodded, for it had that power. She would have given him peace and mended all that was awry in him, drawing him back and back to Eald. But he made bitter mock of any kindness, hating all that he did not comprehend.

"No," whispered Arafel, grieving, dreaming still before that fire in Caer Wiell. She would have made the hand put the stone off that foul neck; but she had no power against the virtue she herself had given it, so far, so wrapped in humankind, while *he* would not. And Evald possessed what he owned, so fiercely and with such jealousy it cramped the muscles and stifled the breath.

Most of all he hated what he did not have and could not have; and the heart of it was the harper and the respect of those about him and his lust for Dun na h-Eoin.

So she had erred, and knew it. She tried to reason within this strange, closed mind. It was impossible. The heart was almost without love, and what little it had ever been given it folded in upon itself lest what it possessed escape.

He had betrayed his King, murdered his kinsmen, and sat in a stolen hall with a wife who despised him. These were the truths which gnawed at him in his darkness, in the stone mass which was Caer Wiell.

Of these he dreamed, and clenched the stone tightly in his fist, and would never let it go: this was all he understood of power—to hold, and not let go.

"Why?" asked Arafel of Fionn that night, when the moon shed light on the Ealdwood and the land was quiet, no ill thing near them, no cloud above them. "Why does he seek you?" Her dreams had told her Evald's truth, but she sensed another in the harper.

Fionn shrugged, his young eyes for a moment aged; and he gathered his harp against him. "This," he said.

"You said it was yours. He called you thief. What then did you steal?"

"It is mine." He settled it in his arms, touched the strings and brought forth melody. "It hung in his hall so long he thought it was his, and the strings were cut and dead."

"And how did it come to him?"

Fionn rippled out a somber note and his face grew darker. "It was my father's and his father's before him, and they harped in Dun na h-Eoin before the Kings. It is old, this harp."

"Ah," she said, "Yes, it is old, and one made it who knew his craft. A harp for kings. But how did it come to Evald's keeping?"

The fair head bowed over the harp and his hands coaxed sound from it, answerless.

"I've give a price," she said, "to keep him from it and from you. Will you not give back an answer?"

The sound burst into softness. "It was my father's. Evald hanged him in Dun na h-Eoin, in the court when it burned. Because of songs my father made, for truth he sang, how men the King trusted were not what they seemed. Evald was the least of that company, not great; petty even in that great a wrong. When the King died, when Dun na h-Eoin was burning, my father harped them one last song. But he fell into their hands and so to Evald's—dead or living, I never knew. Evald hanged him from the tree in the court and took the harp of Dun na h-Eoin for his own. He hung it on his own wall in Caer Wiell for mock of my father and the King. So it was never his."

"A king's own harper."

Fionn never looked at her and never ceased to play. "Ah, worse things he has done. But that was seven years ago. And so I came, when I was grown—wandering the roads and harping in all the halls. Last of all to Caer Wiell. Last of all to him. All this winter I gave Evald songs he liked. But at winter's end I came down to the hall at night and mended the old harp. So I fled over the walls. From the hill I gave it voice and a song he remembered. For that he hunts me. And beyond that there is no more to tell."

Then softly Fionn sang, of humankind and wolves, and that song was bitter. Arafel shuddered to hear it, and quickly bade him cease, for mind to mind with her in troubled dreams Evald heard and tossed, and waked starting in sweat.

"Sing more kindly now," she said. "More kindly. It was never made for hate, this harp, this gift of my folk to the Kings of Men. There were such gifts once long and long ago, did you not know? It sounds through all the realms of Eald, mine and thine and places far darker. Never sing dark songs. Harp me brighter things. Sing me sun and moon and laughing, sing me the lightest song you know."

"I know children's songs," he said doubtfully. "Or walking songs. The great songs—well, it seems an age for dark ones."

"Then sing the little ones," she said, "the small ones that make Men laugh—oh, I have need to laugh, harper, that most of all."

Fionn did so, while the moon climbed above the trees, and Arafel recalled elder-day songs which the world had not heard in long years, sang them sweetly. Fionn listened and caught up the words in his strings, until the tears ran down his face for joy.

There could be no harm in Ealdwood in that hour: the spirits of latter earth which skulked and strove and haunted Men fled elsewhere, finding nothing in this place that they knew; and the old shadows slipped away trembling, for they remembered.

But now and again the elvish song faltered, for there came a touch of ill and smallness into Arafel's own mind, a cold piercing as the iron, bringing thoughts of hate, which she had never held so close.

Then she laughed, breaking the spell, and put it from her. She bent herself to teach the harper songs which she herself had almost forgotten, conscious the while that elsewhere, down in Caerbourne vale, on the hill of Caer Wiell, a Man's body tossed in sweaty dreams which seemed constantly to mock him, with sounds of eldritch harping that stirred echoes and sleeping ghosts.

With the dawn, she and Fionn rose and walked a time, and shared food, and drank at a cold, clear spring she knew, until the sun's hot eye fell upon them and cast its numbing spell on all the Ealdwood.

Then Fionn slept in innocence, while Arafel fought the sleep which came to her. Dreams were in that sleep, her time to dream while *he* should wake, Evald, the lord in the valley, and those dreams would not stay at bay, not as her eyes grew heavy and the midmorning air thickened with urging sleep. They pressed at her more and more strongly. The Man's strong legs bestrode a great brute horse, and his hands plied the whip and his

feet the spurs, hurting it cruelly. She dreamed the noise
of hounds and hunt, a coursing of woods and hedges
and the bright spurt of blood on dappled hide—Evald
sought blood to wipe out blood, because the harping still
rang in his mind, and he remembered . . . harper, and
hall, and the harper who had sung the truth of how he
served his King. He hunted deer and thought other
things. She shuddered at the killing her own hands did,
and at the fear that gathered thickly about the valley
lord, reflected in his comrades' eyes, reflected in his
wife's and son's pale faces when he came riding home
again with deer's blood on his clothes.

It was better that night, when the waking was Arafel's
and her harper's, and sweet songs banished fear and
dreams. But even then Arafel recalled and grieved, and
at times the cold came so heavily on her that her hand
would steal to her throat where the moon-green stone
had hung. Her eyes brimmed once suddenly with tears.
Fionn saw that, and tried to sing her merry songs
instead.

They failed, and the music died.

"Teach me another song," he begged of her, at-
tempting distraction. "No harper ever had such songs.
And will *you* not play for *me*?"

"I have no art," she said, for the last true harper of
her own folk had gone long ago to the sea. The answer
was not all truth. Once she had played. But there was
no more music in her hands, none since the last of her
folk had gone and she had willed to stay, loving this
woods too well in spite of Men. "Play," she asked of
Fionn, and tried desperately to smile, though the iron
closed about her heart and the valley lord raged at the
nightmare, waking in sweat, ghost-ridden.

It was that human song which Fionn had played in his
despair on the hillside, bright and defiant that it was:
Eald rang with it; and that night the lord Evald did not
sleep again, but sat shivering and wrapped in furs before
his hearth, his hand clenched in hate on the stone which
he possessed and would not, though it killed him, let go.

But Arafel quietly began to sing, a song of elder earth
unheard since the world had dimmed. The harper took
up the tune, which sang of earth and shores and water,

the last great journey, at Men's coming and the changing
of the world. Fionn wept while he played, and Arafel
smiled sadly and at last fell silent, for it was the last of
all elvish songs. Her heart had gone gray and cold.

The sun returned at last, but Arafel had no will now
to eat or rest, only to sit grieving, because she had lost
her peace. She would have been glad now to have fled
the shadow-shifting way back into otherwhere, to her
own fair moon and softer sunlight. She might have persuaded the harper to come with her now. She thought
now perhaps he could find the way. But now there was
a portion of her heart in pawn, and she could not even
take herself away from this world: she was too heavily
bound to thoughts of it. She fell to mourning and despair, and often pressed her hand where the stone should
rest. It was time, the shadows whispered, that Eald
should end. She held in ancient stubbornness. And she
felt some feyness on her, that many things together had
gone amiss, that even on her the harp had power.

He hunted again, did Evald of Caer Wiell, now that
the sun was up. Sleepless, driven mad by dreams, he
whipped his folk out of the hold as he did his hounds,
out to the margin of the Ealdwood, to harry the creatures of the woods' edge—having guessed well the
source of his luck and the harping in his dreams. He
brought fire and axes across the Caerbourne's dark
flood, meaning to fell the old trees one by one until all
was dead and bare.

The wood muttered now with whisperings and angers.
A wall of cloud rolled down from the north on Ealdwood and all deep Caerdale, dimming the sun. A wind
sighed in the faces of the Men, so that no torch was set
to wood for fear of fire turning back on the hold itself;
but axes rang, all the same, that day and the next. The
clouds gathered thicker and the winds blew colder, making the Ealdwood dim again and dank. Arafel still managed to smile by night, hearing the harper's songs. But
every stroke of the axes by day made her shudder, and
while Fionn slept by snatches, the iron about her heart
grew constantly closer. The wound in the Ealdwood

grew day by day, and the valley lord was coming: she knew it well.

And at last there remained no rest at all, by day or night.

She sat then with her head bowed beneath the clouded moon, and Fionn was powerless to cheer her. He sat and regarded her with deep despair, and reached and touched her hand for comfort.

She said no word to that offering, but rose and invited the harper to walk with her awhile. He did so. And vile things stirred and muttered in the shadow of the thickets and the briers, whispering malice to the winds, so that often Fionn started aside and stared and kept close beside her.

Her strength was fading, first that she could not keep these voices away, and then that she could not keep herself from listening. *Ruin,* they whispered. *All useless.* And at last she sank on Fionn's arm, eased to the cold ground and leaned her head against the bark of a gnarled and dying tree.

"What ails?" he asked, and patted her face and pried at her clenched and empty fingers, opened the fist which hovered near her throat, as if seeking there the answer. "What ails you?"

She shrugged and smiled and shuddered, because even now by the glare of fires and torches in the dark, the axes had begun again, and she felt the iron like a wound, a great cry going through the wood as it had gone ceaselessly for days; but he was deaf to it, being what he was.

"Make a song for me," she said.

"I have no heart for it."

"Nor have I," she said. A sweat stood on her face, and he wiped at it with his gentle hand and tried to ease her pain.

And again he caught and unclenched the hand which rested, empty, at her throat. "The stone," he said. "Is it *that* you miss?"

She shrugged, and turned her head, for the axes then seemed loud and near. He looked that way too—and glanced back deaf and puzzled, to gaze into her eyes.

" 'Tis time," she said. "You have to be on your way

this morning, as soon as there's sun enough. The New Forest will hide you after all."

"And leave you? Is that what you mean?"

She smiled, touched his anxious face. "I'm paid enough."

"How paid? What did you pay? *What* was it you gave away?"

"Dreams," she said. "Only that. And all of that." Her hands shook terribly, and a blackness came on her heart too miserable to bear: it was hate, and aimed at him and at herself and all that lived; and it was harder and harder to fend away. "Evil has it. He would do you hurt, and I would dream that too. Harper, it's time to go."

"Why would you give such a thing?" Great tears started from his eyes. "Was it worth such a cost, my harping?"

"Why, well worth it," she said, and managed such a laugh as she had left to laugh, that shattered all the evil for a moment and left her clean. "I have remembered how to sing."

He snatched up the harp and ran, breaking branches and tearing flesh in his headlong haste, but not, she realized in horror, not the way he ought—but back again, to Caerdale.

She cried out her dismay and seized at branches to pull herself to her feet; she could in no wise follow. Her limbs which had been quick to run beneath this moon or the other were leaden, and her breath came hard. Brambles caught and held with all but mindful malice, and dark things which had never had power in her presence whispered loudly now, of murder.

And elsewhere the wolf-lord with his men drove at the forest with great ringing blows, the poison of iron. The heavy human body which she sometime wore seemed hers again, and the moonstone was prisoned near a heart that beat with hate.

She tried the more to make haste, and could not. She looked helplessly through Evald's narrow eyes and saw—saw the young harper break through the thickets near them. Weapons lifted, bows and axes. Hounds bayed and lunged at leashes in the firelight.

Fionn came, nothing hesitating, bringing the harp, and

himself. "A trade," she heard him say. "The stone for the harp."

There was such hate in Evald's heart, and such fear, it was hard to breathe. She felt a pain to the depth of her as Evald's coarse fingers pawed at the stone. She felt his fear, felt his loathing of the stone. Nothing would he truly let go. But this—this, he abhorred, and was fierce in his joy to lose it.

"Come," the lord Evald said, and held the stone dangling and spinning before him, so that for that moment the hate was far and cold.

Another hand took it then, and very gentle it was, and very full of love. She felt the sudden draught of strength and desperation—she sprang up then, to run, to save—

But pain stabbed through her heart, with one last ringing of the harp, with such an ebbing out of love and grief that she cried aloud, and stumbled, blind, dead in that part of her.

She did not cease to run; and she ran now that shadow-way, for the heaviness was gone. Across meadows, under that other light she sped, and gathered up all that she had left behind, burst out again in the blink of an eye and elsewhere.

Horses shied in the dark dawning and dogs barked; for now she did not care to be what suited men's eyes. Bright as the moon she broke among them, and in her hand was a sharp silver sword, to meet with iron.

Harp and harper lay together, sword-riven. She saw the underlings start away from her and cared nothing for them; but Evald she sought, lifted that fragile silver blade. Evald cursed at her, drove spurs into his horse and rode down at her, sword swinging, shivering the winds with a horrid sweep of iron. The horse screamed and shied; he cursed and reined the beast, and drove it for her again. But this time the blow was hers, a scratch that made him shriek with rage.

She fled at once. He pursued. It was his nature that he must. She might have fled elsewhere and deceived him, but she would not. She darted and dodged ahead of the great horse, and it broke down the brush and the thorns and panted after, hard-ridden.

Shadows gathered, stirring and urgent on this side and

on that, who gibbered and rejoiced for the way the chase was tending, to the woods' blackest heart—for some of them had been Men; and some had known the wolf's justice, and had come by that to what they were. They reached, these shadows, but durst not touch him: she would not have it so. Over all the trees bowed and groaned in the winds and the leaves went flying as clouds took back the dawn in storm: thunder in the heavens and thunder of hooves below, cracks of brush scattering the shadows.

Suddenly in the dark of a hollow she whirled, flung back her dimming cloak and the light gleamed suddenly: the horse shied up and fell, casting Evald sprawling among the wet leaves. The shaken beast scrambled up and evaded its master's reaching hands and his threats, thundered away on the moist earth, breaking branches as it went, splashing across some hidden stream in the dark, and then the shadows chuckled. Arafel stood still, fully in his world, moonbright and silver. Evald cursed, shifted that great black sword of his in his hand, which bore a scratch now that must trouble him. He shrieked with hate and slashed.

She laughed and stepped into otherwhere as iron passed where she had stood, shifted back again and fled yet farther, letting him pursue until he stumbled with exhaustion and sobbed and fell in the storm-dark forgetting now his anger, for the whispers came loud, in the moving of the trees.

"Up," she bade him, mocking, and stepped again to *here*. Thunder rolled above them on the wind, and the sound of horses and hounds came at distance.

Evald heard the sounds. A joyous malice came into his eyes at the thought of allies; his face grinned in the lightnings as he gathered his sword.

She laughed too, elvish-cruel, as the horses neared them—and Evald's confident mirth died as the sound came over them, shattering the heavens, shaking the earth—a Hunt of a different kind, from a third and other Eald.

Evald cursed and swung the blade, lunged and slashed again, and she flinched from the almost-kiss of iron. Again he whirled his great sword, pressing close. She stepped elsewhere, avoiding the iron, stepped back again with her silver blade set full in his heart and suddenly *here*. The lightning cracked—he shrieked a curse, and, silver-spitted—died.

She did not weep or laugh now; she had known this Man too well for either. She looked up instead to the clouds, gray wrack scudding before the storm, where other hunters coursed the winds and wild cries wailed across belated dawn—heard hounds baying after something fugitive and wild. She lifted then her fragile sword, salute to lord Death, who had governance over Men, a Huntsman too; and many the old comrades the wolf would find following in *his* train.

Then the sorrow came on her, and she walked the otherwhere path to the beginning and end of her course, where harp and harper lay, deserted, the wolf's comrades all fled. There was no mending here. The light was gone from his eyes and the wood of the harp was shattered.

But in his fingers lay another thing, which gleamed like the summer moon in his hand.

Clean it was from his keeping, and loved. She gathered the moonstone to her. The silver chain went again about her neck and the stone rested where it ought. She bent last of all and kissed him to his long sleep, fading then to otherwhere.

And the storm grew.

SIX

SETTING FORTH

The storm had come over the Steading, a wall of cloud and wind which whipped the branches of the oak and ripped the young spring leaves.

And in it Caoimhin came home, running breathless, panting and stumbling as he came along the fence row, fighting the wind which drove across his path.

So he came to the gate and up the path, and young Eadwulf who had come out to see the sheep saw him first: "Caoimhin!" Eadwulf cried.

But Caoimhin passed on, running and holding his side. Blood was on his face. Eadwulf saw that and clambered over the pen and ran after him.

So Niall saw him, not knowing him at first, seeing only that a man had come to the Steading; he left his securing of the barn against the storm and came running from the other side as many did from many points of the Steading, from the house and from the pens, leaving their work in haste.

But when he had come into Caoimhin's way his heart turned in him, seeing the quiver and the bow, the gauntness of the man, the recent scar that crossed his unshaven face, the blood that ran on it from scratches.

"Caoimhin!" Niall said and caught him up arm to arm. "Caoimhin!"

Caoimhin fell, collapsing to his knees, and Niall went down to his own, holding his arms while Caoimhin's body heaved with his breathing. The bloody face lifted again, glazed with sweat, pale and gaunt. His beard and hair showed dirt and grass from his falling. "Lord," Caoimhin said, "he's dead, Evald is lost and dead."

A moment Niall stared at him blankly and Caoimhin's hands gripped his arms as the others gathered round. "Dead," Niall said, but nothing else he understood. "But you are back, Caoimhin—You found the way."

"*Dead,* hear me, Cearbhallain." Caoimhin found strength to shake at him. "Caer Wiell is without a lord— it is your hour, your hour, Cearbhallain. He went into the wood and never out again; he has crossed the fair folk and never will he come out again. Fionn—"

"Is he with you?"

"The harper's dead. Evald killed him."

"Coinneach's son."

"*Listen to me.* There is no time but now. There are men would ride with you, I have told you—"

"The harper dead."

"Cearbhallain, are you deaf to me?" The tears poured down Caoimhin's face. "*I came back for you.*"

Niall knelt still in the dust. Beorc was there, and set his large hands on Caoimhin's shoulders. Most of the Steading gathered and was still gathering, some standing, some kneeling near, and the latest come were shushed so the silence thickened, a deep and terrible waiting.

"Tell me," Niall said, "when and where. Tell me from the beginning."

"From time to time—" Caoimhin caught his breath, leaning his hands now on his knees. "We met, Coinneach's son and I. Fionn Fionnbharr. On the road, when I went after him. And so we parted. Only he brought word to me now and again—how he fared, and where. He wintered in Caer Wiell as he had said he would and the men—I have gathered old friends, my lord, men you knew. I have never been idle, about the roads and the hills and the fringes of the river; I have been to Donn and Ban and all such places and back again, and sent men to Caer Luel—"

"—in my name?"

"What less would bring them? Aye, your name. But we have kept quiet, lord, and hunted and done little— in your name. And we took our news from the harper when he could bring it, even from Caer Wiell. But lately he fled the hold—fled with Evald behind him, and so

they report him dead, murdered—but Evald himself died
after, this very morning. A man of ours was hidden near
his camp; and brings word his men believe him dead—
fear other things less lucky to talk of—in this storm—"
Caoimhin fought for breath and caught his arms. "They
will be riding back to Caer Wiell this morning, today,
lordless, and leaderless—Caer Wiell is yours again. You
cannot deny it now. Men are ready to follow you—Fearghal and Cadawg and Dryw, Ogan, the lot of them—"

"You had no right!" Niall flung Caoimhin's hands
aside and rose, swung his arm to clear himself a space
and stopped at the shocked and staring faces of those
about him, of Lonn and the others, and turned back to
look on Beorc himself, his eyes stinging in the wind
which howled and whipped about them. Lastly he
looked down at Caoimhin, who looked up at him, hurt
and worn as the world had worn him, bearing such scars
as he had been spared in the Steading, where no war
could come—and all at once his peace was shattered
beyond recall. It was not a clap of thunder, although
thunder rolled; it was only a sudden clear sight, how
men fared that he once had loved, how life and death
had gone on for all the world without him. He felt
robbed, for in the stormlight everything about him
seemed dimmed and less beautiful than it had been.
There was gray about the Steading, which had never
been. There were flaws in the faces about him he had
never seen. Tears started from his eyes and ran crooked
in the wind. "So, well, we ought to be on our way," he
said, and helped Caoimhin to his feet. It was hard to
look at the others, but he must, at Beorc's solemn face,
whose red mane whipped in the gale; at Aelfraeda,
whose golden braids were immovable in strongest winds;
at Siolta and Lonn, steadfast; at Scaga whose thin young
face had hollowed almost to manhood in the passing
years. "I have a thing to see to," Niall said to them.
"Like for the wolf and foxes—there comes a time,
doesn't there? The deer are gone. They'll hunt one another in the hills."

"You'll want food," said Aelfraeda.

"If you will," Niall whispered and looked at Beorc.
"If you will—Banain—"

"She will bear you," said Beorc, "I do not doubt. And if she will, then what she wills."

"I need my sword," Niall said then, and turned away, not having the heart for facing Beorc or Aelfraeda any longer. He flung his arm about Caoimhin. "Come up to the house. There'll be ale and bread at least."

So they went. He found Scaga at his left, trudging along with him and Caoimhin, and so he set his left hand on Scaga's shoulder, but the boy bowed his head and said nothing to him, nothing at all, while the thunder rumbled over the Steading and the wind blew the young leaves of the oak in shreds.

They came into the house, into warmth and a busy flurrying after drink and bread and the wherewithal to feed two and more hungry men on their way. Niall went to the corner by the fire and took his sword, but he did not draw it, not even to see to the blade of it. The sheath and hilt were covered with dust. Perhaps rust had gotten to it as it lay by the hearth. But it was not a thing for bringing to light in Beorc's house and in Aelfraeda's. Diarmaid brought the remnant of the armor he had had, and this he put on with Scaga and Lonn and Diarmaid to help him, while Caoimhin sat shaking with weariness and cramming food into his mouth. He had no cloak any longer. He put on the warm vest he had had on before, hung the dusty sword on his shoulder and went out into the chill of the storm to find Banain in the barn.

"I'll come with you," Scaga cried after him, following him outside.

"No," he shouted back to the porch. "Stay warm. Help Aelfraeda. I'll not be leaving without seeing you. Stay inside."

The thunder cracked. He turned and ran, past the gate of the yard and down the hill to the barn and so inside, where was shelter from the wind and the warm smell of straw and horses.

"Banain," he whispered, coming to her in the shadow of the stall. He brought the bridle she had been wearing when she came to them. They had mended its broken rein for the children's riding; but he had never put it on her. He hugged her about the neck and got a nudging in the ribs in return, a whickering from the pony near her in the dark. "Banain," he said. "Banain."

"Cruel," a small voice piped.

He whirled about with his back to the mare. The Gruagach sat on the pony's back, peering at him across the rails of the next stall.

"Cruel to take Banain. Cruel Caoimhin, to take his lord away. O where is peace, Man? Never, never, for Caoimhin; now never for Banain; never for Cearbhallain. O never go."

"I would I never had to." He recovered himself and turned about again, stroking Banain's neck. His hands were still cold from the wind outside. He coaxed the bit into Banain's mouth and drew the strap past her ears. She turned her head and butted him gently in the chest, snorted as a dark shape landed on the rail in front of them.

"Never go," said the Gruagach.

"I have no choice."

"Always, always comes a choice. O Man, the Gruagach warns you." It shifted and hugged itself upon its rail. "Wicked Caoimhin, wicked."

Niall took the cheekstrap and backed Banain out of her warm nest of straw and comfort. The Gruagach followed, a scurrying in the straw: it came out into the light of the half-open door well-dusted, with straws in its hair, and hugged itself and rocked. "Never go," it said.

A sadness came on Niall. He would never have expected such a feeling toward the Gruagach, but he knew that where he fared would be nothing like the creature, never in all the cold strange world. Already it seemed small and wizened and more afraid than frightening. He held out his hand as he would have to a child. "Gruagach," he said, "take care of the people I love. And this place. I have stayed too long."

The Gruagach touched his hand with fingertips, so, so lightly, and cocked his head and looked up at him, then shivered and bounded away to the top of the apple-bin, burying his head in his arms. "She sees, she sees," he wept, "o the terrible face, the terrible lights of her eyes, she sees!"

"Who?" asked Niall. "What—sees?"

"She was waked," the Gruagach cried, looking from

between his arms. "She is waked, waked, waked! and the harp of Kings is broken. O the terrible sword, the sharp, the wicked sword! O never go, Man, O Man, the Gruagach warns you never go."

"Who is *she*?"

"In the forest, deep and still. The harp came there because it had to come. Things of Eald must. Beware, o beware of Donn."

The thunder rumbled and muttered over them. Banain threw her head. "I have no choice," Niall said shivering. "I never had. Farewell."

He flung open the door and led Banain out. He would have shut it for the pony's sake, but the Gruagach was in the doorway. He swung up to Banain's back and rode up toward the house, from which the others were coming down.

So he should not have the chance to come into the house again. He felt cheated—of even that little time. The world seemed the colder as the wind howled and whipped at him and Banain, who danced and fretted under him for distaste of this weather and for the thunder—and never yet it rained. Something keened. It was not the wind. He looked up and behind him and saw the Gruagach perched on the rooftop of the barn, a lumpish knot of hair.

"Man," it wailed. "O Man."

The others came about him, Caoimhin and Beorc and Aelfraeda and all the house so far as he could judge. "Here," said Niall, flinging a leg over Banain's back. "Caoimhin, you must ride. You're spent."

Caoimhin would not, not without arguing about it; but Niall slid down and put him up, and on his own shoulders he took the healthy pack Aelfraeda had put up for them. He kissed her cheek and pressed Beorc's hand. He looked round on all the faces, and they seemed already far from him, slipping away from him, a love he did not know how to hold onto any longer.

"Scaga," he said, missing one. "Where is Scaga?"

Everyone looked around, but the boy was not to be found. "He was with me," said Siolta, "only a moment ago."

"He is hurt," said Lonn.

So Niall shook his head heavily, well understanding

that. "Come," he said to Caoimhin, and hitched the cords of the pack on his shoulder. "Good-bye," he said. "Good-bye."

"Fare well," said Beorc, "and wisely. A blessing beyond that I cannot give you, though I would."

Niall turned his shoulder then and walked beside Caoimhin on Banain. The wind battered at them, and never a drop of rain fell from the black clouds above. The grass and the tender crops flattened in waves, and now and again the lightning flashed in the clouds. He looked back more than once and waved each time, but now they all seemed hazy, shadowed under the storm that had come over the Steading. His heart felt heavier and heavier and his steps were leaden.

"Have care," a small voice wailed from the hilltop at his right. "Have care." It was the Gruagach, sitting on a stone in a sea of blowing grass. "O Man, it is no common rain this brings."

"That fell creature," Caoimhin muttered.

"Speak it fair," said Niall. "O Caoimhin, speak it only fair."

But it was gone, the rock deserted. Banain tossed her head and snorted in the wind.

"Here, lord, she can carry two," Caoimhin said. "Ride with me."

"No," said Niall. A last time he looked back, but a hill was passing between him and those behind: he waved a last time, but they perhaps did not see. He felt a loneliness and desolation, blinked as some wind-borne dust hit his eyes and rubbed at them as he walked along, blind for the moment. When he had gotten them clear he looked back again, squinting in the gusts.

The fences at least should have been in sight. There was only the blowing grass. "Caoimhin," he said, "the fences are gone."

Caoimhin looked, but never said a word. Again Niall rubbed his eyes, feeling a great cold settle into his bones, as if the wind had finally gotten through. Caoimhin had found his way back again, the thought came to him; Caoimhin had come as the harper had come, never reckoning how hard it was—for need, for need of *him*. A haste had come on him, all the same, a blind numb haste to go back to the world again: Ogan, Caoimhin had named the names—Ogan and Dryw and the others, names that he had known, bloody names of bloody years, of *his* years with the King—

And Caer Wiell, to go home again, to whatever home was left—

"Niall!" he heard cry from the hill above him, a human, cracking voice, wind-thinned. "Caoimhin! Niall!"

"Scaga," Niall said, and his heart turned over in him. "Scaga, no."

But the boy came running—boy: he was near a man. He came down the hill and joined them, panting as if his ribs would crack, for he had come the longer, harder way.

"Go back," Niall said, shaking him by the arms.

"I will follow," Scaga said reasonably, "lord."

Niall flung his arms about him; there was nothing left to do. Caoimhin had gotten down off Banain and hugged him too.

So they went, down among the hills, Caoimhin riding mostly and they two jogging along beside, then taking turn about.

"By the river we will find them," Caoimhin said. "There."

SEVEN

MEARA

Women grieved in Caer Wiell, a slow sort of grief, lacking substance or hope. The hunters came home by evening without their quarry and without their lord—men scratched and torn and haunted by long wandering in the wood. They drank together now in the hall, a silent, brooding crowd, whose eyes kept much to the table and to their ale. One man wept, his head bowed into his arms. He was the only one.

In her upstairs chamber Meara sat with her arm about her small son and the boy leaning his dark head against her skirts—not asleep, but drowsing sometimes in his weariness and his fright. Meara sat still and silent, so that the maid, the only servant left her, dared not move or question anything.

"They brought neither home," Meara said at last when the boy had drifted off. She looked toward the tall slit window, toward the night and still-brooding storm. "And they do not come upstairs. So they are not yet sure that he is dead." She stroked her son's drowsing head, looked toward young Cadhla the maid, who had pretended to be at sewing and left it now in her lap. There was stark, constant fear in Cadhla's eyes. There was no law in Caer Wiell this night but fear. The thunder that had rumbled all the day, unnatural, cracked and shook the ancient stones. Then the rain began, at long last, a natural, driving rain. Cadhla looked toward the ceiling, a great and shaken sigh as if some long-held breath had passed her lips as if all nature had been holding its breath. The boy lifted his head. "Hush," said Meara, "It's only rain."

"Does he come?" the boy asked.

"Hush, no, be still. Shall I hold you?"

He reached. Meara took him up. He was a lad of five and mostly too proud to be held, but she took him into her lap and rocked him now.

"Lady," said Cadhla, "let me."

"No," said Meara, just that: "No." So Cadhla stayed, and, looking down, pricked at ill-made stitches, flinching from the thunderclaps. The rain sluiced down the walls, a constant spatter and whisper, and the trees sighed down by the Caerbourne's flood. Ever and again a gust whipped at the curtains and sent the lamps and candles flickering, but the child slept on. From the hall came a clattering of metal, but quiet fell again below, leaving only the rain.

"They do not come," the lady Meara said again in the softest of voices, only for Cadhla's ears. "But tomorrow if he has not come home again, then they will come upstairs."

"Lady," whispered Cadhla, "what shall we do?"

"Why, I go to the strongest," the lady Meara said, "as I did before." She looked down at her sleeping son. Her hand smoothed his dark cap of hair. His small fist clenched the tighter on her sleeve. he was never a hearty child, Evald's son, but small and quick to understand too much. "Hush, what can we do? What could we ever do? But if you can you must be away with him, you understand?"

"Aye," said Cadhla softly, her blue eyes round. "I will." But both of them understood the chances of it, Meara most of all. Gently she caressed her sleeping son, well knowing the men downstairs, that one of them would soon take ambition; and then there was no chance for the boy, no chance at all for any bearer of Evald's blood to survive—perhaps not even past the dawn. There were Beorhthramm and the others, fell and bloody men, wild and bloody as her lord . . . and growing more drunken with every passing hour. The cups were filled again and again downstairs; and cowards gathered the courage they had lost in the woods.

But distant, from outside the window in the dark, from beneath the walls, came the hoofbeats of a running horse.

Meara lifted her head and listened through the thunder and the rush of wind and rain.

"Off the road," whispered Cadhla. "It comes from under the walls, not the gate."

It grew nearer still, seemed to rush beneath the window, and echoed off the stone, distinct in spite of the water's rushing and the blowing of the leaves. A moment it lingered below, then seemed to move on again, and the thunder muttered.

"O lady," Cadhla breathed, clutching the luckpiece at her throat, "it be faery, that."

"It would be my husband's horse come home," said Meara, and her eyes were far and cold. "But it could circle the hold all night and they will not unbar the gates to see, no, they are haunted men. Hush," she said, for the boy stirred in his sleep, and she rocked him, hugged him. The hoofbeats came back again and lingered.

"Faery," Cadhla insisted when the pacing went on and on. "O lady—"

But the hoofbeats passed away into the dark, and below, in the hall, no door was opened or closed: no one went out to see. So the sound died, and the hall grew quiet in the abating of the rain. There were not even footsteps below. The child slept exhausted in Meara's arms, and Cadhla stopped her shivering. The curtain flapped; it had come undone in the wind which now had sunk away. Meara waved a hand toward it and with dread Cadhla got up and approached the dark window to tie it fast, then then began to trim the lamps one by one, a homely act and peaceful in a hall that waited murder.

"You'll sleep a bit," Cadhla said when she had done. She offered her shawl. With a gesture Meara bade her spread it so, over the boy, and some peace they had after that. Cadhla fell asleep in the chair they had set against the door, her hands fallen in her lap, her head resting on her ample breast.

But Meara kept her watch, and listened to the rain which had mostly spent its fury. No tears fell from her eyes, not now. They are for yesterday, she thought to

herself, and for tomorrow. Had the window been wide
enough she would have thought of escape; of braiding
together all the cloth they had and so letting themselves
down. But it was far too narrow for any but her son.
She thought desperately of waiting until those below
were sunk in their cups and so trying to run with him,
passing through that hall. But there was the watch below
to pass, and they might be less drunken.

Perhaps, perhaps, she thought, she could win time for
her son, only a little time; and wise Cadhla, faithful Cadhla might find a way for him and her, a country woman
and not so lost as she. Or Cadhla might somehow get
outside the gates and she might let down her son to
Cadhla's arms.

Or perhaps, after all, her lord would come home—he
was safety, at least, from worse than himself. And this
was the hope which turned her coward, for from the
tower there was no way to escape but the hall below
and the drunken men.

She might feign a mourning for her lord; but any of
them who knew her would laugh at that; nor respect it
even if it were true.

They might fight among themselves, that being the
way of them when they had no one to stop them; and
that was all the respite she could hope for, perhaps a
day to save her son. But that contest only the bloodiest
of them would win.

A door opened in the dark, far away and muffled.
Meara heard, and shivered in the long cold, near the
dawn, waking from almost-sleep with her son's weight
leaden in her arms. He comes home, she thought without
thinking. He has come to the gates after all, bloody
and angry.

But she doubted that. She doubted every hope of
safety except Cadhla still sleeping against the door. She
looked down at her son's face. That wayward lock of
hair had strayed again onto his cheek. She dared not
move to brush it away, fearing to wake him. Let him
sleep, she thought, o let him sleep. He will be less afraid
if he can sleep.

She heard steps of more than one man coming up
from the wardroom below, as one came into the hall.

So, she thought with a chill up her back, it *is* himself; he has come up with the gatekeeper, or waked someone below. We are safe, we are safe if only we stay still—for she knew in her heart of hearts that if the ruffians had left their lord horseless and alive in the forest, then there would be a grim reckoning for that.

Then came a ring of steel, and a cry—a clatter of metal and the dying screams of men.

"Ah!" cried Meara and hugged her frightened son to her breast. "Hush, no, be still, be still."

"It would be himself," sobbed Cadhla, bolt upright, her hands before her lips. "Oh, he has come back!"

In a moment the cries and the blows and the screaming became loud. The boy shivered in Meara's arms, and Cadhla ran to them and hugged them both and shivered along with them.

"It is not," said Meara then, hearing the voices, and turned cold at the heart. Someone was coming up the stairs in haste. "O Cadhla, the door!"

The latch was down but that was never stout enough. Cadhla flung herself for that chair before the door to add her weight to it, but the door crashed open before her and flung the chair against the wall. Men red with blood stood there, with swords naked in their hands.

Cadhla stopped still between, making herself a barrier.

But one came last through the door, a long-faced man in a shepherd's coat and carrying a sword, undistinguished by any badge or arms, but marked by a quiet uncommon in Caer Wiell. His hair was long and mostly grayed, his lean face seamed with scars. A grim, wide-shouldered man came in at his back, and last, a red-haired youth with a cut across his brow.

"Lady Meara," the invader said. "Call off your defender."

"Cadhla," Meara said. Cadhla came aside and stood against the wall, her busy eyes traveling over all the men, her small mouth clamped tight. There was a dagger beneath her apron and her hand was not in sight.

But the tall stranger came as far as Meara's feet and sank down on one knee, the bloody sword clasped in the crook of his arm.

"Cearbhallain," Meara said half doubting, for the face was aged and changed.

"Meara Ceannard's daughter. You are widowed, if that is any grief to you."

"I do not know," she said. Her heart was beating fast. "You must tell me that."

"This is my hold. My cousin is dead—and not at my hand, though I will not say as much for men of his below. Caer Wiell is in my hands."

"So are we all," she said. It was all before her, the hope of passing the gates in safety, the hopelessness of wandering after. "I may have kin in Ban."

"Ban swings with every wind. And what then for you—the wolf's widow? Seek shelter of An Beag? The wolf's friends are not trustworthy. Caer Wiell is *mine,* I say; and I will hold it." He put out his hand to the boy, whose fists were clenched tight in Meara's sleeve, who flinched from the stranger's touch. "Is he yours?"

Never yet the tears had fallen. Meara held them now, while this large and bloody hand stretched out toward her son, her babe. "He is mine," she said. "Evald is his name. But he is *mine.*"

The hand lingered a moment and left him. "Evald's heir has nothing from me; but I will treat him as a son and his mother—if she stays in Caer Wiell—will be safe while I can make her so."

With that he rose and gave a sign to his men, only some of whom remained. "Guard this door," he bade them. "Let no one trouble them. They are innocent." He looked down again, a grim figure still, and holding the bloody sword still in his arm, for it could not be sheathed. "If my cousin should come home again he will have a bitter welcome. But I do not expect he will."

"No," said Meara, and shivered. For the first time the tears fell. "There would be no luck for him now."

"There was no luck for him in Caer Wiell while he had it," said Niall Cearbhallain. "But I will hold it, by my own."

She bowed her head and wept, that being all there was to do. "Mother," her son wailed; she held him close for comfort, and Cadhla came and held them too.

"I would not come down to the hall," said Cearbhallain, "until we have cleansed it." And he went away, never smiling, never once smiling. But Meara laughed, laughed as she had almost forgotten how.

"Free," she said. "Free!—o Cadhla, he is Niall Cerabhallain, the King's own champion! O cleansed the hall! That they have, they have. I knew him once—oh, years and years ago; and the morning has come and our night is over."

A furtive hope had burst in Meara's eyes, a shielded, suspecting hope, as every hope in Caer Wiell was long apt to be twisted and used for hurt. It forgot that the young harper Fionn was dead and lost; forgot an almost-love, for she was still young and the harper had touched her heart in her desolation. She forgot, forgot, and set all her future hopes on Cearbhallain. That was the nature of the niece of the former King, who had learned how to live in storms, that she knew how to find another staying place.

"Mother," her son said—he said little always, did Evald's son: he had learned his safety too, small that he was, which was silence, to clench his small fists on what help there was and never to let go. "Is he coming?"

"Never," she said, "never again, little son. That man will keep us safe."

"There was blood on him."

"It was the blood of all the wicked in Caer Wiell. But he would never hurt us."

So she rocked her son, and the strength left her of a sudden, so that Cadhla must catch them both. And still Meara laughed.

There was a marriage made in Caer Wiell, when the warmth of summer came. There were new faces in the hold, stark, grim men, but soft-spoken and courteous, and no few of them Meara had known in her youth, who smiled to see her, those of them who remembered to smile at all. Some folk remained from the Caer Wiell that was, but the worst had died or fled and the rest had mended what they were; and more and more came to the gates, even farmers who hoped for land—which they got as long as there was land fallow. There were some kinsmen of Niall's, but few; there was a motley lot of folk met over the hills and in them, wild sorts and never to be crossed. There was Caoimhin, lame from the attack;

and gangling Scaga; and grim, mad lord Dryw from the southern hills. But whatever the nature of them, there was law, and more, word spread abroad in what ill-luck the wolf had died, which kept the mutterings from An Beag and Caer Damh only mutterings: they had no desire to trifle with the wood and the power in it. They had felt the storm. So they were content to close the road and to pen Caer Wiell in its remoteness—as if there were anywhere to go.

So Meara wed, decked in flowers and quiet as she was always quiet, and became Niall's lady in Caer Wiell.

And the boy Evald dogged Niall's steps and Caoimhin's and Scaga's and learned play and laughter.

"He is your son," Niall would say to Meara, which he knew pleased her. "And my cousin, and the blood of the Kings is in him on your side."

But at times he saw another thing, when the boy was crossed, when his temper rose. And then twice as resolutely Niall used patience with young Evald, for there were times when the boy could melt his heart, when he laughed or when, though tired, he tried to follow, matching a grown man's steps. He would go everywhere with Niall, onto the walls, up the stairs and down, into the stables and storerooms. A word from Niall could light his eyes or cloud them, and there was no stopping such adoration.

So the boy grew, and if at times Scaga cuffed his ears when he needed it, Evald no more than frowned; it was only Niall could get tears from him. He had a pony to ride, a shaggy beast rescued from the mill, and it thrived and became a merry wicked kind of pony, jogging along by Banain on summer rides. Evald outgrew all his clothes by winter, and all his sleeves were let out, and his waists likewise, keeping Cadhla busy. And on winter nights he listened to the warriors' tales.

But never to anything of Eald, for at any such tale Meara drew him to herself and shivered, so in this Niall forbore.

Meara bore a daughter for him, a fair blue-eyed child; and after her a sister, so he had no son, but this was, if a matter to him, still no real grief—for his luck had brought him two, Scaga, who went to broad-shouldered manhood, a dour young man who managed well the

sometime defense against An Beag; who learned his sol-
diery of men who had fought the long hard war; and he
had Evald, who grew to youth—his heir, for Scaga had
no thought of ruling anything. As for Evald, Evald was
innocent in his assumption that the hold was his . . . for
he was fierce and prideful in his devotion—and learned
to be gentle too, giving all his heart to those who gave
to him—for so Niall had taught him.

So Niall had his daughters and loved them whole-
heartedly, and they inherited Evald's pony when he had
outgrown it. To Evald he gave Banain's latest foal
instead.

Caoimhin died, the greatest grief that came to Niall
in those happy years: it was a simple fall, his lame leg
betraying him on the stairs. So Caoimhin slept in the
heart of Caer Wiell, of a kind of death he had never
looked to die, a peaceful one.

The trees grew again across the river. Snow fell and
melted into spring, and Caer Wiell began a new tower—
for, said Niall, one never knew what the times would
bring. Mostly in his heart was the thought of the King,
who was now toward his manhood, and that wars might
come which he would never see—for age was coming on
him. His hair had gone from gray to white, and one day
he sent Banain away, for she was failing and he could
no longer pretend the years away. He sent Scaga to lead
her, and a troop of his armed men, as if the piebald
mare had been some great chieftain under escort, for
they had to pass the road that An Beag held: and so they
did, with never a stirring from An Beag, which chose to
watch more of late than act, having learned bitter
lessons.

So Banain went, free up the dell.

"She ran," Scaga reported later, his eyes alight. "She
seemed doubtful a moment, and then she threw her head
and lifted her tail and ran the way she could when she
was young. I lost sight of her; the hills came between.
But she knew the way. I do not doubt it."

"You might have followed her yourself," Niall said,
and the tears shimmered in his eyes.

"So might you," said Scaga. "I have my wife, my
son—my home here."

"Well, well, and Banain is home." He set his lips. "So,

well, but so am I, and so are you, that's true. That's true. There's a time to let things go even when we love them."

"Lord," said Scaga, his strong face now much concerned. "You are out of heart about the mare. You were right. It was her time, but it's not yet yours."

"Caoimhin is gone. Of all the rest he had no ties; would I could have sent him."

"He would never have left you."

"Would never have left Caer Wiell," Niall said. "It was the land he loved, these stones; and now he sleeps in the heart of them. I have Meara and Evald and my daughters—That foal of Banain's will serve me, but a strongwilled horse she is. I never liked her half so well."

"We will hunt tomorrow, lord, and change you mood."

"I never found much joy in it, I tell you truth. It minds me of things."

"Then we will ride and let the deer do as they like."

"So. Yes," said Niall, and gazed into the embers from his chair before the fire. A stone wolf's head was above the hearth. It stared back at him. He had never taken it away.

EIGHT

THE LUCK OF
NIALL CEARBHALLAIN

The seasons passed. For long, for very long there was peace—for the young King was a rumor in the hills, and if men spoke well of him, still his day was not yet dawned. So traitors aged who had had most guilt; and true men grew old as well.

"You must do what I cannot," Niall would say to Evald of the King; and poured his hopes into him and taught him arms. "He is your cousin," Niall would say. "And you will set him on his throne. As I would."

Any war in which Niall would not be foremost seemed very far to Evald, for out of his childhood this man had come, already gray, and soon white-haired, but vigorous, a storm that scoured out the hold and scoured the land of every injustice he could find; and rode at times, he or his men, to remind his enemies whose hand ruled in Caerdale. And Evald, who remembered only hurt before this man came and took him to his heart, had never thought those days would end. But end they did, at first without his realizing it—for first Caoimhin went, and then Banain, and Dryw went back to his mountains, and then Scaga took most of the border-riding on himself, while Niall sat at home. And so age came on him. So it came to a small talk in the hall, not the first such sober talk, but the deepest.

"Time will come," said Niall, "when I am gone; and

men will talk—mark you, son, I love you. But true it is
you are my son by love and not by blood. The King's
own cousin: never you forget it. But Evald's too; you
are my cousin and not my son. There are those faithful
who will stand by you come what may: you know their
names. But men will whisper and try to bring you down,
that being the way of men."

"Then I will fight them," said Evald. "And you will
not be gone. Never speak of it."

"That would not be wise." Niall reached for a pitcher
and poured wine into his cup, poured another for him.
"So. I have a match for you in mind."

The color fled Evald's face and flooded it. He took
the cup. He was sixteen and until that moment he had
been a boy, thought like one, mostly for the hunt and
games and dreams of glory in the skirmishes with An
Beag; but he shared a cup with his father, rare honor,
and asked quietly: "Who?"

"Dryw's daughter."

"Dryw!"

"His daughter, I say, not the man."

"Dryw is—"

"Not the cheeriest of men that were my friends. But
the youngest and well-gifted with sons—a fierce lot. He
has one daughter, dear to his heart. His sons have one
sister. And they care for their own. I could set no truer
folk at your back than Dryw's. It would ease my mind."

"Because the man who sired me was one who killed
the King." Evald lowered his head. He had never said
as much, but he had heard.

"Because you are my heir," Niall said sternly. Then
more gently: "I would not see the alliances I made slip
away from you. Dryw I trust; his sons I would trust if
you had a bond to them. Her name is Meredydd."

"What does Mother say?"

"That it's the wisest thing to do."

"What says lord Dryw?"

"He is yet to ask. First I ask my son."

"So, well," Evald said uncomfortably. "Yes. If it's
right." It was unfair. There was nothing Niall could not
have asked of him. For love of Niall and his mother he
would have flung himself on spears, this being the direst
kind of fate he had imagined for himself, warriorlike to

keep Caer Wiell. He had never thought that there were
other ways. This dismayed him more than enemies, that
he had to suddenly become a man in many ways, and
to be wise, and to get children of his own.

"This year," said Niall.

"So soon."

"I don't count my time in years."

"Sir—"

" 'Twould please me and please your mother. I think
of her. I would see you with the strongest allies I can
find—for her sake, if I am gone."

"She will always be safe."

"Of course she will." Niall drank and put on a merrier
face, and smiled for him, which was always like a stone
that had learned to smile, so lean and hard he was.

But looking at him Evald grew afraid, perceiving for
the first time that he was, after all, old; and that his
riding out of the hold was growing hard for him, and his
limbs were not so strong as they had been. So Banain
had begun, growing thinner, bonier in the knees, until
she stopped being young, and they took her to the hills.
Evald believed no fables: Banain was dead; his pony had
died this spring leaving his sisters heartbroken, and he
cherished no illusions.

Why must things die at all? he thought. Or grow old?
And he thought with terror that the curse was on him
too, that now he must be a man and learn to trade in
councils what men traded, and that fighting for the King
when he should rise might be something less glorious
and more the slow and lifelong battle it had been for
Niall.

Evald's son, they would call him, and never trust him
without the claim of his mother's blood and Cearbhallain's allies to support him. He lost his boyhood in that
thinking, and knew what, somewhere in the depth of his
heart, he had always feared: that he might lose Cearbhallain himself and slip back into the dark from which
Cearbhallain had rescued him. They sang songs of Cearbhallain, of bloody Aescford, of bravery and wit and
gallant deeds; and this man fostered him and shielded
him and his mother, which he was old enough to understand was not the least of the gallantries of Cearbhallain.
He remembered the harper, if very dimly, a golden vision

and bright songs; he remembered mostly pain of his true father, blood and pain and a harsh loud voice; and one night of shining metal and hands with the blood of all those who had ever hurt his mother. She had laughed that night, and ever after smiled, and Niall had let no more blood come near her—he washed when he had come home from fighting on the border and never would see them until he and all the men with him had put off their armor and all the manner of war—because this is Caer Wiell, Niall said, not a robber hold like An Beag. And so the men about him learned to say.

But that was years ago. Before the tower rose.

It is for me, Evald thought, full of dread, and looked up at the scaffolding and the jagged stone against the sky. He builds it for me, not for himself. And then the foreboding came on him that it was the last thing Niall might do.

I do not reckon my time in years, he had said.

So month by month of summer the tower rose toward its roofing, and in all those months Niall rode but seldom, and ached much of nights. Meara tended him gently in his sometime illness, and Evald saw how the gray had touched her hair as well, and how worn she grew as his father failed. Only Niall smiled and won her smile from her. But most times Meara wore a worried look.

Month by month the messengers went back and forth with Dryw; and that grim man came, all grayed himself, a lean clamp-jawed man with young men about him who looked little more than thieves—his sons. "So, well," Dryw said having looked Evald up and down, "I have had my spies. They report well of the boy."

"My father speaks well of you," Evald said, which impertinence brought the mountain lord's cold eye back to him and gained a frown.

"Which father?" Dryw asked with Niall there to witness.

"The one who calls you friend," Evald said sharply, "and whose opinions of men I honor."—Which pleased Dryw and made him laugh his dry chill laugh and clap Niall on the arm.

"He is not easily at a loss," said Dryw. And so they sent him away and arranged particulars together, Dryw and Niall, like two farmers chaffering over sheep.

*   *   *

So it was done, and Niall reckoned he had done the best he could. Spring, Dryw promised; Meredydd should come by spring. So Dryw and his sons went home again before the winter snows and Evald walked about with that stricken, panicked look about him that he had had that day of the talk in the hall—but it was well done, well done, Niall told himself, and so Meara said—For, said Meara, now he has kin of mine on the one side and friends of yours on the other.

"And he has Scaga," Niall said. "He has Scaga, truest and closest," which eased his heart to think on.

But that, with his tower, seemed enough. It seemed too wearying to bundle into heavy garments and go riding in the autumn chill; the fire was comfort. Many things which he had done of duty he left now to younger hands, and while he thought it would be splendid, as the snow fell, to saddle up and ride, to hear the hooves crunching the snow, the steady whuff of breath, and to feel the keen edge of the wind against his face—it would not be Banain under him. And to wrap up to take a ride to exercise some horse his men could do as much for seemed pointless, when his men must shelter him from any hostile meeting, when the most that they might look for was a cup of cheer at some farmhouse—but that put him all too keenly in mind of other things he missed. So he forever thought he would like to do these things, and the wanting was joy enough, not to be spoiled by doing. The best thing was his fireside, and listening to the harper who had come to his hall (but nothing like Fionn Fionnbharr, so even that joy paled). At last there was the fire's warmth against the cold that crept into his limbs, and good food, and Meara's kindness and his folk about him. He was fading, that was all, a gentle fading, so that he went all to gauntness.

"I shall see the spring," he said to Meara. "That long I shall live." What he meant was that he should see his son wed, but that seemed too grim a promise set against a wedding: and Meara shook her head and shed tears over him, scolding at him finally, which well contented him: so he smiled to please her. In all he was very tired, and thought the winter would be enough for him. His dreams when he dreamed were of that place between

the hills; of orchards bare with winter; of walking kneedeep in snow to the barn and of the smell of bread when
he was coming home.

He became a burden: he feared he was. He lay about
much in the hall. His son and his daughters cared for
him—for his daughters too he intended marriages, young
as they were, and sent messages, and arranged one for
Ban and his youngest for one of Dryw's grim sons, the
best that he could do. So even in his fading his reach
was far, and he took care for years to come. But Meara
surprised him in her devotion and her tears—a deep surprise, for it had never seemed love on her part, only
habit; for his part it was tenderness, a habit, too. It was
the only thing which grieved him, that he had always
been scattered here and there, doing this or that for
her, and for the children, and never knowing that very
simple thing.

Had he loved her, he wondered? He was not sure
whether he had loved anything as it deserved, only he
had done his duty by everything, save only a little while,
a few years for himself, to which his mind kept drifting
back for refuge. But he had been very fortunate, he
thought, that his duty had brought so much of love to
him.

And he had made a place for gentler things. That,
most. He had brought a little of the Steading with him.
It all seemed a dream, and that of Aescford dimmest,
and Dun na h-Eoin, and the very walls of Caer Wiell.
What was real was a fire, a fish, a shadow among the
oaks; but—strange—he was not afraid this time. And a
small brown face with eyes like murky water.

O Man, it said, O Man—come back.

Niall Cearbhallain was dying. There was no longer any
hiding it. An Beag had made trial of the borders, but
prematurely: Scaga drove them out again, and harried
them within sight of their own hold for good measure,
before grief and concern drew him back again. So Scaga
was there by the hall both day and night, and had armed
men stationed here and there about the countryside; and
farmers to light watchfires if anything stirred.

It was all, Evald recognized, well done, as Niall himself would have ordered it—as perhaps Niall had or-

dered it in his clearer moments, to the man who was his right hand and much of his heart.

So Dryw came, winter as it still was, and the frosts still too bitter for any greening of the land. He came riding up the Caerbourne with enough armed men about him to force his way if he must, like a cold wind out of the southern heights—so unlooked for that at first the outposts took alarm. But then they could see his banners from the walls, the blue and the white, and the first cheer came that Caer Wiell had known for days.

Evald watched them ride beneath the gates. It was, he knew, like what his father had told him of Dryw, not to waste time with messengers, and for the first time he felt an affection for that skull-faced madman. They came with rattle of armor and the gleam of spears and expected to be housed; but among them came a pony with ribbons in its mane, and on that pony rode a cloak-shrouded girl.

"Meredydd," he whispered, slinking from the wall as if he had seen something best forgot. He had no heart for marryings. Not now, never now.

But, "Yes," his father said when Dryw had come to him. "Yes, good for you, old friend." His mind was clear, at least this evening.

So Evald met his bride, who was a thin girl whose clothes ill-fit her, and whose eyes looked nervously over him. Meara had scarcely any time for her with so much on her thoughts, so Evald was left to murmur courtesies in the lesser hall. He was only grateful she had brought her nurse to take care of her.

"I wish," Meredydd said mouselike, from the door in leaving to go upstairs, "I wish I had got my best dress finished. It doesn't fit."

This was all very far from him, but he saw the red in her cheeks and saw how young she was. "It was good of you to come sooner than you promised," he said. "That was more important."

Meredydd lifted her face and looked at him, seeming heartened.

She was not, he decided, what he had planned, but not what he had dreaded either, having a capable way about her when she looked like that. And truth, she quickly had her own baggage up the stairs and ordered her own room and was down seeing to her father's housing and running back and forth with this and that, taking loads from the servants and sending them on other errands so deftly all that number was fed, while his mother took the respite offered her and simply stayed by his father's bedside.

So Evald stayed there what time he could, but never now did Niall stir that evening, but slept a great deal, and seemed deeper in his sleep.

"Go," Meara said to him. "Tomorrow the wedding, Dryw has said. And it would please him to know. She is a fair child, is she not?"

"Fair to us," Evald said, numb in his deeper feelings, but Meredydd had settled into his thinking as she had settled into the hold, without question, because it had to be. "Yes, fair." His eyes were for Niall's face. And then he turned away, and passed the door where Scaga stood watch, haggard and grim and never leaving.

"He sleeps," he said to Scaga.

"So," said Scaga. Nothing more.

It was a premonition on Evald that he should not go up to bed tonight, but stay near. He went down into the wardroom where there was a fire, and lingered there a time, into the dark of the night and the sinking of the fire. There was little murmur from the courtyard or the barracks where Dryw's folk had settled: there was little sound from anywhere.

But the beat of hooves came gently through the dark, gently past the wall, so that it might have been a dream if his eyes had not been open. The hair prickled at his nape and for a moment there was a heaviness over him too deep to throw off.

After that came a scratching at the stones of the wall, and that was too much. He got up and flung his cloak about him, moving quietly, not to disturb the peace. He went out onto the wall, padding softly as he could, unsure whether his ears had tricked him.

Suddenly a darkness bounded up onto the wall, a hairy thing, all arms and eyes. He cried out, a strangled cry, and it leapt back again.

"Cearbhallain," it piped. "I have come for Cearbhallain."

Evald lunged at him: it was too quick and bounded

away, but he threw his knife at it. It wailed and dived over the wall, and now everywhere men were crying after lights.

But Scaga reached him first, pelting down the stairs.

"It was a hairy man," Evald cried, "some dark thing—come for *him;* it said, it had come for him. I flung my knife at it—it went down again."

"No," said Scaga. No more than that. Scaga went running for the stairs; but that *no* was one of anguish—of fear, as if he knew the nature of the thing. Evald hurried after, but "Stay by your father," Scaga shouted at him and was gone.

He stood still upon the stairs. He heard the lesser gate open, heard the hoofbeats going away and rushed to the wall to look. It was a piebald horse with something on its back; and after it Scaga ran, down by the river, under the trees.

"Dryw!" Evald shouted into the yard. "Dryw!"

So it stopped, small and forlorn. The horse had fled, going whatever way it could. And Scaga stopped, crouched near, panting.

"Iron," it wept, "o the bitter iron. I bleed."

"Come back," said Scaga. "Was it for him you came? O take him back."

A shake of the hairy head, of all the body, indistinct in the moonlight, among the leaves. "The Gruagach pities him. Pities you. O too late, too late. His luck is driven all away now. O the bitter iron."

Scaga looked down at himself, his weapons. He laid aside his sword. "That was his son. He did not understand, never knew you. O Gruagach—"

"He is gone," the Gruagach said, "gone, gone, gone."

"Never say so!" Scaga cried. "A curse on you for saying it!"

"Scaga goes wrapped in iron. O Scaga, ill for you the forest, ill for you. The Gruagach goes back again where you might go, but never will you. Ill for you the meeting. You were never like your lord. Eald will kill you in the day you meet. O Scaga, Scaga, Scaga, they wept for you when you left. And the Gruagach weeps, but he cannot stay."

There was nothing there—neither shadow nor moving branch or leaf, only the moonlight on the river.

And Scaga ran, ran with all that was in him, to reach Caer Wiell.

"He is dead," Evald told him when he came inside, when he had reached the doors. And Scaga bowed down in the hall and wept.

There was a decent time of burying and mourning, and Dryw stayed, buttressing Caer Wiell against its enemies. Evald—lord Evald—with Scaga at his side, dispensed justice, ordered this and that in the lands round about, set guards and posts and took oaths from men that came.

Even from aged Taithleach came a message that only Dryw understood. "The King," said Dryw privily, his skull's-face even more grim than its wont: "This passing has set back the time that might have been. Had your father lived and been strong—but he is gone. Alliances must be proved again."

"Send back," Evald said, "and say that I am Cearbhallain's son and the lady Meara's, no other."

"So," said Dryw, "I have done."

And another time: "You cannot go back to your lands," Evald said, "without the promise kept my father made. And I shall be glad of your daughter." It had come to be the truth, for Meredydd had nested in the heart of Caer Wiell to his mother's comfort and to his own, and if it was not love at least it was deepest need. If he had had to sue for Meredydd on his knees now he would have done so; and it was his father's will, the which he tried to do in everything.

"It is nigh time," said Dryw.

So Caer Wiell put off its mourning in the spring. The stones remained, and the grass grew and flowers bloomed, violets and rue.

And vines twined in the wood, among forgotten bones.

NINE

MIDSUMMER AND MEETINGS

Summer lay over the old forest, when leaves veiled the
twisted trunks and graced the skeletal branches with
a gray-green life. They were stubborn, the old trees, and
clung tenaciously to their long existence on the ridge
above the dale. There was anger here, and long memory.
The trees whispered and leaned together like conspirators in their old age while the rains came and the quick
mortal suns shone, and shadows slithered round their
roots within the brambles and the thickets. No creatures
from the New Forest ventured here without fear; and
none stayed the night—not the furtive hare, which nib-
bled the flowers that stopped at the forest edge, not the
deer, which drew the air into quivering black nostrils
and bounded away to take her chances with human
hunters. Not the wariest or the boldest of such creatures
which grew up under the mortal sun might love the
Ealdwood . . . but there were hares and deer which did
wander here, shadowy wanderers with dark fey eyes,
swift to run, and not for hunting.

At rare times the forest seemed other than sullen and
dreambound, and stirred and wakened somewhat, while
the moon shone less white and terrible. Midsummer was
such a time, when the phantom deer gathered by night,
and birds flew which would never be seen by day, and

for a brief hour the Ealdwood forgot its anger and dreamed of itself.

On this night, after many such nights, Arafel came, a motion of the heart, a desire which was enough to span seeming and being, to slip from the passage of her time and her sun and moon which shone with a cooler, greener light, and out of the memory of trees and woods as they might have been, or were, or had once been. She brought a bit of that otherwhere with her, a bright gleaming where she walked. Flowers bloomed this magic night which without her presence might never have waked from their buds, as most flowers did not, in the Ealdwood men saw. She looked about her, and touched the moon-green stone at her throat, which was much of her heart, and shivered a bit in the cool dankness of a world she had much forgot. The deer and the hares which, like her, wandered the shadow-ways twixt there and *here,* moved the more boldly for her presence.

Once there had been dancing on such a night, merry revels, but the harpers and the pipers were stilled, gone far across the gray cold sea. The stone at her throat echoed only the remembrance of songs. She came this night out of curiosity, now that she remembered to come. Mortal years fled swiftly past and how many of them might have passed since her grief and her anger had faded, she did not know. She was dismayed. It pained her heart to see this heart of the wood so changed, so choked with brambles. A great mound rose in this place, thorn-ringed now, about which her folk had once danced on green grass, among great and beautiful trees. This night she walked the old dancing-ring, laid a hand on an oak impossibly old, and strength drained from her, greening his old heart and making thin buds swell at his branch-tips. Such magics she had left, native as breathing.

But overhead the stars should have shone clear. Clouds drifted, wrack in heaven. She looked up, wished them gone, that this night be what it ought. The deer and the hares looked up with their huge dreaming eyes, as for a little time the sky was pure. But quickly a wisp of cloud formed again, and fingers of wind drew the taint back across the sky.

"It is long," Death whispered.

She turned, startled; laid her hand on the stone at her throat, for near the ring had appeared a blot of shadow, a darkness which hovered next a tree the lightning had slain, and for a moment ugly whisperings attended it.

"Long absent," said Lord Death.

"Go from here," she bade him. "It is not *your* night, and not your place."

Death stirred. Deer, beside her, trembled, their shifting steps carrying them nearer and nearer her, and the air breathed with the dankness of most nights in this wood.

"Many years," Lord Death said, "you have not come at all. *I* have walked here. Should I not? I have hunted here. Do I not have leave?"

"I care not what you do," she said. But such was her loneliness that even this converse drew her. She regarded the shadow more calmly, watched it spread and settle on the riven stump as brush swayed. Something doglike settled too, a puddle of shadow at its master's feet. It dipped its inky head and yawned, panting softly in the dark, while the deer and hares froze. "Do not settle to stay, Lord Death. I have told you."

"Proud. Lady of cobwebs and tatters. The old oak is younger tonight. Do you not care to tend the others? Or can it be . . . that a little of you fades, each time you do?"

"He is rooted elsewhere, the old tree, and he is more than he seems. Do not set your hand to him. There are some things not healthy for you as well, Lord Death."

"For many years, many summers, you have neglected this place. And now your eyes turn this way. Have you cause to come."

"Need I cause . . . in *my* wood?"

"The Ealdwood is smaller this year."

"It is always smaller," she said, and looked more closely at the shadow, in which for the first time she could see the least distinction, a suspicion of an arm, a hand, but never, never a face.

"Old friend," he said, "come walk with me."

She smiled, mocking him, and the smile faded, for the hand reached out to her. "Upstart youth," she said, "what have I to do with you?"

"You have given me souls to hunt, Arafel. And they

are *with* me when I have taken them, but there is no sense in them. No gratitude. And less pleasure. Why do I come? What do you see in your side of Eald? What is there, that I can never see?" The shadow drew itself up, and the hound rose too. The likeness of the hand was still extended. "Walk with me," Lord Death asked softly. "Is it not a night for fellowship? I beg you—walk with me."

The deer fled away, bounding this way and that; the hares darted for cover in panic. The hound stayed, a breathing in the shadow. Suddenly there seemed others of them, a shadowy pack, and the shuffle and stamp of hooves sounded where the darkness was deepest.

A wind started through the trees. Where stars had shone, the blight in heaven had become a dark edge of cloud. Arafel glanced from sky to trees, where the shadows flowed, where small chitterings disturbed the peace.

"Send them away," she said, and the other shadows slunk away, and the wind fell. There was only the greater Darkness, and a chill sense of presence.

She walked with him, from out the ring and more and more solidly within this world where Men lived— incongruous companionship, elven-kind and one of Men's less-reputed gods. He said little. This was his wont, and hers. She had no deep fear of him, for elven-kind had never been subject to him; when their wounds took them, they simply *faded,* and where they went, Death was not, nor ever had been. All had faded now, but she had not; they had gone away beyond the sea, but she had not been willing. She was last, loving the woods too well to go when the despair came on others. It was perhaps habit kept her now; or pride—her kind had ever been proud; or perhaps her heart was bound here. Death had never known the motives of the elves.

She did not walk the shadow-ways, that path which was mostly under her moon. Death could not reach to that other place, and she meant that he never should. She stayed companionable with him, her Huntsman, guardian of her forest what time she was absent, who had come to the land when Men came, and who haunted this forest most of all places on the earth. He showed her the land he had had in care, the great old trees with roots well sunk in her own Eald, that could not easily die. She saw their other selves, their aspect beneath this moon, and now and again she found one dangerously fading, and gave her strength to heal.

"You undo my work," he reproached her.

"Only where you trespass," she said, and looked again at the darkness, wherein two soft gleams seemed to shine. "If I do not go where the others have gone, at the last I shall have drawn all Eald-that-was to heal this blight that Men make; and where shall I be then, Lord Death, having used my strength up so? Is that what you wait for? Do you think my kind can die?"

"I wait to see," he said, and his voice was soft and still. A shadow-sleeve rippled in wide gesture. "All of this you might restore, drive out Men, claim it all, and rule—"

"And die, as it did."

"And die," Lord Death said softer still.

She smiled, perceiving wistfulness. "Merest youth."

"Invite me with you," Death wished her. "Let me once see what you see. Let me see you as you are. Show me . . . that other land."

"No," she said, shuddering, and felt the brush of a touch upon her cheek.

"Do not," Death pleaded. "Do not hate me. Do not fear me. All do . . . but you."

"Banish hope. My kind *fades* from wounds."

"But there is none can wound you," he said. "None, Arafel. So you are bound here, to share the fate of Eald."

"There are many who can wound me," she said, looking placidly toward that place where she judged a face might be. "But not you."

"Save when the woods are gone. Save when all that gives you strength has gone. And you live long, my lady of the fading trees, but not forever."

"Yet I shall cheat you all the same."

"Perhaps you will." The whisper wavered, trembled. "Do you know where your kindred has gone? Do you *know* that that place is good? No. But me you know. I am familiar and easy. We are old companions, you and I."

"Companions without fellowship."

"Do you not know loneliness? That, we share."

"But you are all darkness," she said. "And cold."

"Do all see you the same?"

"No," she confessed.

"Perhaps," he said, "you will come to see me as I am."

She said nothing to that, for she was not as cruel as some of her kind, having felt pain.

"I also," he said, "heal."

Still she said nothing.

"Come," he said. "I shall show you my other face."

She stopped at his touch, for the way to another, third Ealdwood lay in his power and the wind from it was chill, that place of *his* making. "No," she said. "Not there, my lord, never there."

"What I take," he said, "most oft I return. What comes into the cauldron comes out again. I have a fairer face, Arafel, which you do not know how to see, having no experience of me. You judge me amiss."

"You have done me service," she said, "in defending Eald from Men. Why?"

And now Death was still, giving her no answer.

"Perhaps," she said, "I shall misjudge my time. Perhaps I shall delay in this woods too long. Only that must you hope for. I give you no hope of my consent."

"I have no hope," said Lord Death. Wind tugged at her, drew her farther. "But come, if not to the one place, to the other. I am anxious that you think well of me. See . . . that I can heal."

His voice was gentle, promising no ill, and in truth there was none that he could do her. Because she had committed herself the once, she yielded, and walked where he would, as mortals walked, their common ground.

And then she wavered, because she knew where he would lead.

"Trust," he begged of her, and the wind tugged more strongly, insistent and cold.

They walked slowly through the brambles and the thickets, mortal-wise and sometimes painfully; and at the last edge of night they came to that grove he sought, a part of the New Forest, that verge of Eald grown up on the edge of the old, nearest Men. Great trees had died, scarred with axes that she had not forgot. The wanton destruction oppressed her heart, for an edge of her own Eald had died that day these trees had perished, truly died, into that gray haze which bordered all her world and bound her sight.

"See," said Lord Death, and the shadow rippled toward a bank of bracken, lush ferns beneath the dimming stars. Man-tall saplings were springing up through it, straight and new. "See my handiwork. Can we be enemies?"

She saw, and shivered, remembering the place as it had been, when the fallen trees had stood tall and beautiful; and their counterparts in her own Eald had bloomed with stars and sheltered her with their white branches. "It is only more New Forest," she said, "and mine is the smaller for it. They had no roots in Eald."

"You do not see beauty here?"

"There is beauty," she admitted, walking farther, and knelt with a pang of memory, for there were bones and shattered wood beneath the bracken, and she touched a long-broken skull. "The trees, you restored. Canst mend this, Lord Death?"

"In time, even that," he said, twisting yet again at her heart. "Do you care for them?"

"I have my own cares," she said; but when she had risen, an old curiosity tugged at her heart, and she walked farther with him, to the flat rock which overlooked the dale, upon a dark sea of trees. She recalled the stone keep the other side of the dale—oh, far too well, among villages and fields and tame beasts and all such business as Men cared for. It was all beyond their sight. Below them the Caerbourne rolled its dark flood seaward, a black snake dividing the wood; and that flow toward the sea made her think of endings, and partings from her kindred, and made her sad.

"Men fare as always," said Death. "Borning and birthing and dying. There is no ending of it."

"Yet they end."

"Not forever. That is the nature of them. You will not look on my new woods; it does not please you."

"Not while mine dies."

"Dies and does not fade?"

She looked at him with cold in her heart. "Go away," she wished him. "I am weary of your company."

"You wound me."

"You, spoiler of all you touch? You are beyond wounding. Begone from me."

"You are wrong," said Lord Death. "Wrong about my wounding. There is loneliness, Arafel; and heartlessness; I am never heartless. Beware of pride, Arafel."

"Go hence," she said. "I weary of you."

There was a snuffling in the shadows at her back, a breathing, a chuckling. She frowned and laid her hand on the jewel that she wore at her throat. The sounds diminished. "You do not frighten me, godling. You never did and never shall. Begone!"

The shadow fled, not without a touch, a chill which achieved wistfulness. She waved it away, and knew him truly fled. There was only the hillside, and the spoiled night, and the wind.

She walked along the ridge, having come this far. All the dale was dark before her, mortals still asleep in this their night and her day. She remembered what of hurt and of fairness Men had brought her . . . how many of their years ago she did not know. She lingered a time, and a curious longing possessed her, to know what passed there, what manner of thing their lives had become.

TEN

BRANWYN

She walked that other way, that slipped with speed no mortal limbs could pace, along paths where brambles did not trouble her. She paused, in the gray glimmering of dawn down the dale, in the pleasant green of new growth, a riverside where she had not come . . . in very, very long. She was beyond the present limits of Eald, and yet not, for Eald was where she willed it, and followed her, stretched thin, so that there was effort in this going.

Morning brought mortal beauty, soft touch of sun in golden haze above the black waters of the Caerbourne, beauty of contrasts which her world did not possess, for there was no ugliness there, no dead branch, no fallen tree or unshapely limb. She glanced aside as a shadowy deer followed her out of otherwhere, black nose atwitch and large eyes full of daybreak. "Go back," she bade it, for it did not know its way hereabouts, and it vanished with a breaking of brush and a flesh of dappled rump, which flickered into the shadow world and safety.

She walked farther, across the water, where now she could see the grim walls of Caer Wiell on its hill, with fields spread beyond it like skirts of gold and green. Evil had lived here once, surrounding itself with harsh men and edged weapons. The keep had a new tower, greater defenses. But today the gates stood open. New Forest had urged its saplings close upon this side of the hill, with grass beyond, and flowers twined upon the grim black stones. She saw Men coming and going on a path, but these Men had no hardness about them. They laughed, and her heart was eased, her interest pricked as it had not been in long years of Men . . . for Death's taunting had cast gloom over her and this sight of life and liveliness was heart-healing.

A few women sat on the green grass, between the forest edge of saplings and the flower-twined walls, and a golden-haired child ran with baby steps on the hillside, laughing. A strange feeling tugged at Arafel's elvish heart to hear it, like the echo of such childish laughter in the long ago. She walked out, into mortal sunlight, saw that the child at least saw her, if others did not. The child's eyes were cornflower blue and round with wonder.

Arafel knelt then and touched a flower, drew a glamour over it, a tiny magic, a gift. The child plucked it and the glamour died, leaving only a primrose clutched in a fat human fist, and dismay in the blue eyes.

Arafel spread the glamour across the whole hillside of primroses, shedding elven beauty on them, and the childish eyes danced for joy.

"Come," whispered Arafel, holding out her hand. The child walked with her into the forest shade, forgetful of flowers.

"Branwyn," a woman called. "Branwyn, don't stray too far."

The child stopped, turned eyes that way. Arafel dropped her hand and the child toddled away, ran at last to the outstretched arms of the woman who had risen to look fearfully into the morning haze amid the bracken.

Human fear. It was chill as Death himself, and Arafel had no love of it. She cast a last longing look at the child and walked away into the shadow of the woods.

"Beware of them," said a whisper at her shoulder. "They die."

It was Death, in the wreckage of an old tree.

"Begone," she said to him.

"They will give you pain."

"Begone, upstart."

"They have no gratitude for gifts," he said.

"The third time—begone."

He went, for at her third command he must, and left a chill behind him.

She frowned and drew back, departing her own way into elven night, and the light of her own and pale green moon.

She thought often about the meeting, but she took her time in venturing again in the face of Death's taunting. Her pride, pricklish elvish pride, refused to acknowledge that he had disturbed her, but she put it off past one midsummer's eve, and yet another, and perhaps more . . . time meant little to her, who measured the oldest trees against her lifetime. But at last she came back to that forest below Caer Wiell, dismayed anew to realize how fast human life fled, for the babe was much taller when she had found her again playing on that strip beneath the walls. The child stared at her from wide, little-girl eyes, her doll forgotten in her lap. She had her attendants, who sat to themselves and laughed shrill sly laughs and never saw their visitor. They chattered among themselves, a ring of bright skirts and fingers busy with embroideries. But the child was grave and curious.

And Arafel sat down crosslegged on the ground, let a child show her daisy-chains and how to count wishes. They laughed together, but then the watching girls came and fetched the child away from the forest edge and scolded her.

It was not every day, nor even every moon, that Arafel came. Sometimes other concerns kept her; but she remembered Men more often than her wont in those days, and sang much, and was happy.

Still the mortal time was long; and when at last she delayed for months, the child took her pony into the woods and set out seeking her, along the Caerbourne's willow-shaded banks.

The wood grew darker very soon; and it was no good place to be. The fat pony knew that, and shook her off and raced away in terror. And Branwyn wiped the wet leaves from off her hands and tried to keep her lip from trembling, for what had frightened the pony chuckled and whispered in the bushes nearby.

* * *

Many the human intruder in Ealdwood that dusk, with calling and blowing of horns; and they found the poor pony with his neck broken. Lord Evald rode farthest and most desperately, driven by a father's love . . . and Scaga led the searchers farther than most would have dared but for shame to Evald's face and dread of Scaga's anger.

Arafel came looking too, having heard the cries and the intrusion. She found the child tucked like a frightened fawn in the hollow of an old and trustworthy tree, dried her tears, banished the dark from that glade. "Did you come hunting me?" Arafel asked, her heart touched that at last, after so many years, there was some hope of Men. "Come," she asked of Branwyn, trying to draw her to that place where childhood might be long, and life longer still. But the child feared those other sights.

And suddenly a father's voice rang out, distant through the wood; and the child chose once for all, and called out, and fled for him

Arafel drew away; and stayed away very long. It was shame perhaps, for intended theft. And pain . . . that, perhaps, most of all. Midsummers passed, and beltains, while mortal Eald grew rank and Death did as he would there, failing her presence.

But come she did when her heart was healed. She expected the child where she would always be, at the forest's edge; and when she did not find her there . . . at least, she thought, Branwyn would be playing on the hillside on so bright a midsummer day; and finally, seeking with persistence, she went even to the stones of Caer Wiell, man-hewn with painful iron.

So she found Branwyn at last, on the tower's crest, in that sheltered nook where the wind could not reach.

The child's shape had changed. It was a budding woman in a woman's gown, who stared at her in alarm and did not truly remember her, forgetting childish dreams. Branwyn had brought bread there for the birds, and stopped in the very motion of her hand, the cornflower eyes greatly amazed, not seeing *how* her visitor had come, but only that she was there, which was the way most mortals looked at Arafel when they saw her at all.

"Do you remember me?" Arafel asked, saddened at the change she saw.

"No," said Branwyn, wrinkling her nose and tilting her head back to stare at her visitor, from soles of her feet to crown of her head. "You are poor."

"So some see me."

"Did you beg of me on the road? You should not have come inside."

"No," said Arafel patiently. "Perhaps you once saw me differently."

"At our gate?"

"Never. I gave you a flower."

The blue eyes blinked, and did not remember.

"I offered you magic. I did you daisy chains, and found you in the woods."

"You never did," Branwyn breathed, cupping the crumbs in both her hands. *"I stopped believing in you."*

"So easily?" asked Arafel.

"My pony *died.*"

It was hate. It wounded. Arafel stood and stared.

"My father and Scaga brought me home. And I never went back."

"You might . . . if you would."

"I am a woman now."

"You still remember my name."

"Thistle." Branwyn drew back, out of her shadow. "But little-girl playmates go away when girls are grown."

"So I must," said Arafel.

And she began to. But she stopped on a last forlorn hope and cast a glamour as once she had done, on the birds which hovered round about, silvering their wings. Branwyn quickly cast crumbs, and the birds alit and fought for them, so that the gleaming faded in a knot of wings and thieving. She threw more. Such were Branwyn's magics, to tame wild things, by their desires. The cornflower eyes lifted, dark and ill-wishing, conscious of their own power and disdaining forever what was wild.

"Good-bye," said Arafel, and yielded up the effort which held her so far out of Eald.

She faded back then, out of heart to linger there.

"Did I not warn you?" Death made bold to ask her, when next their paths crossed. Then in anger Arafel banished him from her presence, but not from the wood, for she was out of sorts with Men. The dream she had dreamed of humankind had proved more than vain, it was turned altogether against her, like the child who had grown as the saplings had grown in Death's new forest, taking root in this world, and not in hers.

She slipped within the safer, kindlier light of her moon, and into the forest of Eald as her eyes saw it, a forest which had never faded since the beginning of the world, save those areas gone for good. Here all the leaves were silvered in the moon's greener, younger glow; here waters sang, and the birds were free, and the deer wandered with all the stars of night in their eyes.

It was her consolation then, to dream, to walk the woods she loved, and to keep that which remained as it had always been, forgetting Men. Of midsummer nights, sometimes she came, and saw mortal Eald grown wilder and more deserted still. How Death fared, she had no knowledge, nor cared, though it seemed that he fared well, and hunted souls.

ELEVEN

Dun na h-Eoin

The banners fluttered over the tumbled stones, the watchfires flickered in the dusk, like stars across the plain. There was war. It had raged from the Caerbourne to the Brown Hills to Aescford and south again, for the King had risen, Laochailan son of Ruaidhrigh, to claim the hall of his fathers, ruined as it was.

Evald had come, of course. He was among the first, riding out of Caerdale to forestall the King's worst enemies in the days before the King declared himself. He came with Beorc Scaga's son, and armed men and no few stout farmers' sons out of the dale, with all the strength that he could muster. And Dryw, the son of the Dryw of Niall's day, rode from the southern mountains with the largest rising of that folk since Aescford. So Luel rose; and Ban; they were expected. Latest came the folk of Caer Donn, high in the hills: lord Ciaran led them. Ranged against them were Damh and An Beag, the wild men of the Boglach Tiamhaidh, and the bandit lords of the Bradhaeth and Lioslinn.

And the war was long, long and bitter, and Evald felt little of glory in it: they named him in songs, but more and more he understood the Cearbhallain, for what they sang as brave he remembered most as mud and fear and being cold and hungry. But all the same he fought, and when he had time to think at all, he spent it missing Meredydd and his daughter and his fireside. He had pains in his joints and his scars when it rained. A great deal of the war seemed to be marching and riding, mov-

ing bands of men here and there and forestalling the
enemy at one point to have them break out in another
burning and looting of what they had lately made safe,
so that they had had great pains to make a border and
to hold it, for the marshes could never be trusted and
the hills were full of warfare.

But at Dun na h-Eoin all that had changed, where
campfires gathered and the enemy massed so many they
looked like a blight upon the land, their backs against
the hills.

Then was a battle, fierce and long, fought from the
breaking of one day to the evening of the next, and the
dark birds gathered thick as the smoke had been before.
But the King prevailed.

"Your leave," Dryw ap Dryw asked of the King that
day on the field: "They'll have no rest of me."

"Go," said the King. Dryw was himself pale and spattered with blood, straining at the recall like some hound
called back from the hunt. "Keep them on the move."

So Dryw leaped onto his horse and gathered his men
about him, afoot, many of them, accustomed to move
like shadows among the hills.

"By your leave," said Evald, "I would go with Dryw.
An Beag and Damh are old enemies of my hold—and
they have force left. The most of my men are here with
me; if they should come at Caer Wiell now—"

"We will come at their backs," said the King. "At all
possible speed. Let Dryw harry them as he can."

"But Caer Wiell—" said Evald. His heart was leaden in
him looking around at the desolation, the clouds of birds
flying with the smokes of fires to darken the sky. It was
not well to dispute with Laochailan King; he was a man
of middling height, Laochailan, fair with eyes of a pale
cold blue that never took fire. He had outlived his counselors. They had held him on the leash most of his life,
and he was cold, seldom roused. Even in battle his killing was cold; in policy he was deliberate and immovable.
And Evald turned his shoulder and strode away with a
turmoil in his thoughts. It was treason in his mind, but
the will of the Cearbhallain still held him, so that it was
would and would not with Evald. He was on the verge
of gathering his folk and riding away despite the King;

Beorc Scaga's son hurried to his side seeing in his eyes, seeing wrack and ruin in the offing, on the bloody field.

"Cousin," the King called after him.

Evald strode to a stop and turned, lifted his head, keeping his anger behind his eyes. "My lord King."

"I will not be scattering my men, some here, some there. You will not be leaving this place without my will."

"Caer Wiell was refuge for your cousin and stronghold for men that held against all your enemies. It holds now against An Beag and Caer Damh and makes their homecoming dangerous. My steward is a capable man to hold against the force they left behind, but he has too few men in his command. I have stripped my land, giving you every man, every weapon I could bring. Now the onslaught comes at Caer Wiell, and what profit to you if Caer Wiell should fall? You would lose all the valley of the Caerbourne; and it would be strong against you— as strong as it ever was for you, lord King, and as dearly bought."

Not even this brought passion to the King's face. "Do you think to ride against my command, cousin?"

For a moment breath and sense failed Evald. The field, the King, the counselors about him swam in a bloody haze. They were close by the ruins of Dun na h-Eoin: the black birds settled on its broken walls to rest, some too sated to take wing. They began to pitch tents, some bright with the green and gold and most leathern brown, even among the slain, amid the wailing of the wounded. Men removed the bodies, looting them too; or carried the wounded to what care they could give them; or despatched the hopeless or the fallen enemy. That was the manner of the King's war, and the sound and the stink of it muddled the mind and made right and wrong unclear. Evald's hand was on his sheathed sword; and blood had gotten into his glove and dried about his fingers, whether his own or others' he had not yet explored. He thought only of his home, and his eyes saw nothing clearly.

"Will you obey," the King asked, "or no?"

"The King knows I am loyal."

"Then come. Come take counsel with me. Now."

Evald considered, looked at Beorc, Scaga's younger

image, beside him. Beorc would ride; and gladly. And thereafter they would be rebels against the King, and no less to be hunted. If they were rebels, then the King might fall, for Dryw would go with them, and so the southern mountains and dale would do the thing that would ally them with An Beag and Caer Damh, in deed though never in heart. And perhaps the King saw that looming before him, since he had called him cousin twice in the same address and spoke to him courteously. Laochailan was cold, but he was clever too, outside the cold determination which had peopled this field with dead. And he knew what was necessary.

"Come," Evald said to Beorc quietly, and so they went, across the littered field with its canebrake of spears standing in corpses, of tattered banners of the Boglach and the Bradheath, of death and agony.

They had pitched a tent for the King among the ruined stones of Dun na h-Eoin, in the courtyard, by the struggling oak which had somehow survived the fires. They had driven the pegs between the shattered paving stones and into what had been a garden. Doves had sung there. Now carrion crows flapped their dark and sluggish wings, startled by their coming. And to this state the King retreated, drawing with him others of the lords.

As they gathered, Evald glowered about him and tried to think what there was to do—for he would far rather now have been the least of men in Dryw's company than the lord he was. There was Beorc by him and no other, for he had no kinsman but the King himself, a king who would as lief not remember that dark history or how he had come to be. Ciaran of Donn was there with his sons Donnchadh and Ciaran Cuilean, a fey and strange lot. Fearghal of Ban came with his cousins, small dark men and bloody-handed, like Dalach of Caer Leul and his brothers. They were northerners all of them and some from the plains, and none of them had any close ties to the dale or the south.

So perforce Evald came into the tent with them, and bided his time while the King's servants helped Laochailan with his armor and one brought them wine to drink. It was the color of blood. Evald took the cup and it had the taste of it as well, a coppery ugliness in the smoky air, the reek of sweat that was on them.

"Dryw has sped after them," the King said to those who had not been there earliest. "He will keep them moving and never give them rest."

"I say again," Evald began, but Laochailan King turned that pale cold glance on him.

"You have said much," said Laochailan. "You try our patience."

"I serve my King from a hold that has been his from my father's time."

"From the Cearbhallain's," the King said softly, as if it had to be explained, and the color leapt to Evald's face.

"And your cousin's, lord." Evald kept his voice steady, set down the cup and stripped the glove from his hand. Some sword or axe had cut through the leather. The blood was his. "As you kindly remember. I ask your leave—no, I beg it, to go now and keep Caerdale in your hands. They will join with their own forces. Dryw may not be enough for them when they have gained what strength they have in their own holds. They will gather forces again—"

"Do you lesson me in warfare?"

They were of an age, he and his King, born near the same year. "I know my lord King has wide concerns. So I would take this small one on myself."

"And shall we all go riding to our own holds?" asked Fearghal. "Two years it has taken to bring us and the traitors to this field, and lord Evald would have us go each to his own defense again."

"This field is half empty," Evald said. "The enemy has gone, has it passed your notice, lord of Ban? We sit here licking our wounds while theirs will be healed when they have reinforced themselves, and their strength be doubled if they should take Caer Wiell. More than doubled. In its full strength, Caer Wiell could hold for longer than we may have strength in us to hurl against it, with all the Bradheath at our backs."

"I will not have dissent," said the King. "That is deadlier than swords. Nor will I release any but Dryw. His men are light-armed and apt to this kind of war. You fear too much, cousin. Your steward is a skilled man in war; and Caer Wiell has defenders. If anything, An Beag is apt to draw off its attackers to come in our faces, not against your lands."

"That was not the way I learned An Beag. No. Pardon me, lord King, but they know the value of Caer Wiell in their hands, and I know An Beag, that they will take what chance they have. Dryw may try but they may hold him in the hills—and I fear some all-out attack against Caer Wiell before this is done, sparing nothing. We have hurt the enemy, never killed them. A wounded beast is still to fear."

"Is fear your counsel then? No, hear me. I will not divide my forces. I will brook no talk of it."

"*Set us through the pass,* lord King; and when you come at their backs then we will be at their faces. If we are divided, then reunite we will, over their corpses. But let Caer Wiell fall and we will leave our corpses at every step we take into the dale."

The King's fair face never turned color but his eyes were cold. He lifted a hand that bore the Old King's ring and silenced the others with a gesture. "You are too forward. I will not yield in this."

"Lord," Evald muttered, and bowed his head and took up his cup again, moved off from the King's presence, toward Beorc who kept to the shadow, for he did not trust his wits or his tongue just now. "Go," he whispered to Beorc, "take horse and take at least the message of what happened here."

"I will," said Beorc, and bowed and was almost out the door with a turn upon his heel, a hasty man like his father.

"*Recall your man,*" the King said. "Hold him!"

Spears came down athwart the doorway. "Beorc!" Evald cried at once, knowing Beorc's mind. Beorc stopped but scantly short of harm, and lowered the hand he had almost to his sword.

"Where in such haste?" asked the King. "Dare I guess?"

A lie tempted Evald. He rejected it and looked Laochailan in the eye. "My messengers have the habit to come and go. Should the enemy know more of what was done on this field than my own folk?"

It was perilous. The King's eye had that chilliness that

went with his deepest wrath. "Cousin," said Laochailan, "messages are mine to send. Do you not agree?"

"Then I beg you send Beorc and quickly. He knows the way."

"I will not have it said a man of this host went home, not the lord of Caer Wiell, not his steward's son, not the least man of his following."

"Lord King," said Ciaran of Caer Donn. "But a messenger—there is treachery in An Beag and Damh. There would be no whispering in the camp at this man's going. It would be well understood—at least by Donn. The dale is at our doorstep, and if Caer Wiell should fall it would be like the old days, with burning and looting in the hills. A messenger to give them heart and ourselves to come at the backs of our enemies—but we will be slow. We have the longer way to go. And what if their heart failed them in Caer Wiell?"

"You make yourself a part of this contention," the King said wryly, and he frowned, for Donn had favor with him. "But Caer Wiell will have no lack of heart. After all, they defend their own lives. and that is trustworthy in these dalemen."

"Lord," Evald said, hot with passion, "but the choice of a defender might be a sortie if he hoped for no help— they are brave, my folk, but they may also be desperate."

"Lord King." It was a voice hitherto unheard in council, Ciaran Cuilean, the younger son of Donn. "You gave your word no man of us should go home before the war is done. But Caer Wiell is not my home. And I know the hills."

There was a deep frown on his father's face and on his brother Donnchadh's. But the king turned to him with his anger sinking. "So. Here is one man who has the gift of courtesy. And one I would be loath to lose."

"Never lost," the younger Ciaran said. He laughed, tallest of all his kindred, fairer than most and more light-hearted. "I have scoured those hills often enough. I can ride through them with less trouble now, if the King will, and maybe quicker than Beorc, who knows? He has not had the hills for his hunting, and I have."

"Then you will carry lord Evald's message," the King

said. "Do you frame it for him, cousin, and let us be done with it. I have given you all I will."

A fell suspicion came on Evald then—that his cousin the King had some fear of him, feared messages and secrets passed—feared this kinship with him. It was a dark thought and unworthy. Others followed it, as dark and fearful. He drove them all away. "Lord King, my lord of Donn, my gratitude." He worked the ring from his finger. "My steward's likeness you can know from his son. Show this to him. Speak to my lady: I send this ring to her. Tell her how things stand. That whatever they hear they must hold a little time, and the King will be coming at An Beag from the back."

"Lord," said the younger Ciaran, taking the ring, "I will."

"There will be peril in it," Evald said.

"Aye," said Ciaran, just that, which so quietly spoken mended all his thoughts of Donn.

"Speed well," Evald said earnestly, "and safely."

"Your leave, sir—lord King." So Ciaran embraced his father, but his brother would not, and excused himself to the door of the tent.

"I am in your debt," said Evald quietly. His pride was hurt, and anger still rankled in him, for it was less than he had wanted. A terrible fear was in him that the King wished the war to go toward the dale and batter down its strength awhile, for it was too rich and too well-situated and its lord was a kinsman. But that was too dire, even thinking what the war had come to. It was too great a waste. He looked on the young man Ciaran, as young and high-hearted as once he had been, and all his heart went with the man as he walked from out the tent and into the dying day. But he ached with his wounds, and there was counsel to be held. He set his hand on Beorc's shoulder, silently wishing him to peace, and Beorc's arm was hard and stiff with anger.

So the King took counsel of them, how they should map the last assault on An Beag and Damh and the Bradhaeth, while the cries of the wounded and of the carrion crows mingled in the evening. Evald shivered and drank his wine. He served the King as his father would, if he had lived to see the day; and for his mother's sake; and little for his own.

"That is a good man they sent," Beorc said quietly while the King called for wine. "They speak well of the youngest son of Donn."

"So shall I," Evald said, "of all Donn, ever after this."

As for Ciaran, he delayed little in his going, seeking after the best horse he could lay hand to, taking his brother's shield with the crescent moon of Donn upon it, for his own was broken.

"Take care," his brother said, Donnchadh, dark as he was fair, less tall, less favored by the King or even by their father.

"I shall," Ciaran said soberly, seeing to the gear, and took the wineflask his brother pressed on him. "That will come welcome on the trail."

"You should have kept silent. You never should have thrust yourself into this."

"It is no small message," Ciaran said, "the saving of the dale."

"He never trusts the dale. Never. It is unsavory. And never you forget it."

"I shall not," Ciaran said, and hung the shield on his saddle, with the parcel of bread and meat a servant brought him. He slung his sword there too, and turned and embraced his brother longer than his wont at partings. "Evald galls the King. But that is not saying he is no true man, far too true to lose. . . . Keep you safe, Donnchadh."

"And you," his brother said, holding him by the arms. "You take it far too lightly. As you take everything."

"And you are far too worried. Is this more than riding into the same hills with the enemy in strength in them? More to fear is Dryw: I should hate him to take me for some wild man of the Bradhaeth. Keep yourself safe. I will see you at Caer Wiell—and I shall have been dining on plates and sleeping in a fine soft bed, while you shiver in the dew, Donnchadh."

"Do not speak of sleeping."

"Ah, you are too full of omens. I shall fare better than you do, and worry more for you before the walls than myself behind them. Only see that you come quickly and we will push the rascals north and be done with them. Be more cheerful, Donnchadh."

So he took his leave, and flung himself into the saddle and rode away, taking the longer path at first, which was less littered by the dead and seeming-dead. The smokes of fires lit the hills, campfires and the fires lit by the pit where they dragged the dead.

It was not an auspicious hour. He would gladly have rested. But he served the King and lived to do it when others he knew had not. And he had to take Dryw's way through the hills and not fall into ambush, either of Dryw or An Beag.

He lost no time in going now, through the wrack of war. Truth, he was not as light about the matter as he had told Donnchadh, but he saw ruin in delaying the army at Dun na h-Eoin, ruin for more than Caer Wiell. It was twice Laochailan's failing, to delay too long upon a field and throw away half of what they had gained; and the dale was too close to Donn. Now it was rushing all downhill, the King on the verge of moving. He was, he hoped, the first pebble before the landslide—for now Donn would give the King no peace. And so they would remember this ride of his, he thought, for he rose to herald not alone the battle for the dale, but what might well prove the telling battle of all the years of war.

TWELVE

THE FARING OF CIARAN CUILEAN

It was not so swift a ride, from Dun na h-Eoin's ruins through the hills. Once Ciaran met with Dryw's folk, but only once, and that was to his liking, for the southrons were sudden men and apt to haste in their killings. He suspected their presence sometimes, a silence of birds where birds ought to sing, a strangeness in the air that he could not put name to. But at last he had passed all of that manner of thing and reckoned that he was past Dryw's farthest easterly advance—for Dryw would go off to the north direct to the Caerbourne as the enemy had fled, while his own course cut deeper into the woods.

But at last he reached the river himself, and forded it, choosing rather the hazards of the far shore than the ill repute of the southern one. He had been in the saddle so long he had forgotten when he had rested—his resting when he took it was only for the horse, and then he was back in the saddle again, sleeping little, aching with the weight of the mail and of his bruises from the battle. Now he kept the shield uncased on his arm, trusting none of this dark wooded way through the vale of the Caerbourne. He was in the dale now. There were no friends hereabouts. He watched about him, no longer hoping that Dryw was close. This was the darkest, the most dangerous portion of his ride. He had managed it

119

so that he reckoned to pass An Beag in the dark, and hoped that he knew well enough where he was.

The day waned, and at times the horse faltered on the narrow trail, which ran over stone and through woods, along the black waters of the Caerbourne, which rushed and splashed over rock in its shallow places, frothing white in the gathering murk. The brush was too thick here for his liking though it offered him cover. He was a horseman; he preferred something less tangled than this thicket, which wore at the horse and in places made every step a risk, in which their moving sounded all too loud. Least of all did he like the whispering that filled the twilight here, rustlings not of the horse's making, little movings which seemed wind alone, and might be something else. All this forest was a place of ill legend; and they did not love such legends in his hills, in Caer Donn, where the old powers were still dreaded, where ruined towers and strange stones poked from out the gorse and broom and reminded them of all things older than the gods, old as stone and like the stone, everywhere underfoot. There were places in his own hills he would not ride by twilight, not for any cause; and names not for speaking by dark or brightest day. The terror was as close here. The horse, long-ridden and drenched in sweat as it was, still threw its head and rolled its eyes and stared into this shadow and the other, nostrils wide. Where it could it kept a steady pace through the forest shadow, a panting rhythm of leather and metal and the beat of hooves.

Then two pale moths came flying, a whipping arrowsound . . . Ciaran flung up the shield; and a blow jarred it, while the horse reared up and leaned leftward in a sudden loosening of life.

He sprawled clear of the dying horse, shield lifting, jarred by a second shaft thumping into the wood while others hissed through brush and his back hit the thicket. He scrambled desperately to cover himself and to run, tore his ungloved right hand on thorns, while the crash of brush warned him of enemies coming. His back met a tree and he braced himself there on his feet. He had his sword from sheath, and they came on him in a mass in the forest dark, with staves and knives. Blows battered at his shield, and he hewed at them with every stroke that his weary left arm could gain him room to take—the blade bit and there were screams. They tried to come at him from behind, and he swung with his shoulders still to the tree and killed one of them and another, rammed his shield under a bearded chin and hewed again, with ebbing strength, for there was a quick numbing pain in his side and he knew something had gotten through, in the joinings. An axe swung down on him, shivered the top of the shield and stuck fast. He let the shield go and swung the sword two-handed, clove ribs and wrenched the blade free in backswing, while a staff came down on him. The blow dazed him; but he rammed the blade's point into that one's belly and slew him too . . . while brush crashed and cries were raised beyond—*Help, ho! help, we have him!*

He took to the brush and began to run, staggered across the thigh-deep rush of the Caerbourne, chilled and sodden, waded ashore and set out running on the other bank, sought brush again when arrows hissed after. Voices cursed in the gathering dark. He sought higher ground with a wildling's instinct, not to be driven into some hole against the stream's winding banks. Branches tore at him and snapped. His limbs turned leaden with the weight of armor, and his side ached. A veil seemed fallen over his eyes and the little light in heaven was dimmed, all murky, yet for a time he ran with hope, for it seemed that his pursuers had fallen behind. He climbed, took ways closer and closer with brush and twisted, aged trees, through tangles so dense that even bracken would not grow, past stony upthrusts and over jagged ground. He hoped; and then the brush about him crackled to a dry chuckling, and the wind stirred through the branches like a rising storm. He ran farther, until all the sound in his ears was his heartbeat, and the brush breaking and his own harsh breath tearing his throat.

But another breathing grew at his heels, the whuff of a running horse, the beat of hooves which broke no brush as it came.

He spun about to face attack, but there was nothing there but the blackness, and the wind and a cold which settled about his heart. Then he feared as he had never feared in battle, and ran as if effort before this were nothing. The ache in his side was more than want of breath; he pressed his swordhand's wrist there and felt the ebb of blood.

He was weakening. He heard a chuckling and now knew the name of that rider which followed him, and the name of the wood into which he had strayed. And when he was nigh to falling he set his back against an aged tree in a space clearer than the others, where it seemed that he might at least have the grace of seeing his enemy come on him.

Shadow came, and a spatter of rain, a rattle of thunder, and the baying of hounds. Shadows flooded among the trees, black bits of night which rushed and leaped for him. His sword swept through them, nothing hindering, and a coldness fastened and worried at his arm, numbing all the way to his heart.

He cried aloud and tore free, ran, leaving a fragment of himself in the jaws, and the sword was no longer in his hand. The shadows coursed behind him, and the hoofbeats rang like the pulse in his ears and the hoarse breathing was like his own. The enemy was not behind him, but lodged in his side, where the wound worked at his life. A part of his soul was theirs, and they would tear him to nothing when they came on him again, a rending far worse than the first. Rain spattered into his face and blinded him, dampened the leaves so that they clung to him and his armor was soaked so that he did not know now what was blood and what was rain. He stumbled yet again, in a crash of thunder, and of a sudden as surely as there was a horror behind him he conceived of safety in the trees ahead, where seemed a mound overgrown, a swelling of the land with life, where the trees grew vast, and strong, stretching out their limbs in sympathy.

He reached it, entered it, sped in strange freedom of limb where trees were gnarled and straight at once, barren and flowered with stars, and aglitter with jewels like hanging fruit, with treasure of silver laid upon the white branches, swords and shining mail, cloth like morning haze, spiderweb among pale green leaves.

A sword hung before him, offered to his hand . . . he tore it from the leaves in a scatter of bright foliage, and the brightness about him faded, leaving him alone with the dark and the swift loping shadows, with the dark rider, who burst upon him in a flickering of lightnings and yet absorbed no light himself, like a hole in the world through which he might fall forever, if the hounds did not have him first. He held the illusory blade trembling before him, and shuddered as its light drew detail from the dark, of jaws and eyes of hounds. He was drawn to look up, to lift his face unwilling, to face the rider—he saw something, which his dazed mind would not recall even in the instant of beholding it.

The rider came closer, and a chill came on his flesh, on all but the hand which held the blade. He lost the brightness, could not hold even his vision of this grim place. The black began to come over him, but he slashed at it and the hounds yelped aside from him, bristling and trembling.

"Come," a voice whispered to him, very softly.

He must, for he could not hold his arm up any longer. The blade wavered, and sank, and yet a warmth broke like a breath of spring at his back. "Stand firm," someone said.

"He is mine," said the shadow, a voice like shards of winter ice.

"Be off," said the other, soft and without doubt.

"He has stolen from you. Do you encourage such thefts?" And for a moment the world was bright, and the shadow was a blight upon it, a robed darkness which stood in an attitude of amazement. "Ah," the cold voice breathed, wonder-struck. "Ah. *This* you have kept from me."

Light blazed. Ciaran staggered in it, and his knees hit the ground, a shock which wrung a sob of pain from him, and he could no longer tell earth from sky or day from night. Wet leaves lay against his cheek or cheek against the leaves, and the rain beat down into his face, chilling his torn soul.

But the shadow was gone, and the thunder stilled. It seemed the moon shone down. A face confused itself with it, and with the sun in a strange, fair sky.

He still clutched the sword. Slim cool fingers pried his hand from it, eased his limbs, covered him with a downy peace in which the only pain was to his heart, an ache and a memory of loss.

THIRTEEN

THE TREE OF SWORDS AND JEWELS

She knelt with the rain still dripping off the leaves, a dew upon them both, and very still and pale the intruder lay beneath the mortal moon. Iron tainted him, and yet he had torn through into her forest—if only for a moment; had brought iron there, and Death. She was stirred to anger, and to fear, and to a longing which had not been in her heart since the child had broken it. To have entered her Eald, to have found that very heart of it and to have stolen an elvish sword . . . it was no common thief, this Man, and no common need could have forced him. Perhaps his mortal eyes had been affected by that terrible wound he bore, so that he fled with truer sight than most; but never in many a hunt had Lord Death failed.

Eald had stretched far once, before the coming of Men; and once, before her folk knew much of Men, there had been a few of halfling kind, for elvish loves and dalliances among these fatal strangers. Still, she thought, there might be elvish blood drawn very thin in some, halflings who had never felt the call across the dividing sea, who had never faded. In hope she tried to draw this stranger with her, but the iron weighted him and he could not stay.

She endured the anguish of handling it, undoing buckles, putting it off him, every bit and piece. So she uncovered a terrible wound in his side, and drew on her power to begin its mending, healed the little scratches with a single touch. And when she had rested a moment, it was not hard to bear him away with her, simply a holding of his head in her lap, and a thinking on elvish things. Then the trees became what they truly were, straight and beautiful, and the sun of her day shone down with kindly warmth in that grove.

He slept long, while the wound healed itself, while the lines of mortality faded from his face and left it beautiful, with that beauty which might be elven heritage. She did not leave him in all this time, waiting for his waking with all her heart.

And at last he did stir, and looked about him, and looked into her eyes, seeming much confused. He began at once to fade into the mortal world, into darkness, being in his own mind again, but she took his hand and drew him back before he could slip away. "Beware of going back," she said. "Death has a part of you. Too, too easy for him to call you into his shadow as you are. You are much safer here."

He tried to rise, still holding to her hand, maintaining that delicate hold on *here*. She lent him strength, the green force which sustained the trees themselves, and after a moment he was able to stand and to look about him. Wind whispered through the leaves and the sun cast its own glamour while deer stared at them both wise-eyed from the green shadow, in the grove of swords and jewels.

"I was dead," he said.

"Never," she assured him.

"My heart hurts."

"So it may," she said, "for it was torn. And that healing is beyond me.— What is your name, Man?"

Dread touched his eyes. "Ciaran," he said then quietly, as a guest ought. "Ciaran's second son of Caer Donn."

"Caer Donn. Caer Righ, we called it, the King's domain."

He feared, but he looked her in the face. "And what is your name?" he asked.

"I shall tell you my true one, that I do not give to mortals; for you are my guest. It is Arafel."

"Then I must thank you with all my heart," he said earnestly, "and then beg you set me on the road from here."

In so many words he healed her heart and wounded it . . . and a regret came into his eyes as if he had seen the wounding. He held up before her his right hand, on which he bore a golden ring, worked with a seal.

"I have a duty," he said. "On my honor, I have to go and do it, if there is still time."

"Where is this duty?"

He lifted a hand as if he would give a direction, and nothing was the same. "There are armies," he said in his confusion, pointing where he might mean the Brown Hills. "There is war on the plain; and my King has *won*. But the enemy has drawn off this way, which is a valley where they might hold long in a siege if they could take it. And lord Evald of Caer Wiell is riding with the King. Do you understand, lady Arafel? War is coming up the dale. Caer Wiell must not be deceived. They must hold firm, whatever the false reports and fair offers from the enemy, must hold only a little time, until the King's army comes this way. Lord Evald's hold—must hear the message I bear."

"Wars," she said faintly. "They will not be wise, who set foot in Ealdwood."

"And I must go, lady Arafel. I must. I beg you." Already he began to fade, discovering the power of will within himself.

"Ciaran," she said, a summoning, and held him by his name, still within the light of her sun. "You are determined. But you do not count the cost. The Huntsman will seek you out again. Once in the mortal world, you are a prey to him; he has never lost a hunt, do you see? And it is not finished."

"That may be," he said, pale-faced. "But I have sworn."

"Pride," she said. "It is empty pride. What arms have you, what means to pass through all of Eald against such enemies?"

He looked down at himself, armorless and empty-handed. But he wavered toward a parting, all the same.

"Wait," she said, and went to the old oak, took from its branches one of the jewels which hung among the others, pale green like the one which hung at her own throat, though dimmed, for its master was ages gone. It sang to her, the dreams of an elf named Liosliath, a part of his soul, such souls as her kind had. "Take it. You borrowed his sword in your need, but this will serve you better. Wear it always about your neck."

"What are these things?" he asked without taking, and looked about at all the trees which held such treasures, jewels and swords glimmering silver and light among the leaves. "What place is this?"

"You might liken it to a tomb; this you robbed . . . my brothers and my sisters, my fathers and mothers. It is elvish memory."

"Forgive me," he whispered, stricken.

"We do not die. We go . . . away; and when we are gone, what use are these things to us? Yet they hold memories. That is their use now. The sword, you could not fully use. But take this stone. Liosliath would not grudge it to a friend of mine. He was my cousin; he was young as our kind go, and so it may be safest for you. The shadows feared him."

He took it in his hand, and his eyes widened and his lips parted. Fear . . . perhaps he felt fear. But he held it fast, and it sang to him, of elvish dreams and memories.

"It too is power," she said. "And danger. It does not make you a match for Death; but 'twill fight the chill . . . if you have the heart to use it."

He gathered the silver chain and hung it about his neck. His fair clear eyes clouded in the power of the dreams. But he was not lost in them. She touched her own dreamstone, and called forth the faintest of songs, a sweet, bright harping. "Do not trust in iron," she warned him. "That and this . . . do not love one another. And come, since you must. Come, I shall walk with you on your way. Eald will take you there more safely than you might walk in the world of Men."

"This is given for a baneful place," he said.

"Walk it with me, and see."

She offered her hand. He took it, and his was warm and strong in hers, human-broad but comfortable. He walked with her, and for all his apprehension a wonder came into his eyes when he saw the land, the trees of elven summer, the glamoured meadows abloom with glistening flowers, the timid, wide-eyed deer which stared at them as they passed.

Stone sang to stone, his heart to hers, and the wind grew warm beneath that other sun. She felt something which had long frozen about her heart melt away, and she knew companionship for the first time in human ages, a fellowship lost since Lioslaith himself had faded, last of all elves save herself.

("Forgive me," Liosliath had said, this Man's unwitting words and her cousin's last, which had tugged at her heart. "I have tried to stay." But he had had that look in his gray eyes which was the calling, and once it had begun in his heart, the fading began, and all her wishing could not hold him—nor could she go with him, for her heart was here.)

"It is beautiful," Ciaran said.

"Not so wide as once," she said. And, remembering: "We held Caer Donn once."

"The grandfathers say—there are your sort still there."

She tossed her head, stung. "Faery folk. Silly nixes. And sad. They have few wits. They shapeshift so often they forget themselves and cannot get back again—That is not to say they are not dangerous when crossed."

"That is not your kind."

"No," she said, laughing, in better humor. "Not mine. We were the greater folk. Elves. The Daoine Sidhe. The faery folk live in our ruin. They never loved us."

"And others of your kind?"

"Gone," she said. "But myself."

He let go her hand to look at her, and in letting go he drifted, cried out in fear, for they were on Caerbourne's edge, a bright stream, willow-bordered, and here its name was Airgiod, the Silver. She took his hand again and steadied him.

"Beware such lapses. You might fall. Caerbourne has eroded deep in human years, and his banks are steep. And worse, far worse, there is no knowing how deep he has sunk in the shadows. Lord Death's geography is a darker mirror of this, but mirror nonetheless, and I

should not care for *his* river. Remember your wound
when you walk in Eald."

He shivered; she felt the dread keenly, a chill in the
stone upon her breast. She touched it and warmed it,
and him.

"Use the stone," she bade him. "He shall not have
the rest of you if you know how to walk in Eald. Your
heart's wish can bring you here, only so you do not stray
too far; your heart's wish can take you away."

"It is a great gift," he admitted at last. "But they say
all gifts in this world have cost."

"Not among kinsmen."

He looked up at her as deer look at hounds, wary
and distraught.

"There's elvish blood in you," she said. "Do you not
know? You could not have come, else. We once ruled,
I say, in Caer Donn."

"So they say." She felt the beating of his heart, like
something trapped in the stone within her hand.

"Is it so terrible," she asked, "to discover such a
kinship?"

"I am my father's own son, no changeling."

"Then by father or mother, you carry blood of mine.
You are no changeling, no. There is nothing of the little
folk about you. Is it sire or mother stands taller than
most?"

Fear filled him, a tumbling down of all truths he knew.
Father, she thought, catching this from his mind. He said
nothing. She felt a chill in him, self-aimed. She perceived
memories of old stones near Caer Donn, recollections
of childhood terrors, of ill legends and human hate, and
shivered herself.

"I am sorry," he said, sharing this. His mind was
awash with fear, and with thoughts of his own duty, and
of dying, and the black hounds. He touched the chain
of the stone about his neck, making to draw it off, but
she caught his hand and gently forbade that.

"You will not die," she promised him. "I will take
you where you will go. Come, it is not far."

The forest edge lay up the bright stream-course, that
place where sight stopped in mist, the edge of her world.
She led him into that gray place, walking blind, but one
hand she kept on the stone which remembered the world

as it had been, and so she brought some substance out of nothingness, enough to find her way beyond the edge. She remembered Caer Wiell as it had once been, a fair green hill with a spring never failing; and so she came to it, and still held his hand fast. Half in the shadow-ways there was a dimming, a glare of fire, the shouts of war, ghosts of battle swirling about them.

Other things were there too. Death was one. "Pay him no mind," she said to Ciaran, who turned and faced the shadow. "No. Hold to the stone and come with me."

She set them more and more surely in mortal night, with the din of war about them, with Caer Wiell's black walls above. She knew the gateway. It did not have wards against her. She set him through.

"Fare well," she said. "And fare back again."

So she stepped clear of Caer Wiell, back into the swirling shadow-din outside.

She felt a presence by her, a shadow which had drawn a moment out of the battle, a blackness sullen and cold.

"Hunt elsewhere," she told him.

"You have had your will," Lord Death said, making ironic homage.

"Hunt elsewhere."

"You give this mortal uncommon gifts."

"What if I do? Are they not mine to give?"

The shadow said nothing, and she walked away through the grayness, and into bright Eald, into her own. The Phantom deer stared at her curiously in elven sun-set; and she walked back to the grove of the circle, touched the stones which hung from the ancient oak, harked to precious memories which they sang as the wind blew among them. One voice was stilled now from the chorus, that which had been Liosliath's.

"Forgive," she whispered to him, who was far across the dividing sea, far from hearing her. "Forgive that it was you."

But a strange companionship shivered through her still, after ages in solitude. She walked, and, mingled with the eldritch harping which was the peculiar song of her stone of dreams, came the whisper of another heart, human-tainted, but true as earth. She was appalled somewhat at the nature of it, for he had known war; he had killed—but so had she, in the cruel, cold anger of elves. Human anger was different, all blood and blind rage, like wolves. He knew passions she felt strange; he knew strange fears; and self-doubts. It was all there, drowning Liosliath's clear voice. He feared Liosliath; he denied, human-stubborn, the things his own eyes had seen in Eald.

But there was no hate in him.

She sank down at the base of the tree of memory, and drew her cloak about her, and dreamed his dream.

FOURTEEN

CAER WIELL

They brought him as a prisoner into the torchlit hall, with the sounds of battle dying. They had handled him ungently, but it was their lord's own ring upon his finger, and they had changed their manner quickly enough when he insisted to show them that. "Sit," they told him now, showing him a bench, and he was only too glad to do so, weary as he was.

Another came—Old wolf, Ciaran thought at that grim broad face, besweated and flushed with battle-heat. He straightened himself at once when that man came in with more men-at-arms behind him. He set himself most carefully on his feet. "Scaga?" he ventured, for he was very like his son, a huge man and redhaired. "I come from the King; and from your lord."

"Let me see his ring," Scaga said; and Ciaran thrust out his hand, which the old warrior took roughly, turning the ring to the firelight. Scaga let it go again, his scarred face still scowling.

"I have a message," Ciaran said, "for your lady's ears." And because he could guess the keep's want of hope: "Good news," he urged on Scaga, though he was charged to take it higher.

"Then it comes welcome, if true." Scaga turned his face toward the open door, where sounds of battle had much faded, then looked back again, looked him up and down. "How came you here?"

"My message," he said, "is for lord Evald's lady."

Scaga still frowned; it might be the nature of his face,

or of his heart: this was, Ciaran thought, a fell man to cross. But Evald trusted him as steward, in a hold beset with enemies: he was then a man of great worth and faithfulness.

"With neither armor," said Scaga, "nor weapon. . . . How came you into the courtyard?"

"Your lord's ring," Ciaran insisted. "I speak only to your lady." He felt the stone which lay hidden within his collar, a presence, a warmth which seemed greater than natural. It frightened him, with that against his heart and the like of Scaga staring into his eyes, full of suspicions.

"You shall go to her," Scaga said, and motioned to the stairs. "Boy!" he called. "See my lady roused."

A lad scampered up the steps at a run. Ciaran shivered in weariness and cold, for wind blew through the door. He wished desperately for a cup of ale, for a place to lie down and rest himself.

And there was none, for Scaga looked on him with narrowed eyes and offered nothing of hospitality—motioned men-at-arms to go before and behind him and led him up the steps to another hall within Caer Wiell's thick walls, which at least was warmer, with a fire blazing in the hearth.

"Beware," a voice seemed to whisper in his hearing, and it startled him. He wondered could all the rest hear it; but the others did not turn: it was for him alone. "Beware this hall. They do not love elven-kind. And do not show them the stone."

A stone wolf's-head was set above the fireplace. It seemed he had seen it before; that he had sat here, a man, and that a harp should hang so, upon the rightward wall—he looked, and was dismayed to find a harp hanging there, just where he had thought it should. He had then dreamed this place.

Or she had. There was a great scarred table where once had sat a chair, before the fire. He blinked it clear, went to it, leaned there wearily against the table, while weary men guarded him.

And women came, so soon that he supposed they had not been asleep. Surely they had not been, with the enemy hurling fire against the hold. They came from the inner door which opened on this hall, one woman older and somewhat grayed. This was Meredydd, he surmised, Evald's own lady; and *Meredydd* the stone whispered in his heart, confirming it. The other of the twain was young, bright of hair—and that name came whispering through his heart as well: *Branwyn.* Branwyn. Branwyn. He stared without meaning to, for so much of anguish and of anger came whispering with that name. This Branwyn stopped and stared at him, blue eyes seemed bewildered and innocent of such pain.

"Your message," Scaga's harsh voice insisted.

Ciaran looked at Lady Meredydd instead, took a step toward her, but hands moved to weapons about him, and he did not go nearer. He tugged the ring from off his finger and gave it over to Scaga, who gave it to the lady. She took the ring as something precious, looked on it closely, lifted anxious eyes. "My husband," she asked of him.

"Well, lady, he is well. I bring his love and my King's word: Hold, defend, and do not be deceived by any lies of the enemy or accept any terms. The King has won a great battle at Dun na h-Eoin, and the enemy hopes for this valley as their last holding place. Only hold this tower, and the King and your lord will come as soon as possible against their backs. They know this. Now you do."

"Now bless your news," the lady wept, and even Scaga's frown was eased. Meredydd came and offered her hands to him in welcome, but he felt Scaga's heavy hand on his shoulder, pulling him away.

"There is more to hear," said Scaga. "This man came over the walls somehow, with no armor, no arms—unmarked through the lines outside. There are questions should still be asked, my lady, however good and fair the counsel seems. I beg you, ask him how he came."

For a moment doubt shadowed the lady's eyes.

"My name is Ciaran," he said, "Lord Ciaran of Caer Donn is my father. And as to how I came—lightly, as you see; by stealth. While your enemies struck at the gates—I came another way. I shall show you. But armed men could not take it."

He was not used to lies. He felt fouled, wounded when the lady pressed his hands. "You will show us where," Scaga said, and gave him in his turn a bearish embrace, gazed at him with emotion welling up—hope, it might be, where hope had been scant for them before. Branwyn too came and kissed his cheek; and weapons were done away as men came at last to clap him on the back and to hug one another for joy. A cheer lifted in the hall, and there was such desperate happiness—He felt a stirring through the jewel too, a presence, a distressing realization that he had said nothing on his own which ought to have convinced them and so relieved their hearts, but that some strangeness overlay him and his words, making them better than they were.

They gave him wine, and brought him upstairs to a princely room—her lord's when he was young, the Lady Meredydd said; and true, everything there showed some woman's love, the fine-pricked stitchery of coverlet and tapestries, the hangings of the bed. Branwyn herself brought a warm rug for the floor, and maids brought water for washing, while Lady Meredydd with her own hands brought him bread hot from the morning's baking. He took it gratefully, while the lady and her daughter lingered to ply him with questions, how fared Evald and kinsmen, cousins, friends, men of the hold, a hundred questions during which maids eavesdropped and men-at-arms contrived to listen on pretext of errands. Some few men he knew; sometimes the news was sad and pained him; and most often he knew only a name, or less—but it gave him joy when he could report some loved one safe and well. Scaga's son was one, for Scaga bent enough to ask. "He is well." Ciaran said. "He led a good portion of Caer Wiell's men at Dunn na h-Eoin, first of those that broke the shields of the Bradhaeth while lord Evald cut off their retreat. He came out of the battle well enough; he was by lord Evald when we parted, in the King's own tent." The old warrior did not smile to hear it, but his eyes were bright.

"He must sleep," Meredydd declared at last. "Surely he has traveled hard."

"I fare well enough," Ciaran said, for he ached after human company, for noise of voices, for all these sights and sounds of humankind.

"Before he sleeps," said Scaga, "he must show us this weak place in our wall."

The warmth drained from him. He nodded consent,

not knowing what he was to do, but compelled to go. He
swallowed a bit of bread gone dry in his throat, drank a
last sip of the wine and set the cup down. "Aye," he
said. "Of course. That will not wait."

Scaga rose, waiting at the door. Ciaran took his leave
of the ladies, walked with the old warrior through the
hall, his heart beating hard within his breast.

"I do not know if I can find it easily," he said to
prepare his excuse, and hating the lie. "From all the
turnings of this place inside . . . I cannot be sure."

Scaga said nothing, which seemed Scaga's way. It gave
him no comfort. And when they had come up on the
walls, Ciaran looked about him in deep distress, seeking
something to confirm his lie.

"Look east," the softest of whispers came to him, like
the touch of a breeze. "Turn east and look down."

He walked that way along the battlement, with Scaga
treading heavily beside him. He paused at a place and
looked down, where the stonework of the walls was oldest and roughest, where here and there brush had rooted
itself in the gaps between the stones and man-made walls
thrust crazily above the jagged stone of the underlying
rocks. Of a sudden his eye picked out a way, weaving
from one such foothold to another among brush rooted
in the wall, a peril to the hold. "There," he said. "We
are a mountain hold, we of Caer Donn. And I climbed
cliffs as a lad. There, do you see, Scaga? There and there
and there."

Scaga nodded. "Aye. That does want clearing, and
watching. Our eyes must have been blind to it. A man
sees things too often and so not at all: I had not marked
how the brush had grown."

"Rains, perhaps," Ciaran said hoarsely, but in his
heart he knew differently. He shivered, for his wool shirt
was not enough against the wind, and felt Scaga's
friendly grip fall upon his shoulder.

"Come. Our thanks, young sir. Come in."

He walked, glad of the wind-breaking shelter of walls
on the one side of the battlements, gazed back as they
walked, and suddenly down at an opening out of the
walk. The courtyard was below, jammed with livestock
and with village folk, a noise which welled up at him
thinly, the wail of children and the listless bleating of

goats. But it was a well-ordered place, Caer Wiell, and some of the men on the walls were country folk, light-armed, but goodly looking men, quick of eye and brisk about their business. Women were climbing up the inside scaffoldings which gave access to the battlements before the gates, bearing baskets of bread. There was then no hunger here, nor would there ever be thirst, because of the spring which named the hill, out of reach of the enemy. Ciaran felt much cheered by what he saw of the defense, even with the ominous smoke of enemy fires rising before the walls. He walked farther out than Scaga would have had him go, walked the wall to the area of the main gates and looked west.

Then he was less cheered, for the extent of the black ruin before the walls. The grass and fields were burned and trampled into mire. The enemy had carried away their dead and wounded; no corpse was left but the carcasses of slain horses, to draw the black birds; and beyond that trodden ground the hills were seared with fire, villages and farms burned, surely, from here to Caer Damh. The smoke rose in countless plumes from the hills, where a vast host camped, a crescent of smokes from the Caerbourne's forested verge to the barren hills to the right, that spread itself on the winds and darkened the sky.

The attack could not have been this far advanced when he was on the road, riding from the King. He had passed one night—surely one night—in Eald.

How much of time? he asked that sometime whisper in the stone, feeling uncertainty all about him. *How long did you hold me?* He was betrayed. He knew it in his worst fears.

The fires would soon grow more and more, as Dryw and the King over the hills drove others into retreat. Or had it happened already? And what more had happened, and what men he just had named living might have died? And what stayed the King from coming?

Hold here. How old was the message, that Scaga was so grim, that lady Meredydd and her daughter caught so desperately at this hope he gave them? And how long had the King delayed to come?

"It seemed the fires had grown in number," said Scaga out of his silence. "Now we know why."

"Aye," Ciaran said, wishing to say nothing at all.

He went back into the tower, and sat in the hall at the table by the fire, victim again of questions from those humbler folk who had not asked before; and a few common folk who served there came only to look at him with their hopes unspoken in their eyes, and to steal quickly away. He sat there most of that long day, alone some of the hours, and sitting with Scaga in the afternoon, who brought some of his trusted men to question him at length—how great the strength of the enemy, what condition their arms, what number yet might come. He answered what questions he could as wisely as he could, hinting nothing, and was glad when they had gone away.

No more of lies, he wished of Arafel. You have tangled me in lies, more and more of them. They break my heart. What is truth? What should I say to them? Should I make them doubt the very hope I came to give them?

She had no answer for him, or did not hear.

But that evening after supper a young man came and took down the harp from the wall, and played songs for him and for the ladies. Then he felt a warmth near his heart, a sweet, sad warmth. Then was peace, for the first time in the day. From the enemy there was no stirring, and the pure notes of the harp found another rapt listener; a joy flooded back from the stone, and filled Ciaran's heart. He smiled.

And looked by chance into Branwyn's eyes, who smiled too, in her hope. The smile faded to gravity. The eyes stayed upon his, flower-fair.

"No," a whisper came to him from the depths of the stone.

The blue eyes were nearer, and had a glamour of their own. He gazed entranced while the harper sang.

"Cling to the stone," the whisper came again, but he had Branwyn's fair hand within closer reach of his upon the table. He touched her fingers and they clung to his. The harper sang of love, and heroes. Ciaran held her hand for more tangled reasons, that it was of this world, and that it too had power to hold.

At length the harper ceased. Ciaran drew back his hand, lest others remark it, for she was a great lord's only daughter, however dire the times.

*　　*　　*

And in time he went alone to his bed in the room
which had been Evald's in his youth, the vast soft bed
of broidered hangings. He stripped off his clothing, shivered in the wind which blew in out of the dark, through
the slitted window—stripped off all that he wore but the
stone on its silver chain and lay down quickly, drawing
the heavy quilts over him, tucking up his limbs until he
could warm him a spot in the bed. He reached out again
to snuff the wick of the lamp on the table, drew the arm
quickly back beneath the covers, as dark settled strange
shapes over the unfamiliar objects of the borrowed
room. There were creakings and movings, from outside
and in; a child cried somewhere in the dark, from the
courtyard on the other side, far, far away. His own slit
of a window faced the river. He heard a distant whisper
of leaves or water: wind, he thought; and somewhere
hounds belled, a sound greatly out of place in besieged
Caer Wiell. He clutched the stone in his hand, drew
warmth from it, and no longer heard the dogs.

He dreamed of groves, vast trees; and of a hill. This
was Caer Wiell; but he called its name Caer Glas, and
there was no well, but a clear spring bubbling out over
white stones, flowing unhindered to Airgiod's pure waters in the vale, and the view was clear and bright toward
the Brown Hills. He rode the plain, tall and bearing the
same pale stone on his breast—rode among others, with
the blowing of horns and flourishing of banners. Arrows
came down like silver sleet, and the sullen host before
them fled, seeking the mountains, the dark places at the
roots of the hills. The Daoine Sidhe warred, and in the
sky glittered the jeweled wings of dragons, serpent-
shapes passing like storm in the blowing of horns and
the clash of arms.

Then were ages of peace, when the pale sun and green
moon shone down without change, and harpers sang
songs beneath the pale, straight trees.

There came the age of parting, when the world began
to change, when Men came, and Men's gods, for the vile
things were driven deep within the hills, and Men found
the way now easy. Came bronze, and came iron, and
some there were of the Sidhe who abided the killing of

trees, small wights who burrowed in the earth close to
Men; but the Daoine Sidhe hunted these, in bitter anger.

Yet the world had changed. The fading began, and
the heart left them. One by one they fell to the affliction,
departing beyond the gray edge of the world. They took
no weapons with them; took not even the stones they
had treasured—for it was the nature of the fading, that
they lost interest in memory, and in dreams, and hung
the stones to stay in rain and moonlight to console those
still bound to the world. Most parted sadly, some in indi-
rection, simply bewildered; and some in bitter renuncia-
tion, for wounded pride.

He felt anger, a power which might have made the
hills to quake—Liosliath, the stone whispered in his
mind, and he drew breath as if he had not breathed in
a long, long age, and looked up and outward, forcing
shapes to declare themselves in the mist which had taken
the world, trees and stones and the rush of wind and
water.

Ciaran waked, caught at the bed on which he lay, all
sweating and trembling, for his heart beat in him far too
loud. He stared into the shadowed beams above him,
wiped the sweat from his face with hands callused and
coarser than the hands he had had in his dream, rested
them on a body rough with hair and sweating, with the
pulse jarring at his ribs—not at all the body he had worn
in the dream, slim and shining fair, with the stone aglow
with life and light, with bright armor and a slim silver
sword which shadows feared and no Sidhe enemy wished
to face.

Liosliath, star-crowned, prince of the Daoine Sidhe,
the tall fair folk.

And himself, who was earthen, and coarse, and whose
power was only that in his arm and his wits.

He shivered, sweating as he was, and tears ran from
the edges of his eyes. He tried again to sleep, and
dreamed of Arafel, of sunlight and silver, and the phantom deer leaping in and out of shadow, for it was her
waking and his night. The pale elven sun shone, blinding,
and she walked the banks of Airgiod, up to the point
where it faded into mist and nothingness, as near to him
as it was easy for her to come.

Kinsman, she hailed him. It was as if she had suddenly turned her face toward him. He waked with a start in his own darkness, and in trembling, put off the stone, laid it and its chain on the table by the bedside, by the lamp. He wished no more such dreams, which tormented him with what he was and was not and could never be, which thrust an elflord into his heart with all the melancholy doom of the fair folk, all their chill love and colder pride. They were dread enemies when stirred: he knew so; and so, he thought, might *she* be, who had been kind to him.

Kinsman she had hailed him; but it was Liosliath who was her cousin, Liosliath whose cold pride wished to live again, Liosliath, the terrible bright lord whose sword had slain Men.

"A terrible enemy," a shadow whispered.

And far away, even waking, Arafel cried to him: "The stone, Ciaran!"

He was dreaming then. He was naked and a part of him blew in tatters. There was a forest like the Eald-wood where a wild thing fled, and he was that creature. Limbs rustled, black branches, and even the leaves were black as old sins; the sky was leaden, with a moon like a baleful dead eye.

"Terrible," it said again, and a wind blew through the inky leaves.

Behind him. It hunted him and he must not look at it, for he was in its land, and if he saw the enemy's true face it would be real.

"The stone!" a voice wailed on the wind.

He reached for it, straining all his heart into that reaching. It met his fingers, and his hand glowed with that moonbright fire. Shadows yielded, as he retreated out of that third and dreadful Eald. He passed other creatures less fortunate, shadows which cried and pleaded for aid he could not give. Elf prince, some wailed, asking mercy; elf prince, some hissed, spitting venom. He dared not shut his eyes, dared not look.

Then he lay again within walls of stone, and Arafel's voice was chiding him. He shivered in his borrowed bed, with the stone safe in his fingers. He lay shivering, with sullen day breaking through the windowslit. A chill breeze stirred his hair. Thunder rumbled outside.

He took the cold silver chain in his hands and slipped it again about his neck, lay still a time holding to the stone with both hands, shivering at the flood of elvish memories . . . of old quarrels with this shadow-lord. The courage seemed bled out of him, through the wounds the hounds had made in his soul. He knew himself maimed—maimed forever, in a way which others could not see and he could not forget. The stone must be forever about his neck to shield him, and it was more powerful than he. His hands were cold that clutched it, and would not warm easily; they were mortal, and that jewel was elvish memory—of one who had not loved Men.

He stirred at last, hearing others astir in the keep, the calling of voices one to the other, ordinary voices, recalling him to a world no longer fully his. He rose, his teeth chattering, and pulled on his breeches and went to the windowslit, hugging his arms about him. He saw the muddy hill, the forest verge, wet green leaves and gray sky. Of attackers there was no sign but the marks which had been there before. The rain was nothing but dreary mist. He turned back and sought after his shirt and the rest of his clothing. He tucked the stone within his collar, tied the laces which concealed it at his throat. He dared not leave it . . . ever.

FIFTEEN

OF FIRE AND IRON

The ladies were in the great hall to give him morning's hospitality. Meredydd and Branwyn and their maids; and two of the pages had stayed to serve them. He walked among them with a hope of a seat near the fire and a bit of bread crowded upon him; but there were places laid at the table, and he heard the lady Meredydd send a page for porridge. Scaga appeared in the door as the boy dodged and scurried mouselike about his errand, and nodded a good morning. "All's quiet," Scaga said. There was no great joy in the report, and Ciaran frowned too, wondering how long till it came down on them doubled. Perhaps the enemy had no liking for rain. Perhaps—the thought came worrisome at his empty stomach—there was something else astir. Perhaps something had gone amiss with the King, some trick, some trap prepared. The King, Dryw, his father—should come soon. They should make some move.

Perhaps—the thought would not leave him—they had tried and failed while he slept in Eald, unknowing. Some ambush in the lower end of the dale could have prevented them. The desolation before the walls of Caer Wiell was as wide as that at Dun na h-Eoin—and he could not judge whether the enemy was greater in the dale than they had reckoned in the first place or whether the forces fled from Dun na h-Eoin had joined them.

He sat where the Lady Meredydd bade him, at her right; and Branwyn sat at her left. Scaga sat down too, and others, but many seats at the great table stayed

vacant, the hall of a hold long at war, its lord and young
men absent. The harper sat with them, late arrival; there
was the Lady Bebhinn, elderly and dour; and Muirne,
all of twelve, who was a shy, pale-cheeked child, silent
among her elders. The hall at Caer Donn came to his
mind unbidden, his parents' faces, the laughter of servants, joyous mornings, full of noise, himself and dour
Donnchadh always at some friendly odds over trivial
things. But it would be lonely there this morning too.

"You did not rest well," the demoiselle Branwyn said,
who sat facing him. Her face was troubled.

"I slept," he said, straightening his shoulders; but the
stone seemed a weight against his heart. And because
his answer did not seem to satisfy those who stared at
him: "I ran far—in coming here. I think the weariness
has settled on me."

"You must rest," said Lady Meredydd. "Scaga, no
harrying of him today."

"Let him rest," Scaga replied, a deep rumbling. "Only
so *they* do."

The porridge came. Ciaran ate, small familiar motions
which gave him excuse not to talk. In truth he felt numb,
endured a moment's fear that he might have begun to
fade into elsewhere, so distant he was in his thoughts.
He imagined their dismay if he should do so.

And in this homelike place he thought a second time
of home, and meetings. Of facing his father and mother
and Donnchadh, bearing an elvish stone forever against
his heart, with close knowledge of that past which Caer
Donn tried never to recall. He could never again see the
farmer's wards against the fair folk without feeling his
own peace threatened; could not see the ruins on the
mountain above Caer Donn without seeing them as they
had been before any Man set foot there; could not walk
the hillsides without knowing there were other hills within
his reach, and knowing what fell things swarmed beneath
them, never truly gone. Worst, to face his father and Donnchadh, knowing what they must never know, that he and
they were closer to those things than ever they had believed, these things which lurked and crept at the roots of
the hills; and to look on his father's and his brother's faces
and to wonder whether the taint always bred true.

Unsavory, Donnchadh had called the date—but he must

live with an enemy always a breath away, Man's shadow enemy, who would take the rest of him—without the stone.

Then he looked about him at the faces of the folk of Caer Wiell, whose war was the same as his, but without such protections as the stone; it was the same Enemy. Death had been outside the walls yesterday, hunting souls. Do we not, he wondered, all bear the wound? And am I coward, because my eyes alone are cursed to see him coming?

The stone seemed to burn him. "Be wise," a whisper reached him. "O be wise. He is *my* old enemy, before he was yours. He wants one of elven-kind. Me he waits for . . . and now you. Your fate is not theirs. Your danger is far more."

He touched the stone, wished the whisper away. I am Man, he thought again and again, for the green vision was in his eyes and the voices about him seemed far away.

"Are you well?" asked Lady Meredydd. "Sir Ciaran, are you well?"

"A wound," he said, bedazed into almost truth, and added: "Healed."

"The rain," Scaga said. "I have something will warm the aches. Boy, fetch me the flask from the post downstairs."

"'Twill pass," Ciaran murmured, ashamed; but the boy had sped, and the ladies talked of herbs and wished to help him. He swallowed sips of Scaga's remedy then, and accepted salves of Meredydd and the maids; and before they were done, warmer clothing and a good cloak all done with Meredydd's own fine stitching. Their kindness touched his heart and plunged him the more deeply into melancholy. He walked the walls alone after that, staring toward the camp of the enemy and wishing that there were something his hands might do. All the mood of the keep was grim, with the drizzling rain and the unaccustomed silence. Women and children came up onto the walls to look out; and some wept to see the fields, while youngest children simply stared with bewildered eyes, and sought warmer places again in the camp below.

Beyond the river he saw the tops of green trees, and shadowy greater trees high upon the ridge beyond the

Caerbourne, over which the clouds were darkest. Those clouds cast a pall over his heart, for it was Death's presence, and the castle was indeed under siege by more than human foes. The thought came to him that he might bring danger on others, that Death who hunted him might take others near him. This enemy of his might bring ruin on Caer Wiell, on the very folk he came to aid. The thought began to obsess him and cause him deeper and deeper despair.

"Come back," a voice whispered to him, offering peace, and dreams. "You've done your duty to Caer Wiell. Come back."

"Sir," said a human, clear voice, and he turned and looked on Branwyn, cloaked and hooded against the mist. He was dismayed for the moment, and recovering, made a bow.

"You seemed distressed," she said. "Is there moving out there?"

He shrugged, looked across the wall and turned his gaze back to her, a pale face framed in the broidered mantle, eyes as changing as the clouds, mirroring his own fears, unfearing while he was brave, frightened when the least fear came to him. "They seem to have no love of the rain," he said. "And your father and mine, and the King himself—will come soon and teach them other things they will not be fond of."

"It has been so long," she said.

"It cannot be much longer," he said in desperate hope.

Branwyn looked on him, and on the field before them, and they stood there a time, comforted in each other. Birds alit on the stone . . . wet and draggled; she had brought a crust of bread with her, and broke it and gave it to them, provoking battle, damp wings and stabbing beaks.

"Enchantress," Arafel breathed into his heart, "They have stopped being honest; and it had always amused her."

But Ciaran paid the voice no heed, for his eyes were on Branwyn, discovering how graceful her face, how pale on this gray day, how bright her eyes which surprised him with a direct glance and jarred all his senses.

A boy ran, scurried past them and stopped where they

stood; he pointed silently and hastened on. With dread
Ciaran turned and looked beyond the walls, for in that
moment there was change. A group of riders had come
out from the enemy camp, advancing toward the keep.
There began to be a stirring in Caer Wiell as other sentries
saw it. He looked back at Branwyn, and so distraught
was her face that he reached out his hand to comfort
her. Her chill fingers closed about his. They stood and
watched the enemy ride closer.

"They wish to talk," he said, seeing the fewness of
the riders. "It is no attack."

Scaga came thumping up the steps to the crest of the
wall, leaned over the battlement and glared sourly at the
advance. "My lady," he wished Branwyn, looking about
at them both, "I would have you back under cover. I do
not trust you to luck. I would not have you seen."

"I shall stay," Branwyn said. "I have my cloak
about me."

"Stay away from the edge," Scaga bade her, and
stalked along the wall, giving orders to his men.

The enemy came into clear view, a score of riders
bearing banners, most of them the red boar of An Beag,
and the black stag of Caer Damh. But they had another
banner trailing crosswise of a saddlebow, and this they
lifted and showed. A cry of rage went up from the walls
of Caer Wiell, for it was the green banner of their own
lord.

"Surrender," one rider of An Beag rode forth to shout
against their walls. "This keep is yielded; your lord is
dead, the King fallen, and his army scattered. Save your
lives, and those of your lord's wife and daughter—no
harm will come to them. Scaga! Where is Scaga?"

"Here," the old warrior roared, leaning out over the
stones. "Take that lie hence! We name you the liars you
are, in the one and in the other."

A second rider spurred forward, and lifted a dark object on a spear, a head with hair matted with blood, a
ruined face. He slung it at the gate.

"There is your lord! We offer you quarter, Scaga!
When we come again, we will not."

The lady Branwyn stood fast, her hand limp in Ciaran's; but when he gathered her against him for pity, she
failed a little of falling, and hung against him.

"Ride off!" Scaga roared. "Liars!"

A bow bent, among the riders. "Ware!" Ciaran cried, but Scaga had seen it, and hurled himself back from the edge as the shaft sped, a flight which hissed past and spent itself. Arrows sped from the walls in reply, and the party rode away not unscathed, leaving the green banner in the mud, and a bloody head at Caer Wiell's gates.

"These are lies!" Ciaran said, turning to shout it over all the range his voice could reach, to walls and the courtyard below. "Your lord sent me to forewarn you all of tricks like these—a false banner and some poor wretch's ruined face—these are *lies!*"

He was desperate in his appeal, only half believing it himself. The whole of the keep seemed frozen, none moving, none seeming sure.

"When was there truth in An Beag?" Scaga roared at them. "Trust rather the King's own messenger than any word from them. They know they have no other hope. The King has won his battle. The King is coming here, with our own lord beside him, with Dryw ap Dryw and the lord of Donn. Who says he will not?"

"It was not my father!" Branwyn shouted out clear, stood on her own feet and flung back her hood. "I saw, and I say it was not!"

A handful cheered, and others followed. It became a tumult, a waving of weapons, a hammering of shields by those who had them.

"Come inside," Ciaran urged Branwyn, and took her arm. "Haste, your mother may have heard."

"Bury it," she said, shuddering and weeping, and Ciaran looked at Scaga.

"I will see to it," Scaga said, and with a word to his men on the wall to keep sharp watch, he went down the steps to the gate. Ciaran wrapped the corner of his cloak about Branwyn and walked with her inside the tower, into torchlight and warmth, and up into the hall, to bear the news themselves.

But he went down again when he had seen Branwyn to her mother and given report, into the court where Scaga stood.

"Was it?" he asked Scaga when he could ask with none overhearing.

"It was not," Scaga said, his eyes dark and grim. "By the way of an old scar my lord has I know it was not; but no other feature did they leave him. We buried it. Our man or theirs—we do not know. Likest theirs, but we take no chances."

Ciaran said nothing, but turned away unamazed, for he had fought the ilk of An Beag for years, and still it sickened him. He yearned for arms, for a weapon in hand, for an answer to make to such men. It was not the hour for it. No attack was coming. Their enemy meant they should brood upon what they had seen.

There was silence all the day. Ciaran sat in the hall and drowsed somewhat, with moments of peace between visions of that gory field and more terrible visions of silvered leaves, of all Eald whispering in anger beyond the walls. He would wake with a start and gaze long at something homely and real, at the gray of a stone wall, or the leaping of flames in the hearth, or listen to the folk who went about their ordinary business nearby. Branwyn came to sit by him, and that peace too he cherished.

"Ciaran," a faint voice whispered from time to time, destroying that tranquillity, but he refused to pay it heed.

They placed double guard that night, trusting nothing; but there was firelight and comfort in the hall. Ciaran recovered his appetite which had failed him all the day, and again the harper played them brave songs, to give them courage: but the stone plagued him—in his ears echoed other songs of slower measure, of tenor never human, of allure which made the other songs seem discordant and sour. Tears flowed down his face. The harper misunderstood, and was complimented mightily. Ciaran did not gainsay.

Then must be bed, and loneliness and the dark— worse, the silence, in which there were only inner echoes and no stilling them. He was ashamed to ask for more light, like a child, and yet he wished he had done so when all were abed and he was alone. He did not put out the light, having trimmed the wick to nurse it as long as he might. The stone and he were at war in the silence, memories which were not his nor even human, memories which grew stronger in the long hours of solitude, so that even waking was no true defense against the flood of images which poured down upon his mind.

Liosliath. He felt more than memories. He took in the nature of him who had worn these dreams so many ages, a pride which reckoned nothing of things he counted fair—which flung against them elvish beauties to turn them pale, and showed him the sadness in his world. He tried taking off the stone with the light there to comfort him, but that was worse still, for there was that aching loss, that knowledge that a part of him was in that darker Eald. Worst of all, he felt a sudden attention upon himself, so that the night outside seemed more threatening and more real, and the light of the lamp seemed weaker. He quickly placed the chain back about his neck and let the stone rest against his chest, which warmed the ache away . . . and brought back the tormenting bright memories.

Then the light guttered out, and he sat in the dark. The room was very still, and the memories grew harder and harder to push away.

"Sleep," Arafel whispered across the distance, with pity in her voice. "Ah, Ciaran, sleep."

"I am a Man," he whispered back, holding to the stone clenched in his fist. "And if I yield to this I shall not be."

Music came to him, soft singing, which soothed and filled him with an unspeakable weariness, lulling his senses. He slept without willing to, and dreams crept upon him, which were Liosliath's proud self, burning pride and sometimes heartlessness. He longed for the sun, which would make real the familiar, common things about him; and when the sun came at last, he bowed his head into his arms and did sleep a time, true sleep, and not a warfare for his soul.

Someone cried out. He came awake with brazen alarm clanging in his ears, with cries outside that attack was coming. *"Arms!"* echoed down the corridors of Caer Wiell and up from the distant court. *"Arm and out!"*

Fright brought him to his feet, and then a wild relief, that it was come to this, that it was no more an enemy within him, but one that yielded to weapons such as human hands could wield. He tugged on his clothing, raced into the hall with others, and finding no Scaga—down the stairs as far as the guard room. Scaga was arming, and others were.

"Get me weapons," Ciaran begged of them; and Scaga ordered it. Boys hastened about measuring him with their hands, seeking what armor might fit him. Outside the alarm had ceased. The battle was preparing. The room had a busy traffic of boys running with arrows and the air stank of warming oil. They began to lace him into haqueton and leather, and one of the other pages came up panting with an aged coat of mail. Ciaran bent and they thrust it over his arms and head; he straightened and it jolted down over his body with a touch like ice and poison. "No," he heard the whisper which had been urging at him, ignored. *"No,"* he raged in his own mind, with the poison seeping into his limbs and weakening them. Tears came to his eyes, and a bitter taste to his mouth, the harsh sour tang of iron. They did the laces, and he stood fast; they belted on the sword, and by now Scaga, armed, was staring at him with bewilderment, for his limbs had weakened and sweat poured on his face, cold in the wind from the door. The pain grew, eating into his bones and through his marrow, devouring his sense.

"No," he cried aloud to Arafel; and "no," he murmured, and crashed to his knees. He bowed over, nigh to fainting, consumed with the pain. "Take it off, *take it off me.*"

"Tend him," Scaga ordered, and hesitated this way and that, then rushed off about his own business, for by now the sound of the enemy was a roar like many waters, and out of it came nearer shouts, and the angry whine of bows.

The pages loosed the belt and loosed the laces, pulled the iron weight off him while he knelt, racked with pain. They brought him wine and tended him among the wounded which began to be brought in from the walls. "See to *them,*" Ciaran cried, clamping his teeth against the poisoned anguish in his belly. Tears of shame stung his eyes, that they delayed with him, while others died. He gained his feet and held to the stones of the wall, sweating and trembling. He made his way out into the open air to use a bow, that much at least. But when a boy gave him a case of arrows, the iron sickness came on him again: the case spilled from his hand and the arrows scattered on the walk. "He cannot," someone said. "Boy, get him hence, get him up to the hall."

He went, steadied by a page on the stairs, staggering because of the pain in his bones. The boy and the maids together laid him down by the fire, and pillowed his head.

"He is hurt," came Branwyn's voice, all anguish for him, and gentle hands touched him. A halo of bright hair rimmed the face which bent above him, against the fire. Tears blurred his eyes, pain and shame commingled.

"No hurt touched him," said a boy. "I think, lady, he must be ill."

They brought him wine and herbs, covered him and kept him warm, while he hovered half-sensible. Outside he heard the clash of iron, heard battle shouts and heard the reports of boys and maids as they would scurry out and back again, how the battle leaned, this way and that. For a time the tower echoed to a crashing against the gates, and there was a dread splintering which brought him off his pallet and to his feet. The words were in his mouth to beg a weapon of them, but the pain in his bones urged otherwise. He hung there against the ward-room door and listened to reports more and more dire shouted up the stairs, for one of the great hinges of the gate had given way beneath the ram, and they braced it as they could, with timbers, and hailed arrows from the wall.

There were ebbs in the battle. Ciaran sat by the fire and pressed his hand against the stone which lay unseen against his breast, but it was silent, giving back only pain. She is wounded too, he thought, with only slight remorse. He was alone in the hall but for Branwyn and the Lady Meredydd, who stared at him with bewildered eyes when they did not go down to tend men more bloodily wounded.

All that day the battle raged about the gate. Men died. At times Ciaran rose and walked down as far as the edge of the wall, but men-at-arms urged him to go back again to safety, and the sight he saw gave him no comfort. The battered gate still held, though tilted on its hinges. Arrows sleeted both up and down the wall, and there was desperate talk of a sortie, to get the enemy from before the gate before it should fall entire.

"Do not," he wished Scaga in his mind, but he could not pass that arrow storm to reach the place where Scaga stood above the gate. Scaga was wise and ordered defense and not attack; oil rained down and discouraged those below, but then the enemy set fires before the gate and the oil made them burn the more fiercely. Another hinge had yielded by afternoon, and more and more the enemy came. Wounded men, exhausted men, passed Ciaran empty-handed in his vantage place, some looking on him with bruised and accusing eyes. Women came up the scaffolding to carry arrows, stayed to tend wounds, to take bows, some of them, behind wickerwork defense, and sent shafts winging into the thick press of attackers. Ciaran came out at last, took a bow from a wounded archer, tried yet again; one and a second shaft he launched . . . but the sickness came on him, and his third went far amiss, fell without force, while the bow dropped from his hand across the crenel. A boy took up the bow, while Ciaran rested there overcome by shame, until he found the strength to carry himself back to shelter.

They brought the boy back later, dead, for a shaft had struck him in the throat, and another, younger boy had taken his post. Ciaran wept, seeing it, and stood in the corner in the shadow, wishing to be seen by no one.

He heard at twilight the battle din diminished; and at long last it faded entirely. He went back to the hall, to stand near the warmth of the fire and hear the servants talk. The women came, weary and shadowed-eyed, and there was talk of a cold supper from which no one had heart. Men were down in the courtyard trying to brace up the gate, and the sound of hammers resounded through the hall.

Scaga came up, pale and sick from an arrow which had pierced his arm and drawn a great deal of blood. From him Ciaran turned his face, and stared into the embers as he leaned against the stones of the fireplace. The ladies sat; servants brought bread and wine and cold meat.

Ciaran came to table and sat down, staring at what

was before him and not at the women, nor at the harper, who had fought that day; nor at Scaga, at him least of all. The servants served them, but no one touched the food.

"It is his wound," Branwyn said suddenly, out of silence. "He is *ill.*"

"He claims to have run through enemies and scaled our wall," Scaga said. "He gives us fair advice. But who is he, truly? How far did he run? And what manner of man have we taken among us, when our lives rely on a gate staying shut?"

Ciaran looked up and met Scaga's eyes. "I am of Caer Donn," he said. "We serve the same King."

Scaga stared at him, and no one moved.

"It is his wound," Branwyn said again. He was grateful for it.

"We have seen no wound," said Scaga.

"Would you?" Ciaran asked, for he had no lack of scars. He put on a face of anger, but it was shame that gnawed at him. "We can go into the guardroom, if you like. We can speak of it there, if you like."

"Scaga," Branwyn reproved the old warrior, but Lady Meredydd put a hand upon her daughter's, silencing her. And Scaga put himself on his feet. Ciaran stood, prepared to go down with him, but Scaga beckoned a page.

"Sword," Scaga said. The boy brought it from the doorway. Ciaran stood still, not to be made a coward in their eyes. Branwyn had risen to her feet, and Lady Meredydd and the others, one after the other.

"I would see you hold a sword," Scaga said. "Mine will do. 'Tis good true iron."

Ciaran said nothing. His heart shrank within him and the stone already pained him. He looked into the old warrior's eyes, knowing the man had seen more than the others had. Scaga unsheathed the sword and offered it toward his hands; he reached for it, took the naked blade in his palms, and tried to keep the anguish from his face. He could not. He offered it back, not to dishonor the blade by flinging it, and Scaga took it gravely. There was a profound silence in the room.

"We are deceived," Scaga said, his deep voice slow and sad. "You brought us fair words. But gifts of your sort do not come without cost."

There was weeping. He saw the source of it, which

was Branwyn, who suddenly tore herself from her mother's arms and rushed from the hall. That wounded as much as the iron.

"I told you truth," Ciaran said.

There was silence.

"The King," Ciaran said, "will come here. I am not your enemy."

"We have lived too long next the old forest," said the Lady Meredydd. "I charge you tell me truth. Is my lord still alive?"

"I swear to you, lady, I had his ring from his own hand, and he was alive and well."

"By what do the fair folk swear?"

He had no answer.

"What shall we do with him?" Scaga asked. "Lady? Iron would hold him. But it would be cruel."

Meredydd shook her head. "Perhaps he has told the truth. It is all the hope we have, is it not? And we need no more enemies than we have. Let him do as he wills, but guard him."

Ciaran bowed his head, grateful at least for this. He did not look at Scaga, nor at the others, only at the lady Meredydd. Since she had nothing more to say to him, he walked quietly from the hall and upstairs to imprison himself in the room they had given him, where he was spared the accusation of their eyes.

Dark had fallen. There was no lamp burning in the room, nor did he reckon that any servant would come to him tonight. He closed the door behind him, gazed at the window through a haze of tears. The night was bright, framed in stone.

Branwyn wept somewhere, betrayed. The joy he had brought them all was gone. They expected now to die. He shut his eyes, seeing his own family, the pain he was sure to bring them. Shame, and grief more piercing than shame, that they would forever know what they were and distrust their own natures.

He sat down on the bed in the dark, and unlaced his collar, drew forth the stone and held it in his hands.

SIXTEEN

THE PATHS OF EALD

"Arafel," he whispered, "help us." But no answer came, and Ciaran had hoped for none. It was doubt, perhaps, which robbed him. He felt a pain in his heart, pain in all his joints, as if the poison of the iron he had touched had gone inward. Perhaps it had more than driven Arafel away; perhaps it had wounded her more than he had known. There was silence, where once her voice would have come whispering to him, and he was afraid.

The stone was power. She had promised so. To cast it off, seek a death in battle . . . he thought of this, foreknowing that he would see before his death what others could not see, and know it when it came. It seemed a small-hearted thing now, though lonely; a selfish thing, to perish to no avail, and to take the hope of Caer Wiell with him once for all. Power was for using in such straits as he had set them in, if he but knew how.

And what had the stone ever done, but link him to Eald? *Fare back,* Arafel had wished him.

He began, holding the stone between his hands. He rose and slipped his mind toward the green fair world . . . saw gray brightness, and moved into it.

There was nothing here. He tried to recall the way he had come with Arafel's leading. He thought that it lay before him in the mist. A certain sense of his heart said so, and he trusted that sense, which he had denied before.

156

Liosliath, he thought, wishing now for the memories of that grim elf, but nothing came to him. It was, perhaps, the taint of iron. Panic swept on him like a flood of water. He wavered out of the mist and blinked in dismay, for he stood on the dark slope of the hill, outside the walls of Caer Wiell.

In panic he reached for the mist again, and ran into it, ran into it, ran, with all his strength, but very quickly he was lost indeed, and he was not sure that he had taken the right course in the beginning. He thought that he could see trees in the grayness, but they were not straight and fair, but twisted shapes, and the mist darkened.

Shadows were with him, loping along in dreamlike slowness. He could not see them well, but he heard the crash of brush, the beat of hooves, slow and strange. A stag coursed the mist, but it was black, and lost itself in the grayness. A bird flew past, baleful-eyed, and black as the stag. It called at him and flew on. He ran the more, panting, and at times his feet seemed to lose their purchase and to stride lower than he wished. Hounds bayed, striking terror into his flesh, and his wound grew into an ache, and to agony. He heard the beat of heavier hooves, and the winding of a horn.

Something tattered swept by him, wailing. He stumbled away from it and shuddered against another shadow, saw trees taking tortured shape. The way was darker and darker, agreeing with mortal night, as the elven-wood never had. He was possessed of sudden terror, that he had fled the wrong way altogether, that he was driven and harried where the enemy would be, toward a place where the stone had no power to save him. A wind blew which did not scatter the mist, but chilled him to the bone.

"Arafel!" he cried, having no hope in silence. "Arafel!"

A shadow loomed ahead of him. He flung himself aside, but it caught at him, and the stone warmed at his heart.

"Names are power," she said. "But you must use commands three times."

He caught her hand and held it, shut his eyes, for a

rush of shadows passed, and the Huntsman was among them. He thought that sight would scar him forever.

And the chill left him. He opened his eyes and they were walking through the mist into brightness, into sunlight, of green forest and meadows with pale flowers. He sank down on the grass, out of strength, and Arafel sat by him, gravely watching until he should have caught his breath.

"You are braver than wise," she said.

"I need your help," he said. "*They* need you."

"*They.*" She flung herself to her feet, and indignation trembled in her voice. "Their wars are their own. You have seen. You have seen your choices. You have come back of your own will. Do you not know now how much we have to do with Men?"

He found no arguments. There was a grayness upon him like the grief of the fair folk themselves, when the world no longer suited them, nor they the world.

Her anger stilled. He felt it die from the stone. She knelt down by him and touched his face, touched his heart, which was still cold with the memory of the dogs.

"This," she said, touching the stone, "and iron—cannot bear one another. You know that now. You are wiser than you were. And when you are wiser still, you will know that they—have no part or peace with you."

"I have dreamed," he said, "and I know what once you were. And I ask you help—*Arafel, Arafel—Arafel,* I ask your help for Caer Wiell."

Her face grew cold, and still. "Too wise," she said. "Beware such invocations."

"Then take back your gift," he said. "There is no heart in it."

"It *is* our heart," she said, and walked away.

He rose, looked about him, at hares which sat solemnly beneath a white tree. He despaired, and shook his head, and would have cast off the stone, but it was all his hope of return to his own night. He had walked it once; he began to walk it again, beyond the silver trees, farther and farther into the mist, for he sighted the direction true, and for whatever reason, the fear had gone.

His step never faltered, not in the direst and strangest of the mist. Trees came clear to him, and the very way

to the room showed itself. He saw it, a black cell before
him in the grayness. He entered it, and found walls
about him once more.

He sat still through the night. There were no dreams.
He slept a time and found the sun coming up, washed
himself and dressed and came out into the hall, strangely
numb of terrors, even when he saw Scaga's man guard-
ing the hall, having watched him. He came down into
the hall where others gathered, and silence fell.

"Is there place for me?" a voice asked softly. He
looked. It was Arafel.

Others had risen from the table, a scraping of chairs
and benches. Branwyn stared, her hands to her cheeks.
Scaga laid hand to his sword, but no one drew. Arafel
stood still, in forester's garments much mended and
much faded. A sword hung at her side. Her pale hair
was drawn back. She looked like a tall, slim boy.

"Long since I was here," she said in their silence.
Somewhere on the walls alarms were sounding, summoning them to the attack. No one yet moved. "I am
bidden aid you," she said. "I ask—do you wish that aid?
Bid me aid you; or bid me go."

"We dare not take such help," said Meredydd.

"It is dangerous," said the harper.

"It is," said Arafel.

"Arafel," Ciaran said. "What danger?"

She turned her pale eyes on him. "The Daoine Sidhe
had other enemies. There are things more than you see.
Long and long it is since wars have reached into Eald."

"We die without your help," said Meredydd. "If help
it is."

"Aye," said Arafel, "that might be true."

"Then help us," said Meredydd.

"Ask cost," said Scaga.

"'Tis late for that," Arafel said softly. "Hist, do you
not hear the alarms?"

"What costs?" Scaga said again.

"I am not of the small folk," Arafel said in measured
words and cold. "I am not paid in a saucer of milk or a
handful of grain. My reasons are my reasons. I speak of
balances, Man, but it is late for that. My aid has been
commanded, and I must give it."

"Then we will take it," said Scaga, with an anguished motion toward the door. "Out there, today."

"Give me time," said Arafel. "Hold against them in your own strength, and wait." She turned, looked on Branwyn and looked last on him, without anger, without passion at all. "Do not go out onto the walls," she said. "Stay within. Wait."

Her voice dimmed, and she did, so that there was only the stonework and a chair, and the silence after her.

"Arm!" Scaga shouted at the men, for still the alarm was sounding, and they had not answered it. "Come and arm!"

They ran. Ciaran stood still in the hall, feeling naked and alone. He realized the stone was in plain sight about his neck, and touched it, but it gave him nothing.

He looked back, into Branwyn's eyes. There was terror there.

"I knew her," Branwyn said. "We were friends."

"What happened?" he asked, disturbed to realize how meshed this place had been, forever, in the doings of Eald. "What happened, Branwyn?"

"I went into the forest," she said. "And I was afraid."

He nodded, knowing. There were then the two of them in the circle of fearing eyes. Lady Meredydd looked on them with a terror greater than all the rest, as if it were a nightmare she had shared. A daughter—who had walked in the forest, that they had gotten back again from Eald. Scaga knew, he too—who had seen a flinching from iron, and known clearly the name of the ill. It was terror come among them; but it had been there always, next their hearts.

"I am Ciaran," he said slowly, to hear the words himself, "Ciaran's second son, of Caer Donn. I lost myself in the forest, and I had her help to come here. But of the King, of your lord—I never lied. No."

No one spoke, not the ladies, not the harper. Ciaran went to the bench by the fire and sat down there to warm himself.

"Branwyn," Meredydd said sharply.

But Branwyn came and sat down by him, and when he gave his hand, took it, not looking at him, but knowing, perhaps, what it was to have walked the paths he took.

Arafel would come back. He trusted in this; and he

remembered what Arafel had said that the others had not been willing to hear, except only Scaga, who might not have understood what she had answered.

Eald had dreamed in long silence; and Men asked that silence be broken. *He* had done so, seeing only the power, and not the cost. He held tightly to Branwyn's hand, which was flesh, and warm, and he wondered if his hand had that solidity in hers.

War was coming, not of iron and blood. They were mistaken if they expected iron and fire of Arafel; and he had been blind.

He was not, now.

SEVENTEEN

THE SUMMONING OF THE SIDHE

She walked quickly, and that was swiftly indeed, through the mists which rimmed her world, into the soft green moonlight on the silver trees. The deer and other creatures stared at her and came no nearer.

And when she had come to the heart of Eald, that grassy mound starred with flowers, and the circle of aged trees, then all of Eald hushed, even to the warm breeze which sported there. Moonlight glistened and glowed in the hearts of stones which hung on the tree of memory, and on the silver swords which hung nearby, and the armor and the treasures which held the magics of Eald. The magics slept, but for what sustenance they gave. Sleeping too, were the memories of all the faded Daoine Sidhe, which were the life of Eald.

She cast off the aspect she wore for Men, stood still a moment listening for the faintest of sounds, and then for no sound at all, but the whispering of elven voices. From one to the other stone she walked, touched them gently and drew their memories into life, so that none slept, not the least or the greatest.

And in the world of Men, Ciaran shuddered, and stared at the fire before them, feeling a stirring which shivered through the very earth. All that Men stood upon seemed like gossamer, threatening to tear.

"What is wrong?" asked Branwyn. "What do you feel?"

"The world is shaken," he said.

"I feel nothing," she said, as if to reassure him; but it did not.

Eald stirred. Arafel stood amid the grove and looked about her and listened; and at last went among the treasures of Eald and gathered up armor ages untouched, which had been hers. She put it on, mail shining like the moon itself, and took up her bow, and shafts tipped with ice-clear stone and silver. She took up her sword, and gathered the sword of Liosliath, his bow and all his arms. She climbed the knoll, laid down her burden, and sat down with her sword across her knees. She shut her eyes to Eald as it was, and listened to the stones.

"Eachthighearn," she whispered to the air, and the silence trembled. A breeze began, which whispered down the green grass of the knoll and set the leaves to stirring and the stones to singing.

It moved farther, coursing narrowly through the trees, across the meadows, making flowers nod, and the hares which moved by moonlight looked up and froze.

It touched the waters of Airgiod, and skimmed them with a little shiver.

It blew among the trees the other side of Airgiod, and branches stirred.

"Eachthighearn: lend me your children."

The breeze blew along the distant flanks of hills, making them shiver, a nodding of grasses; and it traveled farther still.

Then it began to blow back again, through hills and forest, recrossing Airgiod's quiet waters, into meadows and into the grove, stirring the grasses of the knoll, with sighings of the swaying stones and a faint tang of sea breeze, recalling mist, and partings, and the cries of gulls.

Arafel shuddered in that wind, and the grayness beckoned. A taint of melancholy came over her, but she held fast to her stone, and opened her eyes and saw the grove as it was.

"Fionnghuala!" she called. "Fionnghuala! Aodhan!"

The breeze fled back again, laden with the green glamour of Eald, with sweet grass and shade, with summer warmth. It fled away, and the air grew still.

Then a wind began to blow returning, softly at first, and with greater and greater force in its coming, rattling the branches and making Airgiod's waters shiver, flattening the grasses and sweeping like storm into the grove, where the stones blazed with sudden light. The sky was clear, the stars pure, the moon undimmed, but storm crackled in the air, whipped the leaves, and Arafel sprang to her feet, holding the sword in her two hands. The force of lightnings stood about, shivered in her blowing hair and played about the swords in the trees. Thunder began, far away and growing in the wind, stirring like deepest song to the lighter chiming of the stones and the rush of leaves.

And with the wind came brightness in the night, one and the other, like moons coursing close to earth, with thunder in their hooves and moonlight for their manes . . . above the earth they ran, together, as they had always coursed side by side.

"*Fionnghuala!*" Arafel hailed them. "Aodhan!"

The elven horses came to her in a skirling of wind, and the thunders bated as they circled her, as pale Fionnghuala stepped close and breathed in her presence with velvet nostrils shot with fire, gazed at her with eyes like the deer, wide and wonderful. Aodhan snuffed the breeze and shook his head in a scattering of light, stamped the ground and shook it.

"No," said Arafel sadly. "He is not here. But *I* ask, Aodhan."

The bright head bowed and lifted. She belted her sword at her side and took up the arms which had been Liosliath's. Fionnghuala came to her, wickering. She seized the bright mane in one hand swung up, and Fionnghuala stamped and turned, with Aodhan beside. The pace quickened, and the wind scoured the trees, swept the grass, a flicker of lightnings crackling in the manes and in her hair.

"Caer Wiell," Arafel said to them, and Fionnghuala ran, easily above the ground. The mist lay before them, but the wind swept into it, and lightnings lit it, making clear the shapes long lost there, the upper course of

Airgiod, the shapes of faded trees. Shadows were caught
by surprise and fled in terror, wailing down the wind as
thunder took a steady beat and mists were scattered.

Lightning blazed in Caer Wiell's court, danced there,
with thunder-mutterings . . . stood still, and horses and
rider looked on chaos, a gateway near to yielding, a scattering of men in flight from the terror which had broken
in their midst. "Ciaran!" she called. "I am here!"

And Ciaran rose from his place beside the fire, no
more there, no more holding the hand of Branwyn,
whose voice wailed after him in grief.

He stood in the courtyard, with the stone burning like
fire against his heart, with lightnings crackling about him
and above him . . . and the dreams were true.

Arafel slid down, a gleam of silver armor, and held
out such armor to him in both her arms. He took it and
put it on, buckled on the elvish sword, and all the while
his heart was chilled, for the cold went from it to the
center of him, and the lightnings surrounded them. The
human day was murky, clouded; but they stood in otherwhere, and elven moonlight was cast on them, pale
green; night went about them, an aura of storm, and of
the two horses, he knew one for his.

"Aodhan," he named him. "Aodhan. Aodhan." And
the horse came to him, stood waiting.

"Not yet," said Arafel, for there were others about
them, human folk, who huddled against the wind, faces
stark and frightened in the reflected glow, women and
children and wounded men. They had no word to say to
her; there were none from her to them. She walked
toward the gate with Ciaran at her side and the elvish
horses walked after.

"Scaga," Ciaran said, lifting his hand toward the wall.
"Scaga," she repeated, and the old warrior looked down
from the chaos on the walls, his face distraught.

"What you can do," Scaga said, "we beg you do."

"Beware, Scaga, what you have already asked. You
have horsemen; ready them to ride with us, if they will."

The old warrior stood still several beatings of a mortal
heart. He was wise, and feared them. But he called men
to him, and came down the stairs, shouted orders at
boys, and commanded the horses saddled. Arafel stood

still, thoughtfully took her bow from off her shoulder, and strung it. She might, she thought, go to the wall, might aid them there. But iron arrows flew in plenty, and there was time enough for that.

"Mind," she said to Ciaran, "when you ride the shadow-ways, you are safe from iron—but you cannot strike at Men. Shift in and out of them; that is wisest."

"We can die," he said, "—can we not?"

"No," she said. "Not while you wear the stone. There is the fading. And there are other fates, Ciaran. Death is out there. Step into the shadow-ways and you will see him. Leave Men to me, where Men want killing. I am kinder than you know how to be. The arrows—save them: they are too dire for Men."

"Then what shall I do?"

"Ride with me," she said softly. "When one can do much—wisdom must guide the hand, or folly will—Hist, they are ready."

Boys and men brought the horses of the keep, handled, a clattering in the yard, and men ran from the defense of the walls and the gate to take them. Aodhan whickered softly and Fionnghuala saluted them too, and the mortal steeds herded together, ears pricked, nostrils straining. But Arafel walked among them, touched one and the other, named them their true names, and calmed them. "He is Whitetip," she told a rider; "and she is Jumper. Call them true and they are yours." The Men stared at her, but none durst question, not even Scaga, Whitetip's rider.

She looked toward the gate, which tottered beneath the ram. Fionnghuala stepped closer to her, dipped her head and shook it impatiently.

"Do not leave me," she bade Ciaran. "You have compelled my help. I do not compel: I ask."

"I am by you," he said.

"Scaga," she said. "Bid them open the gates." And quietly, to Ciaran: "Oftenest, Men see what they will, and cannot truly see us. Even these. Well for them they do not."

"Do I," he asked, "see you as you are?"

"I cannot know," she said. "But I know you. And you had power to call my name. One must see to do that."

He said nothing. She seized Fionnghuala's mane and

swung to her back. He mounted Aodhan, and the horse suffered it with a shiver, a flaring and quivering of the nostrils, for it was not his rider, but Ciaran knew the dream about his neck, of which Aodhan was part. Fionnghuala tossed her head, and the wind rose.

EIGHTEEN

THE BATTLE BEFORE THE GATES

The gates yielded, a groaning and splintering of wood as the braces which held them were let go and the gates grated inward. Ciaran felt the horse dance aside, light as thistledown, ears still pricked toward the enemy: no need of harness, no need of holding. Aodhan picked up his feet and began to move as effortlessly as the wind which stirred about them, and his feet came down in the boom of thunder. Lightnings cracked, making hair and mane fly. Arafel rode beside him, as the white mare, tinted with the elven moon, paced stride for stride with Aodhan.

And the enemy who had rushed against the gate saw them, mirrored terror in lightning-lit faces, a soundless, horrid screaming. They brandished weapons, and still came on, impelled by hordes behind.

"Follow me!" said Arafel, and Fionnghuala flickered into shadow as she drew the silver sword. Ciaran clung to Aodhan and the horse strode into the shadow-ways.

Horror followed. A sickness passed him near: that was iron, a blade which passed through his substance, harmless in shadow-shape. Arafel thrust at that man; she flickered out of otherwhere in the midst of that thrust and back again: the silver blade had killed. The movements of Men and mortal horses were slow, and slowing still, as the elven horses strode their gliding and fear-

some way, seeming to gallop but gaining less ground
than speed. Ciaran had the sword in hand, but skill failed
him—he struck, and failed his mark and struck again.
The stone sang in his mind and something far colder
than himself seized his heart; Aodhan sprang forward
feeling it, and the thunder grew. There were other
shapes with them, low, loping shapes of hounds, the
taller blackness of horse and rider, which raced with
them. Ciaran reached for his bow, overcome with horror.

"No," said Arafel. "Strike no blow at those."

Death drew away, parted from them in the course,
and Ciaran looked back—saw Scaga and the other riders
in that same slow movement of Men, cutting their way
behind them. Cloaks and hair flew in frozen swirlings,
with lightning flashes. Arafel called to him and the elven
horses lengthened stride, began to move forward as well
as swifter. Men passed by them, faster and faster, shadows through which they could move. Iron shivered past
them with pain and poison, and the hoses shied farther
into otherwhere, flickered out again enough to see
their way.

We are phantoms on the earth, Ciaran thought, and
knew not which heritage *we* meant—for between those
flickerings of otherwhere, like lightning-strokes, there
was no army, only murky day, a strange placid landscape
void of farms and wars and Men.

Yet not deserted. A horn sounded, braying, and came
small folk scurrying from the hooves of the elven
steeds—some fair and some foul, some direly misshapen.
A weapon glanced from Ciaran's mail, and there was
no fleeing. The thunder cracked and the horses leaped
forward. Ciaran struck with the sword while it profited,
saw Arafel herself beset by a tide of shadows which
poured out of the thickening air. She vanished and he
thought her slain, but the shadows poured after her into
that nothingness.

"Go," he cried at Aodhan, and the horse leaped, following Arafel into mortal daylight. The shadows had not
come through, or they hid, or transformed themselves.
Arafel slew Men, a dire dream in which Ciaran's heart
was chilled . . . I am of them, his heart cried; but another
mind rose up in him, flowing into his limbs and his
hands.

Give over, give over, the stone sang in his heart, showing him his helplessness to wield these weapons.

He fought that voice, that one who strove to live, to come back. Aodhan ceased to obey him, raced wildly, while the wind grew and grew, while nightmares passed on either side. An anger rose in him at these ill-shapen things, these shadows that twisted into vision, the prickling of old hostility.

"Liosliath!" he heard them shout in rage; and the anger grew in him, lifted his arm, swelled in his heart. He shouted—he knew not what he cried. Aodhan leaped under him willingly, bore him along while his hands strung the elvish bow and he gathered up an arrow. The air swirled with storm: the arrow flew, ice-tipped, feathered with light. A horror shrieked and fled, and others coursed the winds. There was a light by him, which became Fionnghuala and her rider, and he saw Arafel's face calm and terrible as she sent shafts winging after his. Men ceased to matter. They were nothing. This was the war, these the enemy, old as earth, as they were old. Shapes fled before them, turning sometimes to strike and suffer wounds.

Suddenly they were alone, in a place gone gray and full of mists—They are fled, fled, the dream sang to him; and elsewhere, wherever he looked, was an iron-poisoned hush.

"Come," said Arafel, and shadow-shifted to a bloody and littered field. Rain came down and failed to reach them, pocked bloody puddles in the mire instead, drenched the broken human bodies and the shattered spears. They were in the midst of the field, with both sides drawn back for breath. Ciaran turned Aodhan and beheld Caer Wiell, with its men ranged before it afoot, the dozen riders still remaining to them standing huddled to the fore.

It was pause, not victory. It was regrouping, while the sky poured out its tears.

Another rider came treading above the mire of the center of the battlefield. He was a shape like a fragment of night, with his robes blowing in a wind counter of the wind which blew in the mortal realm. Lord Death stopped before them, leaned seemingly on the withers of the shadow-horse, and Ciaran shuddered, for in that shadow steed's head there was a pale hint of naked bone when the lightnings flashed.

"You are mad," said Death. "Go back. Cease this."

"I am bound," said Arafel. "They have invoked my aid."

Death straightened, and lifted a black sleeve toward the distant lines of the enemy. "*They* are there, come from under the hills to aid them. Do you not know? There are powers which have come to align with *them*."

"They would do so. But we are bound."

"There are my brother gods," said Death. "I bear you word from them: Withdraw, before worse is loosed."

"Let them stay away," said Arafel. "Enough is amiss here."

"Go back," Death whispered. "If the Daoine Sidhe had all left this land, these fell things would never have come again."

"Because I have never gone away, dear youth—they have stayed to their hidings." She laughed and the shadow horse trembled. "Do you know *now* what watch I stand in Eald?"

Death and his horse stood still, bereft of answers. Ciaran gazed at the blackness, and Aodhan shifted and stamped, for things moved underfoot, and forces gathered.

"I do not bid you," Ciaran said to Arafel, although it was effort. "I know what has to be. I bound you to this. I release you. Give us over to Death, us and them, only so this ends."

Arafel gazed at him, and his skin prickled, for the lightnings stirred. "It is Men who lend them power," she said. "And your sight is truer than it was.—We are held to battle here on this field until the army yonder bids their own allies go back."

"And they who are winning—or losing—will not."

"That is so. When your mortal enemy has won, then their new allies will only be the stronger. They will go on, those powers; they will gather forces; they will sweep over all the world. Do you comprehend now, Man my cousin?"

"Forgive me," Ciaran whispered.

"It is heartsease you ask. I give you that. And I confess I had hope of more strength than we have in Caer

Wiell. If we might rob the enemy of lives and human hands . . . but we have not strength enough."

"You have power unused," said Death. "Use it! Will you let them all break forth?"

"The cost of that too you know."

"Our need is *now*."

"That sacrifice will not kill them, only drive them hence for now. And what then, Lord Death? What in a hundred lifetimes of Men—when they go unwatched? You have no power over them, no more than over me. There is no hope that way. No, I will tell you what you must do: stay your hand from Caer Wiell. Our forces are too diminished as it is."

"I cannot," said Death, bowing his head. "I too am bound to what I do."

"My King," said Ciaran, "will come here, if only we can hold."

"Your King delays overlong," Arafel said quietly. "Wiser had you bound me to his aid, not to doomed Caer Wiell's. As it is, we are bound to serve and fall. And the cost of that fall you do not guess even yet."

"There was a battle," said Death, "a day ago. Trust me, that I know. There are still skirmishes; and that force is well-occupied in the hills, Man. Have no hope of them. This enemy has engaged them too, at the pass of Caerdale; and all your King's strength cannot rout the enemy from those heights."

Ciaran listened. There seemed a gleam within that dark hood. There began a beating that was his heart, or Arafel's, or both. He laid a hand upon the stone at his throat, heard a whisper from it, felt an elvish presence that found courage to laugh at the thought that came into his mind; and Aodhan shifted to move at once.

"No," Arafel forbade him, but a light was in her eyes. "Wise you are, but that is no road for you, o Man. Yours to hold here. Where it serves Caer Wiell, *I* am free to ride."

"His human allies will all fall and the enemy will take him," Death said. His darkness became a nimbus about him. "I shall depart this field with all my forces. That much I can do."

"Go," said Arafel.

Death faded. There was only the rain, and then that stopped.

Arafel spoke to Fionnghuala. The white mare began to run. Aodhan whinnied after her, and pawed the ground, but stood fast.

And across the field the enemy began to gather their line.

Ciaran shivered. Beware, a voice in him whispered: You are only seeing Men. Others are closer.

"Liosliath," he said, holding up the stone, and shuddered, surrendering. "I shall stop being. Wake. Wake, Liosliath. It is you they need now. Wake! Your enemies are here!"

Cold fire spread from the stone. It frightened him, the power which spread through his limbs and the pride which drew breath and laughed, despising Men.

Aodhan wheeled then, and sped with long strides toward the battered lines of Caer Wiell, to pace delicately along before them. He saw Scaga's face, marred with a bloody slash; saw this fearless man give ground from him, saw others flinch. He flickered into otherwhere and saw the enemy gathered like a tide. He drew an arrow from his quiver and fired, saw the icy point lodge deep in a shadow which faded in torment.

And with the stone he drew on Eald, cast a glamour over all the force at his back, sheening them all in silver.

"Come," he called to them, and not he: the elf prince, who drew his sword and clapped his heels to Aodhan, the prince who knew well how to fence with iron, nothing reckoning the poisoned pain which whipped through his body when it must. Faster and faster Aodhan sped, and slower and slower the Men, while he brought the flickering elvish sword out of otherwhere, lodged in human flesh—gone again before human weapon could strike.

Yet none died. Enemies weakened, and human weapons hewed them ghastly wounds, and folk of Caer Wiell were spitted in turn, and did not die, but kept hewing others, so long as they had limbs which would move.

There was a wailing on the wind, a darkness. He gathered strength against it and lightnings flashed on monstrous shapes. Blows rained against the silver mail; in rage he swept against them, wounded them, and time and time again Aodhan dropped into the mortal world, until some of the dire things followed him there, and undying Men stared in fear.

One of the Men was Scaga, whose anguished look Ciaran knew, who still held his sword, standing unhorsed in the mud. Then Ciaran's heart was moved to pity, and he would have taken the old warrior up, but Liosliath was stronger, and Aodhan swept him on, skimming the ground with thunder. The Caerbourne down the hill flowed with blood. Saplings on the banks were trampled. He used his sword against Men wherever their ranks tried to stand, and herded them and hurt them, though they would not die. The light about him began to grow paler and brighter, for human sun was sinking into twilight, and elven sun was rising.

Then the dark things drew power more than they had before, thrusting maimed human folk forward to press against maimed Caer Wiell.

And now he was pressed back and back, for the enemy was in all places, and on all sides, converging on the ruined gate, and rending those defenders who lagged in their retreat.

A Man stood by him, at Aodhan's shoulder: Scaga. The old warrior shouted orders to his men and from the walls of Caer Wiell arrows flew, iron which the creatures hated as much as he. Some writhed in pain. Others crept up against the walls of the hold, and tore at the very stone.

And a wind grew in the east, and thunder.

"Arafel!" he cried.

She was there. He flickered into otherwhere and saw a light among the mists of the faded lands, with shadows rearing up between, caught and desperate. He held the gate against them, though his arm grew tired and Aodhan trembled beneath him. There was a thunder in the earth as well, and more and more human attackers added force to those who had come before. But a cry of dismay went up at the far side of that living tide, human screams and battle cries.

"Liosliath!" the call came down the wind, and he saw the flickering of the white mare and the gleam of Arafel's sword. Aodhan gathered himself and began to move, striding faster and faster.

And suddenly a shadow was beside him, a void shaped like horse and rider, and shapes like coursing hounds. Other dark riders had joined them, blacknesses as great as death: and some who ran afoot, some like Men and some horned like stags.

Fionnghuala shone in the murk, and her rider no less than she: a pale and terrible gleaming, her hair astream on the wind. "Liosliath!" Arafel hailed him, and he reached out a hand as bright, caught hers across the gap, a joy which burned and died, because of the dire things about them.

Armies clashed in the dark and the storm, and that noise was far from them. Dark things leaped and attacked, slaying and being slain, and wounded shapes climbed the winds. Lord Death lifted the likeness of a horn and sounded it, and the clouds increased as the dark horse began to move; Aodhan paced the dark rider, and Fionnghuala joined him. Side by side with Death they rode, and the dogs bayed, coursing more and more rapidly through the air. They strode above the ground, and mounted the skirling winds. Aodhan threw his head and shook himself and Arafel circled Fionnghuala out and back again, hastening something fell and fugitive toward the dogs. Clouds tattered beneath the hooves, and the thunders rolled. The horn sounded yet again, and more and more riders joined them, bearing banners like black cloud. Armored Men, with darkened eyes set ahead upon the quarry, and lances agleam in their hands, rode on horses with eyes as dead as theirs. The slain had gathered to hunt the newly dead. Ciaran looked, and the Man in him shuddered, for he knew some of these faces, and he had loved no few of them. He saw a cousin there; and a childhood friend, and another rider on a horse with a white-tipped ear—"Scaga!" he called, but the rider coursed past, eyes dark, unheeding; and many a man of Caer Wiell followed after. The last turned and beckoned to him.

"Liosliath!" Arafel rebuked him. She held out her hand to him. Ciaran came, yielded to the elf prince, and Aodhan ran his gliding pace across the clouds, while the shadows fled.

They two turned back alone then, and rode the field in the human world, but the battle was done. Dark shapes slunk aside where they passed, sought refuge elsewhere, and vanished.

Men gathered at the gates of Caer Wiell, atop the hill. They rode quietly now, covering ground, a rush of wind about them, and had their weapons sheathed.

Then Arafel stopped, sat still on Fionnghuala, gazing toward the gates. "I am free," she said. " 'Tis done."

"Let us ride nearer," he begged her, for Donn had come riding in with lord Evald and the King's army; and there were the folk inside Caer Wiell. He ached to know how those he loved had fared.

"Would you see them?" Arafel asked him. "Aye, I do understand the bonds of kinship. Go."

She would not come inside the walls. He knew her pride, and ached for that as well. But Aodhan felt his will to go, and moved.

Men gave way before him, with fear on their faces. and when he had come as far as the gate, he saw lord Evald's banner, and Evald of Caer Wiell himself standing near it, giving orders to his men. Evald stopped and stared at him. And there kneeling by Evald's feet was Beorc, Scaga's son, who held Scaga's maimed and muddy body in his arms and mourned.

"He fought more than well," Ciaran said. Beorc looked up, and grief in his eyes became dread at what he saw. The look pained Ciaran like the iron, which ached more and more in the air about him, a taint in which it grew hard to breathe. Aodhan fretted to be away, and Ciaran rode farther, within the ruined gates, sought his father and Donnchadh and the moon banner of his own Caer Donn. Elf-sight found them quickly, and he stopped Aodhan by them in the swirl of Men in the courtyard.

They looked up at a strange rider and did not know him—surely they failed to recognize him, or they would never have had such a look of dread at the sight of him. He rode away from them, and Men shrank from his path in the crowded yard. "Stay," he bade Aodhan, slid down and walked among the Men, among his own, past cousins of his, seeing everywhere that look he dreaded.

He moved elsewhere, a reaching of the heart, a shifting, and found himself in the stone hall of Caer Wiell, by the fireside, where Lady Meredydd and Branwyn stood. Their eyes showed no less fear than the others hand.

"They are well," he said, holding the stone at his heart to ease the ache in it. "Your lord is home. You are safe. But Scaga is dead."

He wept in telling it, not having wished to weep, and began to fade. But Branwyn called his name and held him by it. She tried to come to him, a mortal yearning. He reached and took her hand to help her, but she could not come the way he could. He kissed her fingers, and kissed her brow, and stayed a time in the room with them.

Lord Evald came, and the King with him. To the King, Ciaran knelt, while Laochailan's young eyes regarded him with that dread others turned on him.

"Welcome sight," the King he had loved said of him; but with the lips, not with the heart. And Evald, lord Evald, who was Eald's near and knowing neighbor, gave him a look as bleak and unwelcoming—then came and offered him an embrace.

No other human dared, not his own father or brother, when they had come up the stairs into the hall, all clattering with armor. "Ciaran," his father said, and gazed on him with a bleak, hag-ridden stare. Donnchadh started a step toward him, but his father held his arm and prevented him. Then Donnchadh's face became like a stranger's to him, grim and mournful.

They have always known, Ciaran thought, both of them have always known what is in our blood. He recalled the elvish moon which had been Caer Donn's banner for years out of memory, and was heartstricken at such a look as Donnchadh gave him.

"We are going back," his father told the King then without looking at him, as if he had not been there. "We have our own cares, too long neglected."

"Go," the King bade him; so his father and his brother went their way from the hall, not to linger long near Eald, and never looked back.

Ciaran stood wounded, looked last at Branwyn, who looked at him, and in his pain he wished himself away, in the cold air, in the mist, the deserted shadow-ways.

He came back into the mortal night in the courtyard after some time had passed, where all was quieter than it had been.

He walked outside the riven gates, where the horror of the field was honest and undiminished. "Aodhan," he said quietly, and a wind gusted as the horse moved out of the night toward him, slow peals of thunder, a blazing like the noon of elvish sun. He stroked the white neck and thought of his home in the hills, at Caer Donn. He might go there, might—once—go there, greet his mother and his kin, see the things he had known, bring them word days before his father and Donnchadh and the men could come and tell them—before that place was closed to him forever, before—so many things. Aodhan could carry him.

He touched the stone at his throat. "Arafel," he said.

It was another presence which came to him instead, which touched his heart far more gently than it had ever done, with elvish brightness. There was pride—always that; but this time the touch was warm. "Man," it whispered; and there was the roar of the sea and the cries of gulls. *"Man."*

Only that he said, the elven prince, and it sufficed.

NINETEEN

THE END OF IT ALL

He came, but not alone, and that surprised her—in plain good clothes, and with Branwyn tramping along with him through the brambles, her golden hair tangled with twigs. He wore the sword and carried the bow and a pack which clearly burdened him. She watched them, and would have reached out to help them, but she sensed the fear in Branwyn, and could not have helped, no more than he could: Branwyn was doomed to the thorns.

They reached the dancing-ring. He called her in his mind, and she came, smiling sadly at the pain in his eyes, and looked then at Branwyn, who managed to look back at her.

"I have brought Aodhan back," Ciaran said.

"Swiftest to have ridden," said Arafel.

"Branwyn tried."

"Ah," she said in pity, and again met Branwyn's blue eyes. "You might have."

Fear looked back at her, but something like the child struggled behind it. "I wanted to."

"That is much," said Arafel.

A wind had risen. She sensed Aodhan near, but it was Ciaran who had the summoning of him. Ciaran held out a hand, and the horse stepped into mortal sunlight, aglow with the elvish moon. Small thunders rumbled in the glade, and lightnings flickered. Ciaran stroked Aodhan's neck, and whispered his name and bade him go. The thunder clapped and the horse was gone, that swiftly, and perhaps something of Ciaran's heart went with him; he had that look.

Then Ciaran knelt down and unbound the pack which he had brought, and took the sword and bow and laid them atop all the shining armor at her feet.

"Thank you," Arafel said, and the gifts faded.

"I thank you," Ciaran said. "I must thank you. But—do you understand?—I have carried them as far as I can. I have seen things—I shall always see them. They are enough."

"I know," she said.

He rose, and reached last for the chain about his neck.

"No," she said. "That, you must keep."

"I cannot," he said. He drew it off, and offered it to her hands, his own hands trembling.

"It is your protection."

"Take it."

"And Branwyn's too. Do you even hope to get from out this forest without it? Would you see her hunted too?"

That struck deep. Ciaran's hands fell; but Branwyn took his arm.

"I knew that too," said Branwyn, and there was more of sense in her blue eyes than there had ever been. "But I am here. And we will walk out again."

"Please," Ciaran said, offering the stone yet again. "I am a Man, and when he comes, that is the way of Men, is it not? But if I keep this, there is no hope for me."

Arafel took it then, unwilling, and her lips parted in shock at the strength that had come to it, and the presence in it which was indeed almost beyond bearing.

"Ah," she said, folding it to her heart. She looked on him with tears. "You have given me a gift, o Man. And now there is nothing you have left me to give you."

"A blessing," he said, "for us. That I will take."

"Few Men have ever asked it of the Daoine Sidhe."

"I ask."

She kissed him then, and kissed Branwyn. "Go," she said.

They went, hand in hand, and she walked behind them, the shadow-ways, unseen. They had trouble in the going, took scratches of the thorns, and climbed high places and limped on unexpected stones; shadows hissed at them, but fled quickly when she bade them gone.

And at last it was New Forest, and Arafel stood upon the flat rock and watched them down the slope, toward the Caerbourne, and Caer Wiell.

A blackness settled near her. She frowned at it.

"Give them a little," she asked. "Only a little time."

"We were allies," Death said. "Should I have so short a memory? I shall wait. As for Branwyn—she was always mine."

Again she frowned.

"I have another face," he said.

She drew herself up and laid a hand on her sword. "Beware of me, Lord Death; I know your name; and the day I see you as you are, you are yourself in peril. Do not tempt me."

"You have asked a favor," he said.

"Aye," she said more softly, anger fallen. "That I have."

"He may come here if he wills; and she may. He will die abed, years hence. That, I give to him."

"Then I forgive you," she said, "other things."

She left him then, and walked her own way, from Airgiod's quiet rim, to the moonlit grove.

Fionnghuala was there, and Aodhan. "Go," she bade them. "You are free."

They did not go; and they were free to choose that too. They stayed near, and the grove breathed with wind and memories.

"Liosliath," she said, holding the stone near her heart.

He was aware. There *was* another place but this. She held it close and walked amid the silver trees.

Eald was smaller. But it had held. She found that place at the edge of Eald, hers and not quite hers, and the Gruagach scampered into hiding, remembering ancient quarrels—but he fared well, and so did all he cared for. The fields were safe. She preferred the earth no iron had delved, the lands shadowed with her trees—but she took care now of lands far wider than Eald, so that the lands of Men had rarely seen such a year, in which no planting failed. It cost her. She did all she could to mend what war had done, and stretched her care as far as it could go. Long ago she had chosen this wood and kept it—but now it had neighbors she valued, with special poignancy, that they were brief and brave and given to doing as they would. She had never known why she watched, except for pride, not to yield forever what once the Sidhe had been; but now it was for love.

Yet one day, one day she almost despaired, so much of Eald she had given away. She came for comfort to that heart of her wood and walked there listening to the stones, her head bowed in a weariness almost too much to bear.

So she found it, a tiny thing unlooked for at her feet. A branch, she thought, had fallen from the silver trees, which had never happened in any wind that blew—so, she thought as she bent down by it, Eald had at last begun to die, from the heart outward.

Then she cast herself to her knees in wonder—for the sprig was rooted in the ground, thrusting up from the earth with silver leaves all delicately veined, the first new life in Eald since the dimming of the world.

BOOK TWO

THE TREE OF SWORDS AND JEWELS

ONE

THE FUATHAS

It was the old hiding game, and they laughed, did Meadhbh and Ceallach, while Muirne searched. They watched the skinny woman up close by the keep looking this way and that among the bushes and covered their mouths to keep from setting one another to laughing aloud. Then Ceallach threw a stone and made the bushes rattle far over to the right so that Muirne spun and looked in that direction.

"Come out," Muirne cried. "Come out this instant. Hear me?"

She was angry now. Meadhbh slid backward through the brush and tugged at Ceallach's sleeve.

Ceallach followed. "You hear me?" Muirne went on shouting while they slid and slithered away on the slope. "Don't play such games!"

But a path appeared in their way as they got up and scrambled crouching through the trees. It was a strange place to find a path, because no one came and went in the world except by the great dusty road, and no one went off this direction from Caer Wiell, toward the river and the vast and haunted woods—excepting sometimes their father, who went alone and without any armor at all, and taking no one with him, not even Beorc, who went everywhere else. The pair had asked why, of course. They asked everything, why birds flew and why the sun rose and where the wind came from. But no one told them any of these things, and no one told them why their father went walking down by the Caerbourne

where no one else would dare to walk, no, not even
Beorc, who was a huge red-haired man that no one
would ever call afraid.

So a thrill went up their backs when they suddenly
found that path so close to them all their lives and unsus-
pected. One keen quick thought brought their eyes to
each other and a secret excitement brought their hands
together, fingers locked in fingers, Ceallach tugging on
his sister's hand when he had the lead. Then as he
helped Meadhbh down over an old log, Meadhbh seized
the first place and dragged him along. So they went, one
and then the other, their eyes afever with the secrets of
this path that seemed to welcome them. It was the way
their father came. They were sure of that, and for that
reason they had no fear of treading on it, never once
thinking that he could lead them where he could not, if
danger came on them, save them.

It was so sure in their minds that they exchanged only
glances as they went, unraveling this path to its ending,
one pulling the other, skipping over the old rocks, the
bones of the ancient hill on which Caer Wiell was
reared. They dodged through thickets which should have
torn their skin yet magically refrained. It was a moment
of magic. They were sure of that in the same fashion
they were sure each what the other thought, as if some
golden thread bound their minds so close there was no
need of talking.

And never once did they think that where that path
led might be farther than their young legs could run
without stopping. They skipped and ran and fended the
branches away, took wild chances with their leaping
and dodging.

It was Meadhbh who slowed first, who first began to
doubt the way that they were tending. She resisted Ceallach's tugging at her hand ever so slightly just as he had
lighted on soft ground, so that he slipped and brought
both of them reeling down an unexpected slope in the
bracken. Meadhbh sat down at the bottom, plump
among her woolen skirts, barking her skin on the tangle
of roots and stones, and Ceallach slid past her right to
the edge of the brambles.

"Ow!" said Ceallach. "What did you stop for?"

"Hush," Meadhbh said, shivering. "We've come near the river. Hear it?"

"We mustn't lose the path," Ceallach said. The brush seemed darker all about, and the water whispered like the breeze that sported in the conspiring leaves. "Come on, Meadhbh—it has to be just up there."

But Meadhbh bit her lip and tugged up her skirt to look at her shins, where her woolen hose were torn. The wounds stung. Everything was wrong suddenly. The woods were dark and the river was chuckling nearby, so that it was hard now not to think of the strict warnings they had had about the deep forest. "We had better go back," she said. "Muirne will come looking." She said it even hoping at the moment that Muirne would turn up suddenly and rescue them. She gave her hand to Ceallach to be helped up, ready to run as hard to be out of this place as she had run to get into it, although now her side and shins were hurting and she was far from sure in which direction home lay.

"Ah," a moan came to them. *"Ah, ah, ah—"*

They froze like fawns, and turned wide eyes in the direction of the voice, which was mixed with the sound of the river.

"Ah me," it said. "Ah me, so lost."

"Listen," Ceallach said.

"I don't know whether it means it's lost or we are," Meadhbh said, and her teeth began to chatter as if with winter cold. Her shins stung, reminding her of misfortune. She and Ceallach held onto each other with a grip that hurt her hand. "I don't think we ought to answer it."

"O lost," it cried. "O me, o me, o where?"

"It's a girl," said Ceallach then, with a fresh breath of courage. "Come on, Meadhbh, it's only someone, after all." He stood up, tugging at her hand.

"O, o!" it wept. "O, I'm caught, o the hurt, the hurt. . . ."

The sounds of sobs came to them, loud as the river, a crying that was everywhere, and Meadhbh, who was pulling back to look for the path again, stopped pulling at Ceallach's leading—not that she thought better of it, but that the someone was crying as if a heart were breaking, and that sobbing tugged as surely at her heart as at Ceallach's. She stopped pulling back at all and followed Ceallach down past the brambles and down and down where the river ran.

"I don't like this," Meadhbh found the heart to say, when they came on that black water, and Ceallach seemed daunted too. The water was sinister and wide, and gnarled old trees hung over it with a stillness that prickled through the snuffling and the weeping. "Ceallach, let's be going home."

"Look," Ceallach said, and held onto her as she held to him, because of a sudden there was someone sitting on the black rocks, like someone wrapped up in weeds still glistening from the river water. That someone lifted a pale beautiful face and hair gold as pollen fell onto its shoulders among the weeds. This someone sat with legs curled sideways on the rock and arms holding the cloak of slickish weeds about her. Eyes dark as the riverwater looked at them both very solemnly. Then weed-covered arms lifted and flowed toward the water in one smooth motion as that someone dived, so subtly it was like the pouring of water into water.

"Oh," Meadhbh said, and pulled at her brother to make him run away.

But a face bobbed up in the water, flowerlike, with the pale hair flowing about in the river currents and the eyes staring at them and the mouth making a round of surprise and wonder.

"I am lost," the someone said. "Oh, please, I am lost, quite lost."

"Where are you trying to go to?" Meadhbh asked, curious in spite of herself and quite forgetting to run.

"Lost," the someone insisted. The bright head sank beneath the dark water and came up again with her hair sheeting away in the currents. "Who are you?"

"Flann," said Ceallach thinking quickly. "Floinn," said Meadhbh with a very uncomfortable feeling, because she had not been taught to lie, but names were not for giving away, and Flann and Floinn were safe at home, being two fat bay ponies and not at all in question. "Who are *you*?" It seemed completely mad to be talking to a creature floating in the river as if she were someone they had met in the field, as if she were someone dressed in honest clothes and not all in river weeds.

But the creature bobbed higher in the water as if she were standing up and brought her hands into sight, cupped as if she held some precious thing. "I shall give you a gift—see, pearls. Have you ever seen pearls or heard of them?"

"We have to go," said Ceallach.

"O, but you must never go!" The whole creature vanished again in a swirl of dark water and the waters boiled and broke at once in the appearance of a black horse's head, and neck and back, and the whole beast was surging up as a horse comes up from swimming, a horse that made all the horses of the hold look stock and dull, a horse so beautiful and sleek and black that it seemed that the night itself had come up out of the river. And they desired it, did Meadhbh and Ceallach, more than anything they had ever seen or imagined to desire. It was freedom, it was all the might of the river, it was a creature that flowed like waters and beckoned them with power. They saw themselves as queen and king, woman and man in an instant, with never waiting for tedious years to pass. They saw awe in the eyes of all about them and they never, never needed fear any man or beast anywhere or ever in the world.

It came closer, lowering its beautiful head. The water dripped off its mane and made its hide sleek and shining. It extended its foreleg and bowed itself, offering them its back, and Ceallach went first toward it with only the dimmest remembrance that he ought to be afraid, while Meadhbh came with her hands held out to it as she would come to her own pony, quite, quite forgetting the love she had for that poor, plain beast, because desire burned in her for what this one could give.

"No," a voice said distinctly, "I should *not.*"

Ceallach stopped, and the black horse tossed its head. Meadhbh looked wildly about and her heart all but turned over, for a stranger stood at the edge of the thicket, cloaked in gray and deep in a kind of light and shadow that made it hard to see him. His hand seemed to rest on a sword hilt on the shadowed side, and his whole aspect was grim and dangerous. Of a sudden there was a splash where the horse had been, a scattering of cold water on them that made them cry out in fright.

And then whatever had possessed them to be here

unafraid melted away from their hearts and left them terrified. The wood seemed dark and the figure dire and sinister. They held to each other in the nakedness of the riverbank, and Ceallach wound his fingers into Meadhbh's in the spell of a moment too terrible to move.

"Hardly wise," the stranger said. "Who gave you leave to be here?"

"This is our place," Meadhbh said to this intruder who was perhaps an outlaw and perhaps worse, perhaps some spy from An Beag or way up on the Bradheath; and she thought that she ought to have said nothing at all, but she was never skilled at keeping quiet. And nothing seemed right about this stranger, in the rapid shifting of this truth and that about the Caerbourne's dark banks. She could put no quality to the voice, whether it was young or old or what it sounded like, or make out clearly what the stranger looked like in the shadow which was not all that deep a shadow, except that some trick of the leaves and sun made it hard to see who stood there at all.

"Your place," the stranger echoed. "Most assuredly it is not." and the stranger brightened, just that, as if the light had stopped playing tricks or the sun had come out from behind a cloud. It was no man from An Beag, and in one way of looking at the stranger it was not a man at all, but a tall, slim lady in patchwork gray and green like a hunter's clothes, wearing a gray cloak over it all. She went striding right past them to the riverbank as if they had never mattered. *"Fuathas,"* the lady said in a voice that sent a shiver up their backs. It was oh, so soft a voice, but the water stirred, and a golden head came up very carefully, just the eyes showing above the water, eyes dark as the water was dark, and very wary.

So they knew then that they had seen two of the Sidhe—one of whom stood on the bank, there and not there, with a brightness that was different from the daylight.

"Come out," the Sidhe said.

"No." The golden head had risen so that the lips were above the water, and now the creature looked frightened. "No, oh no, no, no."

"Out. At once. Shall I call your name? I shall teach

it to these children and they will call you whenever they like."

"No," the creature wept. It slid to the shore and lay bowed in a miserable huddle of weed, only a knot of old riverweed which moved and bubbled.

"So you remember," said the Sidhe, "whose wood this is, and where you are. —Would you have its name?" she asked suddenly, and looked at Meadhbh so that all the forest seemed to have gone dim, and in Ceallach's breast his heart began to beat so heavily it seemed to fill the forest. "No," said the Sidhe then. "You wanted it once and you would want it again; and you would want it to be, and to do for you, and to do more and more until you saw everyone afraid of you. Is this what you should be?"

"No," said Meadhbh. She recalled the dream that was the water horse and the power of him, and suddenly she shuddered at the thought of her father and mother becoming very small and herself very great and tall. That was not the way the world was meant to be. She never wanted that. And: "No," Ceallach said, thinking of himself and Meadhbh powerful over everything and all alone, with no more games to play and only fear around them, and between them.

"Its name is Caolaidhe," said the Sidhe.

"Ah" the creature wailed, "ah no, ah no, o mercy no!" She looked up at them, held up thin white hands as if she cupped the pearls. "O mercy, o mercy, o no, no, not to leave the river, never, no. I'll give you gifts, o such gifts!"

The thought of the pearls leapt into Meadhbh's mind. It was a good thought and unselfish surely, how the pearls would look about her mother's neck, how her mother would wonder at her having them to give. Surely to give them away would be the right thing to do. But the tall, gray-cloaked Sidhe was staring at her with a look so strange and piercing that no leaf could have moved in all the forest. She could only think that something was expected of her, something more than she had ever done and might ever do, a thing that was wise and at once as simple as understanding. "Let it go," Meadhbh said.

"Go back to the river and don't come out," Ceallach told it.

The creature cast a wild look about and bent and flowed away. "O kind," it cried as it slid into the water. "O good children, o kind—" The sound became bubbles, and the river flowed with its accustomed rush.

"My calling-name is Thistle," the Sidhe said gravely, as if the fuath had been no more than a passing breeze. "You might be trusted with my true one; I do think you might, young as you are. But I am no small matter, no, not like that one. You have done wisely at the last if not at the first."

"We have to go home now," said Meadhbh as staunchly as she could.

"I shall take you there."

"We can go ourselves," said Ceallach.

"Then I shall walk with you and see you safe."

"You mustn't."

"Ah," the Sidhe said gravely. "But I am your father's friend."

"Are you what he comes to see?"

"Perhaps I am."

"I had thought—" Ceallach said and let his voice fall away.

"Be still," said the Sidhe. "Name no names near the riverside. Caolaidhe is listening. Come. Come, now. There are worse things about this stream than the each-uisge."

She offered her hands, one to each, and as Meadhbh considered gravely, so did Ceallach, looking up at their tall rescuer.

"Now you are wary," said the Sidhe. "Good. But wary of the wrong one, and that is ill. Go as you please then."

"Come on," said Ceallach to Meadhbh, and took his sister's hand. They went climbing up away from the Sidhe, up the bank, fighting the undergrowth among the gray stones. Bracken grew here, but bracken gave way to rougher growth, and thorns scratched them and tore at their hair and clothes.

"I don't think this is the way," Meadhbh said after a while. "I think we should go more to the left."

Ceallach went, and it was better for a time, but it was not the path, and very soon they both stopped and looked about them, each holding the other's hand and feeling very tired and frightened and wishing desperately to be home again.

"We have to go on," said Ceallach.

"But which way?" asked Meadhbh. "I'm afraid I've lost us. The path is nowhere near here."

"I will show you," said a voice, and Thistle followed, shadowy and standing right amid a thorn thicket where no one could have walked.

"Is that herself?" asked Ceallach, "or only something like it? —Meadhbh, don't trust it."

"Wiser still," said Thistle, and walked out of the brambles and held out her hand again, clearer and sterner than before. "But that way leads to An Beag and I doubt you would like that. Come, I say—Ceallach and Meadhbh, come now."

There was a wanting, a desire as strong as for the water horse, and first Ceallach and then Meadhbh started to go, but each held the other back in small hesitations that made one great one.

"So, well," said the Sidhe. "But I am called. I hear your father calling me. If he calls a third time I must go and leave you, and that would be dangerous. The woods are roused and he is in danger as deep as yours. Come, I say, come *now!*"

Meadhbh went. It was the part about her father in danger that won her; and Ceallach came running an instant later. "Ah!" Meadhbh cried in fright, for the Sidhe at once flung her gray cloak about them both and cut off the sun. Strong arms held them, and there was a scent of flowers and grass and a grayness which stole the sight like mist, passing then to dark. Meadhbh was falling asleep and knew she ought to be afraid, but she was not. Ceallach knew too and struggled, or thought that he did, but the sleep came on him: he heard the Sidhe whisper his name.

They slept, not wishing to, wrapped all in gray.

So Arafel carried them both as she came, and laid them gently on the bracken.

"No harm is on them," she said to their father. Her heart hurt her to see how the years had dealt with this Man. It hurt her most to see his fright, how he ran and fell to his knees next to his children, and gathered them each in an arm, sleeping as they were, hugging them and holding them as if he had just had part of his heart torn from him and restored. Arafel sat down crosslegged where she stood so that she need not look down at him, wistfully gazed on the three of them until Ciaran found his wits again. "They are sleeping," she assured him, for he might not understand that sleep. "It was easier to bring them so."

"Arafel," he said, holding his children against his heart, two red-and-golden heads nodded together beneath his fair beard. Tears ran on his face. The years had graven lines about his eyes. He was heavy with a man's full strength, and yet held his burden so gently his hands could not have bruised a flower.

So quickly the years fled. Each time she looked at him something of him had changed, and life seemed to have more and more power over him. "They have grown so," she said with a nod toward the children.

"Yes. They've grown." Pain touched his face, a patient kind of pain, long-suffering. "I hoped this time—I had most hope of you, that when I truly needed you—I hoped you had them."

"I." Arafel laid a hand on the stone at her breast. It was like a wound, his look. "No. You wrong me, Man."

"Not that you would do them harm. Never that."

"Or misguide them. Or take them into Eald without your knowing."

"Where were they then? Lost? Only lost, after all?"

"O Man, *Man*."

"I thought," he said, "perhaps there had gotten to be too much of the world about me for you to hear me any longer. That perhaps it was a place only they could go."

The pain was deep and everywhere, but there were no tears for it. He was at once too proud and too humble and it wounded her more than tears. "You do not understand," she said. "I've always heard you."

"And never came."

"The time—is not the same for me. There was a moment I could come, and I have left things now—O believe me, my dear friend, that you never walked in Eald unattended, going or coming."

"I had hoped for a word through the years," he said

simply, and his brows knit together. "That, if nothing more." He wound his fingers gently in his children's red hair and looked down at them and up again earnestly. "But this is more. Far more. This is all I ask."

"There was a difference in this calling. I felt it. Ah, Ciaran, I ran, I ran. I cannot tell you all of it, not here. Never think that it was nothing to me that you came."

"They *were* in danger, then."

"They fared better in it than some would have. There's much of their father in them." She saw the fear and put out her hand to his. "A silly nix, a danger most to children. Keep them from the forest. And yourself— O my friend, no more of walks into the wood. I shall come to you, rather. Things are darker than they were and the way has changed."

He had always had more sight than most. Fear crept in where pain had been. "How, changed?"

"This is not the place to talk of it. Hist, Branwyn is calling."

"Branwyn." A thousand distracted cares drew at him, graving lines on his face. He hugged his children and tried to get to his feet, but Arafel was quicker, and laid her hand on his shoulder.

"Let me take the girl," Arafel said, "and come with me."

He yielded up his daughter and Arafel took the girl into her arms, within her cloak, while he took his son and rose.

It was the merest shifting through the shadow, the lightest journey—and very swift. The walls of Caer Wiell showed beyond the mist, and grew out of shadow into daylight.

"So they are safe and home," said Arafel, and already the children were beginning to rub at their eyes as at the passing of an ordinary sleep. She set Meadhbh on her feet on the ground and steadied her, and looked into her face a moment. "Are you quite well, then?"

Meadhbh blinked and nodded dazedly. And Ceallach waked thoroughly and hugged his father's neck as Meadhbh discovered her father and her home at once and hurled herself against him to throw her arms about him.

"They know me as Thistle," Arafel said, beginning to depart into the night of her own world. "And that is best."

"Come back," Ciaran cried after her.

She stayed, half in his sunlight.

"Come soon," he wished her.

"To Caer Wiell? Yes, if you wish that. I shall come tonight—Yes, I shall. It is time I did that. Look for me at moonrise."

The children blinked and then losing sight of her, tumbled words one over the other, of water horses and river nixes and paths and rescues. Arafel heard them, even so.

And went her own way.

"She sent it back," said Meadhbh to her father, "into the river then, and we were afraid of her—minding what you always said about strangers—" It stuck in her throat to tell him what choice she had been offered, for that was too deep and too dark and too much knowledge of her growing heart to show to anyone, most of all anyone she loved. Somehow she passed over all the rest of it, even knowing the Name of the creature; and so did Ceallach. She was not the same; she would never be the same again after knowing how to choose, and neither would Ceallach; and she discovered this as she faced her father, at once afraid and desperately sure what she was doing. She had begun to grow up and apart in a way she thought was right—but it was not something to speak of.

And Ciaran saw the secrets nesting in both his children, not being blind. "You have been with the Sidhe," he said, and felt the least and most desperate jealousy of those he loved most in all the world. "And some things are not for ordinary ears. There are those who would be frightened by hearing it, do you understand? Be wise and quiet on it." So he took them each by the hand and brought them toward the gates of Caer Wiell.

A horn began to sound from the walls, waking echoes across the hills. The lost was found, and now the searchers through the forest must come safely home. Following these echoes other horns began to sound through the forest and along the river as searchers heard and passed the signal on.

Women came running before ever they reached the gates, and quickest was Branwyn, who had been watching from the walls and seeking too with what small portion of Eald she held in her heart. She came running, her braids whipping loose, her skirts aflurry, her slippered feet hardly touching the stones. She caught her errant children in her arms and looked at their faces and up at Ciaran's and wept.

"They were with her," Branwyn said hotly. "I knew, I knew—"

"No. They were not with her," Ciaran said. "But she found them."

Branwyn's face went pale beneath its flush, all her knowings in disorder. She held Meadhbh's face and then Ceallach's between her hands and looked them in the eyes, kneeling there on the muddy stones beneath the gate—looked last and most desperately at Ciaran, hearing silences. Muirne came, wiping her nose and her eyes and begging everyone's forgiveness. "You must beg Muirne's pardon," Ciaran said sternly to his children. "You left *her,* as I hear it."

Meadhbh made a grave curtsy, difficult to manage within her mother's arm; and: "I beg pardon, Muirne," Ceallach said faintly.

Ciaran looked at all those round about, and still there was a hush on all the crowd except the children. "Our thanks," he said. "Nothing is amiss. The lost is found." He set a hand on his son's shoulder as Branwyn took Meadhbh in hand, and they passed through the gates of the hold he had held as lord the last ten years.

TWO

CAER WIELL

Branwyn wept, in the upper hall of Caer Wiell, her hands against her eyes as she sat huddled in her chair before the hearth. To her credit she wept alone, her children in their tower room with Muirne, her husband with his men down by the gate; for they were tears compounded of rage, of helplessness, of years and years of dread.

She hated Eald. It was a hate not born of anger, and yet having anger in it, for she had been betrayed. She had loved it once desperately, when she had been a child, and so she feared it for her children, with more than instinct. It and she were enemies, but quietly, gently—for all that she loved was tangled in Eald: her husband, her home, her children latest of all. She saw a vision of green leaves and dancing light, touching all she had, and this light was without substance: she could not strike it or hold it in the hand, but no shutters or gates could stop it. It slipped through chinks and the wind that came from the woods breathed enchantments more potent than her mortality.

Something had touched her children, something of Eald had held them today, and so she clenched her fists and remembered herself as if she hovered in the air above the girl on a fat Caerdale pony, and that child was herself and that which hovered was herself grown and trying to warn the girl—*go back, go back, never trust them*.

The vision always ended there, before the pony shied.

It was more dreadful so, with every merry jogging step became horridly sinister, every stirring of the leaves a menace the child could not yet feel.

Go back, go back, go back.

It was strange, that she could never recall Arafel. In her mind she knew that there had been such a person, that this was the power that sat at the heart of the wood. She had spoken with her face to face, oh, many a time. But the face and the voice had left her mind, leaving only the memory of a memory, of something which had shaken her life and left a great gap about itself, making her doubt that it was ever true. She never admitted this to her husband, never spoke of it, but she knew that this was not so with him, that Eald was graven too deeply in his heart for him ever to forget. She hated Eald and embraced it, perceiving even in him, in Ciaran, in the father of her children, a green silence she could never breach, and thoughts she could never share, and a longing against which she worked all her mortal witchery—*Stay, o stay, never think of her, never listen to the wind, never remember—whatever it is I cannot hold in my mind.*

If she could shape this thing, she thought sometimes, she might gain power over it. Once she had walked into the heart of Eald, Ciaran's hand locked with hers, so that for a time she saw; but that memory too had fled like water through the sieve of her reason, and while she remembered that they had spoken with someone, that someone was lost to her. There had been a horse Ciaran had ridden; but she had not been able. In truth, she could not tell even looking at it whether it was a horse at all, whether something of surpassing beauty or surpassing horror, except that it was power, and it had carried her husband once to war, a thing of light and terror, and sometimes the memory of soft horselike breaths and sometimes the striking of a hoof, not horselike, but like the muttering of thunder in the distance.

She shivered, and gazed into the tiny fire they kept to warm this room in springtime. The memories faded, as faery things would, which was their camouflage in the world; faded from *her,* though once she had seen these things and touched the elvish horse and met Arafel face to face.

Stay away, she cried in her heart, *never come back, never trouble us—* for she knew that all the gifts she had and all her happiness came from that most untrustworthy source.

And faery gifts faded, like faery itself in the minds of its beholders, except for those of elvish blood.

She knew the rumors of her husband, that he was Sidhe and fey. He had never said so, but knew she had heard and did not gainsay. So the rumors were true, and that was indeed his heritage. She knew—knew things that troubled his deepest dreams, where Death pursued him and gained a part of him, only biding for the rest. And whether this had truly happened, somewhere in Eald, or whether it was only a portending dream, she was not sure, in that way that all her memories shifted like quicksand. But it was real enough that a night of storm could send Ciaran into dark despair, when they were private, after he had put aside the cheerfulness he wore for others.

On such nights he scarcely slept, and started awake at cracks of thunder, relieved only when the dawn brought back the day. And then he would smile and laugh as if there had never been a cloud; but she had learned to dread these times, and something in her grew taut and miserable when such nights began.

Away, she mourned. *Away, away.*

But that was not the bargain she had struck; and now and again in a far and shifting fashion like the recollection of a dream she remembered a face she could not hold longer than a breath, and a brightness that held something of green and something of the sun and moon at once. Children might stray after such baubles, after such bright promises. She had no children, did Arafel, none that Branwyn knew; and it was in Branwyn's heart that the elf might feel an envy and desire of children.

They told such tales of the Sidhe, that they could be so cruel, so thoughtlessly cruel.

Had not Arafel been so cruel with her, promising a small girl faery-sights, and luring her into the forest to the loss of her pony and almost of her life?

Come away, a voice still whispered in her dreams. *Let go and see things as they are.*

But it was only memory, a voice without distinction, like the face.

The things she cherished now were warm and solid like Caer Wiell, her husband's arms, her children's laughter. She had traded all of faery promises for these.

Come with me, the voice had said, *and see how the years pass, so soon withered like the violets; but there is no fading where I go. Take my hand, come with me, never hear them calling.*

"Branwyn."

She turned where she sat, startled by her husband's voice, so softly he had come up the stairs; but that was his way, this quiet. He offered his arms to her; she held out her own and he came and knelt down by her, holding her, patting her shoulders, making her look at him.

"Were you crying?" he asked, with the evidence of it on her lashes. "O Branwyn, love, my love, my heart, there's no need for crying now. They're safe, full of bread and honey, no worse than scratches and skinned knees—"

"What was it they found?"

"Something— She called it a silly nix, a thing—Oh, don't speak of it. It's nothing; it's gone, not to trouble us more."

"They will not go back to the river."

"They will not. They understand." He smoothed her hair, held her with great tenderness.

"It comes of this gadding about the fields, this—"

"You cannot grow flowers in the shade: they want the sun and wind, Branwyn."

She shivered, sat back from him, he kneeling and holding her clenched fists in his. For a long moment she fought for self-possession. "They cannot," she said, "grow like weeds. They cannot be deceiving Muirne and running off."

"No, they cannot. But they have the luck on them, they do, and that was on them today, and more than luck. —She will come tonight, Branwyn. *Here.*"

She needed a moment to understand.

"No," she said.

"How can it be no?" He was utterly dismayed. His face was stricken. "Branwyn—"

It was in the open then, his distress, her distrust; and then because she had never fought open war with her enemy: "Forgive me, I am distraught. I only want my house in peace, in peace—"

He gathered up her hand and carried it to his lips. She hardly felt the warmth. "Branwyn. You fear too much."

"What does she want?"

He had no ready answer. Some worry sat within his eyes, confirming her own dread. "Perhaps to warn us. Or to explain. Nothing more than that. Perhaps to be courteous. She is that. The Daoine Sidhe are much on courtesy. Branwyn, she is our friend. She had always been. Look you, what land since the war is blessed like ours, what fields are green as ours—"

"Or children," she said harshly, "so many and so fair? —I waited. I waited fifteen long years with every house in the land more blessed than ours. I held the serving maid's daughters and I ached after daughters of my own—and watched children I had held become brides before I held my own daughter and my son. O, if this was blessing, Ciaran, it was slow to come to us, and forgive me, forgive me if I am too fond—"

"And are they only yours?" he asked.

She had no answer. His look robbed her, so that she shivered.

"They were long years," he said, "but we cannot lay them on Meadhbh's and Ceallach's shoulders and crush the spirit from them. And they were good years, Branwyn."

"They were good years," she admitted, "but o, Ciaran, if we were so blessed—if there was luck on us—why not that simple luck that farmwives had and I did not? So I hold them close. And today—today I feared perhaps—"

"She is our friend. Branwyn, they are safe thanks to her."

She thought about that a time, and her heart grew a little broader, and her memory a little clearer, that once there had come a light into Caer Wiell, and in that light a shape, and a voice. Almost she saw her, a ragged figure in faded clothes, but she could not see the face.

"I would like to make her welcome," Ciaran said.

"For so many debts. For friendship. Branwyn, this hall
was *theirs* once and long ago. Its name was Caer Glas,
and I do not know if there is another place in all the
world like this, where she might be here and still in Eald.
I would be dead; and so might we all—but for Arafel."

There is Donn, the thought leapt into her mind unbidden, *where you were born. That also was theirs once.* But
she brushed that thought aside, as she did every unpleasant thing, keeping her own nest pure for those she loved.
"We will set a table," she said, finding comfort in the
proprieties of things, to tame the wild with bonds of
courtesies, as if this were a charm to assure its civility.
If she could once set it within her hall, she thought, and
once fix it in her mind, if she could believe and once
remember it, then she would feel safer; then she could
get sureties of it, and learn to call its name.

Arafel she was, and *Feochadan*, which was Thistle; and
other names besides. But the sound was not enough. She
had to learn it with the heart, as Ciaran had, and she
meant to do so, for the best of reasons, that Caer Wiell
was her home, and she was born to it, of southron blood
and of the line of kings and of an enemy Arafel had
slain. The stones were hers, her home, the magic that
she knew; and what entered here trod her ground. Here
she might learn a thing, and remember this time, not
letting it fade as it faded for others.

She still had power. It was herself her husband chose,
to age in ordinary years, beside her; it was herself who
held his children; and these were the things she dwelt
on in her mind, that in Caer Wiell she was secure.

"There's my love," her husband said, and rising,
touched his lips to her brow. "You'll see." He turned
wistful and very grave. "At moonrise," he said.

It was long before Beorc rode in, for of all the searchers he had ridden farthest and deepest into the woods,
and because of things he had seen or thought that he
might have seen he would have no easy sleep for nights
to come.

"Safe," he echoed when his lord himself had come
down to the gate to meet him. "Gods be thanked." And
then he turned his face again toward seeing to his horse,
for shame that he went so weak and his eyes stung, per-

haps with sweat, but perhaps not. He drew his bow and quiver from the saddle and slung both over his shoulder before delivering his good bay gelding to the grooms who waited.

"Get him a cup of ale." Ciaran said. "Come to hall when you have had your ease. I want to speak with you."

"Aye," Beorc muttered, turning about again, nodding a courtesy to his departing lord. Others had come down—Domhnull one, his cousin on his mother's side; and Rhys ap Dryw, a lord's son himself, but youngest of seven sons; and others who had been among the searchers. A boy took Beorc's bow and quiver, another his muddy cloak. "Who found them?" he asked concerning the children. "Where found?"

There was strange silence among the men. "The lord himself," one said, but seemed to hold something back.

"Come," said Domhnull, taking his arm. "Come upstairs,"

Beorc followed up the stairs to the wardroom, and there sank down on a bench, working himself free of his buckles, his armor and his sweat-drenched clothes. Domhnull and Rhys stayed with him, and a flurry of pages ran in and out with a succession of basins and towels and the promised stoup of ale.

"Oh, that's good," Beorc murmured, his hair and beard plastered with cooling water and his lips wet with the frothy ale. He drew a quieter breath and looked up at his comrades who leaned nearby, Rhys with one foot on the bench and his arms on his knee, Domhnull braced against the wall, hands tucked in his belt. They were not of a kind, those two—his young cousin's an uncommon fairness, hair brighter than new straw, eyes blue and clear as a babe's; and Rhys must have looked sullen from his cradle, a dark, lean man with a brooding stare: his mountains bred grim folk as they bred kites and hawks. "No harm to them?" Beorc asked again, for something in the answers he had gotten and not gotten nagged at him with the sense of something amiss. "Where were they, asleep under some hedgerow?"

"No one knows," said Rhys.

" 'Her,' my lady said," Domhnull answered. "And, 'Not with her,' my lord answered back."

"How far did you ride?" asked Rhys of Beorc. "Myself, as far as the old wood, and then up the road and back; and I did not like the feel."

"Farther," said Beorc, and frowned for memory of the dark thickets, the haunted silences. "It was not An Beag I feared. Not in this."

"So thought I," Domhnull murmured. "And so I think it was. They simply strayed."

"They are fey," said Rhys. "How should they not be? And I did not like the feel."

"Hist," said Beorc, "say no such thing, ap Dryw. Say no such thing of them."

"No," said Rhys, "but 'tis true—Mark you, Scaga'sson, this is true. And those two will find their way to it, to the Sidhe, being whose get they are—O Man, do not you bridle at me; I am their mother's cousin and their own, and friend, and his, no less than you. Fey father, fey offspring; and I didn't like the feel of it today, not so far as I rode."

"I feared them lost for good," Beorc said hollowly, the cup between his knees. "When the recall sounded, I feared the worst. There was a day I would not have—It was all a childish prank, then."

"Our lord was close about it," said Domhnull frowning. "And I don't think he feared An Beag either. He—"

"Hist!" Rhys straightened suddenly, his hand on his knife, and strode to the stairway. "Up here! You!"

A head appeared down below where a shadow had flitted, round the corner of the landing of the stairs, a balding pate and hangdog look and a general slouching of the whole man round the corner.

"Coille!" Domhnull muttered in disgust. "Who else?"

"Out," Rhys ordered, "—skulk."

Coille held out a pail. "Bringing water up, lord Rhys, only bringing water, they told me to."

"Out!" Beorc shouted at him fit to wake echoes from the stairwell, and Coille fled, sloshing the steps as he went.

"Cursed gossip," Domhnull said.

"Bide here," said Rhys. "I'll put the fear in him."

"Stay," said Beorc. "Stay,"—for the southron was a fell man and wild. "Keep that knife of yours in sheath."

"Did I say I would mark him? Not I."

"No, but make much ado over his hearing and we'll not need Coille to gossip it. There's talk enough flying as it is."

"And will be," Rhys muttered. "Will be. That's the nature of you folk, to bandy everything about in market. You've no instinct for secrets, you valley-dwellers."

"There's nothing will make them love lord Ciaran less," said Domhnull. "Fey he may be, but tell them that in the steadings or gossip it in the barracks and they'll ask you fresher news." He laughed and settled the more easily, one foot on the window ledge. "Myself, I confess to have walked in the woods now and again. Wishful thinking, mine. I'd give a great deal for the sight of one of the fair folk; and if there's harm in that, why, Beorc, your own mother and mine would put out saucers of milk at evening. And you who were in the war—"

"You are too innocent," Beorc said.

"You never will speak of it," Domhnull said, frowning now. He seldom pounced on this, but did so with greatest concentration in this moment. "It's nature to tell tales, isn't it? Like Coille, chattering everything he hears, sparrow-like. It's nature that when wars have been people talk about them, and make songs of them—like the old songs. Even the Aescford has its song, with the King dying, and the Cearbhallain—But no one sings songs now. Those that fought there are getting old, and we that weren't there can't make them, and even the harper won't sing any—because no one who was there will talk."

"The harper was there," Beorc recalled shortly.

"But you won't say. The Sidhe was there. Wasn't it so? Everyone who was out there must have seen—and no one says. I was in the forest today. Across the river. I felt nothing ill."

"Then you are numb and deaf and blind," said Beorc, "cousin."

"Perhaps I am." Domhnull looked at Rhys and sighed after things unseen. "But you see things."

"My grandsire had the Sight," the southron said wryly, "but alas, you valley-dwellers called him mad."

"Do they talk about the war there?" asked Domhnull. "Or are they all like Beorc, gone dumb?"

"No whit more," said Rhys with a sober stare, "and

I was at the keeping of our borders, so I saw nothing. But things of the fair folk fade and take strange shapes, and there is luck on this land. Why question? If we were all Coilles we would have no peace of chatter."

"You make less sense than usual," Domhnull said. "And maybe where the young ones hid has faded, quite, and all of it was moonbeams: So they say the Sidhe rode inside Caer Wiell. Myself, I would only like to see one."

"Well, I have seen," said Beorc in a faint, difficult voice.

"What was it?" asked Domhnull.

"A light," Beorc said. "Like light." He shrugged and remembered his ale and drank it. "But that is why Caer Wiell sits so much to itself, young cousin, that others saw it too. And no one sings songs, because I for one wouldn't know how to make one; and maybe it's not a thing to gossip, because, well, there was nothing to liken it to, like sun, like moon, but not. It was more a feeling, was what it was. A man doesn't forget that. I know I won't. It wasn't the same today. It was darker-like. It wasn't good. —They're all right, are they? Did they seem—afraid?"

"They looked pert enough," said Rhys. "No, by the looks in their faces. There was no fear."

"I think you make too much of it," Domhnull said. "They strayed into the woods, is all; and maybe they did see something, but they hadn't any effect of it. I think you and this Sighted southron make too much of shadows."

"You see," said Beorc, "why no one who was on that field will speak of it? There is too much unbelief nowadays. You set out saucers, aye, your mother does, each and every night. I know. But what I saw would take no such offering, no."

"*What* did you see?" asked Domhnull, not for the first time that he had brought Beorc this close.

Beorc, not for the first time, shook his head and refused to say.

But there began to be a coming and going, late as it was, and Muirne rushing outside the walls by twilight, her arms laden with branches. (My lady will have fresh boughs, she said, making nothing of the fact that no guest was expected, nor had been since lord Dryw had called with his retinue a year and more ago.) And there was a stir in the kitchen, a coming and going of chatty pages who could no more keep secrets than they could walk on errands and not run. (For my lord's table, they said; and for those who searched, a fine good meal—which lifted hearts and expectations all through Caer Wiell, and sets mouths to watering and stomachs to longing, for the smells went out from the kitchen of bread baked fresh, even at evening time, and there was honey called for and good butter, and cakes and no few of the best hams and sausages, and a side of venison that had served my lord's table went into roasts and pastries. And there were casks of ale and cider. Faces went blissful contemplating it.)

But amid all this Beorc took himself upstairs and Domhnull and Rhys with him, for Ciaran's word to them all was the same, that they should come up to speak to him in hall; and if there was little now in their minds but supper, and if they eyed the great table in hall with some longing, thinking of the greater tables set in the yard of the keep, they did not look that way with unseemly attention, but assembled there with great sobriety, well-scrubbed and combed and in their best, before their lord and lady in the hall, with the children abed or at least nowhere to be seen.

But there was nothing but anxiousness on Ciaran's face.

"My friends," he said, "my dear friends—there will be a guest tonight and you must serve in hall. No others would I trust. Would you do me this service?"

"Aye," said Beorc, but he knit his brows in puzzlement, and from anticipation settled his mind at once to business, setting his hands within his belt. It was quite mad, of course, but strange things had happened within these walls. It was not his to ask, though his mind was racing, whether some messenger was expected from the King, to deserve such a plethora of lights and fresh boughs and such a feast as that prepared both below and here above; or whether there was to be any guest at all. This might be some odd figure of speech, or pretense, or something Ciaran had made up for some purpose, perhaps—perhaps, Beorc thought, that he would

have his small household to table together to celebrate
the children's safe return, and ask his trusted men to
serve them in lieu of pages, which would be strange, but
no more reasonable thing could he think.

"*She* will come. The Sidhe," Ciaran said then. "Will
you serve?"

"Aye," Beorc said after a moment's dismay. "My lord
knows I would."

"And you others?"

"Aye," said Rhys, "without question."

"Shall we see one?" Domhnull asked, with all his
heart. His eyes were blue and wide. "Here? Tonight?
In hall?"

"Perhaps," said Ciaran, adding, "If she wills it you
will see her. But if she will not, then not. You must not
tell it—if you do."

"No, lord," Domhnull said, but his desire was in his
eyes, wide as his heart was wide.

"Carry no iron," said Ciaran. "My guest will not
bear that."

"No," said Beorc, "that we understand."

"She is not to fear," lady Branwyn said in a soft thin
voice. "It is not that you should need it, or that we
should not be safe."

"No," said Ciaran, "there is no question of that."

For Beorc's part he was not sure; and Rhys' look was
the usual, which was unreadable; but Domhnull's face
was full of color, his eyes bright with hope, as if there
were no ill thing in all the world, and this from a youth
who had ridden borders since his sixteenth year.

Perhaps Ciaran saw it, for he looked longest at Domhnull, and a faint smile touched his face. "Don't count on
it overmuch. She may not stay. But perhaps she will."

THREE

ARAFEL

She came—not without hesitation, for it was a harder journey than once. The mists had grown thicker between her Eald-that-was and the world of Men. She had delayed at the last, beneath the pale silvery trees, among the elvish treasures which glistened with soft brilliance under the wan, strange sun of her day; she had chosen certain things to take with her, and put on light elvish garments which she had worn for festival—oh, very long ago, when there were songs among the elves. She went tonight in trust, as she would not have gone for any Man but one, and so she came weaponless except for the lightest of daggers; and uncloaked, which was mere thoughtlessness: for they were friends.

So she arrived in the upper hall of Caer Wiell—was *there* upon the instant, striding out of the mists into a place she knew; and blinked at the glare and half-faded away again in alarm.

There were fires before her like a row of perilous flowers. Metal glinted. Her every instinct cried *away*. But there was Ciaran holding out his hand to her; there was Branwyn, less her friend, but not treacherous, who stared at her with wide and anxious eyes. And the fires were candle flames and torches; the metal was the glitter of silver plates and cups and the finery of her hosts. The place smelled of closeness and Men and fire and food and dying flowers and cut boughs. She stayed, dismayed as she was by the flames.

For it was honor they wished to do her, she saw that

now. She was caught between horror and weariness and a great sorrow for them in their best that they put forward to welcome her. She had on the garments of peace for respect of an invitation; and as Men did things, they had turned this grim gray hall into a dripping of fat of slain animals, and burning fire, and slain trees, and dying branches—but silver plates, no iron which would harm her; and a blaze of light and warmth and all the best they had.

"Please," Ciaran said, and offered her first place at the table that was set. "Be welcome."

She stepped all the way within the room, a guest in Caer Wiell, in this small closed hall. She looked about her and at the place that was offered. "You have surprised me," she said truthfully, and looked toward the closed doors of the place. Torches burned all along the wall, candles lit the table, and fire blazed in the hearth. The dying boughs on the table sent up a great fragrance like silent anguish.

"We will serve," said Ciaran softly. "Or I have men I trust as close as brothers and they would do that service. They know about you. They're ready to do as much if I should call, no, more than willing. Anxious. But I wasn't sure you would bear with that."

"I have never guested with Men," Arafel said doubtfully, looking at him and at Branwyn; and then with her love of this Man, a strange mood fell on her, between despair and a remembrance of what had been, of the groves alight, of harping and of dancing.

"Might there be music?" she asked in diffidence; and, wistfully, from her heart's desire: "Might I see the children here too? And then we will talk. There is afterward for talking."

Branwyn's hand crept anxiously to Ciaran's, but Ciaran's eyes shone with pride. "Call them," he said to Branwyn. "Call them down." And himself hastening to the door: "Beorc," he called out. "Come ahead—and call Leannan upstairs, and Ruadhan, and Siodhachan too."

"Muirne," Branwyn called by the other stairs, "Muirne, bring Ceallach and Meadhbh and come down!"

Arafel stood still, feeling a certain dread at this multiplication of names. Once before she had faced the prospect of this hall and so many Men. But now was now, and if the place was strange and crude with glare and death, she schooled herself to trust, stood where they wished her to be and waited, to be amazed by them as they were amazed by her.

The stairs erupted with the patter of feet: Muirne, then, that was the name, a thin, pinched woman of no definite colors; and like sunrise and sunset the boy and girl beside her—who stopped at the bottom step and stared with open mouths—for Arafel had not come as she had appeared to them before, in gray and patchwork, but in silver and elvish jewels.

Then the Men came, and foremost in honor the harper, who came with his harp in his arms and kneeled before her: Leannan was his name—and she recalled another harper of Caer Wiell in looking into his weathered face. So *he* would have aged. The thought appalled her and filled her with sorrow.

"I have seen you once," the harper said, "lady, when you saved Caer Wiell. I remember. I was there. I only wish I could get it clear. I tried to make a song of it . . . but it was never what I wanted."

His voice faded. He only stared, bewildering her, until gently Ciaran took his arm and moved him aside. She looked for those faces she knew. Meredydd and Evald were gone—no part of this gathering. Gone, she realized suddenly, of course gone, as Men went: Lord Death culled more than trees, and gently—she had never felt their passing. The faces about her were all different from what she had expected. On most of them she saw the marks of age.

"Beorc," Ciaran named a tall, red-haired Man, himself graying. "Scaga's son. And Domhnull his cousin. My right hand and my left, and I value them as much. Rhys ap Dryw. Ruadhan. Siodhachan." This last was an old, old Man, the oldest of them all.

"I rode," the aged Man said, his lips trembling with the effort of speech, "after my lord Ciaran on the field that day. When you came—" His voice wobbled away to silence and tears, something very like elvish warmth, so that she was touched in spite of herself. "Yes," she said full gently, not knowing this Man and wondering what face he had once worn. She grew desperate in these changes, among these Men. She looked toward the children who stood both in Branwyn's embrace, read there other change happening with fatal swiftness.

"Will you sit?" Ciaran asked of her, reminding her, and she sank carefully into the chair that was prepared for her, before silver plates, before the perilous fires.

"May we sit at table?" Ceallach asked anxiously, and receiving his father's nod, his face lighted and he hugged his sister and his mother, while there was some stir about, of benches brought, and extra plates, and places made, all with a clatter and a rising relief.

A few tentative harp notes sounded, sweet and pure, bringing silence and a settling quickly into places, silence even from the children. So the harper played, and played well for her, light songs and merry. And then was the meal. Muirne took the serving mostly on herself, being most careful of their guest, brought Arafel wine and pressed honeyed cakes and fruits on her when she refused other food.

Arafel was doubtful, but if there was something of Men about the offering, still it was sweet in her mouth, and the wine was good if smoky and strange to her tongue. Everyone ate, in a silence so deep the noise of a cup seemed loud, and Muirne's mouselike steps seemed like echoing footfalls. Even the children were grave and very silent, but their eyes drank in everything.

"We are not wont to be so quiet," Ciaran said desperately.

"May we talk then?" Ceallach cried in his high clear voice, which caught Arafel most by surprise. She laughed, which laughter found its echo first in Meadhbh and then in Domhnull.

"Yes," Ciaran said, "we may talk."

"Perhaps," said Arafel, "the harper will give us songs to make us light."

This pleased the harper, who took up his harp again, and soon had the children clapping their hands and all but bouncing in their seats; at last even the grimmest of them laughed, red-haired Beorc. The song minded old Siodhachan of a tale, which he told well and deftly, and there was more wine, at which Arafel, feeling strange diffidence among such brevity, told a small elvish tale, dismayed when it gained only silent stares. Then: "Oh!" breathed Muirne, and everyone breathed, and she saw that they were pleased and more than pleased, their eyes shining, the harper wiping tears.

"Tell another," said Meadhbh.

It had been a moment of peace, a precious time. The young voice tempted. But, "No," Arafel said softly, for she suddenly felt the hours, saw the candles low in their sconces, heard the fall of a log in the fireplace, saw one of torches out, its flame-bearing head having showered its last cinders to the stones a while ago like stars. "No, now we must to your own affairs. Perhaps you will tell me—" She addressed herself to Ciaran "—how you have fared since last I came."

"Oh, well," said Ciaran. "The land never fails us. And my horses—my horses are surpassing fine."

"And peace. Have you that?"

There was a shifting among the Men. "The King has ordered peace," said Ciaran. "And I keep it as I can."

"Ah," she said.

"Perhaps," said Ciaran, "the children should be abed."

"No," said Arafel; and Meadhbh and Ceallach, whose faces had fallen at once, bounced in their seats and their faces glowed. "Bear with me," said Arafel to Branwyn, and wandered in her gaze to aged Siodhachan, to Muirne who had stopped in her serving. Wisps of hair had fallen about Muirne's thin face and her cheeks were flushed from her many trips this way and that with plates and servings. She had never gotten to eat. Now she had a pitcher of wine in hand and quite forgot it, heavy as it was. And Ruadhan, who was supposed to watch the door, but whom Arafel had called to table too, a Man who smiled much and forgot to smile now; and Domhnull, a handsome fair-eyed Man less than the others' years; and dark Rhys, of wise glances and quiet; and Beorc Scaga's-son, a Man much like his father. "Siodhachan's years are longest backward," Arafel said, "and have their honor; and the years of Meadhbh and Ceallach are longest forward, and extend this company into times and places no one but I may see. So I speak to them as well as to the rest. So counsel taken should be in their hearing, because I cannot say when I will come back again."

Faces grew anxious all about the table, Ciaran's most of all excepting the children's, but no one spoke.

"In all the years of Caer Wiell," she said further, "the guesting has been of Men in Eald and not the Sidhe among Men. But you wake old memories tonight. You remind me of times I had almost forgotten. The blessing of the Sidhe is on you: Your step will lie light upon the leaves, your way will not easily wander in the wood, your eyes will see truth when others fail, and this for all your days. Eald will not fade for you. What you see you will see truly. This gift I give. And one more I give to Meadhbh and Ceallach—Come," she said when the children hesitated to leave their places, and they excused themselves and came to her seat at the head of the table, staring at her with eyes as wide as fawns'.

"So," she said, and opened her hand, laying what might have been a mote of light upon the table, but the light faded and there were two leaves more silver than green. "For memory," she said, "for memory that Eald is true. They come of the youngest of my trees. Keep them near you and they will never fade. You have never seen the trees as they are: I cannot bring you there. I wish I might. But they are for hope when there is no hope, and vision when there is no seeing. I have set a virtue on them of finding. And for children lately lost, this seems a right gift."

They were confused and their eyes were wider still as they took each a leaf.

"Mother," said Meadhbh, showing hers. And, "Lady," Ceallach said in a hushed voice, and looked down at his, and took it to his father to show.

"I have seen such trees," said Ciaran softly. Ceallach sat at his father's side and Ciaran put an arm about him, holding this dearest treasure time had given him very close as Branwyn held Meadhbh. Their friends and trusted folk were about them in this room, like a bulwark against the night, against shadows, against all the ills of the world. But knowledge sat in Ciaran's eyes, as if they saw the shadows beyond the walls. "You speak of going," he said. "And you have been about some business. Is it—something I might ask?"

"Do not." She passed her finger down the side of the cup before her, and looked up as Muirne, sensing want, moved to fill it. The gesture touched her strangely, the earnestness of brown human eyes which saw only need and offered what there was, if only wine. She bent a thought on Muirne, shed a grace which had not been there as the pitcher brushed the cup she held in her hand, and thought no more of it than the flowering of some blighted tree under hand . . . indeed her thoughts traveled on and circled and came back again to the children—to Beorc, whose eyes met hers squarely as few Men's would. He was afraid: this she saw. And loyal and terrible in a way that stretched into a dark future. A shiver came over her, and she was not accustomed to such weaknesses. She looked past him to Domhnull, whose heart was clearest; and Rhys, who had a darkness in him, but so, indeed, had elves; last to Ciaran, finding strange still the sight of this bearded, older man with a son against his side.

"I will be direct," she said. "There is trouble near you. I cannot say the nature of it: plainly, I do not know. I warned you once of balances, and things are out of balance. Meadhbh and Ceallach have chanced against the merest straying visitor to your lands; do it no harm. It does not deserve it. And there are things truly baneful. This is not your affair. But a corner of Eald has gone into shadow, and Eald is both wider and darker than it was. There are things awake that slept. I have a watch to keep and I have kept it—aye, do you understand now, Lord-of-Men? So I have watched and will watch. You are my weakness and my strength, you, Caer Wiell, this little circle of firelight in the dusk. And that dusk is gathering. The night will come. Grant there may be a dawn."

A log crashed in the fireplace. The children flinched, and Branwyn cried out. The fire leaped up and shadows danced and died. The company shifted uncomfortably in their chairs.

"War?" asked Beorc in a horse, harsh voice. "Is it war you mean? Is it An Beag?"

"War," She laid a hand on the stone at her heart and for a moment it was hard to remain where she was. The place seemed insubstantial, a web of gray against truth. And then it took shape again. "I have asked you once. Do you have peace?"

"With An Beag and Caer Damh?" Ciaran replied. "An uneasy peace, but the King rules."

She stretched out her hand toward the west, a vague reaching. "There is no brightness there."

"The King rules," Ciaran said. "He is lord in Dun na h-Eoin."

"And Caer Donn?"

"Is free."

"There is no brightness, I say, toward the west. Look to your borders."

"In Caer Donn my brother rules."

"I say what I have said. War is too simple a word."

"The King," said Branwyn suddenly, "ignores Caer Wiell. We are not favored. We are true to him, and few are, even of those who fought for him at our walls. And as for Caer Donn—"

"He is my brother," said Ciaran.

For a moment the shadow intruded, and Arafel shivered, blinking in the firelight. Again she touched the stone, and waked a harping these halls had known years ago. There was vengeance in it even yet. The Harp was broken, but the song went on. She stood up, and the company rose in confusion as Ciaran stood—as he held out a hand to her, wishing her to stay. She fought the drawing, the feeling of cold. There was a darker and darker melancholy on her and she fought it as she fought all the weapons of the shadow.

"Walk with me," she said to Ciaran, "as far as the hall outside."

He offered her his hand—confused, perhaps, for places were nothing to her, and had never been. But the shadow-ways were dangerous and she took the human way, passed the wooden door in Ciaran's company, alone.

"Close the door," she said when they had come into the hall before the stairs. "What I say now is only for you to hear. But what you say to them after, that is your choosing."

He did so, the lord of Caer Wiell, and faced her again. A solitary and dying torch burned and cast shadows everywhere about, made the lines of his face deeper than they were. He looked old and worn, so fearfully worn.

"What will you?" he asked.

"You have understood more than they. You know what is loosed. And I tell you that there is shadow on Airgiod's lower reaches; and over all the hills. Trees have come back out of it, but strange and dim and not comfortable. Not comfortable. Speak truth with me: speak your heart with me—have you felt no hint of trouble? Can you come and go in this land at your ease?"

"You know that I cannot."

"I know little enough of Men. Tell me truth—why can you not?"

"They remember me. They remember what I am. If I have luck they say it is faery-gift; if I have none they call it curse. Mostly they suspect—"

"—What?"

"Ambition. That, I think. Or power." He shivered and turned half away, and looked back again with the firelight moving on his bearded face. "How can they forget? How can the King sit at board with me and forget? And my brother—"

"Fears his neighbor?"

"Fears his own heritage. We pass no messages. There is only silence. Fear—aye. And distrust. I have had too great good fortune in Caer Wiell." He drew a breath and composed his face, shook his head, but the gnawing dread remained. "No, he would never do us harm. Donnchadh is a good man."

"But not wise."

"Is that so ill?"

"For one who sits at Caer Donn? Whose hold is named in Eald? Yes, it is ill, it is very ill. And a great many ills are abroad. I watch; I do not say I shall be enough. So I have come here. To ask your help."

"No." He shook his head. "Now I know what you mean to ask, and *no*."

"Keep it for me. Only keep it. And should the worst happen, should you know that there is no more defense—then you will judge what you should do. You are the only brightness, do you understand—the only. The small trouble in the Caerbourne—that is nothing, nothing against the other. Take it. I do not ask that you use it. Only that you have the choice. For your defense, for the defense of this place."

He said nothing for a moment, and she drew it from its keeping-place against her heart, the stone he had borne before, like that stone she still wore about her neck. It shone with a strange pallor beneath the torches, casting no shadows with its brightness, reflecting nothing of the fire. It rested so in her hand and at last he put out his and took it, clenched his fist about it, and the hall seemed dark after.

"Do not walk in Eald," she said. "You must not come there. Call me if you have need, but never command; as you value your peace, do not command. Be wise, be wary."

"Arafel!— Shall I see you again—in my life—shall I see you?"

She had started to fade, to drift back to Eald. She stayed, and touched his broad scarred hand. "I have no surety," she said, but it was in her heart that this was indeed the last time. "There are hazards. Who can say? Fare well, cousin, half-elf, friend. In all things—"

The touch faded. Eald closed about her. For a moment she strove with it, reached out over all the hold, so that she seemed to embrace it, so that the strength that greened the trees was shed wide.

Scrub that had struggled in the cracks of the walls burst into sudden flower under a clouding sky.

A sickly child mended and sighed into restful sleep, smiling as she did.

The drowsing sentry clutched his spear, confused in a premature and fading dawn, or the belief that he had seen one.

Folk waked, and some wept, convinced of some wonderful dream they could not remember, or of some luck which had come on them, or simply that they were glad, and some sank deeper in sleep, feeling the world at ease.

One twisted thing resisted, and hid on the stairs where he had crept to listen; and the name of this one was Coille.

I must warn him, she thought, but fate was on her, and the thought with the power faded, like the moment's dawn at Caer Wiell. Eald took her back, a mesh woven of branch and limb, of the dark before the dawn in which even stars had less power. A tear had fallen on her cheek, and traced there a thin cold line.

*   *   *

"You take risks," a shadow whispered.

She turned her head in startled anger, dashed the tear from her cheek and stood straight, facing the darkness in the mist. "Godling, you have no leave to be here. *Keep from them.* I have warned you."

"You take risks, I say." The shadow became utterly black, a hole in the mist. A horse stamped in the fog. "I have fared along the edges. You have set something stirring. You set me to hunt the marches—but you will summon me here. No! name me no threats. I know them all. You have raised them all. But threats will not send *them* back. And it grows."

She shrugged and turned away. "You tell me nothing new. Try again."

Steps trod beside her in the grayness, a soft and bodiless pacing. "There is a place called Caer Donn. You would know it."

She turned again, disturbed and caring not that he saw it, her Huntsman, her Warden of the marches. "What of Caer Donn?"

"That its lord is close to the King. I have heard their counsels at Dun na h-Eoin. You should regard me. I come and go with kings. And beware Caer Donn, I say. Its history blinds you. You delude yourself. You take risks, I say, risks in which your allies have no profit and no patience."

"My allies." She drew herself up and set her hand on the small hilt at her belt. "You and your brothers have no interest in my defeat, that is the only sure thing. Let us say the truth. *What* have you heard at Dun na h-Eoin?"

"The counsels of kings. I have seen the lords of An Beag and Caer Damh sit with the King; I have seen Caer Donn and Caer Luel in the same company . . . and the veriest center of it is Caer Donn. Did you not know?"

"Perhaps I knew."

For a moment the shadow was silent. Something dark and houndlike crept to his side and merged with him. "You are cruel."

"So they say of the Sidhe."

"This Man, this Ciaran mac Ciaran—this brother of Donnchadh of Donn—"

"—is my affair."

"You have tangled me in bargains. Your Man has loosed this on the world. It was his doing, from the beginning, and always you have protected him. Take Donnchadh to your heart: he is no less perilous."

"Donnchadh is beyond my reach."

"Yes. Beyond your reach. But not beyond the reach of other things. You are a fool, my lady of the trees. You are everlastingly a fool, and not alone, no longer alone. You have your enemies. And those seduced by them."

"Leave me."

"Oh my lady fool—were your own kind immune to jealousy? To ambition?"

She strode away. He followed, a flutter of darkness slipping through the mist.

"The King is weak and weakening; they poison him now with more than words. But I delay to take him. There will come the day I must. And what then—*who* then, but Donnchadh? Slay him, my lady: one thrust of an elvish sword—and the world is saved."

"No. Not saved. Leave me. I am weary of you."

"Of me, your messenger. Of the upstart you send to watch your borders—Oh lady fool, well if you had listened long before this. What a merry visitor has come to the Caerbourne! And I can name you others lurking here and there. Stop and listen! This Man of yours—let me have him. You cannot take Donnchadh; your reach is too short. But *I* could remedy matters. For fear of this Ciaran the King has taken evil counsel—For fear of what he saw on that field that day, of help you gave this Man of yours. Do you not know? There is no one in all the kingdom the King fears so much as Ciaran of Caer Wiell—no, certainly not those he ought to fear instead."

Lord Death had pricked her interest, however painfully. Again she stayed, and stopped in mortal Eald: "You know something you have to tell: you choke on it— Say it and be done!"

"I know this, while you have been interested in other things: that the King distrusted the old lord of Caer Wiell because of this Man, and others stepped in to widen the gap until there is no closing it. And worse with

Donnchadh of Donn—ah, much worse. He has stirred up something. I know not what. You say you cannot touch him. But something of Eald has risen up there. It hovers about Caer Donn, skulking and vanishing and I can put no hand on it. Would that I could."

For a long moment she was silent, and the stone burned cold at her heart. "Would you had told me this at the beginning. This is no glad news."

"Come here. If Eald is there, there you can set foot. Deal with it. Let me have this troublesome lord of Caer Wiell. We may yet turn all this aside."

"No," she said, holding the stone within her hand. "*No*. I've no doubt your brothers urged it. But I take no counsel from you, Huntsman. None."

"Is it fear, then?" Death whispered. "Oh, you pretend to be wise—you pretend secrets. But say it: you are afraid—and you keep your life unchanged. For what? For what do you live? To watch, you said, to prevent what you yourself caused, and now you retreat and save yourself and your trees and this one favored Man—for how long, and to whose benefit but your own?"

"Spare me your venom. Tell your brothers this: that they will have felt a change in Eald and now you have told me why. Find me its name, Huntsman; find me its nature and its shape. And believe this—that my woods are wider than they were, in every direction, and I have not spent this time dreaming, no. Would that I had. Would that there were rest for me, or that I could find this thing. And keep your hand from Caer Wiell!"

"Elvish treachery!" Lord Death wailed, and caught at her sleeve, but she was gone, faded into otherwhere. "Hear me!" he called. "Arafel!"

But he had no power to use that name. He had no power over anything of the Sidhe, and in his anger he winded his horn and gathered the Hunt.

Wolves were prowling the hills again, they said in Caer Wiell; and a storm was moving in over the forest heights, sweeping in an uncommon direction for storms, toward the east.

But some in Caer Wiell guessed.

Arafel clasped her stone in both her hands and shut her eyes and drew on herself to find the way. It had grown that hard. When she came to the grove of silver trees, she drew an easier breath—but there were clouds across the elvish sun, and she fought them back again, until they stood over the farthest reaches of Airgiod, in shadow which constantly changed and shifted.

"Fionnghuala!" She clapped her hands, and the horse came, shaking lightning from its mane. Arafel swung up and told it where she would go—and Fionnghuala shivered.

But the elf horse moved, if slowly. Aodhan was left behind, and whinnied after them, a forlorn sound and lonely in the shadow that began to be.

FOUR

THE HEART OF CIARAN CUILEAN

Branwyn came for him, cracking the door carefully and spilling the bright light of the hall into the stairwell where he sat on the steps, arms on knees, head bowed, hands clasped about his ankles as a child might sit.

"My lord," she said tentatively. "Ciaran, my love."

Her voice was so gentle and strange he shivered at it, called back from the place where he had wandered, lost in mist. Branwyn's voice also seemed charged with power, of a different kind, and he must answer it, must come back when she knelt and called his name with such anxiousness. He had worried her and he must not. He felt her hands warm on his, lifting his hands to her lips. Her eyes bore into his, with the shadow falling across half her face, his shadow from the torch behind him. It was his own hall, the steps, the flickering light, and that blinding seam was the hall aspill with lamplight and the smells of banquetry and the plaintive voices of his children—("Has father gone somewhere? Is he all right? —Let me go, Beorc!" "Hush," someone said. "Be still, young sir.")

"Ciaran," Branwyn said, and gazed at him, at that place which hurt him so, there, just at his throat. She reached out and touched it, gathered the naked stone into her fingers, and he flinched at that, jolted by all the dread, all the love, all the horror at once. He might have cried out or she did; and then he was in her arms and his were locked about her as if he were drowning. There was a sound of footsteps, a cry from the hall, and light drowned them both as the door was flung wide, a looming darkness and gathering of shadows.

"Lord," said Beorc's deep voice, "my lady—" A higher voice a smaller shadow thrust forward. "Wait," Beorc said, but their children came to them, and Ciaran reached out one hand to Ceallach's, to Meadhbh, and felt their love like a draught of water where Branwyn's was wine, hers rich and theirs pure; felt the texture of their souls, which was too close even for father to know children, like gossamer, like wind with lilacs blooming.

"Ciaran," Branwyn whispered. Thunder broke; but that was outside, above their walls. Almost he fainted, and felt her arms struggle to bear him a moment. Then he slipped his fingers between her hand and the stone he wore and thrust it safe within his collar, so that the room came clear again, so that he could make a pretense of command and look her in the eyes clearly enough, and look at Meadhbh and Ceallach. There seemed a light about them; but it was the light from the door. He drew a deep breath and gathered himself up to his feet leaning on Branwyn for an instant.

"I am well," he said. He looked beyond at the others who had gathered there. "I dreamed a moment. So Branwyn found me." He looked down at the children, set his arm about them, walked with them back to the hall, into the brighter light and the cloying smell of branches and the leavings of the feast. More faces waited for him—Leannan the harper, Siodhachan, Muirne, Ruadhan, faithful and concerned. He looked about at them. He reckoned that some small time had passed—that he had frightened them badly, not least of all his children, who were uncommonly still and clinging. And Branwyn—Branwyn— He felt her presence at his back, like something bleeding.

"Our guest has gone," he said. "She wished us well and spoke to me awhile, of such things—of such things that mean good will to us. Never fear otherwise from her. I sat a time to think on them. Only go to your beds. And keep the counsel of this room—even the youngest of us." He looked at the children, one and the other, into their eyes. "That means silence."

"Yes, sir," Ceallach said ever so softly. And, "Yes," said Meadhbh half whispering.

"Go with Muirne."

There was never a word further from them. They embraced him, one and the other, and he bent to their embrace, feeling their arms so very frail against his own, and their warmth so much greater than his own it might have been that of the living embracing the dead, but they never flinched. Muirne took them in charge and led them upstairs in silence.

"Go," he said to the others, but while Leannan gathered up his harp and Domhnull and Rhys their cloaks to obey him, Beorc stood still and staring.

"Go," Ciaran said again.

"My lady?" Beorc asked, prepared to defy him if Branwyn should judge otherwise; he saw as much. There was love in such disloyalty, and devotion. Rhys and then Domhnull came and paused at Beorc's side, seeing what was toward, and the others stopped in their departures.

"Go," said Branwyn softly. "Only—Beorc, will you sleep below, by the door tonight?"

"Aye," said Beorc.

"There is no need," Ciaran said, but he saw that Beorc did not intend to regard him, not this strange night. They made themselves his warders, his wife and his own chiefest man. He felt it like his children's embrace, powerless but warm. Beorc went, last to leave; and perhaps Beorc would not be the only one to watch. Domhnull too, he thought, and Rhys. They might take turns. Branwyn had many allies.

The door closed. Their steps retreated down the distance of the stairs. He stood still, not alone, for Branwyn remained.

"Have you subverted them all?" he asked in gentle whimsy, and kissed her on the brow. "Go to bed, you too, only go and rest."

"Come with me."

"I am too uneasy." A chill passed over him like the wind from an open door. Outside the thunder muttered and rain sluiced off the roof. "An uncomfortable bedfellow. Will you sit by me, by the fire?"

She would. He drew the wide bench from the table and the ruin of the feast, set it before the sinking fire and made room for her by him, his arm about her. For a long time she asked nothing, but he knew everything that she would ask, and all that she would blame him for—for she knew that stone as no one in all Caer Wiell could know it. Dreams urged at him, and he fought the dreams—must fight them, with Branwyn so near. The mist threatened to take him, and he measured his strength against it, finding it for the present sufficient to fend the mist away.

"What she said," he began at last, in that silence Branwyn left for him, "was not all of comfort, Branwyn. But this—this *gift*—if I had had it today, do you see, Meadhbh and Ceallach would never have come so near to harm; and no harm could ever come close to Caer Wiell but that I would know it—I must keep it. I have to bear this thing awhile." He could not bring himself to tell her all that he suspected and all that he doubted, that there was an end to his luck and to that of Caer Wiell, indeed, an end of many things. "I need not use it, I think, only keep it safe, I shall be wiser than to use it. But she may not come back again. And yet if she will help us, then this may be the way—a means to keep us safe."

"There is no safety in that thing!" Branwyn cried, and as if she had only waited the dropping of a shield she leaned on his arms and looked closely into his eyes. "Or let me carry it for you."

He was coward, he thought, for one brief moment hearing only the words that would free him and only then realizing that it was Branwyn, fragile Branwyn, who heard the forest singing in storms and had nightmares of being lost. "Love, no," he said.

"You would keep me from such safety?" she asked, deadly in her reason and defter than he with his mind all muddled. "What, will not share it?"

He stared at her helplessly, undone in all his arguments.

"Then it is not safety," she said.

"If my King had called," he said, "and told me to take the sword, then I would have gone and would you have held me? No."

"If the King had called," Branwyn said, "I would know it was a cozening lie."

Her treason shocked him. He had given her children and slept by her for twenty-two years. He had never heard such words from Branwyn so directly. They confused him now, coming as they did at the flank of his defenses.

"I was not speaking of the King," he said.

"Of her, then."

"And if she called," he pursued his reason, doggedly, distractedly, with the stone burning cold at his heart, "then also I would have no choice. There is war of a sort, Branwyn, and I am useless in it, except to hold to this. There is war." He saw banners and dragons in the fire, embers like falling walls, the silver sleet of arrows under the elvish sun. . . .

Liosliath!

His shiver surprised him. He felt her fingers at his neck, felt her loose the chain and lift it from him, and shivered a second time, rescuing the smooth teardrop stone from her fingers as it passed his head. He clenched it so, her fingers still caught in his, entangled in the chain.

"As a guest she was discourteous," Branwyn said in a short, small voice. "She gave our children gifts, and gave to you, and none for me—no gift for me at all."

He saw past the words, straight to the heart of the matter, to the fear in Branwyn's eyes. Perhaps it was the stone, in both their hands. But he saw, and Saw, and that Sight went on plaguing him, that he knew the difference between his blood and Branwyn's; and that Meadhbh and Ceallach were his own, for Arafel had given them gifts and, in truth, brought none for Branwyn. There was nothing Arafel could have given to Branwyn. And Branwyn knew; and he did, with all his insight.

The last log fell, scattering sparks, and something crashed down in his heart then too, a lurching fall like that fall at the edge of sleep, like the chute in dreams, and the dream was the life they had had, their peace, their faith in age and death and passing beyond death together.

He would not age or die at all, not while he held the stone. And Branwyn knew that. Fade, he might, but never die. This was what Arafel had given back to him, a power he had carried once and returned to Eald because he had seen where it would lead him. He might have entered Eald, once for all, but Branwyn never could.

Already he felt the chill of it, which would leave him only elvish love, distant and cold; and make the human world seem crass and garish; which would show him horror and beauty and divide them forever.

"Branwyn," he said, like a talisman. "Branwyn, Branwyn." Names spoken three times had power. He longed for her love, her warmth to hold him. He did not want the dreams. "Be with me, Branwyn."

She took him in her arms. He let his head sink against her shoulder, his hand with the rescued stone fallen into his lap, a great tall man, for all the sons and daughters of Caer Donn were tall, as Branwyn's folk were not. A daughter of Men held one of elvish kind, a man the King himself feared, whose sword the Boglach and the Bradheath knew to their regret; and rocked him like a child.

So he slept a time, but only a little while, and woke and held her in his turn, her small fair head against his heart.

The fire died, and the candles guttered, until only the embers winked in the dark hearth, and the stone was peaceful for the hour.

He looked out over all the land in his vision, a swift unrolling of distances, and if he looked in one way it was mist and shadow; and if in another, only an ordinary dawn with the rain diminished to drizzle, dripping off the leaves. So the stone gave him power to do. There seemed less threatening than had seemed a few hours ago. He was conscious of Arafel, but dimly. Her days flowed differently than his, and this long night had been a moment to her, an indistinction of intent and motion and the feeling of the land, which fretted in its unease.

Liosliath, he wondered, trying to cross a gulf he had crossed once, but the stone was still now. He suspected that Arafel had willed it so, had set a kind of peace on it in giving it to him. That this gift was betrayal, he could not believe of her. She had no need for subterfuge with him: the debt was too deep and too absolute on his side. In this his trust was unquestioning.

Liosliath. But there was a sudden grayness between himself and the presence the stone had once held, as if all of Eald were cloaked in mist and the sea were cut off from him.

He slept again, with the chain tangled in his fingers, and his dreams were gray and dim.

But a darkness sat amid the mist, a piece of night perched on the stump of a dead tree by a sluggish river, for Lord Death rested from his Hunt. His horse and hounds were nearby, a restlessness beyond the leaves.

"You need not be afraid," said Lord Death. "You have the stone, after all."

Ciaran was afraid, all the same. It was not their first meeting, not the first in which he had faced that shapeless dark inside the cowl and wished not to be facing it, for fear that he would see what was inside it. "She asked me to carry it," Ciaran said. "Do you know why?"

"I am not privy to her counsels. She shares them only with Men, it seems. But then—" The shadow moved in a semblance of a gesture. "Then you might invite me to your hall."

"Someday," he said, feeling the cold of a wind that blew from that third and dreadful Eald. "But not yet. I wish to ask you—what I ought to do. Surely you have some advice, my lord."

"Ah, not your lord. But I am lord of those you love."

"Have mercy. Were we not allies—and are we not allies still? You've hated me for cheating you once. But let me beg you. I know nothing else to do now, and I am not too proud, if it will make a difference. These of mine, my family, my friends—I need them. Everything I am asked I will do. But stay away from Caer Wiell."

There was a long silence. "You suspect me of kindness."

"Perhaps. Sometimes."

"Give me your hand. Do you dare that?"

The darkness extended the likeness of a hand to him. All his instinct rebelled, but he reached out deliberately, ignoring the cold, and felt the touch of fingers so dark the shape of them seemed cut out of the world, and the touch of them numbed, but not utterly. They brushed his forearm as if there were no cloth between, and a pain leaped through his body at that touching of an old wound half-healed. The hounds of the Hunt had made it years ago. He had left a part of himself in their jaws and they had devoured it, he suspected. This much of him Death already owned.

The touch passed on, and the robes enfolded him. Very tenderly Lord Death embraced him, and as if it were his brother or his King he returned the embrace, his arms about a body less body than burning cold. Perhaps Lord Death meant to mock him; but there had touched him such peace, and peace parted from him as Death drew back from him, leaving him chilled and prey again to the wind.

"You are bold," said Death, and the voice seemed gently wistful. "Few would dare that, even the most eager. It's your pride, is it not? If I asked that too, would you give your pride, to ransom Caer Wiell?"

Ciaran sank to his knees, one and then the other, out of practice, having been ten years a kingless lord. He felt a flush of shame, and lifted his face. "That too," he said.

But Death was gone, leaving only a swirling in the mist.

"Lord," he called after him, rising to his feet. He suspected Death of laughter at his expense; of cruelty passing his expectations. "Lord Death!"

But a third time he dared not call, and he waked in Branwyn's arms, in the dark of his own room.

The children crept down in the morning, late, but not that they looked to have slept well, only desperately, exhausted. They came hurrying silently down into the hall with Muirne behind them, Meadhbh's bright hair flying loose and both their faces ruddy cheeked from a violent scrubbing, but pale all the same, large-eyed and anxious and very unlike his children, so unlike it chilled him.

So Branwyn left her breakfast and hugged them and wanted to do Meadhbh's hair herself, but they tore themselves from her and came to Ciaran's arms, touching him only carefully, as if he could be bruised by their small hands. *Laugh,* he wished them. *Oh, smile at me and never look that way.* But they did not. In a single day they had learned to fear and to doubt and to know their father and their mother were not omnipotent to save them; more, they suspected helplessness. It was in their eyes, the touch of their hands.

But he gathered Meadhbh's small hands in his large ones and kissed them, and smiled at her, trying to restore her courage, if not her innocence. He set his hands on Ceallach's shoulder, feeling how slight the bones were, how frail his shoulders were for any weight.

"What," he said, lancing straight to the center of their fears, "did you think I would vanish with the moon? There is nothing real about what happened; and there is—It was all very real. Do you understand? There are Men and there is Eald and they are most real when they are farthest apart, but when dreams come into hall and sit at table and leave a gift in your hand, it confuses things. Your mother understands. Perhaps Beorc does, though maybe not. —Do you, Muirne? No. Not truly. One should wake from dreams. But this one left substance. Do you both have your gifts?"

"Upstairs," said Ceallach. But Meadhbh, having pockets, brought hers forth, unfolding her hand carefully as if she had trapped some moth. The leaf shone silver and incorrupt on her palm, which trembled.

"So," he said, "you must always do as she said and keep it by you."

"It feels strange."

"So does mine, you see." He brought the stone into view and prevented her hand with his own cupped over it, a slow and desperate move which left his heart pounding for dread, though he smiled gently at his daughter. "But one should not let another touch such things. Only keep it safe and secret. Did you dream last night?"

"There was a forest," said Ceallach after a moment.

"Was it a good place?"

"Mine seemed to be," said Meadhbh.

"So." He kissed her on the brow and folded her hand upon the leaf. An unpleasant thought came to him and he looked into her eyes. "But when you wander in your dreams, never let it go, this gift. Never let it go. Names called three times will bring a thing. Be careful what you call, that you can send it away again. Do you hear me? Do you understand? You must be able to send it away."

Their eyes were not so perplexed as he would have wished they were. They reached back into something they knew and agreed with him, silent understandings.

"My name you can always use," he said. "And I will come. I will be there. I promise it. Go have your breakfast. You can sit at table with us this morning, will you like that?"

They would. Their eyes were lighter. In a moment they looked like children, squirming into their seats. Ciaran looked past them to Branwyn, appealing for absolution, for all that had divided them; but she was seeing, mother-fashion, to Meadhbh's hair, to Ceallach's collar, and giving orders to Muirne, where they should be allowed to go this day and how Muirne should watch them.

"Mother," Ceallach said, downcast and shamed.

"Well, what would you?" Ciaran said. "I think you went far enough and saw enough for two young folk in a day. Let us have some little rest, your mother is due that, is she not? Is she not? And the next time I ride the west road you can come part of the way. Rhys will ride escort for you."

"When?" asked Meadhbh, twisting in her seat, her eyes childish again.

"Oh, in a day or so. If I find you have kept your mother happy."

"Meadhbh is my daughter," Branwyn muttered, "not your son, to be out with armored men."

It wounded. Meadhbh's face went blank and hurt at once. I was that sort of wound only friends and kin could deal, so strong he felt it in the stone. But Branwyn never saw, or if she knew, wrapped her commonsense about her like a cloak, and poured cider to give to them, golden liquid spilling down into silver cups, smelling of apples and age. She was quite intent upon it. Of such tiny details was the hurt elaborated.

"I have promised," Ciaran said with finality.

Branwyn shrugged, hurting him as well, but this much he allowed. They deserved their wounds, he, his children, being what they were. He dealt none in return, except by being what he was. Neither did Meadhbh, being dutiful. In that moment he saw he had become their father in a protective way, for they had come out of him and only sojourned in Branwyn. He recalled Caer Donn, his own folk, his brother, parted from him— Donnchadh; and his father, dying without his being there, because of his exile. Only Caer Wiell would take such a man as himself to its heart, being itself close to Eald and accustomed to it over long centuries; only Caer Wiell could smile over such children as these two and give them stones to climb and walls to shelter them. He could not send his daughter off to marry, to be what she was in some strange hold, to wither or to smother what she was . . . if there were any one who would court her, the daughter of Ciaran Cuilean. Nor would any lord or king ever trust his son in alliance. The orderly, ordinary hopes collapsed about him, had never stood secure. He reached across the table and laid his hand near Meadhbh's.

Branwyn pretended ignorance of this, of all her injuries. But he loved her and knew that he was loved. When she was harmed, she struck and thought that she was right. When the world threatened to harm one of them, there was iron in Branwyn. He knew this and even Branwyn did not, who seemed to lean on him; but it was the other way around. It was so now, or the gulf would have taken him. She had been there, in the dark, when no one else knew how.

"Eat your breakfast," Branwyn said.

Beorc was looking askance at him when he went out along the wall into the daylight, on that narrow walk; but Ciaran was content to walk, to feel the sun's warmth on his back, to hear the sounds of voices in the yard, the laughter of children playing tag among the supports of the walk. He inhaled the smells of straw, of stables, of leather and oil and woodsmoke and someone's baking, all the scents of Caer Wiell and home. These things were good on this morning, after the night, doubly and trebly precious. The colors, the green and brown, the broad swell of lands he tended, the sky, were all dazzlingly bright. The banner over the gate snapped and cracked in the wind. The gray stone was spotted green and white with lichens. Flowers spread themselves in yellow dust like treasure on the hills. There was a delirium in such sights. They had been there all his life, spread wide, stretched thin. He cast back through his memory for the darkest mortal things, but every dark thing in all the world had left some color in his mind, like Dun na h-Eoin in the morning, with the mist lying near the trees all pearled and strange in the first light; and the bristling of spears that morning, orderly as a woods on the move against them, spears by twilight scattered like jackstraws among the dark, humped bodies of the dead—lumps like sacks across the trampled ground, like the spillage from some cart, but a wreckage so vast it covered all the plain as far as the eye could see—while close at hand life glowed like pools of ruby wine in footprints driven deep into the mire. And in twilight moths came to the torches in small frantic sputterings, their wings trailing sparks in the flames. Dun na h-Eoin was the midst of horrors, but these small details were there among the rest; like the silence, the vast, vast silence after so much clamor, the simple taste of air. The moths came back, even on the last of their wings, for love of the golden light. Even death had colors. He had been in worse places, where there was no comfort, no refuge for eyes or mind. The moths flew like prophecies, blind with their desires.

"My lord?" Beorc had come up behind him; or had been there for some time. He turned to face this huge man with hair like a burning fire, a violence at rest—broad shoulders, strong back, hands capable of everything—and of nothing, this morning; they hung empty and offering, the honest face bemused. The massive head held wit in a cup of bone; sense and love peered out at him through a skull's eyes. Ciaran blinked and shuddered, seeing it; or perhaps Beorc saw him that way.

"Lord?"

"I am well enough this morning." He drew a great breath and looked toward the light, the fields, the hills. "The sun is bright, is it not? A good day."

"Aye." Beorc moved up beside him, leaned his arms against a crenel of the wall, likewise gazing outward. The sun glanced off his golden bracelet, whitened scars which crossed and recrossed Beorc's strong hands, glistened among red-gold hairs on his arms. The bearded face still frowned in its web of blowing hair. "Did you sleep, lord?"

"Somewhat. More than you, perhaps. No more watching at my door. Go to your own bed tonight."

Beorc looked at him, a sideways motion of the eyes.

"Your own bed," Ciaran said again.

Beorc nodded once, not moving otherwise.

"It was a strange company," Ciaran said, "last night. Did it trouble you—that?"

There was long silence, in which Beorc stared outward over the wall. "So I have seen one of the fair folk," Beorc said. "That was something."

"Not for the first time," Ciaran said.

"They say." A deeper frown settled on Beorc's face. "What I saw last night—I'm not sure. Like the war. The young men ask and those that were out there on the field will never say what they saw. Or we try, sometimes, and it never comes twice the same. Like men that meet bogles and the like in the dark—they tell the best they can and never agree, even in their own remembering." Beorc looked about him. "It was like that, lord—last night. Like that."

"But you will remember. From time to time—nights are easiest. It comes back then."

"In the war—*that* faded."

"When Eald comes out in sunlight nothing seems reasonable. Except in the woods, in shadow."

"Whenever I have been there," Beorc said, "anything might happen."

"You followed her once."

Again was silence. "So you tell me that I did. —Lord, how did my father die?"

"After all these years?"

Beorc shrugged uncomfortably. "I never doubted him; don't now. But you were there. I wasn't."

"He was at my back—I never saw just how it happened. But now and again I saw him in the battle. He was foremost, that day, of all that rode for Caer Wiell."

"But behind you."

"Where I rode—it would have been difficult to follow. More than difficult. But *you* know. You followed her."

"They say," Beorc said, and let his voice fade away. "We fought at the narrows of the river—the King led;

and the battle spilled to Caer Wiell—twenty miles. We could never have ridden so far, spent as we were. But a kind of dark came down, or the morning never came. There was a light—or a banner; I took it for a banner. The lights they name that shine in the wood, and a lost man has to follow; he takes it for someone else walking in the dark, and follows, and it leads. It was something like that, but blazing in the dark—I thought it was the King—or his banner—or it might have been a rider; but it was a light, so clear in that murk, and not a man but saw it and went after it, with all the others, as if it was the only right thing in the dark, man and beast, but never sound of hooves—or sounds were far, and if anyone shouted, it was somewhere far away. —Then the light broke, and battle was round us no different than before. —But it was not where we had been, or we had fought our way there, over twenty miles."

"She brought you through the shadow ways. Iron can never pass her realm—gods know what path she used." But he knew, was cold with thinking of that trespass in Death's own domain, where neither Sidhe nor living Man belonged.

"There was light in front of us. That was all I saw."

"Be glad." Ciaran felt the stone cold at his throat, like ice, like a weight too much to bear. The world was mist again. He heard a horse sneeze, heard the thump of hooves close at hand, then blinked and found himself atop the wall, in light, in human color, the stones rough and warm beneath his hands. "What was I? What did you see—of me that day?"

"Like light. Only there was shadow too, or like something wrong with my eyes, like a shadow on your face. But, lord, it was a feeling much as anything. There was this quiet, this awful quiet, like stopping in the woods, or in some dark place too old, where nothing moves or had moved—" Gooseflesh stood on Beorc's arms. He was not wont to talk of this. He shivered in half a shrug and covered it with a laugh, turning with his elbow on the stone. The laugh died. "Lord, it was like that last night. Even through the wine."

"Beorc, what do they say of me? Now. Across the countryside. Tell me the truth, even the worst of it. How do they see me, our farmers, our weavers, the men who guard my doors? What kind of lord am I?"

Beorc leaned there as if something had pinned him to the stone, as if that silence he had named had wrapped them both in too much intimacy. "Lord, I am your man. They know that. What would they say to me? But I have kin in the country, my mother's folk. Domhnull's too. And in the guardroom they curse you sometimes, the way men will curse hard duty, but, lord, they are your men. They say you have the Sight. They say in the country that the land never fared so well, that there is some luck on it since the war. In the country they set out pannikins of milk, that they never used to do, so the old women say, but they say they do it now—to keep the fair folk on their side. That they fight for us."

"Pannikins of milk." Ciaran gave a frightened, bemused laugh, walked a step away and looked back again. "Aye, I have seen the like."

"There are the small things," Beorc said with a set of his lip that was not to be argued with. "The little fey."

"In them, *I* have no trust." Ciaran laughed, for he had dismayed Beorc. "Aye. In some things *I* do not believe."

"Believe you may, lord. My father knew the like."

"Then he was in danger of them. I trust none of the small fair folk. There are such about. The each-uisge. The fuathas. The old women's saucers may catch more than flies. They are dangerous, that sort."

"All the same, lord, the fields have the luck on them. Burned even to the trees, and no planting fails since, not a seed falls but it grows, and apple trees shoot up like weeds. Trees bear before their time, the rain misses the haying and falls at seedtime, all these years. Where the blackest burning was, the cattle and the horses were kneedeep in grass inside a year. Shall I say what else country folk say, lord? That you are too easy in judgment, but always true; that there be no hiding a thing to your face, that one look of you on them and a man thinks of all the wrong he might ever have thought to do, so there were two neighbors up by high Bainbourne settled among themselves rather than have it come to court: the neighbors say for shame of all their doings for years. They say a horse will not go lame crossing your lands and a cow will drop twins; that the lightning turns in the sky and hits An Beag, missing anything of yours . . . they say. In short—aye, you are loved, lord. Have you never seen that?"

The light hazed in Ciaran's eyes; the colors blurred. Of a sudden he found it more convenient to look out over the walls, for the stone hurt him where it lay, a burning pang of things wild and green and intricate.

"Lord?" said Beorc.

He wept. He did not know why, except that he was cold, as lost as ever he was lost on the field before the gates. It was hard to breathe, as if someone he loved were dying, that keen a grief. "They make fantasies. The grass always grows."

"All the same," said Beorc. "It is the truth."

He shivered. It was panic. "I have Sidhe blood. Do they say that?"

"Oh, yes. That too."

He folded his arms. "They expect too much. You are my right hand, Beorc. Does it not frighten you, to be the right hand of the Sidhe?"

"So was my father," Beorc said.

Ciaran looked at him.

"He told me tales," Beorc said further. "Did you not know? He served the Cearbhallain, and the luck was on him too, and the Sight. Ask Rhys. They tell tales in his hills."

"Watch after Meadhbh and Ceallach," Ciaran said hoarsely. "Mind, tell Rhys and Domhnull—to keep an eye to them, where they go. Always."

"This warning of the Sidhe—Lord, there's always trouble of some kind. Or is there more than usual?"

Ciaran forced a laugh. "Perhaps we have had the luck. But hereafter luck rests on what we do. Mind you talk to Rhys and Domhnull. Say—say I rely on them in that." The laughter failed. He looked out over the land and for a moment the colors dimmed. A mist over the land, and strange forests rose about him. Toward the hills, the west, the north, everywhere he faced, there seemed a shadow, but to the south he could not see, nor to the east.

Liosliath! he cried in his heart. But now there were only echoes, and the pacing of a horse, the slow striking of hooves. And shadows lowered, flowing in small curl-

ings about the hills, pouring between him and that
presence.

"Rhys and Domhnull will not fail you," Beorc said,
heedless of such things as coiled across his sight. "And
I will watch them too."

"Do." He looked back at Beorc, flinching from what
he had seen. He felt after Beorc's solid shoulder, found
it, let slip his hand.

"Lord," Beorc murmured, courtesy. Ciaran went
away. He had wanted something different than worship,
had wanted friendship, brotherhood, something somewhere lost. But there were no more comrades, no one
but Branwyn, and even there he suspected a gulf too
wide to cross. He had served his King; he had a living
brother: neither wanted the sight of him. He felt the
grayness about him like a shroud.

So the elves had gone, the tall fair folk, the Daoine
Sidhe. The melancholy came on them and they no longer
suited the world, but faded, deed by deed. Death could
not touch them. Like Liosliath, whose heart he wore.

It was his heritage. He was alone, except the few
brightnesses of his life—like Branwyn; like Meadhbh and
Ceallach; like what he had hoped was comradeship and
feared was distrust—but it seemed it was all too great a
weight of trust instead. He felt the stone as a burning at
his throat; he was cursed to See while he carried it, and
nothing he saw was hopeful.

The trees which had loomed black and barren out of
the mist gave way to stranger geography, hills looming
up out of shadow, themselves touched with the elvish
moon. A stream ran here, still pure, and Fionnghuala
leaped it with ease, running more smoothly now. Here
were fences of stone and rail, neat pasturage and fields
where never war had come. A farmhouse squatted
against the farthest hill, under a tree broad and gnarled
and strong; a cluster of barn and sheds stood near, with
orchards beyond.

It was a human place, and not. It was refuge, where
Arafel rode more quietly, like a wisp of wind along the
reedy bank. Fionnghuala moved with the lightest pulse
of thunder, like a storm muttering in the sky, but

hushed, hushed, and ceasing, for Arafel whispered to her.

The elvish horse paused a moment, set one hoof into the clear running water, dipped her head and drank, for here she could drink, of waters which fed clear Airgiod. The wind whispered in the reeds. A heron watched in tall solemnity from a little distance away, seeming unastonished, but herons betrayed little. An owl called.

"Come," Arafel whispered, and Fionnghuala moved, delicately, softly. If sleepers had stirred in the farmhouse thinking a storm might be blowing up, they settled into their pillows again and thought that they had dreamed. Fionnghuala's steps glided soundlessly; she slipped like moonlight along the banks and finally along the fences, tossing her head somewhat, for this was strange to her, the fences, the hewn wood, the buildings in the very fringe of Eald.

There were horses here, who put their heads out of the barn as they came near and drank in the strangeness with eyes as dark as night and nostrils quivering, a piebald mare, a fat dark pony, plain and mortal-born. They watched, and ventured no farther from their barn. Wings stirred in the loft, then settled again.

"Gruagach," Arafel called softly.

There was, if only to her ears, a tiny movement within.

"Gruagach."

Stillness then.

"Will you make me angry, Gruagach?"

It was the third calling. He must come. A small, shaggy darkness crept out past the feet of the pony and the horse, a moving untidiness shot through with straw, a small brown man looking up at her with eyes darker than dark.

"I hear," he said, "I hear."

"So. I had thought you must. Has it slipped your notice, the trouble hereabouts? Are you so comfortable at night?"

It squatted, arms clenched about its chest, peering up at her as if it would tuck its head between its shoulders if it could. It shivered. "I have seen it, Duine Sidhe. I watch, oh, I do watch my Men to keep them safe; I make confusions in the hills. There was a nasty thing. I threatened it and it went running."

"So." It touched a sense of mirth in her, and not, for small and twisted that it was, the dark eyes sparked sullenness at her tone. She dropped lightly to the ground, still towering, and then, for she sensed its pride, bent down as it bent, until she looked at it eye to eye. "A secret thing have I to ask, Gruagach."

"*Ask,*" it repeated, flinching back ever so slightly, its shoulders tucked about its shaggy head. "Ask, she says. The Duine Sidhe belongs in the deep shadow, the far places. Oh leave my Men alone, elf. Leave them be."

"Is there no trust, small Sidhe?"

It flinched the more. "I love them. I will fight, I will."

"In truth you would," she said resting her arms on her knees and gazing full on the round, dark eyes. "It is a warm place you have made. Even with the fences. Do you know I have guested with Men?"

The eyes grew rounder a moment, perplexed. It shook its head.

"In their hall," said Arafel.

This was too much to credit. The eyes blinked and the doubt grew. "An elf likes my fences."

"I did not say I liked them, Gruagach! I said I forgave them."

"Ah. Ah. *This* is the Daoine Sidhe."

She had drawn herself up somewhat. The Gruagach flinched back again, then frowned.

"There is bravery in you," she said. "Greater than your size. I have long thought so. So I have come to you. Will you listen?"

"The Duine Sidhe says what she likes and the Gruagach has to listen."

"There was a time—" she began, nettled despite herself, but made a further effort, her hands clasped upon her knees. "Gruagach, I beg."

The hair shifted backward, the lifting of unseen brows, showing bewildered eyes. The Gruagach clasped hands about its own knees, straighter now. "Please, elf, nothing against my Men."

"There are two children across the hills—such bright children, they are, uncommonly bright and good. Polite too. You would like them. And a land—not so fine as yours, but for Men's doing, very neat. I have seen them put out milk and cakes of evenings. They are mannered folk, even if the gifts go unnoticed. The children—you would know them if you saw them. You would never mistake them."

"But I have my land, Duine Sidhe, my farm, my Men to take care of—"

"It would take so little notice, only now and then, I do not say you should do the work of their fields; but shadows have come close there. If there were now and again your eye turned that way, or your care— They are very mannerly folk. They would appreciate the attention, I do think, small Sidhe. I have business to tend to. But the shadows do not trifle with you, I know that."

The Gruagach leaned forward. "What are they to you?"

"Something precious. Men that they are—precious to me. I ask, Gruagach. The Daoine Sidhe asks, and hopes. I know it is no small thing."

"You made the hills to quake," the wight accused her. "You loosed them. Now you come asking help."

"I do."

It shivered then. Its eyes rolled up. It moaned. "The Gruagach sees. Oh, I see, I see, I see, the dark thing."

"Is it near, Gruagach?"

A convulsion trembled through its limbs. A murmur began in it, that became words.

Dark, dark and dark it lies and lost is he who finds it;
Cold it burns and heartless lives and never heart can
*   bind it.*

Arafel shivered and rose, laying a hand on Fionnghuala's neck. "I read your riddle. I would I did not."

For a moment the Gruagach seemed lost to sense. Then it recovered itself, hugging itself, rocking to and fro. "Cold," it complained.

"Yes, cold. And my fault, among others. I own it. Will you grant my favor all the same, Gruagach?"

It stood, never tall, coming scantly to her waist, and having to look up at her, the more as she took Fionnghuala's mane and swung up astride. "The Gruagach will do what he can," it said. "I will try. I am very strong."

"Small cousin, I do not doubt it."

Its eyes went bright. "Cousin, am I?"

"Cousin," she said.

It laughed and capered by her as the elf horse began to move. But the thunder boomed now as the horse increased her stride, and the Gruagach had no such swiftness. Lightning flickered. The trees sighed with wind. The Gruagach fell behind, where soon a storm might break, light patter of rain and mutterings of thunder.

Arafel rode not fully in the shadow ways, not daring them. There was true shadow ahead, a darkness where no stars shone nor clouds rolled, an opacity and increasing cold not so far north.

They were old, these hills near Donn, older than Man. They were prisons, but their roots were shaken and what had been loosed had only gone back for shelter.

The greater things were slower to wake, for the greater binding was on them, but beyond this fair place the mists thickened foreboding ill. It was not in her mind to ride against it blindly; but to find it out, how far it reached, and into what, and how arrayed. She might have stayed safe in Eald, for a time, but it would have come there when it chose.

She came for it. Heartless, the Gruagach had named it, in its half-crazed way, but that was a very true name for what she suspected of it, as true a name as any.

FIVE

THE SENDING

Ciaran slept, if fitfully, and Branwyn was by him, so that for most of the hours of the night he did not sleep at all, but lay with his hand closed about the stone, so that he was aware of it, but only dimly participant.

Dragons stirred in his vision, a glittering of lances, of elvish armor, ancient wars.

A face, elvish-fair, hovered near: elf-prince, the shadows whispered, dreading this brightness. *Liosliath,* he addressed this apparition, but it was only dream. The years were many as forest leaves, as raindrops in the storm. The earth had passed its youth since this one had set foot on it . . . cousin to ageless Arafel.

But when he looked, truly looked with the stone, to see what lay about them, his vision went gray and strange, and he seemed lost among the trees which were not the trees he knew. He remembered the darkness which had coiled among the hills as he gazed outward, severing him from the sea, and still the disquiet crept through him, a sense of power that might do such a thing, silencing the stone.

Arafel's? he wondered. But the aspect of it had been dark, unlike her workings, and there was a dread about it different from the bright terror he knew of her. *Has she a dark aspect? Or had Liosliath? Or can anything dim such a stone?*

Arafel, what am I to do with it?

For your defense, she had said. *I do not ask that you use it. Only that you have the choice.*

Has it come? Or do I only see what has been behind our peace for years?

Do not walk in Eald, she had said, and he believed this, and avoided thinking of it in these gray, weak hours when the veil seemed very thin. *So I am not to come to you.* And again: *Do I truly leave this place when I am there? Or do I dream?* The thought of Branwyn's fright if she should wake and find him fading kept him struggling against it, a resolve no less than Arafel's command.

When light came he feigned to wake and smiled at his wife, gave her a morning kiss, with the birds singing beyond the slitted window and the gentle-hued light coming to them, for it was spring and they piled on blankets against the chill, but liked the freshness of the air and had the shutters off that they used in winter.

"They know nothing amiss," he said of the birds. "Listen to them this morning."

"Did you rest?" she asked, searching his face.

"Oh, aye." He was not wont to lie, but he did so smiling.

He smiled through breakfast—"Will we ride today?" asked Ceallach; and "Hush" said Branwyn sharply. "No, you will not. Let your father be."

Ceallach dropped the matter at once, so unlike his son; and Meadhbh tugged at her brother's sleeve and comported herself as if the question had not come up, very sober.

He grew desperate, even then, in the silence, but he roughed Ceallach's hair and made nothing of it. "We shall see," he said. "Nothing is the matter, is it?"

"Oh no," said Meadhbh instantly, wide-eyed and all too quick.

"No," said Ceallach.

So they all had learned to lie. *That is not so,* he started to say, and smothered it, not to break the peace, only wishing that they would do something amiss, or fidget in their seats, or quarrel over the butter, or something like other mornings.

Instead he smiled, weary as he was, too weary and too little in command of his heart to contest with anyone dear to him. He was alarmed by his ready angers, put them deep and smothered them all and ate the breakfast which sat ill at his stomach, worried by the tiny frown which sat on Branwyn's brow as she chattered at the children about this and that duty, to which they kept answering meekly and unlike themselves. *O let me escape this,* he thought, with no thought toward the days of bearing this gift he had been given, or of their days to come. He was reduced to the moment, like some wounded thing. He set his cup down. "I have work to do," he said, and rose, and suddenly had all their eyes focused on his, even Muirne's, who was participant in the table, in this privacy. Her look was like the children's, her pale face all eyes, her hair combed taut about her face which had gone all smooth and strange to him. Was this Muirne, did even Muirne read him so well? And Branwyn and the children. . . . "I have work," he said.

Silence pursued him. He went out onto the stairs and made noise going down them, through the warding room with its armor hung like the empty shells of beetles, with its smell of oil and war and its iron closeness that quivered through his limbs like some noisome sickness.

He reached the open air, the walls, the sight of the sun, and lifted his face to it, eyes squeezed shut until he had purged the moment's touch of iron.

Liosliath! he called, not daring to call Arafel. But still there was nothing. The stone hung insensate at his heart, giving him only the things the wind and sun gave.

He took his breath and opened his eyes, and drew another and walked along the wall and down again by the stone stairs to the yard.

It was better in the light. He smiled at the pages, at the smith who was setting to his day's work, in his smithy over against the inner wall, with its tangles and knots of iron. This he avoided, making small deviations in the pattern of his day.

Youths gave him their silent respect as he wandered within his walls. They were farmers' sons, come at his asking: Ruadhan had their training at arms, which saw them drilling with sword and shield and bow. The skill with the bow was against beasts; that with sword and shield—against the sometime bandits that strayed down from the Bradhaeth above Lioslinn and the forest to the east . . . for there were still bandits. It had been the Cearbhallain's way to guard the land; and Evald's after

him; and it was his, that he kept no great number of
men-at-arms lounging about the hold—less than a hundred, hardly outnumbering his craftsmen, and them
mostly sons and brothers of freeholders, as much of Caer
Wiell's land was given in freehold, save the fields and
pasturage closest about the walls; but even from the farthest steadings the boys came eagerly to learn arms. It
was Caer Wiell's way. The King looked askance on it.
But the land was sown with swords, since the war; every
farmer's cottage boasted some weapon gleaned from the
fields; and bows were kept against wolves and such
(though no wolves were seen). Caer Wiell had not gone
to the winning of Dun na h-Eoin as some holds had, a-
hedge with spears in untrained hands; but briskly,
shielded, glittering with well-honed swords, a thousand
blades sprung up from the land at Evald's summons,
invisible the day before. This was Caer Wiell. An Beag
sat in its hills like some bandit lair, fed by its serfs who
had each some cruel lordling to support, each worse than
the other. Caer Damh was much the same; so also they
distrusted everything, particularly their own. Such lands
bred nothing good, not those who ruled them, not even
the occasional farmer lad who left his sheep and ran.
Caer Wiell had taken in a few such, forlorn attempt at
rescue, of folk who had grown up in knavery and expected nothing else. Most of them came to nothing.
Some came to worse. Like Coille there, sulking at the
scullery work, with no grace to recommend him. There
was suspicion that Coille stole. Cook thought so. Coille
knew nothing of arms; and that was, perhaps, as well.
He was forever surly.

Send him off, was Beorc's advice. But Ciaran had not
found any cogent reason for it, except Coille's unpopu-
larity. Coille did his work. He had asked for land, but
complained of danger in what Ciaran offered him, which
was to go north and east, to clear land bordering the
New Forest as others had done. So Coille did the work
of the hold; and he sulked about that, cruel with the
cattle and with every living thing, so that it was Coille
got the work of killing chickens for the pot: he does that
well, Cook had said, if nothing else. And there was no
one in the hold but loathed him.

"Good morning, lord," said Coille, with a smile of the

sort of all of Coille's smiles, and speaking up when the country lads were content to nod and pass. Coille was drawing water from the well in the shade of the scullery roof, and heaved a bucket up, wiped his brow, being very sure his work was seen. Ciaran paused, stared distractedly at the man, with the clatter of the scullery beyond, the kitchen, the maids already at their washing and water sluicing everywhere on the stones, before it got to the channel and headed downslope and under the walls. There was the granary, the pen beyond, though they kept most all the animals outside; there were the stables and the sheds of harness, and the Old Hall, that had been the first and oldest part of Caer Wiell, with part of the wall still standing, which was the wall of the scullery now, and had once enclosed the well; but the Old Hall they used for storage, mostly old harness and oddments of this and that; and the Old Granary, that was the barracks, lodging for his men-at-arms; and the older Barracks, that was below the Cearbhallain's tower, which came up by the gate—that was all lodgings now, for those who served the hold; and the Cearbhallain's tower, which added its mass to the gates and enclosed the wardroom stairs in its depths, that was Beorc's domain, where he maintained what little luxury he wanted. No wife, not in these years, no child, but a young widow off by Hlowebourne that he supported with gifts of more than small substance, and visited from time to time. But generally he courted Cook, a stout and dour-faced woman who managed the understairs as Beorc managed a troop of horse, with ringing orders and a precision of expectations.

"Coille," Cook shouted now, "Coille!"

The outlander moved, hunch-shouldered, carrying his bucket.

"Lord," said Ruadhan coming up beside—a cheerful man who looked always a little simple, but men mistook that to their misfortune. "There's some of the lads will hunt, by your leave."

Ciaran blinked and thrust his hands within his belt behind, with an inward flinching. Ruadhan stood there, having come up on him from the yard where the barracks stood, whence came the rhythmic thumps and noise of practice. "Is there need?" he asked.

"Naught but bones left. If my lord would go himself—"

"No. Not I. Rhys might go. He's chafed for exercise. Domhnull. Ask Domhnull."

"Aye, my lord." There was the lightest of frowns on Ruadhan's face. "Is something wrong, lord?"

"Nothing," he said. "Nothing." He walked away, up the stairs by the scullery, along the wall again into the storage, where a few unused rooms offered privacy, and sank down in a smallish windowed closet, finding a bench only half-loaded with dusty oddments of pottery. He set the pots in the floor and stretched himself out, tucked up on the bench, having found a safe place.

So he had done as a child, finding some nook of Caer Donn to make his own. He clenched the stone within his hand and brought it to his lips as he lay there, then sought the sleep the night had denied him, in this quiet darkness far from the iron and the noise outside. Here he need not fear, he thought. Here what befell when he slept was without witness, and if he should dream, he need not fear for Branwyn.

So he abandoned himself.

"Man," said Lord Death, settling closely in the room, on a stack of crockery which failed to break beneath his weight, "is this the lord of Caer Wiell, sleeping like a scullery lad above the kitchens?"

"Give me peace," he replied.

"Ah, that I cannot. I have lost that power over you."

"My friend," Ciaran said softly, never stirring from where he lay, his head against his arms, one toe resting against the floor, for the bench was narrow. "Why have you come here?"

There was no answer. The walls gave way to mist, and he was disquieted. This was what he had feared, the realm of dream, in which elvish trees grew like white pillars of some hall, in which the landscape was chill and gray. He drew back from it, recovering his little room again, alone, his body stretched on the unyielding bench, which was uncompromising in its discomfort.

The stone had troubled him before, when he had carried it in his youth. But iron had not seemed so painful then. He had passed the armory bearing it and not felt it half so keenly then. *It is the years,* he thought. His old wounds ached. He limped some winter mornings. *I could have slept on bare stone once, and never minded it.*

But his nerves were taut. He realized his fists were clenched and mindfully unclenched them. He thought that he might have a little peace if only he could take the stone from off his neck. It tempted him, as once, his third battle, he had thought that he could run away; all that dawn he had waited for the ambush to break, hidden half-frozen in the autumn-red thicket as they fought in those years of the King's war. It had occurred to him that he could stay there when the others burst forth, and that he need not go, because he had contracted a sudden, gripping fear, and felt sure that he would die. But his body had leaped when the horn sounded; and he had gone, after lying to himself all the while that he had had a choice. After that he knew that things seemed choices which were not, and that men lied to themselves sometimes for comfort in the small dark hours. So he could think now of putting off the stone, but he knew that his hand would refuse the act, because he had said that he would bear it, and he could not do otherwise.

Liosliath! he cried in his mind, and suddenly there returned to him that sound he had all but forgotten: the sea, waves lapping at the shore, gulls crying like lost children.

Does the stone remember? Or was more than that always my imagining; and was there ever a living voice?

She thought there was, at least.

Silence came. For a while it was all gray, and he waked fitfully, aware at least that he had slept, caught himself sort of falling off his precarious rest. His eyes drifted shut again, fluttered, for it seemed some sound had come to him, but it was only someone stirring about below, some clatter in the kitchens.

He sighed, and was home again. He lay asleep in the loft of Caer Donn, in that closeness he shared with Donnchadh, and any moment now his mother would be calling them both downstairs to breakfast, to that great table they all shared. His sister was alive again. He heard her voice; he thought he heard it, the way he had never been able to remember it; and if he could wake and go downstairs she would be there, his sister and his mother and his father who were dead but alive again in this new and precious dream.

Father, he would say, *you never let me explain;* and his father would sit by the fire in the great hall in the tall carved chair with the huge old wolfhound he had loved lolling at his knee and listen to him without really seeming to listen, which was his manner when he was thinking about something. *Listen to the boy,* his mother would say, taking his part as she always would. *He's your son.*

His father looked up and frowned, disturbing the tenor of the dream. Ciaran retreated from that moment, choosing another.

How did you come here? his mother asked him; but the horse that stood outside she could not see, nor could anyone see who did not know how: Aodhan was its name and it had carried him home as it had carried him to battle.

I can't stay long, he said, feeling keenly the stone about his neck, but he stood in the upper hall of Caer Donn where every detail was precious to his memory, wooden walls, where those of Caer Wiell were gray stone; and fine carving on the benches, for the folk of Donn had always been fine craftsmen and carvers. *O Mother, there was battle. The King has won. I've come home awhile.*

(But he had met his father and his brother afterward, and they had walked away, having seen what he was, and what he had become. The hills about Donn held old stones, for the elves called it Caer Righ, and there was elvish blood in them all, fey and different from men.)

And your father? his mother asked; *and your brother and your cousins?*

Well, he said. *Father and Donnchadh are very well. But Odhran died at Dun na h-Eoin and Riagan at Caer Ban; and Ronan and Hagan too—*

All dead?

Aye. Dead. He sat down in a chair he remembered. *Is there ale?*

She brought it for him; it had taken longer than this, with much stir about the hold, but in his dream it was instant, and she sat near him and asked him when they would come, his father and Donnchadh.

Soon, he said, *soon.* Cherishing the time that he had left. He would stay for supper. He would do that. He would stay all the days before he knew his father and his brother would come home and tell her that he was banished, fading only when he knew them passing the gates.

But he had not stayed the hour. The questions were unbearable, the reality of home insupportable when his mother persisted in her questions, when she grew angry and confused.

It happened now, and he fled outdoors, realizing only later that he had been mistaken, that he should never have come here.

He rode, and he was a boy again, with Donnchadh; they raced upon the heath and climbed irreverently on the ancient stones, their ponies tethered down the hillside.

It is a cursed place, said Donnchadh. He would become a lean, tall man, dark, for he was of their father's first wife; but as a boy he was gangling and his hair always fell so, into his eyes. *Do you dare?*

Of course he had dared. In those days he had no fear. They stood atop the world like kings, he and his brother, and looked from the hill to the mountains round about, shoulder to shoulder.

And stood eye to eye at Dun na h-Eoin, among the dead.

Take care, his brother said. And moths died in the torches outside the King's tent; and the dead lay in heaps.

Ciaran, take care.

The mist was back, among hills that he knew; and Caer Donn stood as it had always stood, high on its hill among the hills about, for its wealth was sheep, and the flocks grazed round about; but now the land was sere and brown like winter, and the treeless hills showed their bare bones of earth and ancient carved stones.

This was not the way it had been. He knew dismay, and entered into the hold, into the upper hall with the blinding swiftness of a dream, where the familiar chairs stood all unused, and only his brother slept before the fire as he had seen him sleep at a hundred campfires, his head at an angle, the fire leaping on his face.

Wake up, he said to Donnchadh.

But there was a sense of menace he had only felt in the wrong places of Eald, something in the stones.

They were boys again on the hill, and something wakened under their feet which resented their laughter and their youth.

It crept and circled in the dark places of the hold, and there was no kindred left. The servants had grown faithless. There was only his brother sleeping here alone, while menace gathered, and the shadow he had seen came nearer.

Donnchadh, wake up.

But the waking was his, and his hands clenched on the board of the bench, his balance for a moment deserting him.

Someone moved on the stairs outside. For a moment he thought himself truly in Donn, and blinked, his heart beating so hard it hurt. But he lay still, and the steps passed, with a clattering of the noise below.

He sat up and leaned his face into his hands, passed the hands over his head to the back of his neck.

More steps outside. The door crashed open. A shadowy man stood there glittering with iron.

"Lord? Lord Ciaran, is it you?"

"Rhys. Gods." For a blinded moment he had feared some attack and known better in the next heartbeat; it was his own hold, after all and only Rhys, whose lean figure and dark hair minded him strangely of his brother's in his dream. He stood up. "Has a man no peace?"

"Lord Ciaran, the hold's upside down with looking for you. Shall I—tell Beorc you're here?"

Ciaran laughed half of despair and took in all that Rhys had said. "Is Branwyn looking too?"

"She had asked; and one man thought you were here, and another thought there, and when the hunt returned and you were neither—Lord Ciaran, are you well?"

"Don't tell her where I slept," he said. "I didn't rest last night." He went toward the door, passed Rhys into the hall and shut the door after him, so that they were in dark unrelieved except for the slit window some steps up. "She was not alarmed?"

"No, not except that she thought you with the hunt and wished you had not gone."

"So did *you* go?"

"No. Only Ruadhan."

"Was there luck?"

"Luck enough till they came back and questions started. Lord, you might have had my bed."

Ciaran said nothing, but surrendered himself to the daylight, rubbing at his eyes as he went down into the sunlight and trying not to look at the men who, one by one, realized he had been found and gathered solemnly to stare at him and Rhys walking across the yard.

Beorc came, meeting them halfway.

"There was no cause for this alarm," Ciaran said, and then, his eyes lighting on Branwyn atop the wall, who stood waiting for him: "Are you all my warders?"

That was short and undeserved. He went up the steps and gave his hand to Branwyn, already ashamed of what he had said, with no way to recall it.

"I was in the storage and fell asleep," he said to her, reckoning that the most of the truth was due and wishing he had said less below.

"Ah," she said, so easily it seemed casual, and wound her arm in his as they walked, taking him inside.

But someone carried tales, or Branwyn read more in his heart than he had thought, for that night there was a posset mixed at bedside.

"You must drink it," she said. "T'will make you sleep."

He was loath. This also was abandonment; he more trusted his own mind. And a dire thought came to him.

"If you took the stone from me," he said, "if you were to do such a thing, you might do me harm."

"I don't believe it."

A great weariness came on him, so great that tears came into his eyes. "But you must not do it, Branwyn. Give me the cup."

She offered it, and he drank: she had made it sweet with honey. then he lay down to rest and she blew out the light, and came to bed beside him, listening long for the evenness of his breathing.

"Do you sleep?" she whispered, ever so softly.

It seemed then that he did, that the stone had no power to resist the cup that she had given.

But she lay long awake, as she had waked much of

the night before, feigning that she slept, and anger gnawed at her, that he had cheated her, forestalling her as he had, with a word and his trust of her.

He had always had that way with her, that he was so simple and so knowing of her heart.

The elvish sun was near, but there was a murkiness which hung late, for here there shone no stars, and uncertain trees which were and were not by turns made the landscape harder and harder to recall, as if the land itself could not decide true from false, now from then. The nightwind that stirred the grass brought forth a hissing sound of dryness and the hillsides were patched with dust, and now and again with stone.

There was ill hereabouts, couched within the hills. Arafel sought it warily, with more caution than she was wont to use in this land that was her own.

There were Men. She saw the houses, but they were nothing like the cleanly houses and neat fields of Caer Wiell, but hovels of rough stone nestled on stony heights, unkept and many untenanted as if even Men had been disgusted with them. There were sheep now and again, and dogs, which little interested her.

She came to a brook in the strange last edge of dark, but Fionnghuala spurned it with a snort, and brought down a hoof like thunder in the night, that echoed among the hills. Something splashed and swam away. "Fuathas," she said, and heard the swimming stop. "I have no quarrel with you, Fuathas," she whispered to the air. "Where are your brothers?"

"Duine Sidhe," the whisper came back from the black water, bubbling, "gone this way and that through the web of waters. Let us go. We do no harm."

"Your name is Hate."

There was soft laughter. "So do you go called the People of Peace by Men, and that name has no power on you. Hate are we; and Spite to Men, but that name will never bind us."

"Come out. I see your name. Shall I speak it to the wind and water, for anyone to hear?"

There was a stirring in the green leaves above the water, a loud rude breath. A black horse stood there, and Fionnghuala shifted her weight and bared her teeth, laying back her ears.

"No," said Arafel. "Give us man-shape, pooka."

The horse faded and it was a dark-haired youth who stood there, clothed in shadow. He had a sullen face, and wrapped his arms about him as if he had taken a chill.

"The Duine Sidhe has come calling names," he said. "But give me my river back, Duine Sidhe." His heavy jaw made his frown the more intense; his thick black hair hung about his shoulders and all but covered his eyes which stared back at her like coals of fire in the shadow. "The wind is cold."

"The water is colder still, pooka. But truth I ask: What stirs hereabouts, and what is its name?"

"If I knew it I would bind it," the pooka said and shivered, for all his pride. "It knows mine, Duine Sidhe. O let me go. The sun is coming and I do not love the daylight."

"What is its kind, pooka?"

"Its kind is yours," the pooka said and shivered yet again. "Let me go now."

"No, pooka." She held it still, having had the answer she dreaded. "Where does it lodge?"

It pointed north, behind the hills, and its arm shook as with ague. It began to fade.

"Seaghda," she called its name.

The face grew clear again, distraught and woeful. "I have given what you asked, Duine Sidhe. But you were always cruel."

"Not I. I only ask you guide me. I do not command."

The youth threw his head and his burning eyes peered madly through the hair that settled. His nostrils flared, pale in the strangeness of the light. "I am bound here. So wise a Sidhe should know that."

"Ah," she said quietly, "where is your soul, o Seaghda?"

Now the eyes were wild, the dusky arms hugged more tightly.

"Show me," she said. "Seaghda, Seaghda, *Seaghda*."

It vanished. The waters swirled, the reeds whispered in the dawning. It was back again, a dark-haired youth holding a small smooth pebble on his palm. The mad eyes stared.

She slid from Fionnghuala's back and came to him and took it in her hand, so small and plain a thing and unlike hers which hung like the summer moon about her neck, but very precious to him. If the eyes were not fire they might have wept or pleaded, but they had no such power.

It warmed within her hand. It took fire from her, becoming and becoming, and so she gave it into his hand. "Be free," she said, "Seaghda. The binding is broken."

The shadow leaped up like a shout, a darkness, a wild flood of mane and eyes like embers. It whuffed wildness into the air and leaped the stream at a bound.

Fionnghuala bared her teeth and sidled close to Arafel.

"Come," Arafel whispered, taking Fionnghuala's mane, "It is Seaghda, a prince among its kind; and it will find the way for us."

The elf horse threw her head, shook it, rattling thunders from her neck, but lightly Arafel sprang to her back and she began to follow the darkness which paced ahead of them, in the delaying dawn.

The light began among the shifting maze, an uncertain gleam that lost itself among the trunks of trees which did not stand there in the mortal realm: she might have sped quicker as mortals went, but less sure, and come blind toward the hazard.

Now the pooka trotted, now walked a space, now moved again, shaking his mane: it was his doom that he could not speak, having no place but his mouth to keep his soul when he was in his true shape, and always fearful of losing it. But when the light had gotten to a murk that gave suspicion of color, when the sun was with them and they had come to the end of the trees, Seaghda stopped and took his other form, spitting his soul into his hand.

"There," he said doubtfully, pointing with his left hand beyond the wood, where strange carven stones rose up on the hillsides like a line of broken teeth.

"Dun Gol," she said, shaken in spite of herself, for that aspect should have passed from the world. She cast Seaghda a dire look. "Have *you* manifested this?"

"Not I," said the pooka. "I could not." He shivered in spite of the sun, or because of it. "But the waters are bitter that flow from this place, and taste of hate. Go back, go back now. Find your forests again. This one is not kind, and the stones are worse."

"It is a drow," she said. "That is what has waked."

"Do not say that here," Seaghda hissed, and his eyes glowed but dimly in the day. He hugged himself and shivered. "Enough, enough, let us be away."

She patted Fionnghuala's neck and felt the tremor. "She will stay with me, pooka. Go. I have freed you. Go where you like; I have no more need of you."

He was proud, but the terror in him was more. He turned away and slipped his soul within his mouth: the black horse stood there an instant lifting its head toward the height of Dun Gol, nostrils quivering with dislike.

Then it fled, the slipping of a shadow into the murk.

Fionnghuala moved forward, softly now, treading lightly above the polluted soil.

Elves had perished here, on this side and on that of war. It had left the world, this hill, with its memories and its stones, so close to what Men named Caer Donn. Something had brought it back again, more, it was the place from which the strangeness came. This was why the trees returned, which had been lost to Eald: that this place remembered them.

And it remembered loss. It was Dun Gol, the hill of weeping, and it was reared above the armies which had met and perished here, to the ruin of the world.

SIX

OF FENCES
AND FUGITIVES

Ciaran slept, past breakfast, and waked with the sun streaming in the windows and Branwyn's place vacant. He lay there a time, his hand finding the quiescent stone where it ought to be, his eyes shut on the day because the quiet was so good to him. But he gathered himself up at last and dressed and went out with a night's rest behind him and a brighter countenance to the days ahead.

He was quite deserted: the hold stirred about its day's business without him, but the maid went scurrying when she saw him in the hall, and Branwyn came in on the return, smelling of sunshine, with hope in her eyes and dust on her hands that she wiped upon her gown.

"Did you sleep soundly?" she asked, as if it were any morning of their lives, and kissed him by the mouth; he hugged her, finding the smell of her sunbathed hair the fairest thing about the morning he had met.

"Oh, aye, I did."

She drew back to look at him.

"My oath. I did." He smiled a weary small smile, not the false one he could use. "You see, there is peace of it. I knew it would come." He gathered her back to his heart. "The Sight was too quick and keen for a time; perhaps that it had gone unused so long, and knew me—

but it has settled now. It has quite settled. There's no more pain."

There were other things she might have said. He waited for them, but she judged the peace still fragile, perhaps, for she only found that she had gotten dust on him and brushed at it and straightened his collar as if he were a child to be cared for. "Meadhbh and Ceallach are out weeding the garden; I thought they should have the sun. Muirne is with them. I will have cook send your breakfast. Cein was here: the notch-eared ewe dropped her lamb this morning and the children went to see it. Beorc is somewhere about: the horses took down the north fence last night and got into the turnip field; but they have got most of them in by now."

He frowned. "I will go," he said.

"You will have your breakfast first."

He smiled and kissed her on the brow, on his way out breakfastless; he was vexed about the turnips, and half-way glad that there was something ordinary to set his hand to, that needed neither arms nor wit, except to reckon where the rowdier mares had gotten to, if they had not gone straight to bickering with the stallion in his stall: and if that had happened, there would be planks splintered and carpentry to do.

He had a gelding saddled from the stables and rode out from the gates, along the gardened north; and along that stout fence and hedgerow that kept the pasturage. He saw a rider on the horizon, close to the end of the row, and rode for him.

"All in but Whitenose," Beorc said. "I have lads combing the riverside."

"That mare was never a wanderer," Ciaran said. Of Slue he would have expected it, who was often leader of the trouble.

"Probably she became confused," Beorc judged, "having more conscience than the rest, and ran off."

"Where was the breach?"

Now Beorc frowned, pointing north. "Up by the trees yonder."

Ciaran frowned as well. Not by the new fields then, but facing open land. That was less like the mares. "Slue got the wanderlust again," he judged, "it being spring, and led the rest to mischief. Let us ride up there and see it."

So they went, the little way that remained, and there was nothing to be seen but some of the lads putting the fence to rights, stacking up the stones again and setting the rails. The ground was much trampled with horses wandering this way and that.

Ciaran shook his head. There was no chance of tracking any single horse here. They rode back again, down along the road where it came near the river. "I think," he said, "that the watch might have seen them from the gate if any had wandered this way."

"I think that in the end we will find our Whitenose off by Gearr's steading," Beorc said, "if she went off north instead. Either the watch missed her in the dark or she went farther than the others. We might have a lad ride up that way. But the rough ground makes her hard to track."

Ciaran shut his eyes as they rode, a brief casting of his wishes: *if I am gifted with the Sight,* he thought, *cannot I find one straying mare?* But there was only mist as there had been; and suddenly a chill that made him draw in the gelding's reins sharply.

"Lord?" Beorc asked.

The horse had faced about under the pressure of his hand, backing still, it was curbed so hard: he felt its discomfort and yielded with a shiver. *"Donnchadh,"* he said, for that darkness was back which he had felt the day before, when he had dreamed of his brother.

"My lord, is something there?"

Beorc's voice came to him through the mists, and trees faded which should not stand there, and the land he knew returned. He felt the sun again.

"Is it some ill?"

"Something ill," he said, and there was a presentiment on him still, so that the matter of the mare diminished in his mind and he recalled the dream that he had dreamed in the night, that was the hill near Caer Donn.

"I will get the men," said Beorc.

"No," he said suddenly, returning to himself, looking about at Beorc's ruddy face. "There is nothing to do for it. It does not concern the mare."

He turned the horse again. They rode and searched

along the riverside, where the road ran, even leaving the road at times to come to the edge of the Caerbourne; and the boundaries of Eald whispered softly in the wind, and the water chuckled as it would among its reeds, mocking them with silences. He did not use the stone again. It was wrong to have used it so, in so small a matter; it was not given him for the finding of stray horses, but in trust, and he chided himself for his foolishness—as if it were some hammer or awl that he had borrowed, this thing that was precious to the Sidhe. Best, he thought, if he learned not even to think of it, if he numbed his heart so that it did not answer when the leaves whispered, so that he did not imagine liveliness in the waters or small things watching from the thickets.

The feeling was not good here. His horse and Beorc's fretted, and it seemed to him in that sense which came curling unbidden through the stone that no horse might love this place, that they wasted their time and their search, for Whitenose would never have come this way.

"Let us go back," he said finally. "Send over to Gearr's steading, see whether she might turn up there: that pony of his might speak to her."

"So I was thinking," said Beorc.

So they came back by early afternoon, and no sign of Whitenose, which put Ciaran in less cheer than he had been. It was a good mare, one of his finest, and he had had the breeding of her through two generations of Caer Wiell's fine horses.

"Maybe," said Domhnull, who had also been out searching and turned up at the stable as overheated and out of sorts as they, with Rhys, who looked no better, "maybe, lord, she strayed west."

Due westerly lay An Beag's lands, and that thought had grazed his mind, ready as any man of Caer Wiell was to blame ill on that neighbor. "I cannot think she would have so little grace," Ciaran muttered. "She was too well-mannered to think of An Beag. Rather she had gone off toward Gearr's, or somewhere about."

"There is the woods," said Rhys, who bore scratches on his face from searching amongst the trees, "and there she might come to mischance—but there is no natural cause for a horse to stray there."

Natural, Ciaran heard, and looked at Rhys' ever-grim

face, and at suspicions. "If it was unnatural," he said, "and the small Sidhe had aught to do with it—well, grant she finds some farm when they are done."

The thought put him out of sorts even further, and he climbed the stairs. "It comes to me," he said to them as they went up, "that we might use the tower for the warding room, and that we might set the one we have to other use. Will you see to that?"

"Other use," Beorc echoed, somewhat out of breath.

"A table, a chair or two: a library; we should move the accounting here." The poison closed about him as they came from the wall to the room, among the dreadful iron; he bore it, shuddering as he reached the second stairs.

"Aye, lord," Beorc said, "but the accounts are small—"

"So, well, but do it, Beorc, see to it this afternoon. Set some of the boys to doing it. Move everything to the tower hall. Move what is there here." He reached the top of the stair, the relief of his own hall, where the table waited, with ale and the morning's bread and some of Cook's fine cheese. "Ah," he said, better pleased in the day, finding he had appetite, and that was good. "My lady has been kind. —Sit with me, you three."

"Is it father?" a young voice called from up the stairs inside, and Meadhbh came running down with Ceallach in her wake; so Branwyn came down the stairs, and he swept Meadhbh up in his arms and spun her so, a flurry of skirts.

"Did you find Whitenose?" Ceallach asked.

"No," he admitted, setting his daughter on her feet. "Likely she went off to some steading; but we will find her."

"If the elves have not got her," said Meadhbh.

"You do not call them elves," Ciaran said soberly, catching her with his eyes. "There is only one of *her* kind, and you cannot see her stealing our mare, can you?"

"Only one?" Meadhbh asked, her face gone very still. "Only *one*?"

"In all the world. The others of the Daoine Sidhe all went away, very long ago, so long ago no man can re-

member it. There is only one, and you must not speak
ill of her."

"No," said Meadhbh, "but why did they go away?"

"Hush," said Branwyn. "Hush, no such questions. Let
your father alone. Can't you see he's been at riding and
might like to sit down? Don't be so graceless."

Meadhbh's face fell, her eyes so very earnest. *I am
sorry,* they seemed to say, but not a whit for questions.

"Come," he said, moving the bench aside, "sit with
us and share the bread."

Their young faces glowed, to be asked thus to sit with
Beorc and Rhys and Domhnull and himself, small companions to a men's gathering. They scrambled to the
benches, fresh and clean and scrubbed, while his company still reeked of horses, except for washing at the
trough. But Branwyn took her place at table too, a waft
of lilac and herbs, her fine hands laced before her.

"There was none lost but the one?" she asked.

"No, lady," said Beorc. Muirne had come, and took
it on herself to be cutting the bread: she took the knife
from Rhys and sliced the bread and cheese, while Domhnull poured the ale.

"A little for Meadhbh and Ceallach," Ciaran said.
"Mind, a little. And no, we have set everything to rights
we can, and the plants wanted thinning, I suppose. It
was likeliest Slue that did it."

"From the far end," said Domhnull. "She has never
gone that way before."

"We will have to stall that mare," Ciaran said. "I'll
not be feeding her on turnips." It occurred to him
strangely that he was given uncommon tolerance, that
Branwyn said not a thing about the ale, that her eyes
shone at him, that she was happy and that the children
were. He gave a short pleased sigh, his mouth full of
bread and cheese, his world at rights again, even if it
turned out to be faery which had stolen the mare.

And then he thought of his dream, how they had sat
at table like this in Donn, and for a moment he felt a
deep distress from the stone.

"We have another lamb," said Ceallach. "It's a ewe
lamb."

"A ewe," he said. "Well, good for that."

"And we pulled all the weeds," said Meadhbh, showing reddened hands.

"Hush," said Branwyn, "your father's men have no need for small chatter."

"Oh, well," said Ciaran, "but the weeds were well done, all the same." He smiled, and got a flicker of a smile from his daughter. "Better luck than ours, I should say." He ate his bread; his men wolfed it, having been hard at work since dawn. "Maybe we should test the fences all round."

"Aye," said Beorc. "I'll tell Cein to put some of his lads to it."

"I'll do that. You have your matter, with the warding room. —I've decided," he said to Branwyn, with a look that tried to tell her secrets, "to have the accounts moved there."

Today Branwyn would object to nothing. It had been the warding room all her life. "Well," she said quietly, and nothing more.

"Can we help?" asked Ceallach.

"Not in your fine clothes."

"We'll change again," said Ceallach.

"I think," said Branwyn, "you might find things to do that didn't get in the men's way. I'm sure I can find things other than that."

"Yes," said Meadhbh miserably, her hands folded before her.

"You might ask the scullery to send up some of the lads," Ciaran said. "There'll be cobwebs to clear."

"Yes," said Ceallach.

So the matter went, and there was scrubbing in the warding room, with a great deal of carrying of water and a smell of wet stone came up from it, and vinegar and burning pine, so that all Caer Wiell seemed dislodged.

And Branwyn went about ordering this and that with a preoccupied frown upon her brow and her hair flying loose from its braids in curling wisps from the abundance of water below.

Ciaran walked out along the wall, relieved, finding in the confusion of the day some solace, as if things had wanted to be turned upside down. He changed a thing which had been the same since the Cearbhallain, and he changed few things in his lordship, but this one was for his comfort.

They must bear with me, he thought, and realized that none of them had questioned him in his strange request, no, not even Beorc.

But they knew what iron was to faery. They knew. And silently they went about this change for his sake.

Only the rider came back from Gearr's steading and reported no sign of Whitenose there, though the farmer would be watching for her. The youth looked crestfallen and unhappy. "Well," said Ciaran, "but she may have gotten frightened and it may take her time to stray toward some farmstead; but any man who finds her would know where she came from." He felt a need to console the youth, who looked thoroughly downcast, for the lad was one who worked closely with the horses.

"She has never been one to run," the youth said, as if the mare's character were in question.

"Well, she may come home," he said, and sent the lad off, sorrier for the boy than for the mare: he had many horses, and little could touch him on this day, that he had mastered the ill which had settled on him and gained peace in the house again.

He watched the lad walk away, leading his weary horse toward the stables inside the gates, and then went upstairs, into warmth and light and the newly cleaned room that would hold no iron hereafter, but only accounts, still smelling of water and burned pine.

He went farther, up into the hall, where Branwyn waited, and had his supper in good peace, with the children, with Beorc and Rhys and Domhnull, Siodhachan and Ruadhan and Muirne and Ruadhan's Seamaire, and had Leannan to play them songs, so that it was more merriment than loss after so disarranged a day.

But Muirne who had gone down the stairs to the kitchens after a pitcher came back and never poured, but went direct to Branwyn, ignoring all courtesy of precedence. She leaned and whispered straightway in Branwyn's ear, and Ciaran saw Branwyn's eyes, the startled dart aside, the fixing on thin air.

"What is it?" Ciaran asked, and frowned at Muirne, so the harping died, ringing softly into silence.

"Coille," said Branwyn softly. "Coille has not been seen."

"How, *not seen*?" He ignored the quick and ugly thoughts, searched further afield. "How long not seen?"

"Please you, lord," said Muirne, whose voice was always soft and now hard to hear even in the silence, "Cook thought he had gone to laze about again, that he would say this morning he had been at the fence-mending; or this afternoon at the moving of the hall, and so some thought he was—but neither-where; at nothing, so they say down in the yard."

"Coille," said Beorc in a low and rumbling tone.

"Aye, Coille," Ciaran said. An anger came on him, so for a moment it was hard to breathe, when he thought of it. He clenched his fists upon the arms of his chair and felt the heat go into his face. "So this is my reward of charity—a good horse and gods know what else. I believed that hangdog scoundrel; I took him in. And straightway he goes home again to his masters at An Beag, with gods *know* what tale—Oh, this is beyond my tolerance."

"Lord," said Rhys, with all his dark fierceness, "send a few of us that way."

"Aye," said Beorc, "we'll have some An Beag cattle for it. And Coille's head for it, if we spy him."

"No," said Branwyn sharply, "*no,* there is no good in it."

"Branwyn," said Ciaran, "I will not abide this thing."

"Then do not abide it; but do not break the peace. You know how it sits with the King; and where your enemies are: give them no such help. Gods know they need none."

"I know where my enemies are. At the King's ear. And in my hold, that I sheltered. Mind me of this, mind me of this, when I grow soft-hearted. They are laughing tonight in An Beag."

"They will be pleased if you break the peace," Siodha-chan said.

"We cannot bear this thing." He brought his hand down on the table. "We have farmers on the borders who will bear worse if we do nothing. If we let this thief, this scoundrel of An Beag get away with what he's done, then who is safe, anywhere?"

"No," said Branwyn. "Who is safe if the King's forces ride against us as peace-breakers?"

"Laochailan King would not have the courage," said Rhys, which treason brought a deeper silence in the room.

"Children," said Branwyn suddenly, "go to bed. Now."

"Mother," whispered Meadhbh.

"Hush," said Ciaran without looking, and then looked all about the room, at all the anxious faces, at folk he trusted, men and women, all. "Friend's son," he said to Rhys, "friend to me—I wouldn't venture to say what the King would and would not do. But he has bad counsel. An Beag and Caer Damh have his ear, more than we. I don't say what the King might do; but what he would permit to others. —Well, Branwyn has the right of it: we have not been wise. The dale might rule the east, and he knows it—oh, he is wise in plots, is Laochailan. And what I say, I say to friends, to those I trust. We have one true ally: your father, Rhys, and how I have valued him through the years—that is beyond telling. But he has had the burden to stand by us more often than we have been able to stand by him."

"Not so," said Rhys, "since he knows full well how this King would rule if not for fear of the dale."

"Perhaps we've guarded each other's shoulder," Ciaran said. "But we have been warned of troubles." The stone lay cold on his breast, like a second, aching heart, and he forebore with difficulty to touch it. "It seems to me that someone other than An Beag might have sent this man among us. That the King himself might have wanted to know what passes here, and poor Whitenose might have a longer run ahead of her than we think."

There was dread silence. "Then he would have a great tale to tell," said Beorc.

"Aye," said Ciaran, "well he might: how Caer Wiell's lord has gone mad, how he is feyer than they had thought; that magics are raised here that are gossiped in the halls—they are, are they not?"

"Aye," whispered Seamaire. "Too freely, everywhere in Caer Wiell's lands."

"That man then can do us great harm. He has been

witness to—gods know what he has seen, or how we may be reported."

"The Sidhe spoke of war," Beorc said.

"Of war of a kind," Ciaran said. "And I cannot sit idle and let us be meshed in it."

"You cannot be riding against An Beag," said Branwyn. "There is no gain in that."

"No. No gain. Especially if this Coille is not An Beag's at all. Far less than gain. But we must find us allies."

"Who, pray? Caer Damh? The Bradhaeth? The lords across the hills? Husband, we are not their friends. We could never be."

"There is Donn."

The company stirred as if some wind had blown, and Branwyn made an outcry.

"Donn! Donn is the heart of our troubles. Who speaks loudest against you to the King?"

"Who can be more bitter than a brother? But he is still my brother. It came to me," he said very softly, and glanced once at Meadhbh and Ceallach who sat crouched small at Leannan's knee, "it came to me that this silence was more of my making than his. I offended my father's hopes; I know why. And somehow when Donnchadh sat in his place, well, perhaps he had tales told him how it sat with me, and perhaps there was some bitterness in it."

"You sent three times to your father, and each time your messengers were sent away."

"The last was at his death. I had hoped, then. But to Donnchadh, after, I never sent, and perhaps Donnchadh would have answered me. He is in danger. I know that he is. The Sidhe said as much and I have felt it—" His hand went to last to the stone, unstoppable. "Here. I have felt traps meshed about us. We are none of us safe. And if things have gotten to such a pass that we have to fear spies and theft and treacheries—A shadow, the Sidhe said, a thing stretching out all round us; and I have seen something of it. You wonder that I don't sleep. The King is in danger. Danger surrounds us. And perhaps, if anything would forestall this—if I could gain my brother's ear and through him reach the King and stop this madness—"

"Donnchadh is your bitter enemy," said Branwyn.

"He is fey as I. And Sighted. It's in our blood, only like my father he has no peace with it. —He is my elder brother." He said this for Meadhbh and Ceallach, reluctant, for he had never spoken much about Donnchadh, but he felt it necessary now that they understand. "We met last in this room, when he had come to Caer Wiell; but he saw me—with the Sidhe's presence about me, and it was too much for him. I think he must not have slept well after that. He went away, he and my father, and I thought they would have fallen from the King's favor after that, but they spoke against me and grew closer to him for putting me aside. Perhaps the King thought there was some luck in them that would outweigh mine. Perhaps he still thinks so. But if I could speak with Donnchadh—"

"It's dangerous," said Branwyn, "and might do more harm than good."

"Ah, Branwyn, not dangerous; to my pride, perhaps. But I had a dream about my pride. One asked me could I give it up for Caer Wiell. And I think there was some foreboding in that dream."

"You are not thinking of going to him."

"That was in my mind."

"Lord, no," said Beorc. "Not yourself."

"What can messengers do, where messengers have failed? But perhaps it would heal the wound if I were to come myself."

"No," said Branwyn violently. "No, no, and no."

"I would go," said Domhnull. "Lord, if you think there's some use in this, send me."

Ciaran was silent, gazing at Branwyn, reading there adamancy.

"I would go myself," said Beorc. "Your brother knows me, at least by sight."

"That calls back the war years," said Ciaran, "and the King's councils, and maybe those are days best forgot."

"There is myself," said Domhnull again.

"I would go," said Rhys, "but I fear your brother and my folk are not close."

"I think it madness," said Branwyn, "and a danger to whatever man you send. Cousin, don't offer. He should not be encouraged in this."

"Lord, I offer," said Domhnull. His fair face flushed,

young that he was and several times passed by. "If I name myself Beorc's cousin and your man, your brother will know it's no small thing that you send me; and as for the war, I never saw it, so he cannot fault me in that either."

"We will talk about this," Branwyn said. "My lord, if you please, we will talk about this thing."

Ciaran sat still a moment. Branwyn gazed straight at him.

"We will talk," he said, and glanced toward Domhnull. "Domhnull, I will think on this."

But as for his mind, it was already set, and he was already framing the message in his mind, what he would send and say after so many years.

SEVEN

BAINBOURNE

Their father rode ahead with Beorc and Domhnull and the other men of the escort, on great tall horses; and they rode next to last, ahead of the men who led the five remounts. They jogged along on their two ponies next their cousin Rhys, who seemed justifiably downcast about it all, in the troop of their house guard, all of whom they knew. They felt very important, did Meadhbh and Ceallach, in this faring out across the country. Meadhbh felt a freedom and fear at once, a fear which had settled into her like habit in recent days, since no one was going to tell her any of the secrets that drifted about Caer Wiell's halls, like the things her mother and her father said when they talked in private; or what her mother meant in those warnings she had heard in hall; but her father who often did things her mother's way (she is the wisest of us all, he had said of her one day to his men, when Meadhbh was there to hear; no snare will ever take my lady)—her father had left the hall that night with that look in his eye which meant he was not going to listen to anyone and their mother went about the next morning at breakfast finding fault with Muirne and with everything. Meadhbh accepted this sharpness in hushed patience, and Ceallach gave her a look which said he thought much the same, that it was their father their mother was worried about, that he was doing something dangerous even in sending to Donnchadh, and so it was easier to blame the breakfast.

It was that fear again, that no one talked about, whether it was fear of their cousin the King, or their uncle the lord of Donn, or faery, or something no one meant to name; it was always there now, like some great fish, Meadhbh thought, gliding here and there under black waters, and the surface gave back only the glance of light or branches, so that there was no way of knowing when the fish was somewhere upstream, or right under the surface staring back at them. No one wanted to talk about it, especially not to them; or to think about it, if there was a choice.

There was, for a while, the sunlight and the ride: she loved riding, with the creak Floinn's saddle made, and the motion, and the smell of horse and leather, and the earth and the land and even the sharp scent of oil and metal and leather and sweat and smoke that the men had, which reminded her—which would remind her every time she thought of it—of her father on winter evenings, when he brought himself and all his doings with his gear inside the hall with him, when the armory was too cold. His corner vied with their mother's which smelled of herbs and of the simples she made for folk who needed them in winter. Her work was all leaves and such and bowls, and his chair stood surrounded with all manner of oddments of horse gear and leather and oil-smelling rags. There was the slow scrape of the whetstone when he honed that great sword of his, the muddled scent of heat and oil and the fine riverstone going just so down the edge which had to be done just right, or spoil it. The blade had lines graven down the center of it which wove back and forth and turned into a running horse. It was precious and very fine and old, a sword which the Cearbhallain himself had cared for, and then Evald their grandfather and now their father had it in keeping. He had seen them watching one evening and let first Ceallach and then herself ply the stone, steadying their fingers, being patient when their strokes went amiss and finally finishing it all himself—redoing what they had marred, Meadhbh had suspected. Her hands had smelled of oil afterward, like his, which delighted her—(O Meadhbh, her mother had said, who always smelled of herbs and roses, and scowled at her for the black marks on her clothes.) But she always

loved the smell, because it was his; and loved what he
gave her, which was his cleverness of hand, his knowledge how to ride, and where foxes denned and hares
might hide, and what were the names of trees and hills
and lands beyond horizons.

But now their father rode armorless among men who
were armored head to foot, carrying shields upon their
backs and many of them carrying the long spears which
they never used for hunting. He had left the great sword
at home, had banished it from hall with the things of
the warding room as if it were nothing. They did not
ask why. But they had marked that he had put off even
his dagger in hall. He had only the stone with him, always that. They did not speak of it, she and Ceallach,
even to each other. She was in sum uncertain whether
this gift was at the heart of the trouble or whether the
trouble had come and the stone upheld him in it; it was
far, far different from their own small gifts, she knew.

And tucked away in her mind was the suspicion of
her own guilt and Ceallach's, that if they had not dis-
obeyed and run off to the river in the first place, none
of this would have happened. The Sidhe would not have
come and their house would not have changed. And that
was a weight of guilt too heavy even to think about, let
alone to speak of. No punishment would mend this. No
one would so much as accuse her. It was like when the
Sidhe had looked into her soul and asked her what she
would do with another living creature.

So at best she tried not to do another such rash thing
as she had done, or even to let herself be a child any
longer. She felt robbed by this: she wanted to grow her
own way; but suddenly all she wanted seemed very
small, and all this war she had begun to fight of being
herself and disobeying when *she* wanted something,
seemed something mean and selfish, because no one in
the world was getting what he wanted, not even their
father, who was lord of Caer Wiell. They had seen him
lean his head into his hands when he thought that he
was alone, as if he had had all that he could bear, and
that brought back that awful sight of him on the dark
stairway, when he had fallen, fainting in their mother's
arms, which figured in their nightmares. They wanted it
not ever to have happened; they wanted things to be as

they had been, but they could not be. Even their father could fall, and they had seen it, and so, separately, they understood that growing up was not, as they had thought, always having their own way. Meadhbh suspected suddenly that it was something like what the Sidhe had asked, that meant *not* having it—or at least not being tricked by thinking one was owed it, even if it was the thing one wanted most in all the world—like home and parents.

People should always be with him now, Meadhbh would have said to her mother if she had had the courage, because her mother would have been there in a trice if ever their mother thought their father needed her help, and gods defend anything that stood between. And her mother might have lost most of this particular struggle, but not all of it, because it was Domhnull who was going to Donn at the end of this ride, and not their father himself; because Beorc had stood firmly with their mother on this, and Beorc and their father had gotten to words fiercer than usual between them.

"We will set him on his way," her father had decided then, of Domhnull; and so that was how it was; and: "You promised we should go when you rode the west road," Meadhbh had reminded him at breakfast, with devious and loving motives.

"No," their mother had said, at once and sternly.

But. "As far as the crossroads," their father answered. "Yes, I did promise. It's a small ride. They'll turn back there, and Rhys will be with them."

"This is no ride for Meadhbh," her mother had tried then. But her father had only looked at her in that way he had had, half sad and half determined. So her mother yielded them both up with nothing more said on either side, and the ponies were saddled along with the horses.

Their mother had not come down to the gate as she sometimes would, but to Domhnull she sent a special gift, food all done up in a napkin that Muirne brought down to him, meat and bread and not the common fare that the men took. Domhnull was frankly embarrassed by it, the more that no one else was so favored, not even their father, who went out just with common stores; so Domhnull had tried to give a share to others, but their father laughed and would none of it, nor would any of the rest of them.

So they were on their way; and Meadhbh let her heart rise then, what with the jingling of armor and the horses jogging along at a fine fair gait. After all the fear and the arguing, they rode out into the morning with sharp weapons and high spirits and the men joking and making light of all that ailed them. These were the best men Caer Wiell had, the best in all the land, and every enemy was afraid of them. If their father should ever somehow need someone's help, Beorc seemed likeliest, the strongest man they knew; and Rhys, the fiercest and hardest and in many things the cleverest; and Domhnull who had taken all the danger on himself, and the men who would go with him, Boc and Caith and the others.

She touched the tiny pouch she wore at her neck, the same as Ceallach wore, that Muirne had shown her how to make for them, for the leaves of the elvish tree never left them now. They did not die, those leaves, nor fade, nor lose their fragrance. And they kept them close, since that morning, as their father had said, waking or sleeping having the gifts with them. Whether they were luck or not they were not sure, but they wore them as their father wore the stone, as faithfully, not understanding why, and hoping for luck from them, like safe homecomings and not losing things they loved.

If she could be like Beorc, or Rhys or Domhnull, she thought, and strong and brave to stand beside their father. (To her father's stature she did not aspire—he was too complex—but if she could be like Beorc. . . .)

Meadhbh watched him, the tall red-haired man who rode at a slouch and looked in many points disreputable beside their father and Domhnull; but men jumped when Beorc ordered. She practiced that slouch herself a moment, deciding then it wanted broader shoulders. She hated what she saw for herself, being slight and keeping to hall, smelling of lilac and of herbs like her mother and waiting, always waiting to learn what the world had done—or what it wanted—or telling her daughter hush, whenever someone mentioned faery, because her daughter would run away if she did not, doing foolish things and thinking hopeless thoughts of Sidhe and losing her-

self in the woods and bringing trouble, the way she had
already brought it.

If she could *do* something to make it good, if she
could slip away and ride with Domhnull to An Beag—*I
am Meadhbh,* she would say to her uncle, in his hall,
with Domhnull in his armor standing by her, *and my
father sent me to talk with you.* It would have been sensible, she thought, that she should go, being young and
having no quarrel with her uncle, but of course no one
had thought of that, and even her father would have
laughed at such an offer.

She imagined bandits from An Beag descending on
them out of the trees beside the road, and herself and
Ceallach proving themselves—but they had no weapons,
not even a dagger. The wish collapsed. Her brother's
Flann and her fat Floinn shuffled along at pony-pace
while the tall horses took longer strides, not working
half so hard. They were childish figures, that was all; and
the plump bay ponies were all their measure. And soon
they would reach the safe limits of their riding, and their
father would send them back, children who had had
their outing.

Domhnull would go on: they all would, but themselves
and Rhys, as far as the north road, and their father
would ride back again later, having seen Domhnull well
set upon his way. And he was going on, but no one
would let him—"Because," Beorc had said when they
quarreled, "You bear *that* about your neck, and if your
brother has no liking for the Sidhe, what when you come
bearing *that* with you? You think that would win his
love? And what when you drift off, as you do with me?"

"I should not," their father had said. "With you, it's
trust, that I do it."

"So, well." Beorc had looked embarrassed, his ruddy
face flushing twice its ordinary red. "But all the same
it's madness. You know it is. And if you will not part
from that thing, and you say you will not, then don't go
to Donnchadh."

"What you say is sense," their father had said then;
so whoever it was who had won with him, whether their
mother or Beorc, he would not go, and perhaps he
would have thought of these reasons himself at last, but
it was Beorc brought it home to him.

Our uncle would not like us either, Meadhbh thought.
*How can a man have the Sidhe in him and hate them?
Perhaps if the Sidhe could only come to Donnchadh—*
she *could win our uncle.*

And again: *I could call her name,* she thought. But
something turned in her heart, forbidding it. *I am no
small matter,* the Sidhe had said of herself compared to
the fuath, *no, not like that one.* Their father could surely
call the Sidhe if anyone could, and did not, for his
own reasons.

So at length they came to the crest of that hill below
which the road divided, one branch going toward the
dark wooded side of the Caerbourne; and that way was
unkept and unridden, because it led west to An Beag.
The other branch, well-traveled, went northerly, through
their own lands, the way farmers took, and their own
patrols

Here their father stopped them all, so that it was clear
this was the parting-place. He beckoned to them; they
rode forward, not jogging, but with that deliberation
taller riders on greater horses used. "Well," he said to
them, "this is as far as you go."

"Yes, sir," said Ceallach very quietly.

"Yes," said Meadhbh as soberly, looking up at him.

"Come, come." He drew his tall horse close to Ceallach and leaned from the saddle to hug him, passed close
by Meadhbh as well and leaned down to kiss her brow.
For a moment he lingered, frowning. "Be good," he said.

"Yes, sir," Ceallach said. Meadhbh only stared. They
had broken off the trail here before when their father
went on his journeys, and always complained when they
had to do it, and had more to say to each other. This
had an ill-omened feel, this brevity. Of a sudden she
kicked Floinn up close to her father's horse and offered
a two-armed hug. He hugged her back, leaning down.
Then: "Back by tomorrow eve," he said, and gathered
up the rest of them and rode away, leaving them with
Rhys to guard them.

There was a knot in her throat. Her pony tried to
follow the horses and she reined back.

"Come on," said Rhys after a moment. "Come on."

She looked at Ceallach, who also looked afraid, and
turned Floinn's head for home.

*   *   *

The familiar fields unfolded, brown and green. The once-traveled road lay dusty and safe, ever so safe, and Rhys had never ceased to frown. He was dark, their cousin once removed, with brooding, heavy-lidded eyes, and frowns came natural to him, natural as the weapons about him. He was smallest of the men about their father, and hardly seemed likely for a lord's son, but he was. And patiently impatient of them, of which they were acutely aware in his long silence, his sullen carriage, his gaze which wandered everywhere—to the riverside, to the fields, anywhere but to two children who had become his unwanted burden.

It only added to her misery. Tears threatened Meadhbh, an irritating swelling in her throat. She kept her eyes open and let the wind dry them. She did not say anything. She did not feel equal to Rhys' wit, not weary as she was; neither, it seemed, did Ceallach.

"Uncommon quiet," Rhys muttered at last.

"Yes, sir," Meadhbh said in half a voice, and they went a further several hills in silence.

"Gods," Rhys said suddenly, "quit moping. The hazard is Domhnull's, no other's. Your father will turn back, long before the border. He has said."

"Yes, sir," Ceallach said.

It was a while more in silence. Rhys scowled for a while, and looked only worried then. "Aye." Rhys said, "aye, I know."

"You could leave us here," Ceallach said, more brightly, "and we could get back home ourselves. We would. Then you could catch up with father and be with him."

"Your father's orders," said Rhys.

"Yes, sir."

After a while longer riding they had come to the ford again at the Bainbourne, which ran down to meet the river, a shallow spot surrounded in reeds, well trampled mud on either side where they had crossed not so long ago. Rhys drew rein and let his horse drink before they crossed, at a spot less mired, and the ponies had their fill too, then behind Rhys's tall disdainful horse, plodded across the stream, up to their fat bellies before they had come out again, all muddy-hoofed and sorry-looking.

"It's hot," Rhys complained, looking at the sun. He had stopped on the level bank where there was grass, and there stepped down from the saddle. "Rest a few moments," he said with a look at the ponies.

They had not brought food for themselves, and Rhys was not the sort who would think of stopping to eat the way their father might. But he looked to his girths and theirs and then wandered off his silent way to the grassy margin of the brook, where he squatted down and drank upstream from the crossing, dousing his face and neck with both his hands, for it must be warm in all that padded leather and metal.

Since Rhys took his ease Meadhbh and Ceallach slid down off their ponies and let them crop the grass, bits and all, since Rhys let his gelding do it. Rhys still crouched there, his hands upon his knees, staring off across the stream as if he were lost in his own thoughts and paying them no mind, so Meadhbh went down to the stream a little up from him where a tree hung over the water and the shade was cool, and Ceallach followed her. It was a place they knew, from the first time their father let them ride out with him; and they had played at being on campaign like the heroes Leannan sang of, and had mock battles among the reeds, with sticks for swords, which made their father laugh, he and his escort; or they had shared food from a basket on the streamside. They had taken cover under this old tree once when a shower caught them, their father and they and Beorc all snugged up under a tent of cloaks listening to Beorc telling them how it had been to live in tents, the years of the King's campaign. Reeds grew on the sandy shallows opposite, which had been mysterious hedged of hostile fields; and tiny flying things still swarmed there and made patterns on the dark and gentle currents.

"I think Rhys is going to rest a while," Ceallach said, squatting down on the bank and gesturing with a glance, where Rhys had lain down in the sunlight, letting the horse and ponies graze.

It was not like Rhys, to be so easy: he was all scowls and moods by habit, and while they liked him well enough they did not expect patience of him, or easiness, or anything but business. When Rhys laughed it had a hard sound, and his laughter was at hidden things and things men laughed at with each other. But perhaps he was weary after being up too late; or perhaps in his silent way he was meaning to be kind, not knowing much of what they wanted, but reckoning not to push them hard on their return. Meadhbh heaved a sigh and sat down on the bank herself, liking the coolness of the shade, the water, the nodding reeds and humming bees. Ceallach took leaves and launched them one by one, faery barks asail on the smooth miniature flood, as they had done before at this place, the first time their father had let them ride with him, when Flann and Floinn had seemed as tall as mountains. Ceallach was not playing now, but thinking. So was she. She plucked a leaf and launched it beside one of his, not playing either, watched it race Ceallach's down the dark swirls, past towering forests of reeds. They had grown too old. There was only memory in it. Her eyes followed the boat, but her mind was on her father, on Domhnull, wishing her uncle in Donn might prove better than they suspected.

"Rhys is in the sun," Ceallach said finally with a second look that way. "I think he's gone to sleep."

It disturbed her too, that Rhys had been sweating so, and lay down in the sun in all his armor, which was not the kind of sense she expected of Rhys ap Dryw. She wrinkled her nose, reckoning indeed Rhys might have been at too much ale last night, but it simply was not like him, and he had not seemed so tired on the way, simply out of sorts and wishing, she thought, that he were going on with the rest of the men and were not left to guard his two young cousins.

The strangeness of it worried at her. She got up and went toward him very quietly, with the sun beating down on her back. "Meadhbh," Ceallach objected, a faint whisper; he had gotten up to follow her, leaving his faery-boats, but she paid no heed to that. Often if Beorc were sleeping he would wake at the least sound and come out of it suddenly: never play pranks, her father had said once sternly—a man who had slept where Beorc had slept was dangerous waked that way, like many who had spent years at war. She remembered Beorc and others of the men, dozing with sometime slitted eyes, looking up foxlike from time to time and napping in the sun, never quite abandoned. Her father napped like that. But Rhys was sleeping with his limbs loose, face-up to the sun and with his eyes shut, his lips parted like a child's. "Rhys," she said aloud, from a safe distance. "Rhys?" She went closer then and squatted down by him ready to spring away if he should wake angry. "Rhys." Her heart was beating hard. She put her hand of his ribs and shook at him. "Rhys, wake up."

Ceallach had come up on his other side. He dropped to his haunches and shook at Rhys hard. Rhys' body was loose, like something broken.

"Is he dying?" Ceallach asked. "Meadhbh, can people die like this?"

She did not know. Rhys' breath still came. There was no other sign. He was a capable man, was Rhys ap Dryw. He lay there with his weapons and his armor, more defenseless than they were. Of a sudden she felt a creeping sickness of her own, a deep malaise which lay at the pit of her throat, where the leaf rested. Ceallach lifted his hand in the same moment to his own throat. His eyes were frightened and wide.

"Caolaidhe," he breathed.

But it was quite, quite another thing which stood there beside the water, in the shadow of the tree where they had sat. That was deep shadow to them, who were in brilliant sunlight; it was hard to see because of that, but it had no proper shape, and when it moved gave out a rustling like grass. It shuffled forward into the light and squatted there, small and brown and shaggy.

"Rhys," Meadhbh cried, shaking at him, and Ceallach snatched Rhys' dagger.

"Brave," the shaggy creature said. "But iron bites, bites you."

"Stay away," said Ceallach.

It came no closer. It sat with its arms about its knees and regarded them with old and shadowed eyes from under its fringe of hair. "Bites."

Ceallach's hand was shaking. He braced it with his other clenched about his wrist, and sweat stood on his face. The dagger tumbled. Meadhbh caught it up and the cold of it burned her fingers. Neither could she hold it. The pain ran through her bones. Run, she thought; and thought of Rhys helpless with this creature; thought

also of the elf who had stepped through thickets effortlessly to pursue them.

"Thistle," she called to the empty air. "Thistle—"

"No, no," the brown man said holding up his hands.
"She would not be pleased. She sent me. You must not
call. I came to see the children, the children I would
like."

She had stopped, falling half under the spell of the
small piping voice. She heard the hum of bees, the sighing of the rushes, and struggled to disbelieve.

"Rhys," said Ceallach. "What have you done to
Rhys?"

"Sleep," the brown man said. "No harm, never harm
from the Gruagach. See, I give my name."

"We will not give ours," said Meadhbh.

"Ah. But I know a name that you own: children of
the Cearbhallain. I feel it in your hearts." The brown
man hopped up very quickly and somehow (it deceived
the eye) hopped to the rump of Floinn, who lifted her
head from her grazing.

"She's my pony," Meadhbh said with all the fierceness
she could muster. "Let her be."

"Nice pony." The Gruagach scampered into the saddle, crouching like some ungainly bird, and leaned close
to whisper something in Floinn's back-turned ear.
Meadhbh sprang up and snatched a stone from the bank.
She held it in threat, and Ceallach took another.

"Let my pony be. And wake Rhys up."

"Rhys. Rhys." It hugged itself, savoring the name they
had given it. "Be more careful where you give names.
You might give away his heart, but the Gruagach has
no need of it."

Shame flooded her cheeks for the mistake they had
made. "Then let us all go," Meadhbh said. "Let him
wake up again."

"I have seen you," it said. It hopped down again.
"Fine sensible ponies, brave and good. They like you,
but mostly they like their comforts, which is what ponies
love best. And they are clever. Many ponies are. But
your way is darker than theirs, o darker. I know now
why she sent me."

"Thistle?"

"You have bright eyes. They see—o, they do see. The

Gruagach knows you. He sees why. Be wise, o be wise, good children. Trust no iron. Be kind but be not foolish. The Gruagach sees, o yes, the green shadow on you. You are old, old as stones and your roots are deep: new growth on a hewn tree."

"You make no sense," said Ceallach. "Let him wake up. Let Rhys be. He never did you harm."

The Gruagach hugged itself and spun on one foot. "Go home, he must go home; the south must come to aid. Go home, go home, walk wisely through the shade. The four-footed friends will serve you while they can. The wind is coming and on it something rides—o I see, the Gruagach sees. Go away! Go away! The Gruagach has these children and the Man you cannot have!"

It was gone, it was straightforwardly gone, with only the sunlight in its place, and the ponies and Rhys' tall horse never starting from it. The bees kept up their humming, undaunted. The wind was gentle in the rushes.

And Rhys stirred in his sleep, and waked with Ceallach and Meadhbh beside him. His eyes were peaceful at the first and then took alarm and shame at once.

"We were worried," Meadhbh explained as Rhys sat up on his hands. "You would not wake up."

Rhys had a desperate look, and ran a hand through his black hair. He looked at them, at the sky, at the streamside and the hills, seeming profoundly embarrassed.

"I have never done such a thing," Rhys said. He started to his feet, missed his dagger and found it on the ground. Again he looked about him and at them. "Did you sleep too?"

"No," said Meadhbh, sure that it had not been a dream, and that it was not for telling, though she wished to. She felt sorry for the man, who was almost a lord of sorts and very proud, and truly never one to be so careless in a charge. He would confess it to their father, she was sure. And their father would see through it all and worry for what had happened.

"You frightened us," Ceallach said.

Rhys said nothing to that, but walked to where the horse and ponies grazed, and they followed, not without looks at each other—not conspirators' glances, but troubled ones. They joined hands as they walked after Rhys.

Meadhbh understood nothing of what the brown man had said; she doubted it made more sense to Ceallach—except that it was to them the brown man had come, and to them he had spoken, and said he came from Thistle, whatever her real name was.

Dark on their path: that he had promised. And something on the wind. but the sky was clear and blue and there was no hint of it. She did not take comfort of that: blue skies were quickly changed, and this one seemed very fragile, and the sunlight like reflection, even at noon. There had been something about roots and leaves; she made no sense of that, either. But it spoke of some kind of change in them, of iron—and neither she nor Ceallach could hold the dagger. Her hand still ached from trying.

Things of Eald and iron would not agree together. That was why their father had ridden out armorless and weaponless; and even now the pain went shivering through her mind, the iron pain, when the stone their father carried had such force or such danger in it he shielded it from her fingers, when he had fallen on the stairs after taking it and she had seen him in pain.

She had felt something like. She knew. And he went on carrying that stone, which was far more than any slender silver leaf. Her mother made him possets to drink so that he could rest. And at times there was still pain. Now she knew where it came from.

She hugged Floinn's shaggy neck and took up the reins and climbed into the saddle as Rhys mounted his tall black horse. Ceallach climbed up on Flann. The ponies started home without any touch of reins or heels, and the black horse went with them as if it were still a dream.

EIGHT

THE WAY TO DONN

The wind blew warm on Ciaran's face and the horses moved in easy rhythm, a sleepy kind of progress up a road still well within Caer Wiell's lands, but the hills of An Beag's domains were at their left, across a rolling shagginess of hedges. There were freeholds hereabouts, where staunch dale families had settled on border land and held it. Caer Wiell aided such folk, who were Caer Wiell's bulwark; and if the company had turned aside to left or right they would have found welcome and a cup of ale gladly given to each, ale and not unlikely a supper offered, had they come at sundown. They prospered, these freeholds, and so the road proclaimed, barely fit for carts, but still traveled often enough that no grass grew in it, a fair fine road as roads went on the marches.

They wended up from the turning of it and met the Bainbourne again where it wandered, a reedy stream crossed here and there by fords and trampled by sheep, of which they saw several flocks in the distance; or by pigs, where Alhhard's steading set its back against the water, a rough cluster of buildings next old and twisted willows, and rough fences made of willow logs and stones the Bainbourne scoured. The place prospered. The boy who kept the pigs called out to the company as they came, and stood on the fence across Bainbourne to wave; others appeared, men and women, and dogs and children who pelted across the stream in a great splashing of water to run beside the horses.

"It be the lord," the children cried, jogging along

beside the column, and there would be gossip from steading to steading by the fortnight; but Ciaran smiled to see them, and the horses tolerated the dogs and darting bodies. "Lord," the eldest shouted, a boy whose stride was longest and near that of a man, running along by his horse, outdistancing all the others. "Will you not come across to us? There be ale and cider."

"Thank your father," Ciaran said, "and wish all the house well from me. I cannot stay this time. Gods, Eada, your legs are longer, are they not?"

"Aye, lord." The boy panted along with all his kin outdistanced, and the last of the dogs about him. "That they be. And I know the bow, lord."

"Do you? But your father would have taught you."

"I have fifteen summers, lord."

The lad was falling behind now. He shouted the last. "So, well." Ciaran turned somewhat in the saddle. "When you have sixteen, then come to Caer Wiell a season."

The boy trotted to a halt among his dogs, waving his hand and grinning. The whole company waved back at the steading, and so the willows took it back again.

The horses protested, having caught a whiff of shed and shelter, and it took curb and heel to keep their minds to the road instead.

But the company moved with purpose, if safe among their own folk, in lands that knew them, and no man of the escort muttered or said anything of regret for the ale.

"The stars and sky tonight for all of us," Ciaran said. He looked beyond Beorc where Domhnull rode—silent, Domhnull, which he was not wont to be. *He is a boy,* thought Ciaran, Domhnull looked very young in that moment, affecting not to hear them—so young, so young Ciaran dared not half so much freedom as Beorc used with him; so young his pride was green and tender. *I was wrong ever to have agreed to this.* He thought of the boy Eada, running by the horses, eagerness for battle shining in young eyes which had seen no sight grimmer than autumn butchering, and he shuddered.

Moths and torches. The glory blinds them. O Domhnull, I never should have heard you.

"It is a long road," Ciaran said then quietly as they rode. "And there are places in it—Domhnull, the more

I think on this—Listen," he said, having the youth's attention, marking the quickness of his eyes to imagined slight or praise. "The way by Lioslinn—I rode this when I was a boy and never since. But mind it lies near both Damh and Bradhaeth."

"I do mind it."

"It winds, between the hills once you have come up from the lake. There are rocks above you." For a space he tried to tell it, every stone and turn that he remembered, where they had hunted once, far afield from Donn, he and his brother and his cousins. Domhnull listened, frowning in his earnestness to remember all he could, and Ciaran felt again a narrowing despair. "I should remember," he said once, "if I saw it."

"I shall manage," said Domhnull and made light of it if only for his pleasing. "Lord, the sun will guide me; and I shall look for the spring. And for the rest, we will go quickly and stir up nothing; or outride it."

It did not comfort him, the more they rode within the sight of the hills where the way bent westerly. He rode silently and the men with him were quiet now for the most part, having fallen silent while he spoke and taking the contagion of stillness from him.

The mood had come on him gradually, and lay darker and darker, from the bright morning when they had left the keep, Meadhbh and Ceallach trotting along with them . . . *because it is safe,* he had said to Branwyn last; *because there is no cause that they should not ride in the fair center of our own lands, with Rhys to watch them. And to watch Caer Wiell while I am gone. No farther than the Crossroads. Is so much to be made of this?*

Now it seemed mad to have done, and a light sweat lay on his limbs, for all that the sun was sinking. *They must be safe by now,* he thought. *Rhys must be sitting in hold, they at the fire with Branwyn, Muirne too, and Leannan, and Rhys doubtless having a drink with Ruadhan. . . .* He built the ordinary things, a fragile structure, stone by familiar stone within his mind, while the sky turned golden and perilous about them and they came near to parting.

I wanted it so, he thought, recalling the peace of the morning. *I wished to believe it, the way I want to believe Domhnull will meet no hazard.*

But he will not. And they have not. He persuaded himself again, gathered up his courage in both his hands and tried to be cheerful. He smiled against the silences, rode with his hand attentive to the reins.

"Lord?" asked Domhnull.

"I was thinking how I am a prisoner, young friend, and how this great cousin of yours and I would be at swords-point if I were to go beyond Lioslinn. And yet—"

"Lord," said Beorc, "no."

"What, my guardian, not try you?"

"Lord," said Beorc, "I beg you."

"You are worried, old wolf." Ciaran heaved a sigh. "There would be no peace for me at home if I were to do that."

"I should be on my way," said Domhnull, glancing toward the distant hills where the sun was setting. "For my part, lord, I had as lief know you had the shorter ride on the morrow, and if you were home sooner than you had promised, you would make your lady wife the happier for it."

A while longer Ciaran rode in silence.

"Lord," said Domhnull.

"Aye," he said. "So you are right." He reined his horse aside off the road, as they had stopped to rest many a time this day, not to tire the horses beyond quick recovery. But this time Domhnull and the four who would go with him unsaddled the horses they had ridden and set the gear on the five remounts, which thought ill of the matter.

"So you must take care," Ciaran said, still afoot when Domhnull and the others sat ahorse.

"Lord, I shall."

"You carry that token I gave you."

"Lord, I have not forgot it." A small smile played about Domhnull's mouth, a twinkle in his eye, so Ciaran smiled, reminded that somewhere, somehow this man had happened, instead of the boy he kept remembering, and that the man was strong and had his wits about him.

"Aye," he said, "speed you well, Domhnull."

So he had to send him, with little ado, making little of the uneasiness that troubled him; and so Beorc sent his cousin off and friends of the escort parted.

So beyond Caer Damh and by the shores of Lioslinn Domhnull would bear westward, a long ride yet to go before they should rest; and Ciaran looked after the dwindling figures, his hand staying his horse by the cheekstrap of its bridle.

Mist lay about them. The others could not see it, but there was mist, all the same, and trees rose about them straight as pillars when he looked with that Sight he had. The trees lay between on that plane and he lost sight of Domhnull, of the way they rode, which did not exist here. There was only tangle, and cold mist, and comfortless forest. He stood staring into it, quieting his horse which stood with him; but the men with him seemed like shadows less substantial than the trees.

"Lord," said Beorc, and thrust something loose and heavy into his hands, a skin of wine. "Here."

He drank. The wine seemed rough and strange.

"We might rest at Alhhard's steading," said Beorc. "There's that ale, remember."

"No," he said. He offered no reasons. Beorc asked none, willing to humor him in his whims, so long as they did not involve following after Domhnull. He thrust the vision away, brought the sky back golden.

He could not see in this place. The stone could bring him no help against it. He doubted, suddenly, everything he had done, but it had seemed wise till now . . . to defend Caer Wiell.

He thought of Donnchadh his brother, of Lioslinn in the sunlight, when they had climbed the hill above it; or again at Dun na h-Eoin, in the twilight; and then he realized with a strange shock of passing time that this was not the man he sent to. It would not be the boy, nor yet the man at Dun na h-Eoin, dark-bearded and slim, as he was not what he had been then. *He will have gone gray,* Ciaran thought with a shock, setting his foot into the stirrup and rising into the saddle. He had never reckoned with the years. *He is older than I and darker; so the years will sit harder on him. He will have gone to leanness: he was always thin.* He tried to build this man in his mind, cast away the image for the one he remembered, brother, companion. Longing came over him then, to be where Domhnull rode. The fair-haired boy he had been would have leaped to horse and ridden, defying all the hazards. He had ridden for the King once, and in that wildness he had gone, and parted from his brother.

So I would come back to him, he thought, remembering better times. He would leap from his horse by the gates. *See, I have come home.*

But it was the lord of Caer Wiell and the lord of Caer Donn now, and the gestures between them must agree with that, full of wariness and the weight of years and anger.

I have concern for you, he had wished Domhnull to say to Donnchadh in his name, but he could not even send that simple thing. *I ask peace,* he had said instead, humbly, caring nothing for his pride, *in these times. This silence profits neither of us.*

There was more, if Donnchadh should be disposed to listen.

Lioslinn lay black by starlight, reflecting nothing, not even shimmers on its surface. It stretched far and shallow, and for sound here there were only the creak of frogs and the soughing of the wind in the reeds.

"I have seen it fairer," said Boc, who was oldest of the escort.

"More bog than lake," said Domhnull, "by the reek of it." He had set eyes on it, but only from a distance, and now riding close beside its midnight shore with the stench of decay going up from it dispelled any illusion he had still cherished of it as mirror of the hills. It lay beside them like a pit, darker than the reeds, and the chiefest concern in his mind was that some misstep of his horse might put him into a reaching arm of it, some hole unseen in the dark. The night was moonless, and the dark sky had seemed friendly until now, shielding them from Caer Damh as they passed it on the road.

They rested the horses as they could, and kept silent for the most part, leaving the conversation to the frogs and nightbirds. Voices seemed to carry all too clearly, and the night was listening.

They were good men lord Ciaran had sent with him, Domhnull knew; indeed, they daunted him with their knowing what ought to be done before he said it; or knowing before he knew it, for they were older than he, and Boc many years so. *Sent to watch me,* he thought, having less and less confidence that he led them at all; but they would never say as much. Only what little he had to tell them he said in brief and noted every breath of theirs, every shift of stance that seemed to say to him: *Yes, boy, yes, we were wondering when you would say so,* or perhaps: *Well, boy, but we would not advise it.*

He had faced this journey with more confidence in the morning, by daylight, parting Caer Wiell and far from Lioslinn's boggy, reeking shore. He had, he thought, taken a great deal on himself. He had seen that much in Beorc's eyes when they parted, a cool kind of reckoning he had gotten in the drillyard.

Well, lad, Beorc had told him more than once, *get to it. Do something or do nothing, and if you're truly one of the world's fools, then the world is sure to learn it.*

The frogs went silent at their splashing. Something started away with a splash of its own, and the horses did not like it. Somehow, by some persistence of his horse or that the others kept reining back, he would end up in the lead again though he reckoned that Boc knew this ground better—he must, for Boc had been here and he never had; but at last he took the foremost position for his own and held it, seeking with his eyes and senses and thinking perhaps that they should not try to ride this ground at all, but walk ahead of their horses.

It was old, this place. Legend said so, but more, he felt it in his bones, that the lake was no wholesome place. He thought of water-horses, of selkies and such like: if there ever was a place where a fuath might lurk it was Lioslinn, among the reeds and moss. There might be shellycoats and bogles, to come rattling out of the bog with reaching fingers.

A thing hissed at them and dove with a heavy splash. His horse went sideways, and trod afterward as if it were poised to spring; he curbed it, his heart clenched and trying to beat again.

"Gods know," said Boc, "what that was."

"Come," Domhnull said. A cold was down his back. His teeth wanted to chatter. "Stay together. This place is too boggish to have one of the horses bolting."

"I have them," said Brom, half a whisper from behind.

"To think," said Boc, "they named this a road once."

"The lake has risen," said Domhnull, "or I've led us amiss." His eyes strained into the dark, where the hills rose up in a blackness deeper than that beside them. "That must be our way yonder."

"Gods grant," muttered Boc.

The nearness tempted him, to urge the horses to speed. He resisted, plodding their slow and patient way, and now and again there were other splashes and the sound of something swimming.

No one spoke. The hooves sucked and slid in mud. The horses snorted, closer and closer to that cloven wall of rock that loomed before them. The ground grew more solid, the steps more firm, and once, indistinct in the dark, a cairn of stones bulked beside the way.

"We are out of it," said Boc.

"I would not be glad to camp here," Domhnull said, feeling his horse laboring with exhaustion. "Best, I think, to change horses and be out of here entirely."

"Aye," said Boc, full earnestly.

They did so, and Domhnull passed round the wine he had from Branwyn: "This should go first," he said, and felt their spirits lighten for it before they took to the saddle again, riding into the narrows.

"Lord," said Beorc, and Ciaran looked up at him in the dark, from his seat beside the spring. The others lay asleep, or feigning it, even the youth on watch.

"I sent the lad to sleep," Ciaran said. "Go to sleep yourself; I will wake Boda when I feel the need."

"I promised—"

"—Branwyn. Aye. To hover by me." He frowned, for Beorc squatted down before him, solid as a boulder. "I need no nurse, old wolf."

"Then go to sleep, my lord."

"You harry me, Beorc. If—" a shudder took him, which he tried to prevent. The land rose about him gray with daylit mist, with ill woven in it. "The sun has risen."

"Lord?" Beorc settled there, arms locked, patient of any madness.

"The sun in Eald, Beorc. When things have most power. But it is cold. Cold. This land has come back; she said it. It was lost to Eald and somehow it has come back again."

"How—come back?"

"Would that I knew how." He felt the chill again and touched the stone within his collar. He shut his eyes, seeking with that second sight, through all the maze that pent his vision. The stone seemed like ice in his hand. "I am cut off on all sides. It frightens me, Beorc. *She* was afraid. Trees, she said, as if one of the Sidhe could be alarmed at trees. But these are ghosts. And I cannot see past them. Neither could she, I think."

"Lord, let it alone."

"And sleep?"

"Let me rouse the men. We will set out now, and get you home again."

"I have sent Domhnull out there. I do not think I should have done it. The longer I am out here the less I find this place comfortable."

"He's a clever lad, and Boc is with him; and Caith besides. And Caer Damh has lost its yen for mischief, look you, not a stir from them all winter."

"They have been quiet," he agreed. "But, Beorc, the woods go *around* An Beag as they do us: I am not so sure of Damh. And I can no longer find the sea."

"What woods?" Beorc asked patiently, questioning a madman. "What sea?"

"Give me your hand, Beorc."

Beorc settled to his knees and gave it, and so Ciaran drew it to the stone.

O gods, Beorc said, or tried to say; and there was all of Beorc's self with him, far too close, and the trees were about them both. The earth began to sink beneath them.

No, Ciaran said, and took the stone in his own hand, trembling. The open land was about them again. The nightwind blew gently on his sweating face, and Beorc still knelt before him. It had been close, that third Eald which was Death's own. The wind from it still whispered.

"O gods," Beorc said, "how do you bear it?"

"Did you see the trees, old wolf, how they grow here?"

"I saw something. Like shadows. I'm not sure what shape they had."

"You have iron about you," said Ciaran. "I should not have done that. Beorc, I should not have sent him. There is something amiss I took no account of. This is

not the Eald I knew. It blinds me. I think it would blind
her. And I have less and less trust of it now that I'm
out here near it." He looked into Beorc's face, finding
fear where fear was not accustomed to be, and doubt,
where doubt had never been. It occurred to him that he
might lose this man, that he might already have lost him,
his loyalty, his love, whatever it was that a man gave
who had served him as Beorc had. The man that Beorc
followed had never faltered, never erred, not to this de-
gree, not with the lives of all else he loved. Small wonder
Beorc hearkened now to Branwyn, born to this land as
she was, heir of the Cearbhallain, as she was. Like Rhys.
Like all he had inherited. He came as interloper, and
led them all amiss. "I don't know what to do, Beorc. I
don't *know*."

"Lord, who does, in this? You have done the best
thing. And if it were wrong, then Domhnull will make
the best of it if it can be made: you sent those who can
bend what can be bent."

"Blind."

"With the Sidhe's blessing on him. Do you not recall
it? On all of us who serve you."

"Can you remember, then? Do you remember?"

"Not with clear sight, maybe, but I remember *something*. That I have seen the Sidhe. I remember—someone
at the table; and there was silver, and she was dressed
in white and gray—"

"No gray. She had no cloak about her."

"Or something like. But she spoke to me. I remember.
My weakness and my strength, she said. And about dark
and morning. I remember that."

"There was a time," Ciaran said, "that the stone let
me see. I have seen dragons, Beorc. Once. I have seen
the Sidhe ride to war. They are memories; or something
like, pent in the stone, but I can't find them now. Only
the mist and the ghosts, and I have led us deeper into
them, and sent Domhnull and Boc even farther. But the
King . . . the King, if he stood with us and not against,
if I could win my brother back to reason—" He shook
his head. "O gods, this mist surrounds him. Maybe I was
to do nothing. But they forget, the Sidhe; or they have
their own concerns and Men are small and brief among

them. Maybe if Men are to be helped—that is for me to do."

"Lord, let us get you back to the hold. Tonight."

"No," he said, just that. *No.* "Let me be."

Beorc nodded slowly, gathered himself up and retreated to his blanket, spread on the ground beneath the oak, where the earth was bare. The other slept. The horses were still. The wind stirred, in this world. The others were bound in leaden stillness.

Ciaran sat, and leaned his eyes upon his hand, for they stung with weariness, though there was no sleep in them. The mist gathered about him again when he looked outward with his heart.

Then a small lumpish thing hopped out of it and perched before him in elvish day. For a moment his heart froze in fear, but there was no ill in this creature.

"Man," it said, hugging its arms about its knees, "Man, o Man, this is a lost place. *Fair,* she said, a fair land, but Eald is strange here."

"What are you, wight?"

It sniffed and wrinkled its nose. "Wight, *wight* he names me. O why do you sit, Man? Things are amiss, amiss here. I have met the children and seen them home to the Cearbhallain's walls; and the dark man with them."

"What have you to do with them?" he asked. His heart was pounding. "What cause had you to meet them?"

A lank shaggy hand touched a shaggy throat. "Eald is about them. *She* sent me. O there is much amiss, Man."

"With them?"

"They are safer than you, far safer. O Man, Man, Man, there is dark, dark about your path. The Gruagach has seen it. Dark and bright together."

"She has sent you."

"To guard the children. She said there were saucers of milk for me. And the Gruagach has had them. He has seen your people, fine, polite folk they are, but o Man, there is trouble near them."

"Where?"

A shaggy arm reached out, long fingers waggled.

"The Gruagach. Is that yourself?"

It bobbed, still crouching, and its eyes glinted in their

darkness. It seemed to shiver. Whites showed as its eyes rolled. Its voice grew thin.

"Dark, dark and dark it lies—
O Man, there is ill, ill, ill."

It was gone. Vanished. He sat on the cold earth and a chill had come on him.

He leaped to his feet. "Beorc!" he shouted. "Wake!"

Men reached for weapons, scrambling to stand, sleep-mazed and frightened.

"Ride back," he said. "Tuathal, get to horse; ride back to Alhhard's steading and send the boy to Caer Wiell: they have a pony. Bid him go, and tell my lady we have need of half the men up here. The rest must stay with her. The rest of you, we are going north a ways."

"Lord," said Beorc, "you must not."

"Come with me," he said, and Beorc hesitated half a breath, then went after him. He had not doubted it, as he did not doubt now which way he was going, and that he was beyond advice.

They followed, muttering questions and doubts among themselves, but Tuathal was off as soon as he could fling a saddle on his horse, and for the rest of them it was northward.

Amiss, he kept thinking as they rode, and perhaps his face was grim, for Beorc fell in beside him asking nothing at all until they were well on the road again.

"Lord," Beorc objected, "we are nine men, and Domhnull too far ahead of us to recall him."

He said nothing to this. There was nothing to say, but perhaps Beorc had hoped there was an answer.

"You are not armored," Beorc said. "And against some things no Sidhe luck is proof."

There was iron. It made his bones ache, even such as the men about him wore. He argued nothing in return, only rode, and Beorc fell silent.

So they came beyond Caer Damh, in that strange fell hour when the sun was only promise; and far away on either side the land seemed wild and empty. The light had caught Lioslinn, which spread itself before them, a glimmering only, to show that it was water; but the day would make it mirrorlike, turning sky and earth upside down. The pass showed beyond, cloven between the hills. The horses shuddered under them for weariness.

Ciaran drew rein, seeking outward with the stone, but the mist was thick, making all his sight gray.

Then he felt the stirring of the land, the poison of iron. It was ambush.

"Men are there," he said.

"What men?" Beorc asked, implicit in his faith. "Can you tell that?"

"No. But about the lake: Caer Damh, perhaps, or the Bradhaeth folk." He shivered, and possessed himself again, in cold clear sight, with the dawning on the water. "Here we stay, Beorc."

"Nine men."

"Well," he said, "Tuathal will find us."

Beorc looked on him, ill-pleased by humor, then gave it the short reaction it deserved and gazed off toward the pass. "Gods grant Domhnull got through."

"So," said Ciaran, and stood in his stirrup, stepping down from the saddle. His horse was lathered. He patted its neck, and it stood three-footed. "Well, if things have gone wrong, we are soon to learn it. I think he has gotten through; I might feel it else. But when he comes back again this way—I think that we should be here."

"I should be here," said Beorc, sliding heavily from his horse, a weight of man and metal. "You—"

"I can see somewhat, and know them coming. What man of you else can do that?"

"One Bradhaeth arrow. That is all it needs, lord, and then how do I face your lady?"

"Ah," he said softly. "Well, but you will save me. You have done it before, old wolf. I have trust in you."

"Gods help us," Beorc muttered.

NINE

BEARING WORD

The sun began going down and Branwyn waited, in the hall, by the fireside; and Rhys hung about the hall, which was not his wont, but his brow had been dark since yesterday.

"I did not like this," Rhys had said when he had brought Meadhbh and Ceallach home. "I like it less now."

So he stayed and fretted, her cousin, and shared their dinner with them. "My lord will come when he will come," Branwyn had said, having made up her mind to it, resolved not to fret herself with expectations, for it was no small ride that Ciaran made. She knew it, having ridden here and there with him in their first years, as far as she ever had ridden in her life, which was to the sight of the Bradhaeth. She had reckoned already that there was no profit in standing all anxious on the walls, nor even in keeping supper waiting. When it came the hour she had her supper with Meadhbh and Ceallach and Muirne, and Rhys as well, and Leannan, who played now softly as she spun, the fine wool making a thread in her fingers, so, so, so, by firelight; and Meadhbh doing likewise, and Muirne; and Ceallach at nothing in particular.

"You were at making something," Branwyn said to him, for Ceallach often carved with his knife, and now his eyes seemed sad and his hands unnaturally idle. "Where have you put it?"

"I forgot," said Ceallach softly, with that same desperate look, and a small suspicion of ill crept into Branwyn's heart, the sense of something wrong with her son

as Meadhbh's downcast obedience was unlike her, her
uncommon attentiveness to the spinning she hated.
Branwyn drew her lips to a taut line and kept the wool
running, this way and that with the turning spindle. She
wanted to ask, and did not—*Iron,* she thought wildly,
*iron, iron, iron in that little knife. Ciaran could not bear
it, and now my son and daughter.*

Rhys stirred abruptly and walked out, again to the
wall, she reckoned, and never her fingers faltered. Something was amiss that Rhys knew and she could not ask
it, not with Meadhbh and Ciaran to listen, and in no
wise would they want to go to bed tonight until they
had seen their father.

"Was it good, your riding yesterday?" She was light
in her asking, as if she had never in the world objected
to their going. Two bright heads nodded, catching glints
of firelight, and there was not a glance from their eyes.
"Well," she said, lips pursed, the spindle turning ceaselessly, "well, your father has his ways about him. I recall
when we were younger we would ride out, when your
grandmother was still alive, you can remember her? And
you would stay with her and Muirne. And we would ride
and ride, once as far as the border, your father and I.
And do you know, he would chat with every farmer.
Come along, I would say—sometimes we had cause to
hurry. But they could always hold him, with ale to try
or some complaint to give—Many a time he would go
tramping off across some soggy orchard soiling his boots
to see how the fruit set on, or off to see some steading's
new plowed field up by the border."

"He would not delay now," Meadhbh said looking
up, and her eyes were fierce. "He would be thinking
of Domhnull."

There was such temper in her daughter. It dismayed
her, how so small words offended. Branwyn was quiet
after, only keeping to her spinning, taking her offering
back. It was the Donn blood in her son and daughter,
that made them wild, and sometimes, as now, that wildness wounded. One of them was enough, her husband
breaking out in stubbornness, brushing aside all her
counsel. She worked, flung all her attention at the
thread. Her children wanted nothing of her comfort. Her
son sat disconsolate, her daughter—*O Meadhbh,*

Meadhbh, Meadhbh! if I could hold you— But they were too old for holding. Nothing she said to her daughter was ever right. And Ciaran would not uphold her.

His daughter. He has his son. Could I not have my daughter? Am I always to be wrong with her? Round and round, the spindle. A bright-haired girl a-horseback, riding in the meadow, red her hair and black the horse, like fire and deepest shadow.

The thread broke in her hands. She shook her head and bit her lip and mended it, mending the vision, the fat bay pony Meadhbh loved. *No,* she thought, afraid of the sight she had seen, Meadhbh and not Meadhbh, and not the bay white-stockinged pony. She saw leaves in her mind, and water and greenness, the child walking into the forest. *His children,* she thought, *both his.* She wanted to talk to them, to chatter idly, to talk of something to fill the silence, but Leannan played that song he had made, sweet and minding her of that night in hall, after which all Leannan's songs had changed, and his old eyes had taken to looking into distances while he played.

A Sidhe song, she thought, the wood flowing smoothly again, and the harpsong moved like water. A memory rose up in her, of that night before this fire, and the smell of the boughs she had brought and the candles; but for all her gifts the Sidhe had ignored her and touched all the rest. *Feochadan. Thistle. So I called her. And now the children name her so. But it is Arafel. I know her name. I might call her. Where is my husband? I would say. Why does my son have such a look and my daughter spurn me?*

She looked at Meadhbh and tried a smile, finding her daughter looking up. Meadhbh smiled back but it was hollow. "That looks very fine," Branwyn said. How often had she found fault? Too often?

Her daughter frowned and bent her head to the hated work again, then glanced up. "I hear a horse," she said.

The harpsound died upon the air.

"Meadhbh," said Branwyn, but Ceallach was already running to the stairs, and Meadhbh was on his heels, trailing yarn and wool together.

"Lady," said Muirne, who need not have said a thing;

there were hooffalls, but of one horse, and the sound of
the lesser gate. One rider.

Branwyn said nothing, but kept at her spinning. Muirne rescued the yarn that Meadhbh had trampled and
sat down again in her place, started the spindle turning
again.

"I will go out and see," said Leannan.

Branwyn nodded, never stopping the work of her fingers as if it worked a charm against calamity. *I must not
run, not I, Caer Wiell's lady. It will be some small thing,
some one of the boys strayed late and far at hunting. O
gods, but one rider, but only one—It is some message,
something amiss; he is not coming; he would not come
alone, not he, not Ciaran; last to retreat, my husband, if
there were trouble.*

There were voices, calling this way and that. Muirne's
hands and work fell into her lap. Branwyn never
stopped, not though light steps sounded on the stair,
Leannan's, returning.

"My lady," said the harper, "it's some lad come with
a message. He's coming up."

"Well," she said, and let her work into the basket,
"well—"

But more than one was coming up the stairs now:
Rhys, and Ruadhan and a sweating farmer-lad with tousled dark hair; and Meadhbh and Ceallach hurrying
after.

"Here is the lady," said Rhys. "Your message, lad."

"Lady." the boy was short of breath, seemed prone
to stammer, an agony of waiting. "Lady, the lord he be
going up by Lioslinn last night, his man he bid me tell
you. Rode back last night, this man—Tuathal were his
name. He said the lord had sent him, and word were I
should ride here, but our old pony, lady, she were hard
put to run much, and I did try, lady, but I could come
no faster—"

"Was there more than that?"

"Aye, this Tuathal said the lord said half the men
must come to Lioslinn and quick as may be. He said, he
said, lady, the rest must stay by you."

"What token?" said Rhys. "Did Tuathal give a
token?"

"No, lord, he said he had nothing, that the lord had

sent him so quick—I be Eada, Alhhard's son, up by high
Bainbourne; and they passed in the day, they did, and I
saw this Tuathal with the lord, and after, in the mid of
the night he come—lord, my father and grandfather and
my brother be gone to him, and my sister run overland
to fetch them from Haraleah and all—there be men
there—best bowmen in all the border."

"Well done," said Branwyn. "Well done in that—Ruadhan—"

"Half the men," Ruadhan said, "as quickly as they
can arm, by your leave, lady."

"Go," she said, "go. Muirne: get this lad somewhat
for his stomach."

"Lady," said Eada, "I'd ride back again, where my
folk be—"

"Where you choose," she said. She looked at
Meadhbh and Ceallach, at their pale faces. "Doubtless
some matter with Caer Damh," she said, for them, wishing to believe it. "And he has wished to keep the way
open for Domhnull's riding back again." Ruadhan had
left, taking the boy Eada with him; Rhys should have
gone, but stayed, looking at her with that black-eyed
stare of his.

"Branwyn, cousin, I am going south. Tonight."

"This is some small thing," she said, "some matter
with Damh, and they have dwindled—"

"This is a small thing," said Rhys, "but it is on me I
should go south, now, tonight. I should have gone long
since; now I know it." He came and offered his hands;
she took them, looked up at him.

"I can spare you ten of the men with me; none that
are bound with Ruadhan."

"I shall go faster alone." His hands slipped from hers.
Meadhbh and Ceallach stood aside for him as he strode
for the door. He went out down the stairs into the dark,
and Meadhbh and Ceallach stared after him, hands
linked one with the other, so solemn, so unnaturally
solemn—

"Meadhbh," said Branwyn. "Ceallach. The men will
see to it."

They turned. They stared at her with the stillness of
thoughts she did not fathom. Not amazed, not bewildered. Anxious.

She held out her arms to them, wanting them. They came, and she folded them in her arms, and they rested there against her skirts. She told them no lies. One could not lie to them. It was the Sight; she guessed it. She might have asked them questions, but feared the answers.

"Rhys is going home to Dryw," she whispered; but they would know that. "To your great-uncle Dryw in the mountains in the south; there are all our cousins, and if there is trouble your father will come riding back in a moment; and we will shelter behind our walls if it comes to that, but it will not. Once our kinsmen come from the south, then there will be a reckoning, whatever the matter is. And perhaps Domhnull will persuade your other uncle from Donn, perhaps he will listen: your father at least is trying. But however it is, we will be safe here."

He has no armor, she was thinking. *O gods, at Lioslinn, in the passes up by Damh and him unshielded.*

"The road goes through the forest," said Ceallach, of the way that Rhys took. "And over the Caerbourne."

"Hush," she said, "hush, Rhys knows that road, and will he not be safe there? The Sidhe would never harm him."

They said nothing, nothing at all to that, but no one was comforted.

Soon the noise of the horsemen sounded departing the yard, and the greater gate groaned open. Branwyn kissed her son and daughter each and looked at Muirne. "Go find Siodhachan. And Hugi. Tell them I set Siodhachan over the hold and bid Hugi take nine men with him, scatter and rouse the farms from Gearr's northward and west and east—but quietly, quietly, no watchfires must be lit, nothing to rouse An Beag. Tell them—no, bid them both come to me, and I will tell them. Haste, Muirne."

Muirne sped.

"What shall we do?" asked Ceallach.

"Go down," she said, "Ceallach, tell Cein and Cobhan and the boys to bring in the horses at far pasture; Meadhbh—Yes, go with him. But neither of you without the walls: hear me."

"Yes," said Meadhbh, and dropped a kiss upon her

cheek; Ceallach pressed her hands and ran, and
Meadhbh scurried after.

He will say it was all unneeded, she thought. *I shall
have alarmed the countryside. Perhaps An Beag will hear
it and o gods, bear word of it to the King and do us hurt
for it. Caer Wiell, they will say, is warlike. And Rhys,
gods, Rhys will have roused Dryw, a moving of their
forces northward. The King will know it beyond any
doubt. And how then will we fare?*

She almost wavered. But her messengers were gone,
Rhys away from the gates, the riders sped for the
marches. She clenched her hands and waited.

The hold loomed shapeless on its hill in the darkness,
a mass which thrust up only one of its corners against
the backdrop of starlight. The rest was hid against the
higher hills about it; but it massed large, like some
crouching giant above its stream-cut valley.

Perhaps, Domhnull thought, they should have stopped
before this and not pressed on, but they had begun to
come under sight of cottages set high on the flanks of
the hills as they entered twilight—no great expanse of
tillage, not like Caer Wiell, but pasturage throughout the
hills; and dogs, most likely, and wary folk who might
view strangers with suspicion. It seemed best to him to
keep moving, quietly, and not to chance the country.

"No lights," said Boc. "Gods, how dark that pile is."

"I think it is the face we see," Domhnull said. "Its
walls and not the keep itself." Rough, lord Ciaran had
called his native hold; mostly shepherds, flocks scattered
in every fold of the hills round about; a keep which had
grown up as chance and invention built it, a wall here,
a shed there, a hall of rough stone and timbers—it had
never had to stand siege, Ciaran had said, except by
wind and weather.

They rode closer, the lonely clop of the horses' hooves
echoing off the cliff.

"Are we not reported?" Brom wondered, rearmost,
who led the other horses. "Surely the shepherds saw
us coming."

"Gods know," Domhnull said, and unslung his shield
from his back where he had carried it. So did the others
then, a rattle of wood and metal. With that thumping

on his left arm he felt at least some cover about him, for they rode near brush and jagged stone as the road followed the streamcourse. It was a place apt for ambush. His weary horse picked up its head, skittish at the sound of the shield, snorted in the darkness. He touched his heels to it and it moved a little faster on the dark trail, past trees and up again, with the walls and gates rising now above them.

"Caer Donn," Domhnull called out, "ho the watch, Caer Donn!"

"Who is it?" a voice drifted back to them. "What purpose?"

He was relieved at that hailing, reined in his horse with his men about him. "I am Domhnull Gaelbhan mac Gaelbhan, Beorc Scaga's-son's cousin, of my lord of Caer Wiell the messenger, and four men my escort. Open your gate for us."

There was long delay. Domhnull sat his horse and kept his shield on his arm while his eyes scanned the rim of the wall. His heart was beating as hard as it had at the worst of their journey, dreading words this time, not arrows: Go away, go back unheard, our lord will not admit you. No man behind him spoke, Boc, Caith, Dubhlaoch; and Brom who led the horses. Hooves shifted, clattered, restless: the horses saw a gate, thought of hay and straw and shelter, unwitting of all politics.

"You will come in by the lesser gate," the voice hailed them from the wall, "your shields at your backs, Domhnull mac Gaelbhan."

It was no more than reasonable, at this hour, with the dark behind them. "Do what they ask," Domhnull said, and slung his own shield to his back, tapped his horse in the ribs and rode forward as the lesser gate eased open outward, showing torchlight beyond it.

He passed beneath the arch, among boys who came to take his horse, no different than at Caer Wiell. He stepped from the saddle, looked about him, not missing the men who stood above the gate: archers, if they were needed. Caith came through, and Boc and Dubhlaoch, Brom last of all, with the string of horses. The gate slammed shut. The yard passed into the confusion ordinary with lads and half a score of horses.

"My lord will see you," a man came to say, a graying,

square-faced man wearing a gold chain that glinted in the torchlight, wealthier than the look of this place.

Everywhere was timber. Not a hold for war, lord Ciaran had said: it was far too much of wood, a mass of wood and stone before them, like some shepherd's cottage turned fortress, as if some giant had tumbled a hundred such cottages together. Here was a wall, there a corner, a second story of wood and stone overhanging, and some of the roof timbers jutting out from all of it. Steps went up to the doors, thundering and creaking under their heavy tread, and so they came into a smoky, timbered hall, a great long table in the midst of it, a fireplace burning, torches lit, so that light chased the shadows; and a great carved chair where a man sat with others standing by him.

Donnchadh, Domhnull thought, finding uncomfortable this place, this sitting in chairs like some minor king, when his own lord would have come down to the yard to meet a guest, or at least stood up to meet him.

"Domhnull mac Gaelbhan," said Donnchadh—there was no brother-likeness, none. This man was lean and gray as a wolf, where Ciaran was fair and golden. Half-brothers, they were. "My brother has some word for me, does he?"

"Lord, he sent a ring to you." Domhnull slid it from his hand—easily it slipped, when Ciaran had worn it on his smallest finger. He offered it, and gave it when Donnchadh held out his palm.

"Yes," said Donnchadh, "I gave it him."

"My lord sent it for a token." He looked into Donnchadh's eyes and for a moment lost all his thread of thought, everything unraveling—*I cannot,* he thought, *I cannot do this.*

"And wishes?"

"Peace," he said. "Peace and other things . . . He said—" His wits rallied; he gathered his forces, embarrassed. "Lord, his word was that he wished peace. That foremost. He says that silence profits neither. He spoke with me—" *O Gods, this is not easy. This man hates him.* "I am close to him. I know his heart. He thinks often of Donn, has thought, through the years, and wants to see you. Go to him, he said to me, and answer his questions, whatever he might want to ask—and bring back news again, and perhaps—"

"Perhaps?"

Shame flooded his face with heat. The word tangled on his tongue, echoed in this hostile hall. "Forgiveness."

Long silence afterward. Donnchadh stared at him, looked down at the ring, looked up again and his eyes were less fierce. "That is strange to hear from my brother."

"His word, lord."

"I have waited many years," said Donnchadh. His lips clamped taut. He looked down and slipped the ring to his own hand. "Well," he said then, "well, Domhnull of Caer Wiell. I know your cousin."

"Yes," he said, "lord." That little seemed safest.

"News. Is it news my brother wants? Well. You have had a long road and a dangerous one, and I am bound to listen. I have long thought he might have sent to me; and tomorrow you will tell me what is in his mind. In the meanwhile—in the meanwhile, there is rest and food, whatever you have need of." He beckoned to the man who stood nearest at his shoulder. "Geannan, see you to it."

"Lord," said Domhnull, "thank you."

"Tomorrow we shall talk at some length," said Donnchadh, "and I shall have thought, and you will. Go with Geannan."

Domhnull made his respects and his escort with him, and followed after the slight man in rich clothing who led them from the hall.

My lord, he thought, *would call for food and drink in hall, would be frank and open-handed.* He dismissed such carping thoughts. It was another hall, another custom, a sterner lord. He felt young before this man, young and simple, and felt the eyes of Boc and the others on his shoulders, expecting him to uphold Caer Wiell's honor, while bowing and giving courtesies in this place, before this wolf-eyed lord who sat high in the councils of the King in Dun na h-Eoin.

Pages came, meeting them in the hallway beyond the great hall. "I shall show you where you will lodge," said Geannan, "and the lads will see your men well fed and comfortable."

"I will go with my men," Domhnull said, but Geannan soberly caught his arm and drew him on.

"We would not have you say in Caer Wiell that we lodged you meanly, sir Domhnull; you will not report my lord in that way. Come, come, no mean lodging for your men; plenty of ale and perhaps cook will find some of that lamb we had for dinner. For yourself, perhaps some wine, and I know some of that lamb is left, and perhaps a slice or two of that good ham we had. I shall entreat the cook myself, and hot water, yes, and a fine feather bed, I'll warrant will be far better than the saddle. Did you ride straight on, then?"

"We had come into your lands. We thought it best to come and give an account of ourselves straightway."

"Wise, yes; the shepherds have the dogs out by night throughout the hills. There's little stirs but what they set to it. Ho, page, where are you going? Go straight ahead with that light: open up the west chamber."

Sir Domhnull he had become. This man Donnchadh had sent beside him spoke him fairly, delivered him to a room of wooden walls and fine appointments, sent the page scurrying with orders for fire, water, servants. Donnchadh from close-handed began then to seem generous beyond all expectation. He was dazed by this, and yet afraid.

Where am I in this great place? he wondered. *And where are Boc and the rest of us in this rambling warren?* He shivered, and looked anxiously in Geannan's direction as the man left him with promises of food and wine to follow, with a flurry of servants seeing to the fire, the fine soft bed, the warming of water for his washing. He was afraid. He did not know why this was so, only that it was in the air, the walls, a silence in which the soft sounds the servants made were all too loud. He remembered the shores of Lioslinn, the silences of the passes, the uncanny stillness of the rocks.

I have done a foolish thing, he thought, wishing he and his escort had never been parted; and then he shook off the feeling as too much caution. *I start at shadows,* he decided, suspecting the lord of Donn of some vague and tangled irony, to house him like a lord, exaggerated courtesy. *I should have been sharp with him,* he thought, wishing he were older or wiser in statecraft, or somehow more subtle in the ways of lords other than his own; or at least that he knew how to treat such courtesies as they offered.

The shadows were deep by the river, where the road ran, and the water whispered louder than the leaves. Rhys went warily in this place, marking how desolate it had become, how in want of tending—the King's road that linked all Caerdale with the plain, and all unused by honest folk, or by Caer Wiell in these years. He rode with all his weapons, with his saddlebags full of Cook's gifts, and now with his shield upon his arm, for he came to that point which ran between the river and An Beag.

Now, now, he asked speed of his horse, knowing silence would not serve him. It was less than likely that An Beag would watch the road, that any of those bandits would be devoted enough to duty to sit out on the riverbank in ambush in the rare hope of a man of Caer Wiell to murder—but anything was possible with trouble abroad in the land.

Brush loomed close on either side. Grass had grown in the roadway, and here and there a bush had taken hold, or brambles flung their spite out where they might rake the horse. The black gelding disliked this nighttime running, this uncertain ground: he used the spurs he seldom gave it and kept it going, reckless of such hazards.

It spent its strength, began to labor under his armed weight when they had come well toward the hills. He let it slow its pace at last, still beside the river, and now tending to Caerbourne Ford, the place he liked least of all.

The trees took him then in their embrace of willow fronds, trailing like a curtain darker than the starlit skies, caressing, cutting him and the beast off from sight—whisper of leaves and water. The horse danced and shied suddenly, finding something to alarm it. He touched it with the spurs, fended the willow leaves with his shield.

Now came Eald. He felt it, the haunted quality of the shore before him.

Now lend me luck, he wished, remembering that one had shed a blessing on him. He kept her memory in his eyes, in the dark before him—*o Sidhe, you promised.*

He found the ford, itself more perilous in the dark, in

length of time untried: the river might have carved new ways, made pits to trap horse and rider, brought down uncertain sands instead of solid bottom. He slid down and led the horse for prudence, waist deep in the Caerbourne's sluggish water.

The horse plunged. A thing slid past his thighs, large and live and horrid. He kept the reins and stumbled on, struggling in the water, and now the whisper of the river had the sound of laughter. The shore wavered before him. A second time the touch came at his legs, his waist, soft hands reached upward, clinging to his armor.

He flung himself toward the shallow water, fell to his knees and made the horse stumble by the pull on the reins, then regained his feet and hastened through the reeds, on soft and yielding mud, past dead and breaking branches.

He set his foot in the stirrup, heavy with his weight of metal, with the horse shifting this way and that and starting to move at once. It threw its head as he hit the saddle, and leaped forward, catching panic; he reined it hard, for branches whipped at them: they went blind and at hazard.

He held it; it walked, shivering. He shivered likewise, soaked to the skin and remembering what had touched him.

Each-uisge, Ciaran had said. Water-horse. River nix. A thing to frighten children. He feared as he had never feared in battle, in this path that he had taken, and ever and again he heard the sound of hooves, like a horse running where no horse could run, like the thunder of a gallop that grew loud and soft by turns, now on this side of the path and now on that, where the way to his own lands bordered Eald.

"Grant you mercy," he whispered to it. "We were quiet neighbors."

He did not give way to panic, not even when eyes like coals stared at him from out the thicket. It might do him harm, he knew it; but it went beside him, and his horse shuddered and shivered and snorted at its presence, that moved on hooves.

"Pooka," he said, "you do not frighten me. I have leave to pass here, and you cannot stop me."

The eyes never came again. The beat of hooves stayed with him.

TEN

CAER DONN

The morning came quietly in Caer Donn, a hush so deep and wide Domhnull waked slowly, eyes searching the place a moment, finding wooden walls and not the stone of his own room in Caer Wiell about him nor the swaying of a horse under him, but the steadiness of a bed softer than his at home, the breaking of full sun through the slitted window.

Daylight, he thought, ashamed, recalling that he had finally, far, far toward the dawning settled into sleep; and waked at first light and found his limbs still heavy, the place so quiet he was sure he had waked even before the servants were stirring. *A moment more,* he had thought then and shut his eyes, cherishing the warm spot he had made on the feather mattress, beneath the covers, and he had slept again, after all his restlessness, his night of listening to sounds where no sounds were, of nightmares of riding endlessly through the narrow passes so that the bed seemed to move under him, or again, his imaginings that there was no safety, that he had become lost in the windings of this place and that it had closed its gates on him to swallow him down.

If they wished, he had thought in the loneliness of the night, *I might vanish from the earth, I and all those with me.*

What men did you send? lord Donnchadh might say to his lord. *None ever reached me.*

Or Donnchadh might say nothing at all, since Donnchadh had said nothing in lo these many years. Silence could drink them up, and walls entomb them.

These are fancies, he had thought at last, with the light come to the window. *Now they will know by my eyes I have not slept, and what a figure I shall cut with them this morning.* So his eyes had closed. So they wanted to close now, as if all the due of days before had fallen on him.

But a certain disquiet began to grow in him. The halls were still quiet. There ought to have been some stirring about by now. He might have been mistaken in the hour the first time he had wakened.

See, my lord, the servants might be saying, *he is still abed for all these hours.* And Donnchadh wondering to himself at his guest's discourtesy.

His wits had come back to him; his limbs must follow. He flung the covers off, met the chill highlands air and braved it, more and more awake. He looked out the narrow window, with its view of daylit mountains, for here the keep met the wall and the window faced the land round about, the Brown Hills, stony and harsh and forever untilled.

It was far unlike Caer Wiell, with its girdle of fields and forest, of pasture where yellow flowers bloomed. The Brown Hills were well named, desolate and fit for sheep. Even the air was different, having no perfume of growing things from this windward side. The little stream in the cleft at the foot of the cliffs sent no sound up the walls; there was no rush of water and wind that was always with Caer Wiell. The hills were full of stones and harsh with brush and no flowers seemed to bloom here in this season.

He shivered, turned from the window and sought his clothes, the finer ones he had brought in hope of gentle welcome.

And so prepared, leaving the armor and all but his dagger that was fit for meat, he went to the door and opened it.

A page slept on a bench nearby, a thin lad, pinch-faced, who lifted his head at the noise and leaped up. "Lord," he said.

"I have slept too long," said Domhnull. "And not a

lord, no. But where is your lord this morning, and will he see me?"

"Oh, he be hunting. A wolf have got some sheep hereabouts, and my lord and the men be gone to find him."

"Ah," he said, chagrined. "Well, may I go to hall and wait there?"

"It will be long waiting."

"And breakfast."

"Oh, aye, breakfast, surely, breakfast."

"The men with me—where are they this morning?"

"O, my lord he breakfasted them in hall and took them with him. They thought they should not wake you. Stay here, my lord says to me, and see to his comforts."

Domhnull frowned, and the least niggling fear came on him, that Boc should have gone off without his leave. Perhaps they hoped thus to win Donn's favor and make amends for his shameful lateness, or perhaps Donnchadh had insisted, or a thousand other tumbling thoughts, not least of which was the suspicion that men who had known the war like Boc and Caith and Dubhlaoch might go their own way. "Well," he said, "well, I shall have the breakfast down in hall."

"This way, lord."

The boy led; he followed, down halls that thumped and echoed, with wooden floors, wooden stairs and walls, the antlers of deer hung here and there and whimsically adorned with candles unlit now that the sun came in the windowslits.

It was not the way they had come last night, in this warren. He remembered other stairs, no such decoration; but they came into a small warm hall where a cheerful fire burned in the hearth.

"This is not the hall," Domhnull said.

"Oh, it be the lesser hall, this," said the page, "and here my lord will come when he will come. It be far more comfortable than the other with its drafts and echoes. Sit here, lord, and I will see to breakfast."

"I am no lord," Domhnull said again, distracted in looking at the place. A table waited. There was a single chair and benches about it. *No lady. Donnchadh has never married.* The thought struck him strange, that he had heard somewhat of Donnchadh all his life, but never that he married, nor got children. He was rich and high in the King's favor—and for certain seasons of the year Donnchadh went down from his hills to the plain across the passes, and to the King's seat at Dun na h-Eoin, with entourage and banners and all such things, while lord Ciaran sat in Caer Wiell and never made the journey, save once or twice and that years gone, with bitter issue.

He had expected, somehow, more wealth and less of the rustic about Donnchadh. *It is very like some steading,* he thought, looking about him as he sat down at table. *Or some shepherd's cottage, if monstrous large.* It might have been a warm place, a cheerful hold. But here were no children, no running feet, no games nor childish laughter—no children of the lord or any of his folk. Perhaps they had kept them out of the way of untrusted guests; perhaps there were such besides the harried pages.

And women—surely women lived here. But there was no lady such as Branwyn, to have been in hall last night: that was the reason the hold had so strange an aspect, such a grimness, that no children disturbed the lord's dignity with games or broke the silences; a man could become like that surrounded entirely by men—*I should marry,* he thought distractedly, *get children, half a dozen at the least, have a wife to my comfort*—for until yesterday he had hoped only for some brave word that others might say of him, a little glory in his life. He had seen only Caer Wiell, and had ambition to see Dun na h-Eoin and the King, to ride to some war or other; and now that he had come into this place so different from his own, his longing was all toward home again, recalling how beautiful the fields were, how green the forest, how fine these things had always been and he had never seen them; how rich his lord was, and he had never known it—not in gold, not in such ways as Donn, but in many others.

Perhaps tonight, he thought, *will be harping, and folk will begin to laugh, deciding us no enemy.*

What will he ask? What shall I say to him? Gods, Boc, and why have you done this? It was not well done, to leave me sleeping.

His breakfast came—no maid came to serve him, but only the servants, a succession of dour men bearing

bread and cheese and meat in greater quantity than any
breakfast he had had in Caer Wiell.

Perhaps, he thought, *their guests were gluttons, or accustomed to choose and have their whims satisfied.*

"I shall ride out," he said, "and see whether I can
overtake your lord. Have my horse saddled."

There was silence for a moment. "Lord," said one,
"we will tell the seneschal and he will come to you."

So he waited, and so the seneschal came, that man
who had met them at the gates, he with the gold chain,
a graying beard, eyes very dark and narrow.

"I did not have your name last night," said Domhnull.
"Forgive me."

"It is Breandan."

"I would ride out," Domhnull said, "and join this
hunt."

"So the servants told me."

"I shall need a guide."

"Our lord gave no such order."

"So," he said, and all at once his heart was beating
harder, his wits racing this way and that.

"For your safety."

He gave a laugh, easy and merry. "Well, but I rode
that way by night, and worse."

"I could not permit it."

The laugh died. He stared at this Breandan. "Then I
take it on myself. Must I find the stable?"

"I could not permit it."

*Do I then break with this pretense? Ask them where
be Boc and Caith and the others?* He walked a pace or
two away, disliking the gray level stare upon him. *O
gods.* "And how long will this be, before your lord
comes home? How long must I wait here? I didn't plan
to stay overlong, sir Breandan. That was not my order."

"Not so very long," said Breandan.

"I shall go back to my room, then."

"As to that I have no instructions. I pray you wait
here."

"Is it so?" He walked to the fireplace and looked back
at Breandan. *And my weapons may not now be there.
No, I can be sure they are not.* "Where are my men,
sir Breandan?"

"I will inquire," said Breandan and walked toward the door.

"I had heard—" Domhnull raised his voice, "—that they were hunting with your lord."

"Why, that may be. I will inquire, sir Domhnull."

Somewhere below a door shut, hollow in the wooden halls. "That may be my lord."

"I did not hear the gates."

"Why, this is a rambling place, hall upon hall. All sorts of sounds come and go, playing tricks with the ears. Come now. I am certain that is he. Bide patient."

"And my men, sir?" He stood quite calmly for all that his heart was racing. "Do you think they might be with him?"

There were footfalls on the nearby stairs, a great number of men by the sound of them; and Breandan stood there smiling with perfect falsity.

So Donnchadh came, cloakless, in light boots, not a thing one would wear in hunting; and men came with him, all armed, all armored, and filled the back of the hall.

"Where are my men?" Domhnull asked him, following with his eyes this brother of his lord, this thin unsmiling man who went and took the chair at the head of the table, and drew it aside, and sat down in it at the front of the hall, as a lord sat who disposed of cases.

"What?" Donnchadh asked him. "What talk of men? I thought we were to speak of trust. Of peace. Of forgiveness."

"How was the hunting, lord? Did you take the wolf?"

"Ah. The wolf. It did not fare well, sir Domhnull."

"Where are my men, lord?"

"You have one refrain, it seems."

"Until I have an answer."

"Young fool. You will give the answers, alone here as you are."

"Alone. Is that my answer?"

"Fey you are. I have felt it since you came. There was a night, Domhnull mac Gaelbhan, that doors were shut in Caer Wiell; and strange things passed there, the sound of harping, all in private—they say that bargains were struck there."

"What, they? Have you made them say such things, to agree with all your fancy?"

"Bargains such as my brother struck before. Such as on the field at Caer Wiell. We know what that portended, and mark you, he was born least and youngest of all our house, and now has hold and lands and a name far and wide as defying the King. Evald of Caer Wiell took him in, and that was his undoing."

"This is all fantastical."

"Oh, but truth, all the same, sir Domhnull. Evald was a strong man, to die still hale and with a good many years before him."

"My lord loved this man. Evald was more kin to him than any of his house."

"But Evald died untimely, did he not?"

"All men die, lord. And none of us know the time of it."

"And there was this meeting, this gathering behind doors; and bargains struck and plans laid, how there should others die, opportunely. No lord has richer lands, more wealth of cattle and horses—the King's own cousin for his wife. Oh, aye, all men die, lad. Luck, for one, may leave them. He has bargained with the Sidhe to gain all that he has gained. I know it. There is nothing natural in his lands. And now he aims higher—oh, I don't doubt he looks to win me now. The King is failing . . . I doubt will last the summer. And now behind these doors in Caer Wiell, bargains are struck. You were in that room. You know what words were passed, and with what, and with what issue."

"The Sidhe warned him of hazards."

"I do not doubt, warned him of me. Come to me, he says now, come and be my brother, help me overthrow the King—"

"He has served his King better than the King has served him. Were even two of the lords of my lord's mind, then Laochailan King would be better served than he is. The Sidhe warned of danger; of some shadow hanging over us; and so my lord sent to you—"

"That I should take him to my heart."

"He has loved you. Twice he sent to your father. Now to you."

"This hall was lighter once, filled with my kin. Their bones are at Caer Wiell."

"They chose to be there, following the King. As you did. As Evald. As my lord. And without him—"

"And his allies of the Sidhe."

"He won your battle for you; and if cousins of his died, do you think he didn't mourn them? So did others die there. So cousins of mine, and my uncle. So no one of Caer Wiell but lost someone on that field. You are not unique, lord of Donn."

"And so he prospered. He and his allies. And now he sends to me, hoping to gain even more than he has. I will know what was said there that night."

"Nothing of concern in this hall. Much of reason. Of friendship."

"With the Sidhe."

"Lord, if what they say is so, there is Sidhe blood in him—on your *father's* side, lord. I do not know why you hate him."

A vein beat in Donnchadh's temple. His nostrils were white about the edges. "One of us knows another. I have the Sight, yes. What bargain has he made?"

"There was no bargain."

"And what is this thing he carries?—Oh, I do know, lad. I know many things."

"But the truth. Did you get that from your watchers? He sent us here honestly. He purposed nothing but your good."

"This meeting—this—visitation—"

"This meeting. You are too fearful, lord. There was no—bargain." *Back again to this,* he thought. *So we are out of words.* He half turned, to measure those between him and the door; and one face caught his eye among the five that guarded the way out, a small and scowling man who seeing him, smiled his ugly best.

"So," Domhnull said, feeling the sands slipping farther beneath him, "Coille. We wondered where you had gotten to." And louder, not taking his eyes from Coille: "Lord, did you know you shelter thieves? Or do you breed them?"

Hands went to swords, steel rising to the light. "Alive," came the word from behind him. "Take him alive."

"*Coille!*" he shouted and flung himself, dagger coming so deftly into his hand—Rhys had taught him: and into Coille's belly. He never stopped to account of it, ducked

low, snatching Coille's fallen sword and ran, staggered
by the blow that struck his back, by hands that tore at
him. He spun against the hallway wall, swung a two-
handed sweep across bodies oncoming from the door.
He ran. He felt a wound, his back, his side—some edge
had struck him. The whole keep thundered to running
steps, to shouts of rage: pursuit was close behind him,
below him, coming up the stairs he wanted.

He went for light instead—for the slitted window that
gave day into the dingy hallway: he was high in the keep,
he knew it, but that death was quick and better. He
leaped for it as they rushed about him. Hands grappled
at his clothes. The hills, the daylight blinded him to the
height. He thrust off from the sill and took it, a long,
twisting fall with the clean wind rushing past him.

Branches took him, snapped, speared at him in rapid
course like weapons.

He caught at them, tried to hold; and after, another
space of air, another hurtling, past rock where there had
been branches, one impact and another before his sight
was darkened.

Dogs were in his hearing, that fell sound echoing
among the rocks, with the sound of voices. " 'Twas on
the cliffside; he never got to bottom."

"Go round," someone shouted, "go round, up on the
hillside. If he is not below he has fallen to that brushy
shelf."

" 'Tis a long climb, that."

"Go, get the dogs to it, fool, and quickly."

His limbs drew up like a child's, like a child's kept
moving restlessly, and that movement relieved one pain
and brought another torment of sharp gouges at his
body, brush beneath his hands, then smooth and heated
stone, and the taste of blood, an ache so deep it had
shaken to the roots of his teeth and the center of his
bowels. *Bones are broken,* he thought, hearing the dogs,
and scrambled all the same, having his sight back, a jum-
bled view of bristly foliage, of light on stone, of leaf-
patterned shadow. He felt no pain clearly. It was all one
ache, and he got his knee up, the one that was not battered and strengthless, and staggered to his feet on the
cliffside. Depths swayed into his vision, sunbright and

deadly as he stood holding to the gnarled limb: they beckoned, sunlit jagged stones, without dread in them, but he veered away, took a step, another, for the hills and sky were in his sight, and he went to them.

Dogs are there, he thought. He could not remember how he had come there, or where he was; then did remember that there were two sets of voices, that men hunted him, that somehow he had come to die here. He recalled wooden hallways which had suddenly become this nightmare, and he had hit his head, and fallen. There had been branches: still he felt the sting of them, and those that had rammed into his body; he bled, wiped his face and brought his hand away liberally reddened.

Donn, he thought then, a sudden settling of vision; these strange hills which had made no sense to him were the hills of Donn. He felt the mass of the keep looming over him, himself toiling along a ledge full in their vision. The edge was there, another hurtling fall awaiting: his courage failed him. There were the trees, there was hope, if only for the moment, and that moment was all of life now. There was a man who meant to come up that hillslope, round its shoulder, so up to the cliffside; and that was one man, only one man of all those who served Donnchadh to hunt him through the hills.

He reached the hillside, the grass and brush, where old stones thrust up black fingers, doom among the wildflowers, the first small touch of color in this brown, dead land. He was naked on that hill, beyond the concealment of the trees, limping now with great stabs of pain up his battered leg and sides. Dogs barked and yelped. They were coming, his enemy; and now his sight was failing. The sky was dimmed to night, the place seemed stark and horrid, and small things chittered among the stones, wry and twisted shadows.

"This way," someone said. "O Man, keep coming. Hold out your hand to me."

He saw now a glimmering like a star amid the dark, and it grew as he went to it, a light, a warmth, a hope he went to for haven. His wounds ached with cold. His hand reached across the gulf and fingers touched his, took his, held them as he began to sink. A grayness wrapped him about, a cloak and enfolding arms. He was on his knees, rested his head against a shoulder, felt a hand upon his head as if he were a child come home. "There, be still, I have you."

There was the scent of leaves, of greenness, of rose and lilac, reminding him of Branwyn. For a moment he was content, but thunder muttered, and wind swirled about with voices. He lifted his face, met hers. The wind was in her hair, her eyes—her eyes were Sidhe and dreadful.

"O Man, what do you here among these stones? This is no place for you."

"Donnchadh, the lord of Donn—my lord sent me, Duine Sidhe, to make peace, and Donnchadh has done murder on us. I fell, I cast myself—o Sidhe!" He heard a thing crying down the winds, and struggled to his feet on the sudden, staring blind into the dark where stones rose like pillars lit by fitful lightning. "Sidhe, they must not take me."

"Hush, they will not." Arafel stood beside him.

"There is something out there," he cried, for something lurched and bobbed among the pillars, lost in dark.

"That will not harm you. O Man, you should never have come here. Did I not say there was no hope in the west? Did I not warn you? Go back, tell your lord—tell your lord—that there is neither hope nor help in others. Here least of all. Donnchadh deserves his pity."

"Pity? A man who has done murder on guests?"

She was a whiteness in his sight, as if some inner light shone through her; and then dimmer, the whiteness blotched with black about the breast and hands; dimmer still, and it was his blood upon her. "For Donnchadh. For Caer Damh, An Beag and Bradhaeth. Pity, yes. They are only Men, and snared in evil they tried to master. It lies beneath, about them. I gave you a gift to see such dangers, but you could not heed it: this place is overpowering, and it drew you here, *here*—" The thunder broke, and the wind battered at them in a circling, so that her cloak flew and her hair streamed on the winds, a scattering of light as if she bled; and the cold knifed into him, probing the depth of all his wounds. "That is from an older Eald," she cried against the whirlwind. "It blows from Dun Gol, from age and ill and malice—You fade, Man; you must not! Take my hand!"

He sought with his. Her cloak whipped about him,

and she found his hand and led him. He struggled on his aching leg, felt the wind even so, that shook them.

"Arafel!" a voice wailed, high and thin. "Arafel! Yield him up!"

"It is coming. O cling to me, Man. There is no iron about you, and you can hold here if you will. Do not let it shake you."

They came among trees, strange gray trees that groaned and gave hoarse voices to the storm. There was another light before them, nigh to the ground, like the fitful gleam of lightnings, and beside them as they went a small wizened thing scampered, hopping and leaping, using hands as much as feet.

"O," it wailed in a faint, piping voice, "o Duine Sidhe, ride, ride, ride. It is too great here, far too great. You must not contest it."

"Get him to horse," she said. "Gruagach, I bid you."

She was gone from him. He stumbled, full of agony, and arms took him up, arms warm and strong, bearing him like a child, as if his weight were nothing, with a scent of straw, of sun, of earth, a leaping that confused his sight and drove pain through all his wounds.

It hurled him up then, at the side of a startled pony, and he tried to hold to its mane, tried to drag his knees across; the wizened creature scrambled up before him, held his arm and pulled him.

"Come, come, come," it chided, "dark it bides, dark and lonely; o Man, o Man, the Gruagach must help her, the Duine Sidhe. O hurry, Man! This pony will not lose you."

"Help her," he wished it, but it was gone. The pony began to move, the trees flowing past: it ran, and he could not feel the running, as if it were not ground it crossed but air, a stocky, shaggy pony.

It came. The winds howled. Arafel held her ground and as it came she drew her sword, slender and silver, star-bright against the night. "Fionnghuala," she called, and behind her in the wind came the sound of thunder.

Then the winds fell, and the night grew very still, there among the ancient stones, which made an aisle: a barrow-walk, to the hill's dark heart.

And darkness stood there, which became a slim tall elf.

"Arafel," he said.

"Duilliath."

He smiled. Cloaked in black he was, and light that came to his garments died there. She held the sword before her and even its silver dimmed: this was his place, his power.

"Free," he said, "and of this place the master. Master of all this land. I have brought back—"

"Ghosts. Naught but ghosts, Duilliath. And sorrow. Let be. Go back. Sleep again."

He dimmed, and then became something more of substance. A sword like hers was in his hand, but blue stained all down its length—a thing of venom and tarnish. "O Arafel," he said, and settled on a stone, sword-hand on his knee, and gave her a gentle smile. "The bonds on me are broken, quite—and shall I tamely sink back to sleep? Oh no." The sword lifted, pointed at her heart, and the wind stirred among the grasses, a breath of cold. "We are too old in malice."

"Drow," she said. "I find pity for you."

"Pity. I have no such. I lost it."

"Is it a heart you want? There are many left; I keep them. Name the one you wish, and I will give it."

"Even yours?"

She laid her hand on that stone at her breast, feeling cold within it. "Is it what you ask? Yes. I will yield it."

"How clever." His lips smiled. His eyes did not. "And were I to take it, then you might bind me with it—so you hope. So you have bound that Man—oh, yes, I know, you've lent such a stone, but all useless to your minion. My workings overpower it. Soon they will overpower him. You are too liberal with such gifts."

"I had hoped you had more courage. What, doubtful which of us is stronger?"

"I am not a fool, to hand you such advantage." He rose, and held the sword before him. "The land is mine, Arafel. Its King is mine; its lords are mine—even that one yonder. Donnchadh. He hates us. And seeks powers of me to match his brother's—is that not humanity? He is in my hand. As Caer Wiell is in yours, but not forever. Ah, cousin, how well you kept things—Eald shrunk to so pathetic few trees, and no Sidhe stirring from it. Where are the rest, Aoibheil? Liosliath our cousin— gone too? You cast the world away. You might have ruled it. Fools!"

"You made one Dun Gol. Will you heap more dead there? More elvish bones? Duilliath, I remember what you were. I mourn what you cast away."

"Is that Man's blood on you?" The sword lifted. "Mortality. It makes breaches in your armor. But I shall let you go. Retreat, Arafel." The point advanced. "Or yield. Surrender I shall allow you. That would pay for my long waiting. We are many—oh, very many, we are thousands upon thousands. And yielding would be wiser."

"No," she said, lifting her sword, for he came nearer. "Take counsel from you, Duilliath? It never served you well. Why should I trust it?"

The wind hit, bitter cold. He leaped and thrust at her, and narrowly she parried. His face shone before her, pale beyond the lacery of blades, the leap and dazzle of light and elvish quickness. The winds fought for him. The numbness grew within her. Lightnings lit the hill and leaped among the stones, making his face a dark-eyed mask, his blade a blue-edged flicker. His armor turned the point; hers, human-tainted, must fail her; and constantly she gave back and back, her fingers gone numb, her defenses waning in the bitter wind. The blue-stained blade crossed her guard, its poisoned edge kissed her hand in passing.

She thrust at him in that approach, slashed his face and marred him. He shrieked and vanished from sight among the stones. The pit of the ancient mound yawned before her, whither he had gone. From it came the wind and the murmuring of many voices, malice beckoning. "Come," they said, "come down to us."

"Duine Sidhe," a small voice wailed behind her. "O Duine Sidhe, don't listen. The Gruagach cannot reach you down in the dark with him. Do not follow."

Thunder grew around her, and the light that was Fionnghuala. A small dark shape sat astride the elf horse that had come to her. It clung to the mane. It reached out a hand.

She took it, sprang with her fading strength for safety, and Fionnghuala bore them both away, the thunder of her hooves echoing off the valley; but that sound was dimming.

"Do not fall, Duine Sidhe," the small voice begged her, and strong arms wrapped about her. "O do not fall. They would all be on us."

"Get me away," she whispered past the thunder. "O cousin, I am poisoned. Get me home, to Eald, my Eald across the river. It wakes, it wakes, and now I cannot stop it."

The shadows deepened in the hall, and servants moved soft-footed. *Lost*, the men reported. *Lord, we cannot find him.*

"Then *search*," Donnchadh had said, so lights winked back and forth like fireflies through the brush and the dogs coursed this way and that, but then the rain had started.

Now he kept close within his hall, and drank red wine to calm the fears that gnawed him. *Lost, lost, lost.* The boy had had something about him, something of the Sidhe, and his men swore that he had fallen, that they had seen him hit the rocks. But he had vanished.

Man, the whisper came, just at twilight, with the rain adrip from the eaves, apatter on the wooden roof; and the Dark Man was there, in the shadows of the corner as he was wont to come, so that Donnchadh reckoned him a part of dreams, or some manifestation of the age of Caer Donn, from the ancient stones. His brother had the Sidhe; but he had ghosts, dark ones that flitted, that knew nothing of the perilous green shade, that whispered to him at night and brought cold where they passed like honest hauntings.

Man, he has slipped you, quite.

The presence came closer. It seemed to bleed, and the blood to steam upon the air, in thin streams down its pale cheek, like warm water on snow and ice.

What shall I do? he asked his counselor. *What advice have you to give? Who marred you?*

The Dark Man leaned near, two hands on the arms of his chair, confronting him so that his icy breath struck him in the face and the wine dregs spilled from his tilted cup. *Arafel is her name, the name of his power that aids your brother. She has taken this your brother's minion to safety, and now what tales do you suppose that one will bear to him? Fool, Donnchadh, fool ever to have breached your gates. You would not heed me.*

Donnchadh glowered, shifting in his chair. The eyes were close to his and dark and dire. He tried to face them.

My brother. I know my brother's allies, what they are. This power you promised me—where is it? Where is this Sidhe-touched boy?

Man, the apparition said, leaning close and smiling, beautiful and dire at once, *Man, what do you imagine me to be?*

Donnchadh thought of this, and it was hard to think of, the way it was hard to hold this face in his mind, even when it was looking into his own. *Ciaran,* he thought, recalling a fairness in his past, and sunlight on the hills, his mind shifting the way the face before him shifted, before there were the Sidhe, before he had known what his brother was, or what it was to rule. They had laughed in those days.

I am Sidhe, said the ghost, very softly, in a voice so indistinct it might have been any voice, but fair and shifting like light on dark water. *Does this fright you, Donnchadh?*

Ciaran! he appealed to that safe past, that time far away from this. But the sunlit hills slipped from him, bringing back the mist. *O Ciaran, was it this way with you?*

Does it fright you, Donnchadh?

The pale, the beautiful face filled his sight. There was the scent of damp aged stone, of old wood, of wind in the night. There was a touch at his heart, more subtle than these, and it was fear and desire of power. "Begone," he whispered—a whisper was all he could muster—and the mist was all about him. "Leave me, ghost."

Would you command me? You would need my name. Ghost, that is what you are.

My name is Duilliath. Banish me if you will. But do you think your brother will do as much with the Sidhe ally he has taken? Oh, you have always known what I am. I have whispered it in your dreams. I have said it over and over and tonight you have to hear it. Banish me, Donnchadh. And be alone. You have killed your brother's men. Come, speak my name; banish me if you like, now you have done murder. Why, I might side with him—or with some other lord of the land of Men, to make him King. Laochailan is fading. Your brother has his own ambitions. So does every lordling in the land. Will you banish me, Man, and wait for the armies to come against your wooden walls?"

The sweat was cold on Donnchadh's face, in the morbid wind. There was such an ill ease in him, such a gnawing uncertainty creeping through him as he had grown all too familiar. He feared. There was fear in the very stones underfoot. He felt stirrings all about him. The Sidhe owned Caer Donn; he had always known as much. The Sidhe, like Men, knew malice, knew connivance, made plots among themselves. This one Sidhe sided with Donn, belonging here.

Will you bid me go? it asked. The beautiful eyes were windows into the mist, the touch at his heart quite deft and sure. There was no resisting it.

No, he admitted. He did not want to admit this, but it was so, that he had no counselor but this ghost, whose advice had always been true. He knew the world; he had fought a bitter war; he had fought a different sort of war after, his house disgraced, his parents failing in health, his kinsmen all dead in the war or turning on one another. His counselor's advice had won the King, after all; gained him power while the lords of the land conspired and connived with a King who knew only plots and murderings.

Listen now, said the ghostly Sidhe, his Dark Man, the voice which had whispered through his thoughts for years so subtly he thought the thoughts his own. *You must gather your forces, quickly, before your brother can prevent you. You must not stand siege here. Caer Donn was never made for it; and if you are pent within these hills he will reach to Dun na h-Eoin and cut you off from the King. Move now, this night, while you have the chance.*

And do what?

Murder came to his mind, so soft and deadly a whisper it was not a word, but a vision, the King lying lifeless on his bier, the armies with their lances shining in the sun, advancing on the Dale.

Prevent him, said the voice. *Prevent him.*

ELEVEN

RETREAT

They were still there, the skulkers in the brush, and sometimes arrows flew: men of Damh and perhaps the wild men of the Bradhaeth with them, lurking round the margins of the lake, in reeds and willows. And in every hiding place of the hills sat the countrymen of Caer Wiell, farmers skilled with bow and spear, and sword if it came to that, grandfathers and striplings not a few, for the word was out and the archers came, not alone here, but all along the marches, bands of kinsmen and not a few bow-skilled daughters ready for any outbreaking along the border.

"Go south," Ciaran had said then to the folk of Alhhard's steading, who had come first and feathered a good many of the lurkers about Lioslinn. "You and all your neighbors, go up and down the Bainbourne, and keep a watch, in case An Beag should grow restless."

So Alhhard's sons went and Ciaran watched them go, not without misgivings. "An Beag will carry tales," Ciaran said glumly, "and the King will hear how I make war and stir up the whole countryside. If there is some attack of An Beag they will say it was I who moved on them."

"Go back to Caer Wiell," said Beorc. "There is no more need for you to be here. Less talk if you are back where you belong, and what passes up here is my doing."

Ciaran gave that no answer. He was weary of Beorc's asking, and walked away, sheltered by the hill. He wore armor of a sort, that country folk had gotten him, of laced leather; and there was talk. There could hardly be otherwise, how their lord was faery-touched and could not bear sword or iron, how he bore an elvish stone next his heart and flinched from Damh's iron-tipped arrows. He saw their looks as he passed them in his wandering along the lines, and felt the silence they paid him as if they had seen some direr sight than a tired, graying man in motley leather. By day he had stopped and joked with them as he had talked sometimes over fences in his riding through the land, but there were always whispers in his wake: he knew it. Now he passed along the ridge without a word except sometimes to greet a man familiar to him, like Cuinn of his household troops or Graeg of Graeg's steading. But mostly there were whispers. Likeliest, he thought, the folk of Caer Wiell had done a good deal of free talking to their cousins and brothers of the steadings; and there was no stopping the tale-bearing.

He wearied of it, beyond all bearing, felt solitude heaped upon his shoulders, and even Beorc resisting him, Beorc, who spoke less and less of Domhnull and took wilder and fiercer chances, flinging himself toward any point of hazard he suspected his lord might take instead. An anger burned in Beorc; he felt it in the stone, a dark thing that looped and twisted all round their long comradeship, through blame and guilt and a rage that smothered itself like banked fire.

You never should have sent him, lord. He went to keep you from it. And you were blind. But Beorc would never say it.

He went back to that post he had kept in the evening before, a stony knoll that gave view of the lake and hills. Here they had held when the riders from Caer Wiell had reached them—reached them in the midst of battle, and taught their attackers somewhat of respect. That had been one of the good moments of their holding here—but less good for Boda who would not be riding home to his wife; and for other lives they lost. The sky threatened; a feeling of ill had grown in the air since morning, and now the darkness that lay over the northwest was deeper and direr, shot with lightning, though it seemed only a cloud to mortal sight, a bit of weather to the west. . . . "Get firewood under cover," he had heard his captains order. "That'll be on us by nightfall."

There was no sunset; the west was bound in murk too

thick for sun to color it; and if that sight was grim, the surface of Lioslinn took on a leaden gleam that made it even less wholesome than before, a well of mire and dread, rimmed in shadowy reeds. *Wrong,* it cried to any with eyes to see it. Elvish sights should be fair, of green trees and silver; and this was not. This was corrupted. The hills rose like iron walls beside it, and trees were fallen, burned, laid waste.

"I do not like this," Beorc had said a day ago, when they waited attack. "This place weighs on me as nowhere I have ever been."

That from Beorc, who was not one to start at shadows. And the house troops, newly arrived, went about with haunted looks, glancing much toward the lake and toward the west, but that was no more than the countrymen had been doing before them.

"Lord," said Beorc now from behind him; but he had heard the tread in his wake all the while he had come this way, and known Beorc was following, his relentless shadow. Beorc reached him and crouched nearby on another stone, his guard, his warder, not to be shaken from his heels.

"It is worse," Ciaran said at last, for with his Sight he saw no difference now in day or night toward the west.

"I would you were away," said Beorc.

He had no more to say to that than before, and for a long time Beorc was silent.

"I feel it," Beorc said at last, "this storm. Others do. I'm sure of it."

"Was it not her gift," Ciaran murmured, "to see such things?" He thought of Domhnull, as he reckoned Beorc was thinking—the boy, loyal to him, going ahead in spite of all his Seeing.

Then it seemed to him that he heard hoofbeats in the dark, and the stone began to burn against his breast.

Beorc had spoken. He could not get it clear. He rose. "Be still," he said. "O my friend, get your distance from me—"

It was coming from the pass, he thought. All the world seemed stretched and distorted, like iron under fire and hammer. He saw fires in the murk, and twisted trees and a darkness coiled and monstrous within the lake, stirring in its sleep.

The hoofbeats grew louder, and hounds bayed, voices mingled with the wind.

"Lord Death," he whispered, and struggling to see the Man beside him: "Beorc, Beorc, run, get away from here."

Iron shuddered in the air, the rasping of blade from sheath, and poisoned the wind. "Not I," said Beorc, there by him, if dimly through the pervading murk. "Lord, *what is it*?"

"The hounds, hear you?" The baying filled heaven and earth, and the brush and grass whispered about them like a gathering of many voices. There were clouds, and dark shapes coursing among them. His arm, once torn, turned cold and painful as the stone upon his breast. Fleeting things shredded on the wind, and voices shrieked in it like voices of lost children, of wounded animals, of dying men and the clangor of battle.

A moving shape appeared in the distance, like a shape cut out of night, and that shape became two riders, one tending northward and one coming straight toward them, smaller than the other and less dire—it seemed no more than a pony, running silently amid the wind and the lightning, its shaggy coat and mane aprick with points of light as if marsh-fire had settled there, and light glowed on the bright, bowed head of the rider slumped across his shoulders.

"Domhnull," Ciaran murmured, and louder: "Domhnull, *Domhnull*!" —with his hand upon the stone and running now, half in faery, to reach the pony. The hounds of Lord Death coursed about it, a tide of darkness: the pony threw its head and shied, and for a moment there was mist about them, and whirling shapes wind-carried.

"My lord!" Beorc cried, and reached him, as the winds turned watery, sluicing them with rain. The world had shadowed, the clouds had gone to greenish murk shot through with lightning and rumbling with thunderclaps that shook the ground. "Lord, stay—the men of Damh—"

He shook off Beorc's hand, running and wiping the water from his eyes, sodden with it, searched among the gorse and brambles and found a body lying, bright hair darkened with rain and twilight, in soaked clothing better suited to some hall; and that torn and stained with blood the water sought to purge. "Domhnull," Ciaran said, sinking to his knees. "O Domhnull."

Beorc likewise knelt and turned Domhnull over, his face to the rain, white and stark in the lightning; but breath stirred and one hand moved as if he would fend the flashes off him.

"Domhnull," Beorc said above the rush of water. The lightning flashed again. Pale flesh shone through the shreds of his garments, and Beorc rested his hand on Domhnull's side, on pale new scars. "A month or more healed—o gods, what could have done this?"

"The Sidhe," Ciaran murmured, shivering in the rain. "He has been with the Sidhe." He took Domhnull's cold face between his hands and wished upon the stone. "Domhnull, Domhnull, *Domhnull,* hear me."

The eyes opened, bruised and vague, blinking in the rain. "Lord," he murmured, "cousin, I fell—the dogs, the dogs—"

"Hush, be still. You fell from the pony. But the dogs are gone."

"Lord," said Beorc, "let us get him behind our lines."

"They are dead," Domhnull murmured, "the others,"—but Ciaran took this without question, and worked with Beorc to gather him up between them, his chilled arms locked with theirs. Domhnull tried to walk, limping as he did, and kept talking as he went, of treachery and dark and shadow, of murder and the lord of Donn, but this Ciaran had already begun to know—long since, that all his hopes were fallen, and he had sent good men to their deaths.

"At least I have you back," he said to Domhnull when they had lain him in warm dry blankets in such shelter as they had. "You must rest now." But he had seen the scars, the dreadful marks on him in the lightning.

"Go home," Beorc said gripping his arm, making him listen. "You would see them return, you said. Now you have got back all. There are no more. What more is there to do—what hope here?"

"None, None here. I shall go home." Ciaran stared into the dark with the rain trickling down his neck. "I shall withdraw all the forces but what can keep the Bradhaeth in its place. And Damh. We shall more watch than fight. My brother has answered me, I understand that well enough." Breath was short in him. He caught another, that pained him like the stone, and his eyes burned in the rain. "I shall go home."

A moment's silence. Then Beorc left him.

He shivered, flinching at the thunder. The rain in the puddles gave back the lightning where horses had churned the ground and rain smoothed it again in pockmarked sheets. *Arafel, was I wise? I think that I was not. O gods, answer me. Arafel!*

Domhnull slept, sometimes, clinging to the neck of the pony they had gotten for him, a farmer's elderly beast with a placid, rolling gait. Sometimes he dreamed that it strode the winds or trod on mist, swift-footed and magical, but in the intervals of his waking he found an ordinary pony and plain dalelands mire squelching about its muddy hooves, so that he grew confused, whether the other had ever been, or whether the horror that had happened to him had ever happened at all.

But now and again Ciaran rode by him, and then he would speak disjointedly the things that he recalled, knowing that he was making a muddle of them and trying to pull them into order—of Caer Donn, of Donnchadh, of Boc and the others.

"Did Donnchadh do this to you?" Ciaran asked, and there was anger in his voice. And at last: "Domhnull, give me your hand, give it me."

He gave it or yielded it, one, across the gap between them; and then a kind of strength flowed into him, surcease of misery. They had gone somewhere together, he and his lord, and it was gray and full of mist. He was sitting—somewhere, on the grass, it seemed; and his lord was sitting by him on some higher place gazing down at him—but a Ciaran strangely changed, whose brow was smooth, whose fairness burned like the sun in this shadow, whose eyes compelled the truth as he questioned him, this, this, and this, and he answered as he must.

He is like a king, thought Domhnull, surprised to think it. *And if the land had had him for king and not Laochailan, then none of this grief would have happened.*

He remembered other things, the Sidhe, the darkness: he told it, remembering now.

"Stay," his lord told him, and rose up from where he sat and tried to go further into the mist. It seemed he sought something, but the mist was everywhere concealing it.

"Lord," Domhnull cried, getting up from where he sat, fearing to be left behind. He tried to follow after him, but he had not the strength, and small twisted things writhed out of the mist to draw him down into the depths with them.

Of a sudden his cheek was against the pony's rough neck, his wounds paining him with a dull ache, and when he struggled to sit his lord was riding safely knee to knee beside him.

"You will fall," Ciaran said quietly. "Don't try to sit up."

He paid no heed to this, riding for a time with his hands on the pony's withers. Beorc came to his other side.

"He has come back to us," Beorc said.

"Aye," said Ciaran. "Domhnull—don't fret yourself. We are bound for home now, well inside our lands. Rest."

There were armed men about them, more troops than they had begun with; but he let that confusion pass. He felt of his wounds and found scars instead, and bone well knit, if aching. The wounds had stopped bleeding and hurting while the Sidhe had held him in her arms. He had come home, revenant among the living. He had gathered things instead of his youth—wariness and toughness. But he had been outside the safe world and came back meshed in Eald so thoroughly he drew shreds of it with him into daylight, to haunt his waking. He had the memory when he shut his eyes of that hurtling fall past rocks and branches, that long, long tumbling in the air and the shock of landing that was no bodily pain, but a shattering slippage between life and dream.

Arafel, the voice had called her name. He recalled her bleeding light and strength into the gale like a candle that must soon fail. *Arafel. The Gruagach, and the Horseman.*

The wind blew cold on his face, on the tracks of tears.

Something bumped his knee persistently and someone drew a cloak about him and touched his shoulder after. A face lingered in his vision, hair and beard like blowing fire.

"Beorc. I fare well enough."

"That you do, cousin. But let me take you up. Old Blaze can carry double."

"Boc is dead," Domhnull said. "Caith and Dublaoch and Brom—all dead; I hope that they are dead. There is an evil in that place—" Panic beckoned. He refused it, speaking calmly, his eyes fixed on the pony's ears and the riders in front of him. "I let them part us. I never should have done that."

"No more of it," said Ciaran, close by him on the other side. "Boc at least was a wily old wolf and so were Caith and Dubhlaoch, and Brom was a borderer; don't suffer so for their sakes. They were not children to need your guidance; and living past a battle where friends were lost is no shame, gods help us else. They had many battles, themselves left friends behind, at Dun na h-Eoin, Caer Lun, Aescbourne, and Caer Wiell."

"A plague on leaving friends."

"Oh aye, but that is life and death, my friend." And with that came so bleak a look on Ciaran's face that his own grief seemed dim and cold. They rode side by side, he with Beorc and Ciaran; and in time the dimness came on his eyes again. Hands steadied him; he went forward gently, lay his head against the pony's neck, lost but homeward tending.

Fionnghuala went slowly now, among the silver trees, and so the Gruagach slipped from her back, leaving Arafel to ride while he walked before the mare.

Here was home, and peace, but the elf horse trod on leaves, fallen leaves upon the grass, where seldom a leaf had fallen, under the elvish moon. Ruin had touched here too, if more softly.

There was a stream. Men called it the Caerbourne; in Death's realm it had a name. But here it was Airgiod the Silver, and its waters were clear and healing. Fionnghuala waded it and the Gruagach went across like an otter, shaking the water afterward from his shabby pelt as the elf horse tended on her way with her quiet, drooping rider. But the Gruagach delayed, cupped up water in his ample palms and hurried after, his wrinkled face all anxious and earnest.

"Here, Duine Sidhe, here, o drink, the good bright water, will not the Duine Sidhe?"

Fionnghuala stopped very gently. Arafel leaned from her back and bent to the brown, uplifted hands and drank, then rested so, her arm about Fionnghuala's white neck, her eyes gazing into the earthen brown of the Gruagach's.

"Go," she said. "Have you not your farm, Gruagach? Have you not your Men? You have stayed long from them. Who will weed their gardens, little cousin, small brave Sidhe? Weeds will grow there, and brambles. Be free and go tend them."

"You must not die," wailed the Gruagach. "You must not leave us."

"See the leaves. Go. You cannot help me more. And your land will need you. I do not know the issue, but of that one thing I am most sure. This is Eald's heart, and if I am not safe here I am nowhere safe. Go. Go home, the third time I command you."

"Duine Sidhe!" it cried, but Fionnghuala began to move again, gently, leaving it behind.

So Arafel rode deeper into the wood, where trees rose like silver pillars, and the leaves shone with light. A gentle chiming sounded here, in concert with the breezes that wafted sweetness. She passed into the heart of this grove, where rose that grassy mound spangled with flowers, and shading it was the greatest of the trees: Cinniuint was its name. Upon it hung thousands of such jewels as that moongreen stone about her neck; and elvish swords and arms such as her folk had carried once in their wars, hung here and upon Cinniuint's fellows, so that all the air in the grove seemed alive with light and sang with memories as the winds would stir the stones.

Here she found strength at least to slip from Fionnghuala's back, and she sank down full length on the grass, where the coolness of the earth touched the fever in her. For a time she rested so, from time to time feeling Fionnghuala's breath upon her.

"Go," she bade the elf horse. "Go back to Aodhan."

There was a clap of thunder, a breath of wind. So she lay alone, upon the mound in the moonlight, and for a long time she was still in her pain.

Then a leaf settled to the earth before her open eyes, and others. She lifted her head, seeing a rain of leaves, the trees all dimmed.

Horror touched her, a shivering of weakness. She gathered herself up and laid her hand upon a bough of Cinniuint, so that his light brightened and greened somewhat, but that healing cost her dear. An ancient, irreplaceable tree perished then from her Eald, at its far margins, faded into mist and into Duilliath's domain forever.

From Cinniuint to others she passed, and to the youngest, precious to her. Miadhail was his name, the only tree to be born in Eald in long ages; and he was slim and new, scarcely of her own stature. Here too were fallen leaves, silver and shining in the moonlight. To him most of all she gave strength; and touched the leaves and the stones of Cinniuint, calling forth memory—but all the stones recalled was war, the dread age of conflicts past, and despair that followed.

"Miochair," she named her lost comrades, "Gliadrachan." From those two stones came no help, but sorrow. She named others, yearning. "You have left me," she cried at last, "and where have you gone across the sea? Is there hope there?"

There was silence, only silence, except the wind striking stone on stone, a hollow chiming.

"Liosliath," she whispered; but the lord of Caer Wiell had that stone, and those memories were lost to her, dearest of all. All about that name slipped away into the mist, leaving only the sorrow, the memory of the gulls she could no longer hear.

Fear was on her. Poison ate at what strength she had. Once the deepest despair fallen on her had been that sound of waves which sometimes whispered from the stones, the promise of the sea: *Dreary,* they said, *is all the world that Men have touched. The sea is wide: who knows what we shall find?*

But now the darkness lay between, and there was no hope of such retreat. The trees went one by one into Duilliath's Eald, and ghosts rose up to haunt her.

Duilliath, the leaves whispered, shivering. *The spring is past, our summer passing; there is only autumn and then the winter. Liosliath is lost, lost, lost.*

War was all about them now. The Bradhaeth stirred; there was the ring of steel in An Beag and in the south, where one she had touched had come to his own; there was ill in Dun na h-Eoin, and worse to follow.

She sank down, shut her eyes, her arms folded about her, shivering. She had no more refuge but this, and somewhere the Gruagach scampered and hid, for evil had gotten to the edges of the Caerbourne, and swam within its waters, not the water-horse, but some more baneful thing.

Fear touched her; it was the poison in her veins. And when the elvish sun had risen she cried aloud to see the trees, for there was the touch of golden autumn about their silver green.

Fool, Lord Death had called her. Men had spun this thing, an outlaw in her forest, a harper, a throneless king she had never seen; An Beag, Caer Damh; and latest of portents came Ciaran Cuilean, son of Eald and Men, who had called her name three times and bound her to his aid.

The most innocent had done her greatest harm. It was the way, between elves and Men, that they were fatal to each other. And now the leaves fell, edged with gold, and the wind from Dun Gol came skirling among them.

A resolution settled on her. She lifted her head. "Aodhan," she called. "Aodhan." And without the third calling of his name Aodhan came racing down the winds, with Fionnghuala close beside him. His ears were pricked, his fireshot nostrils drank the breeze for all that it could tell him, his coat gave back the elvish sun in light; for a moment he had joy in all his bearing, then sinking sorrow.

"No," Arafel said softly, touched to the heart, for each time that he was summoned there was so clearly one thought in Aodhan's heart, one hope. Of all the great horses who had served the Sidhe, all had gone beyond the winds but these two, Fionnghuala because she served and Aodhan because he waited, hoping still for one special voice, one remembered touch, that had been Losliath's, last of elves but herself. "He is not here,

Aodhan. Go. Seek for him as far as the sea if you must. Be wise, be wary; call to him there and maybe he will hear."

It was scant hope, when all others failed, when the stones went silent, that Aodhan could link her to the sea. But Aodhan flung up his head and was gone upon the instant, the both of them sped in a clap of thunder. Then the thunder came back again in little mutterings, for Fionnghuala had stayed, stamping and pacing and shaking tiny lightnings from her mane. The elf horse gazed at her in seeming sorrow, walked closer and nosed at her where she had sunk down upon the grass, giving her soft breath upon her offered hand.

"No," Arafel said softly, "not for me the sea, dear friend, not now. You do not understand, do you? I would you would follow Aodhan. It is almost without hope, his going; but let him try; and when the darkness comes, then run free, run far, be wiser than Aodhan."

Fionnghuala nosed her cheek gently, breathed in her ear and went away, head dropping, disdaining the tender grass. A few leaves drifted down, sliding off her white back, and she vanished within the silver wood like a ghost of a horse.

Then Arafel drew her sword and strove with trembling hands to clean it of the tarnish of the blood that was on it, while constantly the wound on her hand burned, healed but not healing, painful as iron. Constantly she must give what strength she recovered to keep her Eald from fading. The sun itself seemed dim—chimerical as elvish suns might be, yet this day seemed dim and strange, and now and again tendrils of cloud drifted across its face when it was high. She did not trouble to banish them; she had not the strength now to spare. But when the sun had passed toward the west a premature darkness took it, and elvish night came early.

Then she shivered and wrapped her gray cloak about her, for the wind out of the north was cold, and the clouds took more and more of the sky to themselves, cutting off the stars.

Something snorted, horselike, and hooves trod the earth. She leapt up, startled by a darkness greater than the night, and twin gleams of red within it; but it took a twofooted shape then, betraying itself.

"Pooka! When had you leave to come here? You are too bold by half."

"The Daoine Sidhe were never hospitable." Seaghda tossed his head and blew a snort hardly less horselike. "Men have entered Eald. Do you not feel them?"

She folded her arms the tighter about herself. The world seemed shrunken and cold. "Go away," she said.

"You are dimmed," the pooka said. "Something has befallen you, Duine Sidhe." His nostrils flared; his eyes were wild, his hair blowing in the wind. "You would go further, in spite of all my warnings; and now the shadow comes, it is loose upon us. The Daoine Sidhe have betrayed us as they did once before—faithless, faithless."

"Not all." Her voice trembled. "I tell you so. Flee for some safer river, pooka, safer than the Caerbourne. And be not forward with me. This is no place for you. Nor any place of safety."

"Where will safety be? Where is refuge? Or do you know one? They wake, Duine Sidhe, they wake. And you are fading. See—" He held out the simple brown stone that was his soul, cupped in his dusky hands. "I have not forgot. Run with me. I am strong to carry you. I shall never tire. No master have I ever served, but favors I remember."

Anger fell from her. She smiled somewhat, despite all the pain and dread, so simple he was, so earnest in his offering. "O pooka, I wish it were so easy. No. I cannot. I was rash, and bitterly I paid for it. I shall try to mend it."

His shoulders fell; his hands dropped. A third time he snorted, seeming to laugh. "A Duine Sidhe is wrong."

"O cousin, all of us have been wrong at one time or another; perhaps the Daoine Sidhe more often than most."

"There was a Man," the pooka said after a moment, perplexedly, and tossed his head as if to mark the way, "dark like me, Sidhe-blessed. He walked in Eald and I did not frighten this one."

"Ah," she said, "yes. I know him."

"Others I might have harmed." His head lifted. His red eyes glowed like coals in the murk. He took the stone into his mouth and the black horse whirled and fled, mad as all its kind, and wild.

She gazed after him, seeing only darkness about Eald, Duilliath's advance. The pooka would, she thought, fare well in the coming storm. Mirth and lawlessness were in his blood, and he was short of memory. No drow could ever tame him.

The night wrapped the more deeply about Eald. Small creatures, the fey, strange deer, hares, a timid hedgehog, foxes and a moon-eyed owl—these had crept to the grove and now returned, the latter with a flapping of wings. Here was a little safety in the dark, in the glimmer of the trees.

But the leaves flew, dying, on the wind, and the stones jangled discordant, dimmed and all but lightless.

Listen to me, a voice breathed through that wind, like hoarse, resounding brass, *failed you are, but the task was hopeless. Come to me, come to me, and I shall give you Caer Righ again, the trees, the smell of them on the air. Come, Aoibheil.*

She shivered. "Begone!" she cried. "Go to sleep, seducer! My kin you won, but never me, never shall, old worm, deceiver—go back! Go back!"

In the depths of Lioslinn was laughter.

She banished it, gathered her strength, wove silence about the heart of Eald, a web of light and quiet. The stones shone again. She forgot the voice. But her heart had weakened. She lay still then, on the mound, amid a drift of golden leaves, and slept in the dreams of vanished Sidhe.

A dragon rose in them; he whispered, and Sidhe cast away what made them Sidhe—*Duilliath,* she mourned, remembering. *My cousin.*

Come, it said. *Enough of Men. It is too tame a thing, that the Sidhe should pass like this, unresisting. You have power. Use it to save the land, to keep the world what it is. What has pity won you? Think of pride, and anger.*

"You wish to live, old worm," she whispered back, still dreaming.

Do not you?

It was the poison in her, the pain that flowed like ice. It filled her dreams. Vengeance, it whispered.

But even in her dream she wove the web, and the wind died into silence.

TWELVE

OF HOME AND HOPE

Nothing was the way it used to be, Meadhbh and Ceallach reckoned that. The men went armed back and forth out of the hold, and their father talked seriously to farmers who had come from the farthest steadings afoot or on hard-ridden ponies. They eavesdropped where they could, hearing news of skirmishes that made small cold discomforts in their stomachs, names like Lioslinn and the Bradhaeth, and a fight over by Raven Hill where Caer Wiell's farmers had thrown stones at An Beag riders. Rhys had not come back; perhaps he would never come back, but no one seemed about to say so.

And there was Domhnull, not the same as he had been, but worn and pale and looking sometimes as if the world had gotten too heavy for him. At first they had thought that he might die: his mother had come in from her steading up by Gearr's to tend him. He had lain days abed and fevered, with her by him, and Muirne hovering over him no less. Now at least he was up and walking, but like someone far older. He was a hero, of course; everyone in Caer Wiell knew it, and whispered how every bone in his body had been broken, but the Sidhe had healed him.

"But will he not get well, then?" Ceallach asked their father, one day that Domhnull was nowhere in their hearing, and they stood out on the wall near the gates. "Could not the Sidhe have done a little better while she was about it?"

"No," said their father sharply, and then more gently, looking down at them: "If there had been time, she would have. So I don't think there was." He ruffled Ceallach's hair, which the wind was doing too, blowing at all of them and making Meadhbh's skirts fly so she had to hold them knotted in her fist. Their father had that look of his that kept things from them. "He is still mending, Domhnull is. Mostly he would be himself again if he could, and not know what he learned up there at Caer Donn—do you understand that, Meadhbh and Ceallach?"

"Yes," said Meadhbh, and Ceallach nodded soberly.

"Do you?" their father said, staring at them strangely sharp. "Then get him ahorse again."

"We?"

"Not in the wood or down the road; not beyond sight of the walls. Say that I gave you leave to ride and ordered him to watch you."

Meadhbh looked toward the high hall, thinking of their mother, not wanting to ask whether their mother knew about this riding, because she wanted it. Ceallach had her hand and tugged it; so they went racing back to find Domhnull and get their ponies and a horse.

That was the best day of any day since their father had come home, even riding a sedate pace along the hedges close about Caer Wiell; for Domhnull's eyes grew bright again and he talked of the crops and the new foals and calves, and laughed to see the lambs playing in the meadow. Then they felt like laughing too, feeling that they had done something good and that the world was right again, at long last and overdue: that they had been wrong to doubt it.

But when Domhnull had come to the farthest point they might ride, at the end of the fence, he drew his tall horse to a halt and sat staring out north and west. The border lay that way. Caer Donn did. He only sat and sat, his horse cropping the grass, while the silence grew long and painful.

Ceallach urged Flann a little closer and looked up at Domhnull. "When we were lost," Ceallach said carefully, "there was a water-horse; but Thistle sent it away."

"Thistle."

"We're too young, she said, to know her real name.

When you have a name you can do magic on it. But I think it would be a mistake to try with her. The river horse—she gave us its name."

Domhnull was looking at them now, both of them. He was a man and grown, having gotten lines on his face and a new scar on his brow (too quick a scar), but he was looking at them eye to eye and heart to heart, as if he wanted to talk and had something boiling up inside him.

"I saw her," Domhnull said; but the greater thing stayed unsaid.

Meadhbh took that pouch which hung about her neck and offered it, although it was like giving her pony to someone else to ride, or letting someone rummage among her treasures. "It's my gift," she said. "You could carry it awhile. For memory, Thistle said. For hope, when there isn't any."

"Hope of what?" he said. He scared her, so harsh his voice was. But she doggedly refused to be put off, and covered her confusion by taking her gift out of its pouch so he might see it, a silver leaf held carefully between her fingers because of the wind. She held it to her nose, then offered it again.

"See. Smell. It's still new, after all this time. It makes me think how the woods smell when it rains."

He took it; and then he slowly rode away from them, beyond the point where they were to follow. He stopped and only sat there in the center of the pasture with his back to them.

She decided then what it was, and she reckoned that Ceallach understood, because he said not a thing either, but simply sat his pony waiting.

"I think we should ride back a way," Meadhbh said finally, "and then maybe Domhnull will feel like coming home."

"He might not, you know," Ceallach said.

She thought of Donn then, of Domhnull riding that way alone. But she turned Floinn's head for home all the same, and Ceallach's Flann turned without his doing anything. "He has my gift with him," she said, though parting with it made her anxious, "and they have a magic on them, don't they? A virtue of finding. So he has to bring it back. Doesn't he?"

Ceallach simply shook his head, still looking worried, whether over the gift or for Domhnull or for both at once.

But in time they did hear him behind them, and turned to look when he came near, not riding fast, but fast enough for his long-legged horse to catch them.

"So, well," he said scowling. "You ought not to be off by yourselves, didn't your father say that? Come on."

Their ponies took the pace of his long-legged horse, and they went briskly for a time—*He would joke if we were men, or quarrel if we were his friends,* Meadhbh thought, *so he has to find some fault with us, that being all there is to do.*

"Look," she said, finding welcome distraction, "the foal is lying down."

"Tired," said Domhnull after a moment "and the sun is warm." He offered back her gift then. "It does smell sweet."

He pleased her by that last, that he thought her sensible enough to give a courtesy to, as if she were growing up all of a sudden. Then she spoiled it all by blushing. She felt the heat in her face and had to pretend to have all her mind on putting her gift away and hanging it about her neck.

She thought that she had made him feel better, all the same. He looked eased, could smile again—perhaps it was the Sidhe gift: she looked at Domhnull in a way she had never looked at any boy her age, and felt desolate and hopeless. He was a man already. Women from the smith's daughter to the scullery maids sighed after him; even Muirne, whose devotion they had had all their own—even Muirne had taken to doing small things for him; and somewhen she had gotten—happier, or younger, or at least different, for all that she was older than he was. So Meadhbh felt twice robbed; and once more—that it was the first thought in her life she was worried Ceallach might learn and laugh at her.

Then with a sigh she recovered all her sense and gave Domhnull up two breaths after she had first loved him, deciding to look him straight in the eye and to be his staunch friend, the way he was her father's; and Beorc was; and Rhys—o Rhys!—and to go on riding out with him on summer days, as long as such days lasted.

Caer Wiell will not be here, she thought suddenly, having seen it the sudden way dreams unrolled at night between two blinks of the eye; and the leaf ached at her throat. She saw the land burned, changed, and smoke going up from blackened fields.

"Ceallach—"

He had got it too, the same awful dream. She saw it in the sudden pallor of his face, his glance toward her.

"What is it?" Domhnull asked, not the way someone might ask children, but anxiously.

"I had a dream just then," she said. "It seemed Caer Wiell was gone."

"There was a hill," said Ceallach while the horses plodded on, relentless, toward the walls. "It had bones under it."

"I never saw that," Meadhbh said.

"Caer Donn," said Domhnull, all hoarse. "It was Caer Donn you saw." He gathered the reins which he had let go slack. "Come." He put them to a quicker pace as if that could make them safe, to get them behind gates and walls.

"They had no business to be riding out in the first place," their mother said, over by the fire where she had gone to stand. Meadhbh looked at her distractedly, as if she had gone mad. With all that they had come panting up to the hall to say, that was what their mother settled on, with their father sitting still in his thoughts and Domhnull sweating and pale from their climb up the stairs. "The Bradhaeth loose and Caer Damh stirred up and they riding out as if there was no trouble at all."

"I saw Caer Wiell burned," Meadhbh cried.

"Hush!" said their father. "Come here. How was it burned?"

Meadhbh shook her head and came to her knees by her father's chair. Ceallach hung on his other side.

"Perhaps," said Domhnull, "when she lent me her gift to hold, she confused things in it. Maybe it was some other place."

"And Caer Donn?" asked Ceallach. "I saw Donn, did I not?"

"Maybe," said Domhnull, "you caught it from me, something I had seen or imagined."

"Doubtless so," their mother declared and came back again, sweeping past Muirne who hovered near the fire with large, frightened eyes. "I've held the stone. It was like that. One remembers things."

Their mother wanted it to be so. Meadhbh looked at her, understanding now and wishing for once the same thing her mother wished, that what she had seen could turn out to be something past, something of Domhnull's rememberings and nothing yet to come.

"Meadhbh," her father said, "give me your hand, and you, Ceallach."

She did that, and for a moment thought he only meant to tell them something; but then he shut his eyes, and the world turned gray and full of mist.

"Ciaran!" their mother called.

The hold was burned and the land was waste, with smoke over all the hills, that spread to the forest; and there was a hill of bones, and a shallow lake with something coiled at the depth of it, and deep places under the hills that had cracked open like eggs, empty in their darkness.

"No!" It was their father's voice. He let go of their hands, a fierce shove, and for a moment Meadhbh was lost and breathless in the mist.

But it was her mother's arms she felt, smelled the lilacs and herbs of her skirts against her face, and her mother was shouting at her father.

"It's going to be true," Meadhbh said, "it's all going to be true."

"They are *children,*" their mother cried.

"Yes," their father said. Meadhbh blinked him clear, and there were tears on his face. That won her silence. She wanted not to look at him but there was no other place she could, not now. Her father reached out quite calmly and ruffled her hair as he had not done since she was very small, and tousled Ceallach's after. "Domhnull."

"Lord," Domhnull answered quietly.

"The Sight can mislead. Sometimes it is not quite what it seems. But all the same, with the Bradhaeth roused, with all our enemies combined—and Rhys not here— well, I have no kinsman, Domhnull; and where I go, Beorc is like to go. My lady's kin—something untoward has delayed them, or Rhys would be back by now. Be in a kinsman's stead to her and Meadhbh and Ceallach—if need should be, stand by them."

"On my life, lord," Domhnull whispered. Meadhbh felt her mother's arms tighten about her as she rose. Her mother smoothed the hair her father had ruffled. *Let me go,* she wished, wanting to shout it, and turned instead and hugged her mother, thinking that someone ought to.

"Caer Wiell will never fall," her mother said without a doubt in her voice. "This nonsense comes of meddling with the Sidhe gifts, that's what it is. Or listening at doors where they shouldn't."

No one said anything. Their father only sat still and gazed at all of them with that look he had when he was far away, and then he got up from his chair.

"Domhnull, go rest. Muirne, see he gets a pot of cool ale—I daresay it would come welcome. Maybe a bit for Meadhbh and Ceallach too if they would like."

"A very little," said their mother, measuring with pinched fingers and frowning at Miurne. She combed Meadhbh's hair then with her fingers and held her face steady, looking in her eyes. "You are too old to be riding about the country, do you hear? You will not be doing such things again."

It would have galled Meadhbh even if she thought it would come to no more than the other threats, but now it had the sound of doom, louder than any intent in the words. *Not again, not again, not again.* She pretended she had not heard; saying anything to it might seal it like the magic of true names. "May I go?" she asked instead.

"Go. Comb your hair." Her mother was distracted. The hair was something she said without thinking. Meadhbh went with Muirne, beside Ceallach, and Domhnull came after, but Meadhbh cast a backward glance where her mother and her father were, her mother standing with her arms hugged about herself, her father standing staring off toward nothing at all and with a grimness about his mouth that tokened words to come.

Not be doing such things again, Meadhbh thought, and her hands were cold. It was not the riding, but the country that would change, no more sun, no more green fields, no more of foals playing and them laughing with Domhnull outside Caer Wiell. She held to her gift and tried the while she went down the stairs after Muirne, to foretell where she would ride and to what, but even Floinn was lost to her, and there was darkness, everywhere darkness and mist and only the stone of present Caer Wiell under her fingers to remind her where and when she was.

Ceallach, she thought, *o Ceallach*.

"I shall be gone awhile," Ciaran said quietly to Branwyn. "Don't fret for it."

"Ciaran."

"Hush. I know." He pressed a kiss on her brow and held her a moment. "Forgive me."

"What did they see?"

"Desolation. Give them comfort. They have need of it."

Her hands caught at him and clenched. "Ciaran, Ciaran, if Rhys would come—He *will* come. He's too clever for anyone to have stopped him—"

"Things may happen; he may have had to give up his horse and go afoot after all, if the road was watched, and that would have taken a great deal more time."

"If anything were amiss, if what they saw—Ciaran, we were destroyed before and burned and here we are. If we had had the Sight before the King came to Caer Wiell, we would have lost all our hope. Those were dark days. But they were not the end of us."

"Tell *them* so. They need hope."

"*I* need hope. Ciaran, do not you leave me! Do not you go anywhere, not unless you leave that thing behind and take your sword, hear me? What can the men think, that you go empty-handed and moon-eyed with that stone—Forgive me, listen to me now. What good has it ever done? None. Love, love, you should have had all the men about you up at Lioslinn, o gods, and gone up there armed in the first place and taught that brother of yours how to treat his guests."

"So would your father have done?"

"So would I do if I could wield a sword."

He took the reproach he had not looked for and stared at her a moment, then let fall his hands and turned toward the door, patient because there was nothing else to be.

"Ciaran." Heartbreak was in Branwyn's voice. He stopped and looked back with hope of her.

"So would I do," he said quietly, "if *I* could wield a sword."

"Put off the stone. Will you kill us all, and the children too?"

He brought a hand to the stone and felt it cold as it had been cold for days, like ice against his heart. He had nothing to say, nothing that would not give Branwyn more to fear than already she had; anger was better than anguish.

"Answer me."

"No, Branwyn."

"O gods!"

His cloak was on the peg. He gathered it up. "I shall not be going far. No riding off."

"Take me with you."

He shook his head. "No."

"Into Eald. Into Eald, is it?"

He put the cloak on, pretending he had not heard. "It may be cold."

"O gods, Ciaran, don't go."

He managed a little smile, not an easy one. "Back by supper," he said, as if he were only going out to the fences.

And then he stepped away, not a little parting, but a great one, so that he caught at the stone and held it clenched in his hand, lost for a moment in the chill gray mist.

"*Arafel!*" he cried, "Arafel!" but he did not call the third time, not daring that. He listened a long time, hoping for any small sound, searching with his heart for any trace or hope of her. "I am here," he shouted into the gray mist, in the green of the forest with the moisture dripping off the bracken and glistening on black bark. "You said I should not call your name—but that you would always know what I was doing. You said that I shouldn't walk here—but the world isn't as safe as it was either. And I do need you."

There was silence, profound silence, in which no wind stirred, nor leaf moved.

"What am I supposed to do?" he cried, forcing his voice amid such stillness. "If there is any help at all

you can give—or even give me some advice. Sending
Domhnull up there—I know that was a mistake. I'm
afraid I have made all too many mistakes. I could go to
the King at Dun na h-Eoin—but that would leave Caer
Wiell with too little strength for safety, or send me out
with too little on the road. What should I do, stay here
and do nothing? Was that what you wanted? What was
I supposed to do?"

Still there was silence. He walked forward, carefully,
remembering the way, believing it in spite of the mist
and the black and ghostly trees; but then he thought of
what he was doing, like a man looking down when he
ought not, and then doubt began to grow at his shoulder,
and shadows began to deepen on this side and on the
other, and things to gibber and rattle in them. He
doubted the power of the Sidhe which supported his
own—doubted she existed, doubted all the wisdom that
she had given him and all the way he knew.

"Help me," he cried in the thickening mist. "Help me
if you can! I need you! Help!"

He heard hoofbeats then far away and from the west
of the world; and something familiar touched his heart.
A wind blew over him, lessening the mist, a wind from
the sea. He heard the cries of gulls and shivered in a
melancholy that leached away all life and love and
purpose.

Then he heard the hoofbeats closer, and the stone
remembered a whiteness, swiftness, fierceness.

Aodhan, leaped into his mind like some answer to
a question long forgotten, implicit in the thunder and
the storm.

"Aodhan!" The horse was his, had always been, if
ever he had thought to call him, if he had ever thought
of journeying those ways through Eald where Aodhan
might go.

"Aodhan!" he cried. "O Aodhan!"

The wind blew stronger from the sea, and there came
a flickering of memory from the stone.

Man . . . it whispered, full of anguish. *Man, is it you?
What have they done?*

"Liosliath! Help me—"

I cannot come. The shadow—Man, the shadow—

The wind fell suddenly as if someone had shut an open

door. Then it rose from another quarter, miasmic, heavy, wafting from some place of water and corruption.

"Liosliath! I am still here! Liosliath!"

But there was only mist, and the voice faded in his mind as faery things would, leaving him robbed and bewildered, whether anyone had spoken at all; or whether he had imagined the salt wind or the sound of hooves.

Something chuckled at his despair, and brush stirred by him. He had slipped somehow. He did not know this place. The mist wove through it in threads, so that one moment he had a clear view of trees and more mist beyond, and then he passed into that mist and lost all bearings, all certainties. He was looking for Airgiod, but the stream he found instead was fouled, choked with leaves and stagnant. A reek went up from it that assailed the soul.

Then his heart failed him, for strange pale eyes stared up at him from beneath that murky water, and blinked when leaves drifted down, silver tarnished black. The eyes rose closer to the surface, glowing like some double reflection of the moon.

He backed away, met the corpse of a tree whose branches clawed at him like fingers. He felt past it, retreated step by step.

"Man," a voice said.

He stopped, looked toward that darkness darker than the skies. "Lord Death," he said, his heart beating as if he had been running. His arm ached with his old wound. "Where is she, do you know? Or where have I gotten to?"

"She is fled," Death said, and his voice came thin and strained. "Man, I had thought to follow *you*."

"To her?" Wariness came on him. "To her, is that your meaning?"

"She sent me out, Man, to learn a name; but she would not stay for it." The darkness drifted near, loomed, shutting out the little light that sifted through the branches, and the air was bitter cold. "If you can reach her, do. I have more messages for her."

"She met something at Caer Donn. But you would know that. You were there."

"She met something, yes. Use that stone of yours and call her."

"I tried. The stone gives me nothing but the sea. Trees are where they should not be . . . and Airgiod, if that marsh yonder is Airgiod—"

"The sea," Lord Death whispered. "And Eald deserted. Man, Man, if *that* urge has fallen on her, we are all lost. Call her. Call her name. You have that power. You proved it once before."

"I can't."

"You *will* not." The shadow swept closer. A hand gripped his arm with strength like bone. "Man, listen to me. The drow are roused. Do you know that name? Whatever this stone of yours may be to a Sidhe, they are without. They have lost it, cast it away—a drow is what a Sidhe becomes, when he has lost whatever that stone is."

A cold settled into his marrow, and the stone stung his heart like a lump of ice. He remembered then a tree shining like the moon, like a thousand moons, agleam with jewels and elvish work. "No," he said, "not always." Warmth came then, reassurance, and he shrugged off Lord Death's hand as if it were spiderweb. The stone grew warmer. "I am sure of that. It is what a Sidhe does to the stone himself, of his own will; that makes the difference. I *remember,* Lord Death." The strength in the stone grew poignant as tears, as a shout going through the forest, then faded, leaving the cold. He turned about, sought that retreating touch with all his heart, as if that door had opened again and let out warmth and kindness and all the things this place had long forgotten. But Death laid his hand on his shoulder and came before him again, cutting off all his vision.

"Fool and servant of a fool! Use the power you have. If there are weapons, take them up. You will need them all. No, do not turn from me. This is all your doing, the loosing of this plague. A thousand or so human lives you bought with it, and your own. Caer Wiell might have fallen, yes, would have fallen that day; but suppose—no, hear me, never turn your back to me—suppose you had not roused all Eald to help you and Caer Wiell had fallen. The King was on his way; he would have come there sooner or later, if you had only sold your lives for enough of An Beag's. He would have come on an enemy in their looting, disorderly, in a hold with gates broken.

Then Laochailan King would *be* king in his own right, by his own hand, and he would never have reigned in fear—fear of you, halfling, married to his kin. But no, you refused to die there; saved your life and a paltry thousand more and waked all of this evil and cost every life you saved. You doomed the *world,* Man, and all that might ever be, to save your life!"

Ciaran tore himself away, but brambles snagged his cloak, his clothes, his hands, and Death was still before him.

"You waked power, Man, and would not use it—destroyed the peace, destroyed the King, destroyed your mother with grief and your father and your brother with fear of you and it. You were lord of Donn if you had reached out your hand. You could have taken that sheepcot and compelled your father and your brother instead of moping about waiting for them to send to you. You could have gone to Dun na h-Eoin and faced Laochailan: Who could have prevented you if you had had the stone then and used it? Your King feared you. The whisperers at his side would have scattered like deer. You would have had him in your hand for good or ill, and then was time for compassion. You could have made him great, shaped him however you would have him, made him a name to remember, gained him a kingdom greater than any king before him. Fear of you broke what little there was of him and made him clay for molding; but you would not. You cast him away, cast it all away. You stayed at home, breeding your horses and raising cabbages. This small realm of yours, have you not made it fair? But at what cost?"

"The kingdom has had peace of me."

"Are you virtuous? But you could have murdered father, brother, King, host, and done far more good in the world after all this murder than you have done with your peace. You could have piled corpse on corpse and burned holds and tortured and plundered and done more good than this."

"Then where were you? Why did you stay your hand from me?" The taste of ashes and tears was in his mouth. The thorns held him impaled. "There were years I had nothing. I was so slight a matter. I expected you— in the forest, in fighting with An Beag, somewhere on the stairs—Where were you, that you could not do so slight a thing, if all the world hung on it?"

There was silence. The shadow drew back and seemed to shrink. "You are not the only fools there be. I bound myself by a promise in your case, old comrade. She asked. And I promised."

"And my brother? Was *he* beyond you too? Or the King? Any of us would have sufficed, would we not?"

"But on them I had no claim. And *she* would not. I begged her!—I! Slay this Donnchadh. One stroke and the world is saved. She would not. The Sidhe are fey and mad. This abdication of yours—it must run in the blood." Lord Death drifted closer. "Listen. A night ago your brother quitted Caer Donn, bound for Dun na h-Eoin where the King lies dying—a long dying, believe me. It amazes them that one Man could survive so much and so deadly poisons. But they are out of patience with such methods. Do you not understand, Man? Laochailan has been no King. They divided him from you, from the one who might have saved him, and murdered the lord of Ban, who was the best of them. And not they. Donn-chadh. From the beginning, your father and Donnchadh."

He shook his head vehemently. "My father—no. I will believe it of my brother, but my father, no, no man was truer to his King."

"Your father was halfling like yourself, and the curse was wakened at Donn. You wakened it. It was waiting for him when he came home, lurking in the stones, the earth, the foundations of Caer Donn. I will tell you the name of it; I will whisper it: *Duilliath*. And doubtless the drow came whispering to him: *Half-Sidhe, half-Sidhe, kinsman, where is your younger son? More powerful than his King, more than his father—what would stay him from coming here? Power must fight power, and there is power in this place. Dig deep, search it out, master it.—* But it mastered Donn. Of course it could. It whispered, it grew—without scruples. Your King already feared you; and when they came whispering in their turn, kins-men against kinsman, why, conspiracy was a thing Lao-chailan King could well believe, when he would not have believed in virtue. *Power against power,* they said. *Magic to oppose the Sidhe that sits in Caer Wiell. How else can we survive?* You wed your King's cousin, begot an heir while your King has failed. Evald died to your advantage—*Now he has Caer Wiell,* they whispered, *and was not Evald's death untimely young?*"

"O gods."

"Oh, but you are beyond gods, halfling. I cannot hear your prayers. You have the stone. Your brother is on the road. You might be there, suddenly, beside him. Against Sidhe I have no power, and his life is guarded now, I know so. It has him. The drow will have Donnchadh on the throne in a fortnight; and armies at his command. If you have power, use it! Call *her* name, not mine."

He doubted. Doubt crushed him. He shook his head. "No. Call her into this place—no. I will try something else—to go to her." he held the stone still in his hand, and it remained cold and lifeless. "And if I find her I shall give her your message."

"Do so, then," said Death. The darkness drew aside. "If that is all that I can win, do so. And be wise. The border is not the greatest danger. I have sent a dream to Beorc Scaga's-son: his father. *Come home,* I have bidden him. *Your lord has need of you.* And mark my words, you will."

"Keep your hands from my folk! They are not yours to be sending here and there."

"They are mine when I call them—when their hour is come. One of them I found wandering and escorted to your hands. Was I thanked for that?" The voice faded on the wind that rattled dry branches and stank of stagnant water. "No. But our interests are liker than you know. Fare well and fare better, Man, than you have fared before."

He shivered. Somehow he had gotten to his own woods again, less dire than the place he had quitted, and the sun shone through tangled limbs and summer leaves. He was not held. The brambles did not grow here and it was Caerbourne that flowed at his feet.

Then with a jolt of his heart he knew where he was, a place where he and Lord Death had met before: it was Caerbourne Ford near Raven Hill. He had strayed half a day from home.

At least he knew his way from here, a path Rhys must have taken, a path which once he had run with the hounds of the Hunt at his heels. A spur of it led from here to the heart of all Eald, to that grove where he had first met the Sidhe, beneath that tree which grew rooted in his woods and hers at once.

That was the place she would be, he told himself; there lay hope if hope there was, if he dared come there now, with Arafel unwilling. But things were changed. It was his own safety she had thought of. Now he was concerned for hers, for all that depended on her. He made haste going down the bank, fevered haste, trusting this Caerbourne far more than the stream he had just quitted, though his shoulders itched between with the memory of arrows and An Beag so near to this crossing-place.

Danger. He felt it suddenly near him as he waded the dark stream, a shivering in air and water, a poison in the winds. He struggled the harder, panting, sought the far bank and gained it, soaked and heavy in that climbing and already reaching elsewhere with his mind.

An Beag, he thought. *Watchers at the ford.* He fled into Eald as if it were a dream, recalling another day that he had met evil in this place. *The grove,* he thought, but he could not find the way. The mist thickened. Brambles caught at him. Iron shivered through his substance like poison, so that he staggered, almost losing Eald.

A darkness loomed up before him in chill and fetid wind. It rattled and gibbered and mud clung to his feet, holding him like nightmare. Other things leaped and clawed at his boots, strove to reach his hands, and the cold was terrible. He lurched aside in defeat, tried another way, but dead wood crumbled beneath his weight, and another of the greater horrors lay that way. The air was presentient with ill and malice, so that it stung his chest and sped his heart. It came toward him. More and more the lesser ones had power: one sat on a dead branch and plummeted suddenly upside down, laughing and clinging with hands and feet, its face still rightwise up.

He plunged on, thrusting it and its branch away, but something drifted before him now, black and unwholesome, with long white hair, and dodge as he would, he was overtaking it.

It turned suddenly and looked at him with a white elvish face. *Arafel,* he thought in sudden relief, because they were so like; but this face was cold and not what it had seemed a moment ago. It reached out its hand, more terrible in its beauty than all the rest in their ugliness.

"Duilliath," he guessed.

It laughed. "You are wrong, Man, and powerless to name me." It came closer. "Yield up the stone. You are hopeless else."

"No."

"Lost, then." Other creatures had come, and iron shivered in the air. "Ciaran, Ciaran, Ciaran—*back to your beginnings!*"

It hurled him. The black limbs spun, the earth came up at him and he struck it, brown wet earth, slick leaves, clinging to his hands.

He heard dogs. He leaped up, in the sunlight, in the dappling of the leaves of Caerbourne Ford; he heard horses and movement and the cleaving of the air, the shivering passage of iron from the bowmen beyond the trees.

Arrows struck him in quick succession. His heart burst in dazing pain. He fell a second time, shattering the shafts and numb after the first hurt—rising then because his limbs still moved: he saw the An Beag bandits, saw bows bent again to add more arrows to those that pierced him.

He ran. He turned and plunged into mist, where the pain began in earnest, robbing him of breath.

"*Ciaran,*" Liosliath cried, fair and far and desperate. "*Cling to the stone—o run, run, run!*"

The wind came then, tearing at the mist, and he heard thunder, the howling of the gale that yet smelled of sea and wrack. A glimmering shone like a star amid the murk, and grew, steadily oncoming, while the thunder swelled.

"*Aodhan!*" he cried, remembering. He had called three times. The elf horse had come, from the ends of the earth it might be: Aodhan had come.

Thunder came down on him, and wind battered him as Aodhan came near, a shining pallor in the dark, a shoulder offered to his need. He caught the mane amid which lightnings flickered, harmless to him; strength burned from the stone toward his hands, needing nothing of his heart, and he flung himself astride, or somehow he had gotten to Aodhan's back. The elf horse began to run above the ground, carrying him with shockless steps and racing not through distances but faster and deeper into Eald.

"O Aodhan," he whispered, "take me to her, take me there now."

The elf horse snorted, shifted in his stride, almost losing him from his back, and whinnied in dismay, shifting this way and that. They ran; a wall of bright mist loomed before them, poured about them. Ciaran cried aloud, so fierce the pain of iron that split his heart, cried a second time in dismay to find them in retreat.

"Again," he cried, "Aodhan, take me through!"

The elf horse turned and tried the chill mist again, laboring. The cold pain shot through him, but he clung to the mane and held, feeling the horse fighting and veering beneath him. Trial after trial the elf horse made, shying back to lunge forward again, and now small things chittered and leaped at them in growing shadow; he cried aloud, and Aodhan whinnied and veered aside.

There was a darkness then, and Aodhan was running to the baying of hounds, away from the barrier, for the pain had ebbed. Thunder muttered. There were other hooves, and leaping shapes of dogs, and swift-flying shadows.

A rider drew even with them, moving with them, on a horse like night, in which there was the pale glimmering of bone where Aodhan's lightning flickered; the rider was Lord Death.

"No," Ciaran whispered. "Let me go on trying. Let me try, Lord Death."

"Turn then," the answer came; and he called out to Aodhan, to no avail. The elf horse ran on, a swift striding that lost not a pace. He sank on Aodhan's neck in defeat, unable to do more, clinging as the sunny road stretched suddenly beneath them.

Death stayed with him, a shadow in the day. They had

left Eald and ran now on the river road, that which led home. The elf horse had failed as he had, ran now with a stretching and gathering of sinew, a flutter of mane, a blur of sunlit dust.

THIRTEEN

THE BAIN SIDHE

Domhnull made the steps, leaning on his stick, for his legs would still betray him, and went out along the wall, seeking somewhat of refuge, some little solitude where no one else could come at him with questions— Ask my lady this, it was, and ask my lady that, and pray, sir, what of the grainstores? —and the riders be home, sir Domhnull, nothing found, no hope, no luck and less of substance.

He leaned his arms upon the wall, his stick resting by him, and bowed his head, for it ached; but he thought again how despairing that would seem and lifted it, looking outward on a sight that today seemed worse than yesterday—for sun shone on Caer Wiell's lands, on green pasture and growing fields and the gentle swells of it west and north and even on the trees about the river. But beyond that circle of sunlight the sky was darkened with walls of cloud, towering fortresses of cloud that had begun as wisps and mare's-tails.

It did not advance as storms did, on wind and claps of thunder. It built new outposts, a mare's-tail first, a gray, dull wisp, and then an outwelling of the stormcloud near it, all silent, proceeding no more swiftly than any growth of clouds on a summer's day. A man had to watch, not merely look, and then he would see it, this wall-building all about them. They had hardly noticed it beginning, first as a line of cloud in the far northwest, and then in the west, spreading over the forest to the south as the clouds built; and then one night it reached out an arm toward the north again, darkening the dawn with strands of murk that became another wall.

Daily, folk had begun to remark on it, and to cast anxious glances from the fields and the crests of the walls. Night and day it grew, until the first strands of it appeared in the north, completing the ring about them, and the cloud over the forest advanced until the line of sunlight could be seen plain on the treetops at noon. Now shadow lay visibly along the tops of the trees that overhung the Caerbourne and off across the hills; and overhead, above the gray walls of the keep, a cloudy rampart towered, up and up into bright sun and blue sky, its gray surface knobbed and gnarled and changing and somehow not moving, as if it had pressed against some barrier that made this well of sunlight above them. Domhnull did not look at it, no more than a glance, but there was no escaping the sight of it outward, where its arm swept round across the hills, and the marching line of shadow had now come all the way over the hills, so that that horizon too was dull and dark.

The circle had narrowed again in the night, from the north. No one talked about it. Only there was a traffic to the walls or out the gates, each looking for himself, from lady Branwyn to Cook in her apron, floured from morning baking—to himself, latest, not wanting to look at all, but drawn here. It was the sunlight he looked at, the impossibly brilliant sunlight shining off the fairness of the land, barricade against the shadow, which had now assumed a perfect roundness on its nearer edge, marking the size of the circle that yet would be.

Gods help us, Domhnull thought, but it was not gods he thought of, but rather Arafel. He still hoped. The sunlight was reason for hope even if it was narrowing, even if their lord was the seventh day missing.

"He has gone away," lady Branwyn had said, with such a look in her blue eyes that he dare not question it. *Gone.* Domhnull knew where lord Ciaran had gone, and watched the cloudwall veil that forest day by day.

But the circle remained above them, and the folk of Caer Wiell went about their business, knowing quite as well as he, he reckoned, that their lord had not *ridden* to this place where he had gone—since his horse was still in stable and no men had been called to go with him. Gossip would happen, but there was a strange calm about this gossip, a matter of factness like the confidence with which his own mother had set out bowls of milk for visitors in the night. This cloud was a sign, it was clearly a sign, and not a good one; but a steady hammering went up from Smith's forge, and smoke and sparks: and riders went to and fro on the road keeping up contact with the borders, while wagons groaned their way in from the steadings, and the storehouse filled day by day, preparing for siege.

So now a wagon came, lumbering from distance to nearness, and when it had come near enough, Domhnull came down and stood leaning on his stick while the wagon came through the gates. A farmwife drove it; a girl was on the seat beside her.

"Where from?" he asked, hoping for news from the borders.

"Raghallach's steading," the farmwife said. "The boys be all at the border, and that cloud—yon's ugly, an't it?"

Domhnull cast an involuntary glance upward, shrugged, leaning on his stick and grinned. "Sun's fair, goodwife."

For a moment the stout face looked bothered, grayed hair sticking with the sweat, lips clamped. Then a spark came to dark eyes and a grin showed gapped teeth. She clapped the girl on the shoulder, smoothed her tangled hair and nodded. "Oh, aye, 'tis."

"Stay in hold," Domhnull said, "if you like."

"Brought the stores, I did, all's to spare. Left my mark on t'door so's my folk won't worry. It's my granddarter, see—" She looked down at the small face, and up again. "There be trouble about the steading. I be a fair shot wi' my man's old bow, but them things comes at nightfall, run off the cow, they did, and got the sheep, e'en Sobhrach's lamb, poor thing."

"Nothing here," said Domhnull, "to trouble you— Cein," he said, the man being among others who had come up. "Take them through."

So he let them pass and turned away, thinking most on his own kin and glad that his mother had already come in and stayed. Beorc was on the border still. He found himself, but for Branwyn and Siodhachan, chiefest in the hold now, a thing he had never looked for. He had become sir Domhnull and respected; but it seemed

to him that all it meant was standing still and not doing
the things he would do: like riding with the searchers,
like going where he knew how to look, like seeing for
himself and not relying on messages days old.

Thunder muttered. He glanced up at the clouds and
saw no darkened source of thunder. About him in the
hold no others seemed to have heard it. Folk were going
about their business. That strange deafness disturbed
him, the more as the thunder grew and no one noticed.
He strode for the walls, his limp pronounced, his stick
forgotten in his hand. Behind in the yard was the squeal
of the oxcart wheels on pavings. Children played. A
rooster crowed, long and loud, fit to break the morning.

Then thunder clapped, deafening, and horses whinnied
and cattle lowed. There was a pause in voices, a sudden exclamation.

Lightning blazed in Domhnull's path, just within the
gates, a thunder-rumbling, the shape of horse and rider
burning like the sun and dimming then.

"Lord," Domhnull whispered. It *was* himself, it *was*
the lord.

"Domhnull. Help." It was the ghost of a voice, and
the shape reached out to him. He went, flinging his stick
aside, offering his hands, and Ciaran came down to him,
sliding into his arms. For a moment there was no weight,
and then there was, as the white horse of the Sidhe retreated. His injured leg could not bear the weight and
Domhnull sank to the pavings on his knees, shielding
his lord's head and shoulders, at least. Ciaran's face was
waxen-pale, his flesh seeming to glow inside with light
beyond what fell on it, and the bones stood out. Arrows
had pierced him, three in the chest and ribs, broken
stubs of shafts that moved with his breathing, and yet
there was no bleeding.

"Gods," Domhnull said, feeling tears dammed up in
him. "O gods." He trembled. He brushed dirt from Ciaran's cheek and the closed lids flickered. Domhnull stared
about him, stunned, realizing he could not lift his Lord,
that he knelt in a ring of people gathered helplessly in
the gateway. "For the gods' sake do something. Help
him. *Arafel!*"

"No," Ciaran whispered. His eyes opened and there
was a murmur from the folk. He moved. It was incredi-

ble that any man could breathe, his body so pierced, but breaths continued. His hand sought the pavement and pressed to raise himself. The stone glowed upon his breast, like a moon by daylight. "Don't call, don't use that name."

"Lord," Domhnull said, and then another arrived running, Branwyn racing breathless through the crowd. She stopped. One might have expected a cry, a wail—something. She only came quietly and knelt and took her lord's hand and brought it to her lips, bloody that it was.

"I have had dreams," she said. "The children saw you coming home—o Ciaran, Ciaran!"

"He is sleeping," Domhnull said when he came out to the children, there waiting in the hall; he had rather face enemies than these young faces, these hearts hanging on every turn of word for hope or something hidden from them. They stood there like two waxen images, with vast bruised eyes, and so, so lost, not knowing how much folk lied at such times, or how much a man might want to tell two children, or what horrid thing might have been happening up there while the door was shut. They hesitated. He opened his arms to them both and hugged them tight, like comrades, like something more than children, and felt his senses aswim with panic and with loss. Perhaps it was the talismans the children wore. For a moment he could not get his own breath, and felt somewhere lost, wrapped in mist, as if they stood in some space without boundaries or safety, naked to evil and to good. "O gods," he murmured, "but he will heal. I did. And she loves him more."

They looked up at him then, two pairs of eyes staring into him; but it was only the hall about them, solid stone, and the light came from torches in this unwindowed room.

"Iron," said Ceallach, half-whispered, "Domhnull, they shot him with iron."

" 'Tis gone now. We drew it." The image was vivid in him, the waxen skin, Siodhachan's knives, but only a little loss of blood—He saw the young faces, their pale, pale faces, as if they were as drained of tears as their father was of blood. They could not know such things, must not be privy to them, with the cloudwall building over them, their father lying so unnaturally pale and still beyond the door.

"Can we see him now?" Meadhbh asked.

They were not to do so. Their mother had forbidden it. But Branwyn had not seen their faces, heard their voices, so calm and reasoned they broke his heart. "Yes," he said, "but from the door. You would not want to wake him. Listen to me. From such great hurts—well, sleep is best."

He took them then to the door which Muirne was leaving. He took it from her hand, and cracked it wider, so that they could see where Ciaran lay abed, Branwyn kneeling at his side. Ciaran's face was calm.

So was Branwyn's now. She gazed at him and them and motioned to them, laying a finger to her lips to sign them quiet, and noiselessly they came to their father's bedside.

Forgive me, Domhnbull sent with his eyes, but Branwyn hugged her children, Meadhbh and then Ceallach, wiped with her thumb the tears that spilled silently down composed, pale faces. Silently she urged them to go after they had seen their father. Domhnull held out his hand again, not without a look at his lord lying there so still.

Ciaran's eyes had opened. "Hush," said Branwyn, "go back to sleep."

The faintest of smiles touched his face, the smile of a man looking on what he loved, and then it faded and his eyes closed. Sweat broke out upon his brow, and his face had again that waxen light, his brows and nostrils and the edges of his mouth so drawn that it seemed another man, the lines of age smoothed by pain into an illusion of youth and fierceness.

Like a king, Domhnull recalled the vision. *Or the Sidhe.*

"Father," Meadhbh whispered. *"Father—"*

"Go," Branwyn said distractedly, her arm about the pillow on which Ciaran's head rested. "Let him sleep."

Meadhbh fled. Ceallach hesitated a moment, his face anguished, and Domhnull took his hand and led him away.

They wept afterward, like children. Muirne came and brought them sweet cakes and a bit of ale and this at last tempted them; Domhnull won smiles from them, the sort without laughter or happiness, but brave, their father's kind of smile when he had looked on them. There was the smell of rain in the air, reminding them of clouds, even in this room, and sometimes thunder muttered.

"That's the white horse outside," said Meadhbh, her eyes wide, her hand upon the talisman at her throat. A chill ran over Domhnull's skin, chill and comfort at once, a sense that there was still something of the Sidhe near them.

"Perhaps," he said, "its owner is not far."

"It is lost," said Ceallach in that same distant tone, as if he were listening to something else at the same time. "It grieves for someone. O Domhnull—something is wrong down by the river."

"Hush," he said, "hush. Be still. Come back and drink your ale. Get them more, Muirne. I think they could well stand it."

"No," said Meadhbh.

A strange sound was growing on the air, so that Domhnull stirred, thinking of thunder, of the clouds, of the creature that he had seen—but it was a different, earthy sound, of hooves, of echoes off the wall that had nothing to do with thunder.

"There are riders coming," Muirne whispered. "Domhnull, do you hear?"

"Aye," he said, and thrust himself to his feet in haste, in dread, for they were coming hard and they were almost at the gates. "Where is the watch, that we get no word? Gods help us." He started down the stairs. He had followers, Muirne, Meadhbh and Ceallach, but he did not delay to stop them.

So they came out onto the walls where others had gathered, as the gates groaned open and the riders thundered into the yard on lathered horses, riders whose colors and whose metal brightness had been obscured with dust until even their faces were masks. They were Caer Wiell folk; and no dust could hide the foremost, for his size and fiery hair and beard.

"Beorc," Domhnull breathed, and headed down the last stairs to meet his cousin.

There was yet another visitor in the room, perched on his bedside. Ciaran saw him without opening his eyes, saw him best that way, a lump of darkness sitting there staring at him, but Branwyn had not seen him: her golden head was bowed, the light coming to her so that it picked out the silver amid her braids, dancing on the stones of the wall, but never, never touching the darkness. The pain was deep in Ciaran's chest, a gnawing pain of iron where the poison had spread. He felt an ache as if he had gotten a hailstone for a heart, pain of wounds, of loss, of seeing Branwyn sitting there so lost and helpless. He could not move. The world seemed too still for that, or too fragile. I shall slip away, he thought; I shall never see her again, and the children, and my fields and all the rest, the table set for dinner, Meadhbh laughing, Branwyn in the sunlight, none of these things. It will tear like spiderweb, this world.

"Take off the stone," Lord Death said. "You have that much strength."

"Is that what you have come for?"

Death stirred, came closer, leaning over him while Branwyn drowsed. "For you—yes, my friend. Give up the stone. Turn it loose and give me your hand—o Man, there is little hope enough; but at least you will be spared the worse things." There seemed others beyond him, mothers, cousins, friends; a tall brooding figure hung back from the rest, and that was his father, still frowning.

"Ciaran," his father said, "I was wrong."

"I have seen your son and daughter," his mother said. "They are very fair. Will you not bring them? And Branwyn too?"

"My daughter," said another, shadow-wrapped, with a golden-haired woman by his side.

There were others, shadows, crowned with gold. One face was brighter. It was Laochailan's, and tears ran on his gaunt face. "Ciaran, Ciaran of Donn," his King said. "They have murdered me."

"Lord," said others, a shadow-host, folk of his hold. Blood and dust marked them. Arrows pierced them, men he had left at the border, farmer-folk who had rallied there. "They never cease to come. What shall we do?"

"There is no luck in Donn," his father said. "Nor hope now."

"Murdered," said his King.

"No!" He opened his eyes then, caught a breath that pained him. Branwyn caught his hand.

"Beorc is here. Beorc has come back safe from the border."

He said nothing to this. He was not surprised at this passage of familiar faces, not then nor later when Beorc came with Domhnull to stand beside his bed.

"He is sleeping again," Branwyn said. "Domhnull says that he will mend. He will."

He smiled to hear that, wishing to believe that and not the dreams.

"Come back," said Lord Death, but the sound of waves was in his ears, and a white horse came running toward him in the dark.

Man, said another voice, *cling to the stone. There is no other hope. There is none in all the world. You must help me.*

"It hurts," he said.

Ciaran, that voice cried, at the margin of the world, *for the world's sake, hold on!*

The white horse waited. Thunder rumbled from its hooves.

A black one waited too. Death was there, with other riders. "There is battle coming," said Lord Death, "in which you cannot share. How long will you lie there suffering? They suffer too, who love you. Free them. There is no more hope. But you at least might be safe in my hands. I shall gather as many of them as I can. Old friends, kinsmen, family. Be free of this world. There will be other heroes. Make way. Make room. Call one you trust and pass on the stone. Domhnull might bear it."

He felt after the stone and held it clenched tightly in his hand, ignoring the voice. The pain came in little waves, like the rocking of the sea, and greater ones, like the blowing of the wind. He held fast, feeling at times the coolness of sweat on his face when the world's wind would stir through the window. Now and again someone touched him and wiped his brow, now and again raised his head to give him drink; at times he looked and Branwyn was there, and he slipped his other hand in hers.

Thunder cracked.

"Is it raining?" he asked.

"No," she said, "not yet."

He drifted back again, having gathered up the scattered threads. "Liosliath," he said, "Liosliath, *Liosliath*." It was a misty way, out among the trees. The white horse ghosted among them, and lifted his head toward the sea. "Hear me," he said, "Liosliath. I have lost her. She has gone somewhere into the wood, and something has gotten loose in the world. I dare not call its name, but I think you would know it."

There was no clear answer, but a touch at the stone, a flooding of strength into it.

"Come," a voice said then, a whisper hollow as the sea. "Hear the gulls?"

"Beware," said another voice, "to hear only true voices. Some will doom you. A mistake will doom the world . . . and some seem very fair."

"I hear something singing," he said, and fair it seemed, wailing on the wind.

He was asleep again, his face so drawn and thin: Branwyn never let the candles die, seldom quit his side, though Muirne came and gave her drink and others came, like Beorc, big man that he was, so soft-footed in his tread, to look in and then depart again.

Now Beorc knelt, bending to one knee, to take her hand in his huge one, to press her fingers.

"Lady," he whispered, "go to hall awhile, go to bed, and let me watch—Do you think some harm could come to him with me beside him? Nothing in this world or the other would I let pass. You have children, lady. They need you. They need you to sleep a bit and eat a bit, and wash your face and smile."

She understood. She gazed at him from that distance of long patience, having wept all she meant to weep while her lord was living, but Beorc's loyalty touched her to the quick. "They're not my children," she said, "but his. Do you think I dare have them near him, Sighted as they are? They saw him fall; they saw him coming home. What more should they see, Beorc? I'm blind to such things. I can only watch him, not—not suffer the other things. And my children know. They know where I have to be."

"They are children," said Beorc, "and see their own hurts too well."

"Do they?" She thought back on breakfast tables, on childish tears, on baby faces, and first steps, and skinned knees; and the forest when they were lost; and the gateway, when they were found. But she gazed on Ciaran's sleeping face and that had more power than all these things. "No."

A singing had grown again, some old tree wailing in the wind, some thing of nature, for the wind was strong outside tonight and thunder muttered. For a while that was the only sound. The wind came into the chamber, and Branwyn tugged the covers higher.

"No," she said, when Beorc got up and went to the shutters. "He refuses to have them closed."

He stopped, his mouth set, his eyes troubled. "Curse that thing."

"It's some old tree down by the river; a limb must have broken." She smoothed Ciaran's hair, used her kerchief to wipe his brow. "Hush, hush, go on sleeping."

"Tree," Beorc said. "Lady, do you not *hear* it?"

She looked at him with a sudden stricture of the heart. "I hear the wind," she said. "Give me none of your imaginings."

"It must be that." His shoulders fell. His eyes settled beyond her, on Ciaran, with vast sorrow. She knew the tale. She had heard it, outside the door, the border in disarray, steadings burned. The last refugees were coming. They did not say such things within this room, in Ciaran's hearing. Here the talk was all of peace, of calm, of home and will you take a little soup, love? But he would not. And the borders were afire, the clouds above them narrowing day by day. There were creakings and groanings they could not disguise. *What is that?* he would say. *Oh, supplies brought in,* she would answer: he seemed easy to deceive, forgetting that she had said that before; and meanwhile the yard filled, and tents were set, and Caer Wiell prepared for siege.

"Not the wind," Ciaran whispered, and his eyes had opened somewhat. "Love, don't you hear it?"

"Out on it," Branwyn said lightly. "Listening after all." She smiled then for him, and dabbed his brow. "Look you, should we not close the shutters?"

"Is that Beorc? Gods, who's in command up there? Ruadhan?"

"Lord." Beorc came anxiously and held his hand. "It's well enough."

"Well." Ciaran's eyes drifted shut again. "Old wolf, to lie to me. I know. I can see, better than either of you. And I hear." The voice came faintly, at great effort. "I can't stay longer. I have a ride to make. Aodhan is waiting. Branwyn, Branwyn—"

"O gods, Ciaran." She put her arms about his neck, held him so, her head against his. "I will not let you. *No.*"

The sights afflicted her if she let them, a place of mist, where dark shapes twined amid ghostly trees, where a white figure washed bloody rags in Caerbourne's water, wailing as she worked. She banished the visions, keeping her eyes open, fixing them on the familiar solid stones; and Beorc, Beorc was there. She heard the wailing clearer now, a hungry thing and nearer.

So Rhys came riding in, all unexpected. There were cheers from the walls where anxious folk had gathered to see what this dustcloud meant in the waning of the sun—waning, not setting, for the sun died daily into murk, choked by the cloudy ramparts in the west. In this greenish twilight the folk of the south came riding with their black and silver banners, three companies bristling with spears.

"Dryw's folk!" the cry went out—"Rhys is coming!" from place to place along the walls, from those who had vantages to those who did not.

"Open the gates," Domhnull cried, for once the great gates were shut, someone in authority had to open them; and he sent a page running to bear word to the hall, to Beorc and to the lady, who might whisper it in their lord's hearing and so give him cheer.

And: "Rhys," he said, embracing the smallish man who dismounted and met him on the stairs, the while the folk still cheered. "Rhys." Domhnull limped. His face was scarred. There was haunting in Rhys' dark eyes and a gauntness about the cheekbones, new lines about the mouth. They held each other at arm's length and tried to read each other, but Domhnull simply hugged the southron a second time with all he had to tell damned up in his throat, and looked at him again. Others had come up to the foot of the steps, smallish men, two of them, much like Rhys in their dark cloth and darkened metal. "My brothers," Rhys said, "Owein and Madawc ap Dryw."

"Our lord cannot be here to greet you," Domhnull said, "or he would. But welcome to his hall, in his name and in his lady's your cousin. Gods reward you for this, all. Ale and supper for your men—we are not scanted of that." He spied a captain on the wall; he shouted orders. "Come," he said then to Rhys and his brothers. "Come upstairs. I would ask you which you would, rest or news, but this much first: lord Ciaran is hurt—" The truth stuck in his throat. "My lady is there. Come see her."

"Sore hurt?"

He nodded, lips clamped on words he would not say. "Will you come there first? My lady will not leave him."

"Aye," Rhys said. His tired face took on a resolution for still worse than he had seen.

Branwyn wept, quietly, at their coming to the room; and hugged them one and all, Rhys and Owein and Madawc, though talk went in whispers: "He will mend," she said as she had insisted a hundred times. "He sleeps a great deal, and that is to the good. I will tell him you've come. He'll want to see you."

But Ciaran lay very still, his breathing hardly stirring the coverlet, so pale that his flesh and the moonstone on his breast seemed little different. "Yes," Rhys whispered back. "Tell him we have come."

And afterward in hall Rhys hugged his youngest cousins and sat down to ale and meat, he and his brothers, trail-worn and haggard, while the dark fell outside and the wailing began again from the riverside.

"You had no easy ride coming here," Domhnull said. They were all at hand, Beorc, Muirne, Meadhbh and Ceallach by the fire they laid of evenings; Leannan with his harp encased and songless; Siodhachan whose wrinkled face was a map of years and present sorrows.

"No," said Rhys, "it was not. But An Beag has men to bury, by the ford."

"Well done," Beorc said. His eyes burned. His huge hands knotted up in fists.

"There were other things," said Rhys. He did not look up, but the thought was there, the ring of cloud, the darkness through which they had ridden. "There were men we could not bury. Gods help them." His mouth was drawn at the corners. He took a drink of wine and Domhnull looking on him caught a glance of his eyes when the cup had lowered. A chill came on Domhnull then, a keen ache in all his wounds, kinship with all those who had fared outside of daylight, in fell places and old.

"What happened here?" Rhys asked.

"Misjudgment," Domhnull said. His muscles all were hard, and ached on mended bones. "How did you get through?"

There was darkness enough in Owein's and Madawc's eyes, of proud men not used to fear; but Rhys' darkness was more. "With small things in the bushes and arrows in the dark; and two horses gnawed to bone and men we never found. Nor could delay for." Rhys shivered, and leaned on his knees, the cup clenched between his knees; a fury was on his face. "Mist. A lot of that. An unnatural lot of that. We hoped for better here. Some of my folk went home: Gwernach and his folk—I sent them for my father's defence. We saw the sunlight; we had hoped for better beyond Caerbourne Ford. Easier An Beag arrows than the forest road by night; but something went with us—whether a fair thing or foul I know not, but at the last it led us fair. There have been such things. I saw a pooka once."

"And followed it?" Domhnull asked.

"O, friend, it followed *me*. That was on my way. This was smaller, a noise in the leaves—it loved the trees too well to leave them, and hung about the streams. And we none of us liked it, but there was no parting from it. We saw it scampering through the brush. Small and quick it was, and always ahead of us til the ford, til the cursed singer—" He fell silent. There was the wind outside, and always, the singing. "We have heard that wailing at night. Two nights upon the road."

"It can sing all it likes," said Muirne. "It's not coming in, that thing."

"It's Sidhe," said Meadhbh, a small voice. She sat by her brother, by the fire. "It wants our father."

"Be still," said Muirne, "hush, Meadhbh, don't speak of it."

There was silence then. There were a great many things not fit for speaking tonight. Domhnull's heart went out to the children. He moved close by them and sat down on the hearthside, his arms about them both.

"You'll want your beds," said Beorc to Rhys and the others. "I'll have bedding brought."

Rhys looked about him, at the hall where bedding was scattered in corners, pillows tucked in chairs, disorder that told its own tale of how they rested. "I'll wash," he said. "I'll watch here."

Beorc nodded, gazing steadily at him. " 'Tis hard to think of riding, Rhys, but those men of yours would be a welcome sight northward: Ruadhan is hard pressed on the border. Gods know I should be up there, but—"

"We will be glad of the beds for a few hours," said Madawc in a voice like Rhys', quiet. "Owein and I will take our men north. That is why we came. Or we will go west. Or where you like."

Beorc clamped his lips together, still staring, moist-eyed. "Gods reward it, Madawc."

"Gods send us enemies," said Owein darkly. "Our folk have need of them after such a ride, facing things no arrow troubles. We have arrows saved for the Bradhaeth, or Damh, and gladly for An Beag."

"We are Dryw's sons," said Rhys. "And there is blood between us and these northrons. Much of it."

Beorc rose up and led them down the stairs. Domhnull sat watching, but his heart was not eased. He held Meadhbh and Ceallach against him. Frail-seeming, watching much, they were. He felt them shiver. Oftentimes they gazed off into nothing at all, or watched the fire, or drowsed and picked at the food Muirne kept offering them. *They are in danger,* he thought, perceiving war of a different kind than spears. He held them tightly.

Be kinsman to them, Ciaran had said. Domhnull thought of his own mother, busy among her neighbors down below with this and that matter, the baking of bread, the ordering of shelters, meddling even in Caer Wiell's kitchens on the strength of her connections—nothing daunted her. She always had an answer; and these waifs, the children of a lord and a lady too wrapped in grief, he wished he could bring them to her; but he could not. They would not be comforted. *Go to bed,* Muirne had told them, had sternly ordered; but Meadhbh had sat down, plump upon the hearth three nights ago, and Ceallach had folded his arms and lifted his chin with a look that was Ciaran's own, that look which few had seen but his men when things were at their worst; and Meadhbh had one of his looks too, that quieter one, which measured distances and battlefields. So there had been pallets laid down, and both of them like weeds did as they liked, when they liked, where they liked; only sometimes they turned anguished looks toward the stairs when there was some sound, not often asking with more than silence; or their shoulders would droop or their heads fall, when, as now, they were willing to be held, to lay their heads against him, being not all grown. In his mind he railed on Branwyn, that she deserted them; and in his heart he knew why, as Ciaran had known—that they were strangers to Branwyn and grew more so.

He bent his head, overburdened with knowings, brushed Meadhbh's brow with a kiss for comfort, as if she were his sister. She never stirred, nor did Ceallach. A stone of the fireplace bore into his back, but he did not move.

Rhys came back upstairs quietly and settled to sleep, the quick hard sleep of a man long without, in the dimmed hall; others settled; the fire burned down to embers and Muirne drowsed in her chair, her head on pillows.

And still the voice wailed, outside.

Go away, he wished it fiercely. *Bain Sidhe, go away: he cannot die, our lord. Give up and go away.*

Meadhbh lifted her head suddenly, violent and lost; Ceallach stirred. "Hush," Domhnull said, "it's just the same noise."

"My father!" Ceallach cried, thrusting him away.

And from the hall: *"Beorc!"* Branwyn cried. *"Beorc— o help me!"*

"He's abed again," Beorc said, closing the door at his back, facing them in the hall; stood for a moment as if he were set to keep that door, but then his shoulders fell and he looked more shaken than Domhnull had ever seen him. "He is weaker," Beorc said. "He is growing weaker now."

The children stood there. Muirne set her hands on Meadhbh's shoulders. Domhnull locked his arms about Ceallach's as if that could protect them.

"Curse that thing," Rhys said suddenly. "Curse it. It's that howling, it's no luck to the house, that thing."

"It is Sidhe," said Siodhachan from his corner by the fire. The old man's lips trembled. "And there is no fighting it. Speak no curses. Speak no curses, ap Dryw."

"Bain Sidhe," said Leannan. "It wants a life. It could have mine. Gods know it could. I would give it." And the harper wept, wiping at his eyes. "O gods."

"Or mine," said Ceallach. "It could have mine instead."

"By the gods, no!" Beorc cried. His face twisted. "Talk of appeasing that thing—by the gods, no giving that cursed thing any life of ours. It'll have to take me first, by the gods it will." His eyes were wild as battle. It was contagion. Rhys was on his feet, his dark face flushed, his hands clenched.

"We won past it once," Rhys said. "It's at the river. Do you dare, Scaga's-son?"

"For the gods' sake," Muirne cried. "No."

"And you, mac Gaelbhan?"

Domhnull shivered. It was mad. To attack a Sidhe—it was a thing hopeless from the start. But its price for leaving was a life. He dropped his hands from Ceallach's shoulders. "Tracking a Sidhe—aye, let's be at it. At that I have some advantage."

"No," Muirne whispered, "no, o gods, no."

Beorc headed for the door to the downstairs; Rhys went; Domhnull did, mortally afraid. But Beorc got his cloak and Rhys borrowed one, and they headed down the stairs. "Wait," Domhnull said snatching his, less agile. The madness grew in him, after so long waiting, so much fear. He hastened on the stairs, using his hand to steady him, gathered his sword where they left such things nowadays, at the bottom on their pegs, far from their lord and his hall. They did not run; they went with purpose, opened the door outward to the wall and went out where lightning flickered and wind battered at them.

They bore iron. It was sure at least the Sidhe had no

love for it. Domhnull belted on his sword and came after
Beorc and Rhys. "Open the lesser gate," Beorc bade
the watch as they went down the steps, and such was his
voice that the man did it, and let out the three of them
afoot, hunters of the Sidhe who wailed death into the
winds—afoot, for it could not now be far and no horses
could be trusted.

"By the river," Domhnull said. A sense had settled
into him for days now, that he knew where it laired. He
shivered in the wind, in the dark; and drew his sword,
keeping up with the others with difficulty. He remembered the stones about Caer Donn, and wind and mist.
It seemed he could hear the hoofbeats of a horse, racing
this way and that in distress, like something pent and
desperate.

The shore was far, far, and there were dangers on the
way, a maze, barriers forbidding and dark.

"I am still here," said Death. "Still here if you want
me."

"My friend," said Ciaran. His heart ached. "Give
me up."

Death settled on the window ledge. His sword was in
his hands, and the hands were darkness, but bone was
in them too. His hooded head was bowed. His face was
still concealed. Outside, the wailing grew shrill, and
hoofbeats circled, circled, wilder and wilder, like the
beating of a heart.

"Give me up," Ciaran breathed, and pain rode the
breath. "Go away. And take the Bain Sidhe with you."

"Over the Sidhe I have no power. Least of all that
one. It gives me gifts. It goes before me. I do not rule
it. It will have its due. And your friends have gone to
hunt it."

"O gods, gods, stop it! Prevent them!"

"I have only one power over Men. Which one of them
shall I choose, lord Ciaran?"

"Ciaran," Branwyn said. The visions shattered, became pain, became the room, hard to keep. Her hand
enclosed the stone. For a moment he felt her grief, her
love. She slipped her fingers beneath the chain.

"No," he said, "no, Branwyn. Let it be. If you take
that I shall die."

She wept. Her hand trembled. He felt her desolation in the thing she had resolved to do.

"No," he said, loving her for that. "O no."

She took her hand away. She held his. She looked into his eyes, hers all astream with tears, but she composed her face and smiled a desperately false smile. "Well, awake?" she said. She began to talk, softly, to weave a spell of words; and he knew what she purposed, that she would keep him while she could, but that when there was no hope left she would cast the stone away, to steal him back from Eald.

"You mustn't," he said.

"She loves you," Death said. "She means to do this. And so I have to be here, until the Sidhe is sated."

Branwyn washed his brow, whispered on, of Meadhbh and Ceallach; Rhys had come—he blinked, wondering when Rhys had ever gone, or where; she talked of siege, fiercely, telling him things he could not remember even while he was hearing them.

"The King is dead," he said. "Had I said that?"

She carried his hand to her lips. "Hold on," she said. "Would you ever give up Caer Wiell? Hold fast. Hold on while you can. You have to defend the hold. Stay here, beside me."

That much he understood, that little thing she asked, who had right to ask so much. He hovered there bewildered, remembering their youth, such as they had had together, in the long ago.

Then:

"Man." It was Liosliath. He knew the voice. It had been part of himself once. He heard it speaking to him from a great distance. A white thing rose up between, wailing and bloody-handed.

"Hold on," cried Branwyn.

"No," Meadhbh said, thrusting off Muirne's hands. She ran, raced to the corner where Ceallach had fled, themselves against Muirne, Leannan, everyone who guarded them; she clutched Ceallach's hands in hers, cast a wild look on familiar faces, anxious faces. "We know where it is. Let us go and tell them. It wants him, that thing." The sound was everywhere the wind blew now, everywhere, in blood and bone and stone and timber of the hold.

"Let us go!" cried Ceallach.

And then they went, so suddenly, into such a blast of cold it took the breath, a passage into the place of mist and trees.

"Where are we?" Meadhbh said, shivering. "Ceallach, where are we?"

"There," he said in a voice fainter than the wind and the singer. "O Meadhbh—I think we're *there,* on the riverside."

"Find the men, o Ceallach, we have to find them."

"We're lost, Meadhbh!"

"Not we." She clenched her hand about the gift she wore. "We can't be! We can't be lost, remember? It's the men who've lost themselves." She heard the river mingled with the singer and the trees the wind was tossing. She trod now on wet grass. There was moonlight from above, lightning from the cloudwall, a curious and dreadful luminescence. She gathered up a stone. Ceallach took another, silently.

They saw it then, a small white thing that perched among the trees—so small a creature, like a withered woman all gauze and rags, washing, washing something in the stream.

"Ciaran," Branwyn said. "Ciaran."

Lord Death only sat there, head bowed, the sword within his hands.

"Branwyn," Ciaran said. His eyes were shut or open: he could not tell. The visions crowded close. The singing grew. A horse whinnied desperately. "Listen to me, Branwyn."

"Woe," the Singer wailed, "woe and worse to come. Woe and desolation—"

"Get it," Meadhbh sobbed. She drew back her arm, cast a futile stone.

"No," piped a reedy voice. *"O no, do not touch it, never touch it, throw no stones."*

They started at that crashing through the brush, at the small and hairy thing that peered up at them.

"You," said Meadhbh.

The Gruagach hugged itself, it rolled its eyes, it shivered in the lightning. "Let be, go back, go back, you do no good."

"No!" She took another stone and cast it at the singer; Ceallach's hurtled after, splashing in the water, two sets of rings in the lightning where the Sidhe had been.

"Woe," wailed down the winds.

"Get it," Ceallach cried, gathering another stone; the Bain Sidhe drifted on the water beneath the wind-whipped trees, clutching bloody rags against its whiteness. He cast.

"Ceallach," Meadhbh cried, for it had grown again by half. It grew straighter, brighter, striding on the river.

"There it is," someone cried, and: *"Gods!"*

It wailed. It towered above the trees, a shape more and more terrible and swift.

"It grows!" Meadhbh cried. "O no—no—no—."

"Beorc!" Ceallach shouted, and stared to run, but brambles held them, tore their hands and faces, and threads of white went everywhere in the brush, the wailing grew and grew, everywhere about them.

"Stop it!" Meadhbh cried, struggling in the thorns. "Thistle, help! Thistle, Thistle—stop it, help!" But nothing came. The tendrils wrapped them round, cold as ice and ghostly. *A name,* she wished, *o gods, a name, anyone.* *"Gruagach!"* But it was small and weak. "Caolaidhe, Caolaidhe!" she cried. *"Caolaidhe!* Come help us!"

The white tendrils drew back from them. The wailing went away down the river, to the other side. The water surged, a large body coming up.

It was there, the river-horse, black and shining wet. It waited for them. It threw its head. Its eyes shone like gold lamps in darkness.

"Get it," Ceallach said. "Follow it—keep that thing far from here."

It threw its head; it whuffed the winds and trumpeted its challenge.

"Branwyn," Ciaran whispered. He thought he did. He heard the hoofbeats coming. She bent close and kissed him. He could hardly feel the touch. The world was dimmed.

"Gods help me," he said.

"We have lost you," said Lord Death.

"Meadhbh!" It was Beorc's voice, cracking in the wind, obscured in thunder.

"Go," she cried. *"Never let it near him!"* The each-uisge sped, a flowing of water toward water, that scattered them with drops. She flinched from it and turned, grasping at Ceallach's shoulder. The men came, Beorc and Rhys and Domhnull, Domhnull last and Rhys swiftest to reach them, running down the hill.

"O," a small voice piped from among the rocks, "too late, too late, o run, shelter, o haste, haste, haste! He is gone, gone, sped!"

Meadhbh ran with Ceallach, each dragging the other, into Rhys' arms, and Beorc's; and Domhnull coming last.

"We drove it off," Ceallach wept. "We sent it away. O Beorc—it mustn't have him."

"Too late," the small voice wailed, *"late, late, late."*

Hoofbeats confounded themselves with thunder. The hillside burst into fire, a shock of lightning; a tree blazed up and scattered fire and fragments into the river.

Then the rain, pelting down on them, drenching them to the skin. Meadhbh held her gift and thought of home, now, at once, but the men bore iron, poisoning the air, and the lightning played over them, flickering through the rain.

"Run," Domhnull cried, seizing at them, his fair face drowned and stark in the flashes. "Run, get under cover."

Rhys dragged her up the long hill to the walls; she ran, ran, ran, after Beorc and Ceallach, till her side split and her senses swam, and the gate opened for them and closed after.

They came up the stairs, drenched and shivering; the men cast away their swords with hollow clashes, and got them up into the hall.

Their mother stood there. So they knew. Meadhbh stopped, too numb to think, except that they had lost. Someone pulled her to his embrace, touched her cheek, but she had no tears, had nothing.

"He—left," their mother said, in a still voice they had never heard her use, a whisper, like the rain upon the roof, all hollow and toneless. "Meadhbh, Ceallach, he

just left, in that way he could. He couldn't die, you
know. The stone wouldn't let him. Sidhe fade. It was
like that, that all of a sudden I couldn't feel his hand,
but I could see it. *Aodhan,* he said. That was a horse·
that was his, once." She came to them, held out her
arms. Meadhbh came and hugged her, wet as she was,
and Ceallach came into her arms. She smoothed their
hair; her hands trembled. "Did you see him?"

"No," Meadhbh said. Thunder cracked about the
hold, shaking the stones. She remembered the cloud.
Her mother was being very quiet, a restraint worse than
thunderclaps; and there was this footing about the truth,
of leavings and goings. *Too late,* the Gruagach had said.
She lifted her head from her mother's shoulder and
looked her in the eyes, hard and straight. "You mean
he went away—like us? Like that?"

"Like that." Her mother's lips moved, forcing breath
into the words. "He said good-bye. There's a place Sidhe
go. He talked about the sea. He didn't die. He can't,
now. Ever." For the first time her lips trembled into
tears. She hugged them again, shook their heads back
and looked at them. "Can't you cry?" their mother
asked.

Meadhbh shivered. Her clothes were cold; it got into
her bones, except where the Sidhe gift rested about her
neck. She patted her mother's cheek, feeling it soft and
warm and remembering the smell of lilacs and oil and
metal.

They had lost him after all. They had not watched him
well enough. She felt herself at fault; and touched the
gift about her throat, remembering what it meant: but
all Eald faltered, crashed in ruin overhead, around,
about them. Her throat ached.

"My lady." It was Leannan's voice, from over by the
corner, a-tremble and very soft. "Forgive me, lady—
He's gone. Siodhachan's gone."

The old man looked asleep, nodding in his corner by
the fire. His face was peaceful.

"O gods," Rhys whispered, and his voice broke. "The
old man outran us."

FOURTEEN

FUGITIVES

They had a burial to do in the morning. It was not the burying that Siodhachan would have wished, being quiet, in the black-clouded dawn, with no cups of ale or tale-telling through the night; they were in too much haste and the matter of their lord weighed too heavily on them. They built the old man a strong cairn of Caer Wiell's gray stone and vowed him a greater one in better days. Leannan for his part meant to make a song for him; but there was no singing it until things were worse or better. So the harper only sat awhile by the cairn after everyone had gone, bowed with his head on his arms; and came in finally, drank a cup and washed his face, and wandered among the tents and shelters, among the hapless who had come for refuge.

"Sing a song," the steader children asked, of the friend who had always cheered them; for the night had been dreadful and the day ahead looked ugly.

"Hush," said their elders sternly. "He is the lord's own harper; and he is sad today. Show respect."

So silence went about him.

But rumors flourished, in the harper's downcast silence; in the grim rebuilding of the cloudwall after last night's storm; in the whispering of one nightwatch to another and them to others of the men . . . for the Bain Sidhe was silent today: *She wailed for the old man,* folk said. *Now the lord will live.*

But down in the kitchens: *No more orders come from hall to scullery. Something is amiss up there.*

And again: *His men went out last night. And came back with his children, but they never passed the gates before that. The Sidhe magicked them.*

The lord is dead: it's himself in that cairn, and the old man's just gone to hiding.

"Lord Ciaran left last night," said Beorc to the men he gathered, with Rhys and Madawc and Owein, his own folk and the southrons. He said it loudly, so there would be no doubt and no mangling of the news. He shouted it out; and country folk gathered beyond the knot of men at arms and southrons. *"He is not dead, hear?* And where he went and how is his business; but he took his leave of my lady before he left and had a good reason for going. The rest of it is not for our bandying about in the yard. Get to business. Mind your tongues and reckon the lord knows what he's about. Meanwhile we have the Bradhaeth to deal with; the lord's order—*look to it!"*

Domhnull watched the people. He saw the stricken looks, the bewilderment on faces that had seen too much of disarray in their lives. But no one disputed what Beorc said: no one met that scowl of his or argued with that voice. Folk listened; and Beorc told them what wanted doing and how quickly.

When Beorc let them go again, Domhnull climbed the stairs, past Rhys, who stood on the bottom step; and Madawc and Owein near him. He had no part in what was toward now—in the defense of the north. The orders now were for others. He went up into hall to watch over Meadhbh and Ceallach, that being what his lord had last charged him to do, and it seemed to have been left to him even now that their southron kinsmen were at hand.

Muirne was there, infallibly, Muirne—sitting on the bench and spinning by the light of the one torch they kept burning, beside the pallets where the children slept at hearthside. The room was in order again; blankets had been taken away—doubtless Muirne had seen to it, the way she saw to everything.

He settled on the hearthside bench in the warmth that remained of the fire, taking comfort in Muirne's presence, watching the deft work of her fingers that coaxed thread out of wool, a work he had watched hour upon hour of his long convalescence. This was Muirne's Sidhe-gift, he had thought then, to spin, spin, spin peace out of chaos, comfort out of hurt. He had been ashamed once, when he had come out of the muddled days and nights of his sickness, that anyone should have seen him as he was. But Muirne never flinched; more, she had looked up from her spinning from time to time with a glance he might have laughed at once, seeing it from Muirne, shy and girlish and wishing, years older as she was. His mother had been there in his fever, when it was worst; but Muirne had been there when the memories came, and beguiled his moods with questions—of the land, of places he knew; he discovered she had never been beyond sight of Caer Wiell's walls, though she had seen war and siege beneath them. She knew little of the world. She had always had the spinning, the children, the duties of the hold, for lady Meredydd, for Branwyn, as isolate in her world of women as some soldier in his world of men—shy, suddenly, to be in such different company but treasuring the moments in their trade of what they had to trade—*Can friends be so opposite?* he began to think. *O if she were younger*—

She went to spinning. He watched her fingers, the firelight on her face. So, so tenderly she had soothed brows in this room and in that through all these dreadful days, and whispered that she was there, close by, between them and whatever they feared—as if she were protection. But she was protection, he thought, if love and steadfastness meant anything in the world.

The hall seemed strangely silent now, empty of the orders and instructions that had always flowed from it. My lady slept, exhausted; my lord—gods knew. And out in the courtyard, Beorc prepared revenge, a gust of red-haired violence, ordering weapons and supplies and wagons and whatever horses they could gather.

And above them all, the clouds—for he had looked at the sky this morning—the cloudwall was taking shape again, after the wreckage of the night. Rampart-building moved apace in heaven, so that the forest was all dark and dawn winked out as the sun rose into the wall of cloud. The daylit space narrowed; and there were ominous mare's-tails to northward, many of them, advanced from that border Ruadhan was holding.

A chill had fallen on him when he had seen that, not a sharp fear, but one that mingled with all the others of the day, so that the shouts Beorc gave to the wagoners, the noise in the yard, the whisperings and the movements and the colors, all seemed perilously thin, like some last outpouring of vitality.

Before death, he thought. *Before the world goes dark.* He finally named what he had feared out there in the yard, that Caer Wiell's strength was ebbing, that everything they were preparing was wrong, while the clouds narrowed like advancing armies. Lord Ciaran was gone. *Not dead,* he insisted to himself but he remembered Ciaran tumbling from his horse, the black arrows, the waxen flesh that sustained itself only by the stone—To go back into Eald, to enter it foredone as he was, to seek the elvish horse and fare outward on the last of his fading strength. . . .

O ride quickly, he wished his lord, *go where they go, find peace, whatever this fading is.* When he shut his eyes he saw the hill outside Caer Donn, a black and terrible wind that blew the Sidhe's white fire in tatters.

He shuddered, a quick convulsion of his limbs. The air seemed thick and foul.

Something touched him; but it was only Muirne when he blinked, laying her hand on his shoulder.

"Hush, it's all right."

"They can't do it," he murmured, having a sudden clear vision of the yard, the wagons readying, Beorc amid it all, going north to the defense of the steadings. "They mustn't. The north is already falling. O gods—"

"Domhnull!" Muirne whispered. She was on her knees, clenching his hands in hers. He felt her grip at last when she shook at him. He was still cold, and what had been in his mind slipped from him like a passing dream.

"Forgive," he said, confused, forgetting it all like some fading glimpse of faery.

"Hush, you mustn't vex yourself. You were sleeping sitting up just then. You were dreaming. Go down to your own bed and rest. It's time you did."

He remembered then, distantly and coldly, how futile everything had seemed to him. He had had such nightmares often since Donn. He feared he might have cried out just then in his sleep, and heat touched his face. He glanced aside, where the children slept undisturbed on their pallets. He felt aches in his shoulders, in all his bones. "If Eald should fall," he said, a scattered thought as all his thoughts were scattered now, like doves before some hawk, "maybe I would go to moonbeams and cobweb. Or be what I was, where I was, on the rocks below Caer Donn."

"Hush." Muirne's fingers stopped his lips. Her eyes were anguished.

He caught the hand, touched it a second time with his lips and held it. She remained distraught, seeming so weary, so very weary. Her eyes were full of tears and fright. "Muirne," he said, "if there are heroes in Caer Wiell, you are one. Did you know that?"

"Why?" she asked, as confused by this as by the other.

"Because you are." He let go her hand, for her cheeks burned red. Perhaps she suspected idle flatteries, herself unarmed and unarmored against the only man she knew. He sensed so. He rose, aching from the stones, awkward. There were few he let see him in pain, but Muirne knew, and so he indulged himself, too weary to hide it. A restlessness gnawed at him. The fears that had made sense a moment ago were vague, and he had the urge to see the clouds again, to do something toward the hold's defense, even to stand idle and watch those who were going to it. *I still might go myself,* he thought in the scattering of his thoughts. *With a horse under me I might be well enough. The shield-arm . . . I can bind it.*

Then he recalled the children, and in that same instant he felt relief that he had an excuse not to be faring north, for he sensed something wrong.

"Domhnull?" Muirne asked. "Whatever is the matter?"

He blinked, gathering his mind back from that gray place where was such loneliness, so little formed and certain; where something flitted lost in the winds.

"Meadhbh!" he shouted. *"Ceallach!"*

"Domhnull—" Muirne cried; but he had gone to them, gathered them in his arms all limp as they were, holding them as tightly as he could, on his knees beside the hearth.

"Wake," he whispered to them, in that place where

they had gone. "Come back. Meadhbh. Ceallach. Your mother needs you, do you hear?"

So they came back to him, obedient.

"Domhnull," Meadhbh said, and he laid his face against her chill one. "We're here," Ceallach murmured, and began to wake, stirring in his arms.

"O gods," Muirne said.

"Watch them, my lord said," Domhnull's heart was beating against his ribs. "*Watch them.* He had this danger in his mind all along. And I thought of leaving them. O wake up, wake up, hear? I know where you are and that's no road for you. Come. Come back now."

"It was dark," Meadhbh said. "The light was blowing away, Domhnull!"

"Wake their mother," Domhnull said fiercely. "Muirne, wake her, go!"

Muirne sped, flying on the stairs.

Then Ceallach shuddered in his arms and drew a great breath, and both of them were there.

He let them go when he was sure. Meadhbh rubbed her eyes. They sat looking at him with a sadness dawning on them, that it was only Domhnull holding them, he thought, and not the one they loved.

"If I could have gone in his place," Domhnull told them, "o gods, I would have."

Meadhbh wept, sitting there amid her blankets, tears rolling down her face. She wiped at them. She ran her hands back over her sleep-tangled hair. Ceallach sat as if lightning-struck. Domhnull gathered them both again, rocking them, though his bad leg ached on the stone.

"Morning's come," he said, "and the world is what it is, and you have to stay in it."

They said nothing, nothing at all.

"Your father said I must watch you," he said, "and so I will."

Steps came hurrying from the door. So their mother arrived with Muirne, herself all dishevelled, in a plain white gown, with her fair hair flying about her shoulders.

Then Domhnull worked himself painfully to his feet, leaning on the stones of the fireplace and on Muirne's offered arm. He saw the children go to Branwyn's embrace, saw tears shed, which ought to be—but then he watched Branwyn fuss at Muirne for their hair, and at them for sleeping here instead of upstairs in their beds. She rubbed at Ceallach's face with the tail of her sleeve and in all delivered as much roughness as love.

She does not know what happened to them, or what danger they are in, he thought with a chill to his heart. *And knows she doesn't.* Branwyn had waked from sleep, only sleep, a sleep heavy or light, but nothing more, never more. *She is only clay,* he thought, *as he was half of air—and knows it.* Mortality was on Branwyn. Her shoulders stooped. There were lines about her eyes this morning. She turned from fretting over her children and looked at him.

"Where is Beorc?" she asked.

"With your cousins. Making ready the men that will go north."

She stared a moment. "No," she said.

"Lady?"

"No, they will not go."

"Lady, little good they will do the land here, in Caer Wiell." He felt heat go to his face. His tongue tied, that he had forgotten to whom he spoke. He stared into her eyes, which were blue and pale and passionless. "The border," he finished, trying to mend things. "The northern steadings. They can't stay waiting." But she was of Caer Wiell, bred and born here. She knew the needs of its defense. That too he remembered.

"They will not go," she said. Her mouth set, making lines at the corners. She folded her children against her like a wall. "Tell Beorc so."

"I will tell him." He cast a desperate look at Muirne, then bowed his head and went in haste, knowing how Beorc would hear it.

She was adamant, when Beorc came thumping back upstairs with him to argue, when Rhys and his brothers arrived on his heels and Rhys shouted at her—which spoke how desperate Rhys had become, how desperate all the men were. Horses, saddled, fretted in the yard; wagons already loaded, stood with their teams outside the gates, their drivers waiting. Folk murmured from wall to wall of Caer Wiell, once again confused, frightened what with the ominous sky above them and the shifting orders of those that led them.

"Good gods," Rhys cried, "you cannot take on like

this. Grief is one thing, madam, but this immolation of your people is profitless. You have a border crumbling at this hour, horses readied, men standing in their armor, rumors running rife in the yard."

"The King is dead," she said. She sat calmly, in her plain blue gown, dressed and coifed now, her hair severe in its braids, her face very pale. She might have been an image graven out of ivory. "Do you understand?"

"Laochailan dead." Rhys paced the floor, when the rest of them would have wished to, fretting as they were. Rhys stopped, held out his hands in entreaty. "Well, that would be no great surprise, cousin, but how do you suppose to know that?"

"My husband said it," she answered in that firm still voice. "Before he left. Send riders out, over all our lands. As far as the borders. Bring our people in and bring Ruadhan home with all our men."

"Lady cousin," Rhys said gently, "lord Ciaran was fevered."

She rose, unfolded upward from her chair, and for a moment small as she was, they were daunted. "Cousin—do you understand me? My cousin Laochailan is dead. He hated us. But he is dead. They murdered him, smothered him in his bed, since their poisons failed. The King is dead."

Domhnull's eyes wandered to the corner, where a slight, red-haired boy sat watching by his sister, and a chill went down his spine. *O gods,* he thought, which he had not thought, for until yestereve there had been Ciaran, and the chance of alliances and maneuverings; and the chance that Laochailan would declare some heir. But nothing was the same this morning. *Ceallach. Gods, gods, this boy is King.*

So others fell silent. The perhaps-King stared back at them in distress, his hand locked in his sister's.

Then: "Cousin," Rhys said, "if it were true—we may have little time. If it were true—there might come trouble up the dale, and quickly. All the more reason to take care of that matter to the north and be ready to face trouble from the west when it comes."

"No," Branwyn said.

"Cousin, give orders in the hold. Not in matters of arms."

"I tell you no."

"This is grief," said Beorc. "Lady, you know me, that I am your man as I was his. And I say the same. Leave this matter of the borders to men who know them."

"The King is dead." Her voice rose, losing both calm and dignity. "And we need all our forces here. And my husband is not dead, Beorc. He has gone away, but he is not dead. You are still his man, and don't forget that."

Beorc bowed his head and lifted it sorrowfully. It was clear what his opinion was. "Lady, wherever he is— But this matter of the border—Lady, it can't wait."

"Beorc, he looked at me. It was the last thing—the last thing he said. He looked at me as clearly as I look at you: 'Branwyn,' he said, 'look to Dryw. Go there if you have to. Go soon.' "

"Impossible," said Rhys somberly. "Would to the gods you could; but that is no sunny ride, cousin, not now. Almost *we* failed it. Safest to secure that one border northward and then close the westward pass."

"They will come through the hills like ants," Branwyn said.

"Lady cousin, that they may; but that will put them in our hands: Owein and Madawc and I—do you think any lowlanders can best our folk in the hills? Let them try. We will hold here."

"Domhnull." Her gaze turned on him, her hands outheld. "Donnchadh—it is Donnchadh who killed the King. Do you understand me?"

A chill went over Domhnull, a memory in once shattered bones, fear driven deep there, and doubt. "Beorc," he said, "Beorc—that one has allies—O gods, Rhys, the Brown Hills and the north—there is too much moving on us now. I saw it—It isn't the armies. Not the worst of it. She may be right."

So they looked at him too with pity and something worse. Beorc had his hands in his belt; at last he ducked his head and lifted it with a frown, looking at Branwyn. "Domhnull will stay here," he said, "to order the defense. You are my lady, but my lord is gone; and until he's here again, I do what he told me last, and I mind me that I never had his leave to be coming back here in the first place. Rhys, Owein, Madawc—"

The color has risen to Branwyn's cheeks. "I have told

you," she said. "But you refuse to hear." Her lips trembled. Her eyes were filled with tears. "So go. Do as you will, Beorc. Domhnull at least will stay."

Domhnull stood still, feeling the heat in his face, looking still toward Branwyn while Beorc and Rhys and his brothers left, a martial clattering on the stairs behind; and his eyes went dim and blurred and painful.

"Well?" Branwyn asked sharply. Muirne stood there, witness to this. The children sat in their corner, in the corner of his sight.

"I will go out, by your leave," Domhnull murmured painfully, "and see my cousin off."

Branwyn nodded and turned her shoulder to him, finding something to do in the clutter of herbs and jars in the corner that was hers.

The gates stood open. The wagons already groaned their way out onto the road. "Take care," Domhnull said, standing close beside the way, looking up at Beorc as he rode past; and Beorc reined aside from the others.

"Domhnull." For a moment Beorc sat looking down, a line between his brows; and then he heaved himself down from the saddle and offered an embrace, tentative and shamed-seeming.

Domhnull took what was offered, looked Beorc in the eyes, at arm's length. "Take care," he said doggedly. There was a fear in him like sickness. He saw the riders pour past, almost all Caer Wiell's strength. He was conscious of the sky above them. *Donnchadh,* rang in his mind with the rattle of the armor. *Donnchadh, Donnchadh.* "Do it quickly and come home."

The fear showed. It woke pity in Beorc's eyes, who was not accustomed to failings. "Cousin—" he said, and bit his lip on what he would have said. "See to matters here. We'll be back as quickly as we can."

The ache of Beorc's fingers lingered on his shoulder. He stood there staring from the gate as Beorc galloped off to the fore and the column of riders bent northward. His heart had gone cold, for all the brave color of the banners of Caer Wiell and the black of the sons of Dryw, the thunder of horses, the clash of armor of riders hard upon their way toward the north, toward the gathering mare's-tails of new rampart-building in the heavens.

There were folk about him, above him on the walls, watching from all manner of vantages, and only a few had cheered, a silence unlike Caer Wiell.

"Son."

His mother stood close, by the stairs. He turned to look at her and her face changed at his look to something quieter—a tall woman, his mother, her hair shot through with gray and her eyes full of living. "Come," she said wisely, as she had coaxed him in younger years, of bruised knees and falls and prizes missed and loves spurned, in the years before he thought himself a man and ran off to Caer Wiell. "Come, I've somewhat to spare this morning. Come breakfast with me."

It was not the food he sought. His lady wanted him in hall; he had duties and no time to spend, but Beorc's look still stung, and he had duties here in the yard as well as anywhere else, if Branwyn and Muirne had the children well in hand. Someone had to be seen out here, someone to still the rumors.

So he let himself be seen; folk stared at him and murmured. Of the breakfast he took only a cup of cider and a bit of bread, while his mother talked of everything but wars. He sat on a sack of goods by the scullery door and the traffic came and went, a bustle of impudent goats and running children, of women going this way and that with water and food and stores. Most in Caer Wiell now were women; and the young and halt and old. So he listened while his mother talked of neighbors' lives and scullery gossip, and while children played tag in the sunlight (but there was shadow beyond the wall) and squealed and screamed until the noise was like to drive him mad in one moment and seemed precious in the next. She asked no news of hall; no, she had no wish to go there. She had her friends and neighbors, and insisted on telling him of them, small, simple things, so he knew it was like Muirne's bravery, innocent and wise. And others lingered near them, pretending tasks and errands, listening ears and watching eyes of women all thinking of their sons, of husbands, brothers, cousins—and himself one maimed man, one marred and somewhat broken man, and now, with a handful of men left to him, commanding in Caer Wiell.

So he lifted his head and looked at his mother and

marked how she was beautiful in his eyes, how other women deferred to her. It was the way she was, full of good sense. His father had loved her for reasons he only then saw, having only then come to manhood, this morning it seemed, in Caer Wiell.

He felt a great calm then amid his fear, finding himself knowing more of the world than he was wont. He knew where he belonged, and where his oath to his lord was pledged. "I have to get back to hall," he said deliberately. "There are plans—" Several score breaths bated. He knew. "—My lord left clear instructions to carry out; there are things to do." His mother sat quietly, her wise fair eyes intent on him, well knowing what he did. "Say that." He pressed her hand where it rested on her knee and looked straight into her eyes. "If others ask. Our lord is not lost. I've been where he fares now. And *I* came back. He's gone for healing. As I did. Say that too."

He rose. His mother did. He had become a liar. He had no shame in that at all. He kissed her on the brow and turned his cheek for her. So he walked away, not limping, though his bones ached.

He crossed the yard, took the stairs under hundreds of silent eyes. He felt them on his back. He heard the tide break behind him as he gained the wall, a flood of women's voices. He did not look back even so, but walked on up the inner stairs and up again through the accounting-room to the hall.

"Well?" said Branwyn, pausing in her combing of Meadhbh's hair.

"Nothing, lady. They've gone, that's all. A while ago. I've been down in the yard. Taking breakfast."

Branwyn tightened her lips, and Meadhbh braced herself and suffered, her head bowed as she stood. Her red hair shone and sparked in wisps beneath the strokes of the comb.

And after a moment: "And where would Leannan be?"

"Somewhere about. Since the burying."

"So. Well." More strokes of the comb. "Now hear my morning's orders. Bring in every horse we have, mares and foals too. Find every cart Beorc has left us, and every weapon. We shall be going south tomorrow. Every soul in Caer Wiell."

"Lady—" His certainties ebbed from him, regrouped behind his reason. "You want a man to ride after Beorc, then. To force him and Rhys."

Two motions went on, Branwyn's combing; and Ceallach, who was at the grinding of Branwyn's herbs. There was the talisman about the boy's neck, that swung with the fierce effort of his arm. There was a madness in all this, that ordinary things went on, that Branwyn insisted on them. The air was full of rosemary and grief.

"If they would listen," Branwyn said, "they would have. Are you faithful, Domhnull?"

"Lady, those men are faithful to you. They only see a danger—"

"So do I."

"I will ride after them, persuade them—if I stood with you, to do this, then they might listen, and fortify Caer Wiell."

The combing stopped. She patted Meadhbh's shoulders, dismissed her. Meadhbh only stood and stared. Branwyn looked straight at him.

"You do not well hear me. And Beorc would hold you to prevent me," she said, "because he sees a danger. No. Send last to them. Before that, bring the last few steaders in. Send riders."

"The folk will be afraid, down in the yard."

"Say what you like. Send Cein's boys: they have close mouths. Find Leannan. And Cobhan. This hold will be ready. Tell that where you like. Take every weapon, everything that can be mended and every hand that can hold one. Most of all keep them busy. Will you do these things?"

"Aye, lady." He looked at Muirne and at the children both, at Branwyn, last and longest. "What is in your mind to do? Lady, you were not there when Rhys told us what he had seen on that southern road. Things that took men and horses. The forest is deadly."

"The Sidhe will protect us. For my children's sake, they will save us all."

There was fey madness in Branwyn's eyes. There was fear there too. Both were contagious.

"Lady—for the sake of those out there—who would

suffer in siege, but most would live—with a half dozen men I might take you south to lord Dryw. If you are sure the risk is worth it. But to set out on a road like that with the old folk and the infants still in arms—gods, my lady, that's a forest trail we're speaking of, no way for carts and wagons. We haven't enough horses for all of them to ride."

"Domhnull—the King that sits in Dun na h-Eoin is *Donnchadh*. You of all people should know his manners."

"Aye," he said after a moment. *O Beorc, come home, come quickly, reason with our lady.* "But if Donnchadh comes into the dale he would waste no time on Caer Wiell if we were not in it."

"You think in numbers Caer Wiell could raise. You never saw the armies Dun na h-Eoin might lead. Well, *I* have seen them. Do you think they couldn't divide that force and come at Caer Wiell too, to let Damh and Bradhaeth and An Beag loose inside these walls? No." She drew her daughter back into her arms. Ceallach had come to stand beside her. Lines seemed graven in Branwyn's face after these last, horrid days. "My husband's word, Domhnull. Do you believe it?"

"I saw Caer Wiell burned," Meadhbh said, so faintly he could hardly see her lips move. "I dreamed it last night, Domhnull. I think that it is true."

The world seemed cold and frail about him. He stared at both; at the boy-King who came to join them, red-haired, his sleeves rolled up, hands dusted with herbs and country simples.

"I will do what I can," Domhnull said to Branwyn. It seemed impossible to him that his lord was not there, that they were left with such choices. The Sidhe would protect them, his lady believed. But he lived with the ache in his bones, the memory of the hill and the fading of the light.

The Sidhe has lost, that is what, he thought, on the stairs leading down from the hall. He limped, using his hands to steady him, he, the guardian of Caer Wiell. About him constantly he seemed to see the stones, the lightning, the Sidhe tattered in the black winds.

Sidhe faded. Ciaran had gone, Sidhe-like; but even in that place was no refuge—or he would have let the children seek it. Branwyn was blind, hoping to pass the forest, hoping because she had no other hope.

But Meadhbh had visions.

Your brother is gone, the Dark Man whispered. *Lost.*

Donnchadh started and looked about him, in the solitude of the gloomy hall in Dun na h-Eoin. Armies were about it: his; the lords had gathered like carrion birds at the King's failing; and among them had come one eagle.

"What—*dead?*" he whispered aloud; but the voice came creeping inward, cold as ice.

Last night, the voice said, soft as spidersilk. *The Bain Sidhe has sung it. Ciaran of Caer Wiell, of Donn, Branwyn's husband—he is gone.*

Donnchadh sat down on the plain wooden throne, that being where there was to sit. He felt it like a blow, a hammer-strike to the heart. He felt like weeping; and felt relief at once. *Dead—of the wounds An Beag gave him?*

Dead— The voice grew softer still. *Ah, well, but nearly. At least as dead as Sidhe can die.*

This was a dagger-thrust. He looked up at the shadows, but there was no one to see. *A man is dead or not, ghost.*

Oh, but a Man is—dead or not. But there was less and less of Man in him—cousin. Now he has no boundaries. He might be here, this moment—or stand beside your bed of nights. He might easily come this way. He would still defend his hold, his son—with every means at his command, and those means are many.

A chill came on Donnchadh. It grew, as if warmth were leaving him forever. It was true: there was his brother's son, heir through Meara, Evald, Branwyn; and all those armies knew it. It wanted so little to produce one rebel, one of those lords to rouse others in the name of a boy who could be brought up as they pleased, if he fell into their ambitious hands.

That is the first danger, he thought; and it *was* his thought, perhaps; or it was the Dark Man's, who had come so close now there was no distinguishing one from the other. *The boy. Ceallach. Laochailan's heir; and my brother's; and Dryw's kinsman. In Caer Wiell, near the Sidhe. He must die.*

* * *

"It is quite mad," Leannan said. His pale blue eyes were mazed with ale when Domhnull found him outside the scullery, with ale and too much of losing folk he loved; and with doings of the Sidhe and a sky that seemed worse and worse. But: "Say no word of it," Domhnull said. "Only give me help—to keep the folk quiet. Go among them. Find out how many there are here; and how many of those could not ride—somehow. Or be carried."

"Aye," the harper said, who had a skill at remembering things, and at numbers.

"Southward," Cein said when Domhnull went to him at the stables. "O gods. With wagons?" But: "Better Sidhe luck than Donnchadh's mercy," Domhnull said. "I can swear to that. Don't say anything here. Send your boys for the steaders. I want them back by sundown. And tell them to be discreet in it."

And last to Cobhan, who was grooming Ciaran's Iolaire, stubbornly, faithfully as every morning: "Every horse, Cobhan. Every one. We leave none of my lord's horses to An Beag bandits. Bring them in. And oxen for the wagons."

"Aye," said Cobhan, tight-lipped and thinking. He called a boy to him and gave instructions, never pausing in his work.

So the matter proceeded. There was further gossip: *The enemy is near. The border is giving way. So these preparations.*

Domhnull did not gainsay that rumor. It served him. He went here and there with a worried frown and cared little now who saw it.

"Is it so?" his mother asked. "Is the north in danger?"

So there was another soul he decided to trust. "It may be. Mother, it's southward we are going. And soon. For good reasons. It's not to be told, not yet. But if Beorc is driven back—we will move quickly; for our lives, we must move, to shelter with lord Dryw until this thing is over. You know the steader women, who's to rely on. Name them to me, the ones to move the others."

She set her lips, frowned a bit, and named them.

There was smithery in the yard, the hammering of iron, the mending of a wheel. Leannan moved here and there like a fish through troubled waters, visiting shelters, playing small songs to keep minds elsewhere, asking after this old man's health, that old woman's, the weeks a baby had. Cein and Cobhan brought in the horses, a great protesting of mares and nervous foals; of old geldings too long out to pasture and showing their tempers; of oxen, lastly, moving their great bulk past shelters and collapsing one tent by the Old Hall, to wails and protests of the old woman in it.

Domhnull went from place to place, keeping pages and steader lads busy sharpening old weapons and the old warriors at more meticulous tasks restoring old horse gear out of storage. He took care to be seen often; he gave, if not detailed orders, at least approval of what experienced folk would do; and wider and wider he spread his trust where he dared, taking oath of this one and that one to keep quiet.

Even silence begat rumors. *There is too much quiet,* folk began to say. *There be those that know things.* He heard other whisperings and murmurings which he could not make out; and these made him uneasy. Whenever he chanced up to the wall he could not forbear looking northward himself, wishing for some sight of riders, just enough to be Beorc and Rhys coming home, with Ruadhan beside them: but what he dreaded was a larger band—the whole of Caer Damh and the Bradhaeth turning up on that horizon. And always there was that unnatural ring of sunlight, against their walls now on east and south: *we must pass under it if we go south—into that shadow.*

When such chill thoughts came on him he would think, unthinking: *Lord Ciaran would know what we ought to do—*

Then with a reeling of his mind he would remember why they were doing all of this at all, that lord Ciaran was not in hall, nor likely to be again: that there was no chance of things being what they had been, no days stretching before them of summer and harvest and winter and spring, no more, no more, forever.

O gods, he would think then, and there would come a leaden pain about his heart and a panic desire to go up to hall if only to look and be sure no further calamity had fallen. *They do not know how to watch them,* he thought of Meadhbh and Ceallach, remembering that they were fey, and willful, and desperate. *I would know. I might. O gods. Muirne; my lady—keep them from wandering.*

But he had tasks enough at hand. The counting of the horses came to him; Leannan brought him the tally of the people. "Cipher me the thing," he begged Leannan, helpless in the profusion of numbers; and so they squatted together by the steps and made an obstacle of themselves while Leannan traced figures in the dust and told him the tale of it.

"The fittest men have to have the good horses," Domhnull said. "To ride at the fore. They cannot carry double; we must not tire those horses or those men— for our defense."

"So," said Leannan. "But what will we do with the twenty-odd left walking?"

He had no answer. So Leannan left him, saying nothing more. He ran his hands over his aching head, sitting as he was on the step; and remembered then that there were always eyes on him, and gathered himself to his feet.

A shadow fell, abrupt twilight. Thunder rumbled. He looked up at the cloudwall, towering up and up above them. A dark thread had torn from it and streamed across the heavens, headed northward. Another mare's-tail, in sky that had been pure. A chill went up his back.

"Domhnull."

The voice was high and clear and urgent, from the steps above him. He looked up at Meadhbh and Ceallach.

"Go inside," he said. A dread was on him because of the clouds. He felt the whole of Caer Wiell defenseless, naked to storm and lightning. "Get back inside!"

The thunder cracked. They flinched together and looked up. He took the steps, reckless of the pain, and suddenly saw another sight beyond Caer Wiell stone— he saw the border hills all shadowed, tangled figures locked in battle, men in rout and dying in the black hail of arrows. *Lost,* he thought, between two steps; and like a thunderclap remembered that he had dreamed this once before, in early morning. *The north is fallen. Ruadhan!*

"Domhnull—" Small hands gripped his, thin arms embraced him at the stair's crest. He swept the pair up with him, carried them both, aching with the pain and stumbling. An icy wind rose; it battered at them, carried dust, smelling of rain. He thrust them inside the doorway where there was some shelter, and looked back again.

"They're going north," said Ceallach. "The clouds are going north."

They were: the gray mare's-tails streamed off the cloud-wall above them, all tending in the same direction like strands of black wool all drawn by some invisible hand.

"Like weaving," said Meadhbh. "Look!—there are more coming from the north below them."

The lightning cracked. Wails of dismay came from the yard, the screams of children. "Get inside," he shouted at them. He went out onto the wall and yelled at the men who were running down the steps to safety, to the folk who were hurrying in the yard. "Get everyone within walls! Go to the Old Hall: go to the barracks! The doors are open!"

Wind whirled up sand from where it gathered by the stairs. Leannan came out of nowhere, clutching his harp like a babe before him, rushing up the steps. The awning of the scullery ripped loose; a stack of pots overturned and went racketing about in the wind. A stray horse bolted through the yard, shying from the pots and running children.

"*Domhnull!*" It was Muirne's voice behind him. He stood staring outward. The sun was going. Shadow covered them. The winds howled. If he let himself he could see dark and flickerings of lightning, like that night at Donn.

"Domhnull!" A hand seized his arm. It was Leannan who pulled him back inside shelter. The door slammed: Muirne dropped the bar. Meadhbh and Ceallach hugged him as if they feared he too would fade; he hugged them blindly to him and went up the stairs inside with them, while thunder shook the stones.

Branwyn waited there, sitting by the fire.

"It's happened," Domhnull said. The children were mute beside him, too prophetic, shivering. He held to them. "Lady Branwyn, the border's fallen."

She was unamazed. She stared at him. Her eyes were dry. She was stone, ice, immobility. "So Beorc will come home now," she said. "If he can free himself. Rhys with him."

"No," said Leannan. "Likeliest they will be at Hlowebourne by now. And if Ruadhan retreats Beorc will stand there, Ruadhan's shield."

"He mustn't," said Meadhbh. Her teeth were chattering. Domhnull clenched his arm about her. "It's coming. Something dark—*dark on your path,* he said; he told me."

"Hush," said Ceallach, "Meadhbh, don't."

She grew cold a moment. Domhnull felt it, as if some winter wind had chilled her skin, even beneath his hand. "Meadhbh," he said. "Stay, stay *here.*"

Eald quaked. The silver trees shed gold in the darkness, a cascade on the hill, an ebbing of their light even with the first glimmering of dawn.

There was silence for the moment. Then the wind began, driving more leaves before it, and the day hesitated, whether it could dawn at all.

The night's cold lingered. Arafel sat still within the grove, head bowed against her knees, her sword embracing them in her hands. The moonstone's light was dimmed, murked with shadows, and she could not bear to look at it.

Darknesses crept close among the trees, regaining courage in the fading of her spell. They whispered there.

Then she lifted her head and clenched her hand on the sword hilt, and the silver light gleamed.

"Where is the horse?" one mocked her. "Do you know that, Duine Sidhe? Has it run away like the Man? Or has sòmething caught it?"

"There were two," said the other, whose eyes were lamps in shadow, "but she has lost them both."

Her heart grew cold. She rose with the sword held before her. "What mean you—run away? Be plain, wight."

They edged back into darkness. Others were there, tall Sidhe, slim and pale of face. They were armed and armored, and the rising day shone through them.

"Begone!" she cried. "Dun Gol hold you! *Begone from Eald!*"

They vanished. They were prudent still. Her wound ached. The sword sank point against the earth, impaling golden, once-silver leaves. The leaves still fell, spiraling about her, gentle and desolate; and a longing was on her—how fair they had seemed, even as they were, how fair and how proud and how much what the Sidhe had been.

"Fionnghuala," she whispered. And aloud: *"Fionnghuala."*

Rain began to fall, cold as death, hazing the struggling day, making the leaves one sodden carpet and sending shivers to her bones. It heralded change, like the falling of the leaves. Even Miadhail, the youngest of trees, had green only in his uppermost leaves; a dozen at least fell to the onslaught of the wind.

"Fionnghuala."

There was a breath near her. The elf horse stood drenched in rain, her bright head lifted, nostrils wide.

"So you *are* here," Arafel said, and shivered at the doubt that had been so easily sown in her heart; like the rain, like the death of trees, it was the waning of her strength. And Fionnghuala hesitated, as if that doubt had come between them.

She went to the horse, offered her hand. Soft breath came against it in return, trust and faith. The night was past; elvish day had come, even a murky one and dim. And time—mortal time—how much of it had fled?

Ciaran—Ciaran—*Ciaran!*

Run away, the voices had whispered. She felt something, but it had changed, vastly changed. She felt another presence when she strove to reach through the mist, the prisoning, black trees.

"Aodhan," she murmured. The stone pained her, went cold. "What of Aodhan—Fionnghuala?" She stroked the damp neck, felt the shiver, brisk and impatient. A fey dark eye regarded her, full of dread and madness. *Come,* it said. *Come. There are things yet to try.*

She sheathed the sword, seized the mane and swung up, and Fionnghuala began to move, in a muttering of thunder, shifting through *here* and *now* with increasing swiftness. In the long night she had lost much. The day promised to be brief and dim—but it was her day, all the same, when the drow must wane.

Ciaran, she thought, and shivered at what the stone brought her, a lost and lonely grayness, far from any sun. *"Aodhan!"* she called, and the names wound together inseparable in their fate.

She rode even into mortal Eald. But here there was no sign or touch of them. "Lord Death!" she called.

But even he was gone.

One touch of Eald remained in this world. *For memory,* she had said once, *for memory that Eald is true.*

And again: *I have set a virtue on them of finding.*

Thunder rumbled in the night. Meadhbh wished to be brave, but she shivered, even wrapped as she was in warmth, in the hall and the glow of fire and the presence of those she loved.

Fire, she thought. She imagined the small safe hearthfire licking out at the floor, running the stones, down the stairs, cutting them off from safety. Her gift prickled at her throat like nettles and when she shut her eyes there was the mist. Her brother wandered there; and they were afraid, both of them, of something nameless.

Their father would have warned them back; but he was not with them; and they did not know this place.

"Meadhbh." That was Domhnull. A callused hand took hers and held it, ever so gently. "Ceallach."

So they were back in hall, within gray stone walls. Muirne and Domhnull were by them. Their mother slept in her chair, and Leannan nodded, while the rain came down against the roof above them. It was like that night, the last night, the rain, the dreadful rain, their father lying abed.

"Leannan," Muirne said. "Play. Play, will you?"

The harper lifted his head, weary that he was, settled his harp on which he had been leaning, sent his fingers wandering over the strings, and the lightest music came, the gentlest, saddest beneath the rain-sounds.

It is a Sidhe song, Meadhbh thought; and so long as the harper's fingers moved it made a magic in the hall.

But when the song was done the silence seemed the grayer and the thicker for it.

Sometimes she heard horses; heard sounds she had only heard in the practice yard, the hiss and strike of arrows: but harsh cries followed. She heard the clash of metal, smelled iron like poison in the air. She rested her face in her hands, and could not escape it.

She slept true sleep but little. Domhnull held her and Ceallach, each in an arm; and so she had a little rest, her head against his heart, with Muirne close beside her.

The light failed, no longer than a mortal day now: the nights grew longer and this one would be longest of all. The sun was rising in the mortal world. Armies moved. On Airgiod's banks darkness returned.

But Fionnghuala strode in and out of this world and the other, searching.

And in Caerbourne's waters she found it, a quiet creature, hiding, baleful in its shadows.

"Come out," Arafel said, in mortal dawn; it fled to Eald, a quick shifting; but Fionnghuala was quicker. It shifted back again: and now it shivered, white and shriveled in the rocks where it had hidden.

"Despair is your name," Arafel said. *"Andochas."* Her sword whispered from its sheath and the water shivered. "You have trespassed, hear me."

It shrank farther. Two pale eyes shone like moons beneath the water.

"Where is he, fuath?"

The moons rose. The white face broke the surface. The air shivered to its wailing. "I warn, I only warn, Duine Sidhe."

"Baneful, spiteful creature! Lord Death is patient! I am not, not today—Andochas. Tell me!"

"He fled, fled, fled. *Another* life went out." The Bain Sidhe shifted into elvish night; but Fionnghuala did not lose her.

"Where?" Arafel asked.

"Dark to me, dark his path. Death lost him." The Bain Sidhe shrank farther, became a pale strange fish, that dived deep into Death's dark realm, leaving only a ripple on Caerbourne's surface. And into that place Fionnghuala would not venture unbidden.

"Men," a far voice whispered. *"Men have failed you,*

*Arafel, Aoibheil, whose name is Joy. Aoibheil, Aogail—
joy and death . . . o Arafel, Arafel, Arafel. . . ."*

"No," she said ever so softly. "No. You do not have
him. *Here, Duilliath—come here to me here, Duilliath,
my cousin."*

Her whisper sped, winding through mists and among
the ghostly branches of that other Eald. She clenched
the moongreen stone she wore and willed a harping from
it, an elvish sound, of a harp now broken. That song had
power in it. It was heard in all three realms of Eald. It
was heard forever; if that harp had been whole she might
have changed that song, but it was not and that was
beyond her power. It bound and drew, having magic in
it; it had Men in it, for a Man had made it.

It reached to the halls of Caer Wiell, where that harp
had hung; it reached to Dun na h-Eoin, where Kings
had had it; it reached even to the plain before the gates
of the King, where in the dawning Donnchadh rode on
a black, powerful horse. The eyes of that horse were
green and sometimes it seemed other than what it ought.
And Donnchadh seemed other to his men than he had
been the day before—or perhaps they had never seen
him so fired with purpose: he was lean and fair and
strange and sat straight as a younger man; no one looked
him in the eyes, no more than they looked at the horse
more directly than they must.

The standards moved. The points of countless spears
glittered wanly in the greenish, stormy dawn; these were
the contingents of the plain. There were archers: and
these were the Boglach folk and their lords. They had
gathered to Laochailan's deathbed, to seize what could
be seized; to have power; but power had seized them
instead, and they had no doubt now who of them was
most perilous.

"Hail," the shout went up against the murky sky,
"hail, Donnchadh King!" The hills rang with it like the
sighing of the sea.

"King," the voice whispered which had become Donnchadh's own. *"O sweet self, I shall make you more than
this. What you dreamed of is dross beside my dreams,
long and long inside Dun Gol. King is only the beginning
of it. Caer Wiell was ours once, like Caer Donn; but those
were not the names. I shall teach you to call them. Of all*

Mankind only you will be left, my self, my very soul. You wanted Eald thrust aside; I shall cast it down, and make the world again what it was. And you will see, self, what wonders there are to see—of jewels like the sun and moon, of elegance and pleasure, of things so rare no Man has seen them. We shall scour the world and own it."

Donnchadh had no fear now, of his brother, of armies, of any shadow. Least of all of the Sidhe. He gazed about him and Men flinched. He moved to the fore, the black horse at a canter.

That harp-sound reached one other, far lost in gray and cold. Aodhan had slowed his pace, wandered in the woods, in the maze of darksome branches. But that sound came like light through the murk the world had become, like springtime through the winter, like a friend's hand offered in a world of enemies.

For a moment he knew the way. He made himself remember. There was very little of him left. He looked at his hand that clung to Aodhan's bright mane, and he could hardly see it.

"Come," he said to Aodhan. "This is the way."

The elf horse began to move again, running uncertainly, shaking the lightning from his mane.

FIFTEEN

OF FIRE AND SWORD

The rain had stopped. Branwyn sat listening to the silence in the hall. About her, her children slept, and Muirne, Leannan, Domhnull—all, all finding a moment's peace at the end of night. She sat staring at nothing, feeling tears dammed up in her throat. She had laid all her plans; and now they lay in ruins, the roads a quagmire, Caerbourne rushing high for days, an obstacle for her poor folk, less for a determined army, none at all when An Beag should rise to cut them off from the ford. She had had dreams in the night, and they were all of ruin. She imagined other desperate things, of sending Domhnull and Cein and Cobhan with Meadhbh and Ceallach, to cross the flood alone near Caer Wiell somehow, and to go afoot through the heart of Eald, seeking Dryw, seeking—whatever refuge there was for a King the world rejected.

Perhaps her life had been all a mad hope. She had believed too little in luck at the beginning and believed in it too much at the end—but she had hoped all the same, not even understanding Eald, with the last hope in all her world.

"Arafel," she whispered to the silence. "Arafel. Arafel. Do you hear me—Feochadan, Thistle, whatever name you use nowadays? Ciaran, do you hear, can you hear?"

But in the one she did not trust, and in the other she could not hope, no matter how she tried.

Then came the sound of a running horse, lonely in the

thick-walled silences, up against the walls. From the watch there was no hail or challenge. The hoofbeats continued.

Ciaran, she thought. She dared not breathe, for fear the hope would perish.

No, one of the horses was loose, that was all; some horse strayed before the walls.

Or Arafel had come.

She rose, shedding her laprobe; she walked barefoot to the door, then heard the door open down below, a soft padding on the stairs—but nothing mortal could have come inside so quickly, ignoring gates and watchers. She held back, her heart hammering with dread.

"Domhnull," she said, never taking her eyes from the door. "Domhnull, wake—"

There was no stirring from behind her. The door opened. A head thrust through at knee level, of a small hairy thing whose eyes glittered in the torchlight. "Domhnull!" she cried.

It came inside, hugged itself and leaned against the door. "They sleep, sleep, o the fair children; the Gruagach knows them, knows this Man, comes for them—for you."

"Keep away!" There was no weapon here, not so much as a dagger; they had moved out every piece of iron for Ciaran's sake, for her children's, who could not bear it. She edged toward the wall, thinking of the torch.

"Never fear," the small creature said, "o no, no, no, friend am I; such nice, kind children—so polite the people, saucers of milk they leave me, fine cakes, brown ale—but the Gruagach has his home, and he cannot linger. Come with me, come with me, fine cakes, brown ale, where sun is kind forever."

Her hand fell. She saw the green shadow, the jogging pony, the blonde girl in search of faery. *Come with me, take my hand, never hear them calling—* Her eyes blurred. "Is there still time?" she asked. "Is there place—for all of us?"

"All," the small wight said, and bounced up to his full height. "All the good, kind people; no iron must they carry. Haste, haste, haste."

He was gone, out the door and the door shut so quickly that the eye could not believe anything had

stood there. Branwyn shivered and looked back at the
hearthside where her children stirred, and Muirne;
Domhnull wakened then, and Leannan in his corner.

"Get up," she said, "all of you. Get your warmest
cloaks; Domhnull, go rouse the yard, everyone."

"Lady," Domhnull said, his face bewildered; but he
gathered himself up.

"No iron," she said. "Not even in the bridles, no cook-
ing-pans, no knives, nor brooches, no least thing."

"Lady—"

She drew herself up, wrapping the shreds of her pride
about her—perilous, she thought; might pride shut the
gates of faery? So she was afraid to claim what she had
claimed before, that she was privy to faery's secrets. "I
think now we have help," she said quietly, "and o, I fear
we'll lose it." Beyond Domhnull her children gazed at
her with solemn eyes. "Get your cloaks. We'll go down
to the gate. Hurry, Domhnull; Leannan—help him."

Leannan took his harp; Domhnull paused for nothing
but his cloak, and the door closed behind them.

"Wash, dress," she said to Meadhbh and Ceallach.
"And then we go down."

For once she held secrets and Meadhbh and Ceallach
did not. But they hurried.

She went to the empty bedroom, washed, dressed,
while Muirne tended the children. She took Ciaran's
next-best cloak, oiled wool, warmer than her heaviest.
It may be cold, he had said once, setting out on such
a journey.

Now she thought of Beorc and Rhys and Ruadhan, of
the men up at the border, and for a moment the glamour
faltered. *O gods, what will become of them when they
find Caer Wiell deserted? What if our enemies should take
it against them? O gods, where are we going? Where am
I taking these folk?*

But then she thought of Ciaran, of the way he had
gone, and what they faced from the west, and no chance
seemed too desperate. The vision recast itself, the small
girl on the pony, the desire she had had once. She had
seen the green silence; this beckoned differently, made
her think of sun and meadows, not moon and sun together, not the dreadfulness of that guest who had come

to their hall. This was warmth and laughter. And wherever it would go, *he* might have gone before them.

She hastened; she gathered up Meadhbh and Ceallach in the hall each by a hand and they went down the stairs together with Muirne close behind them bringing a bundle of clothes— "In case," she said, "someone should need warm cloaks. 'Tis a waste to leave them."

The dawn broke as best it could over Hlowebourne, a dim redness before the clouds should take back the sun. The reeds were black, like so many spears; the bank loomed, and Beorc was glad when they put that rise behind them. All the land seemed full of ambushes now.

Of Ruadhan they had seen no sign; of the Bradhaeth folk nothing; the road was mire and even Hlowebourne denied its name and fought them.

But now something came toward them in the murk, a band of riders; they heard them in the distance. They were already carrying their shields uncased on their arms: now they took their swords from sheath and those with lances spurred their horses forward to meet whatever came.

The riders poured over the hillcrest into their midst, shadows in grim red light with neither face nor feature; but the foremost horse had a broad crooked blaze and two white feet—"Hold, hold!" Beorc cried when he saw it, and spears went up and horses shied under the rein as friend met friend in the feeble dawn. "Where's Ruadhan?" he asked Swallow's rider. "Blian, where are you going?"

The young man's face was haggard; he bled from the temple; his armor was battered and it seemed his wits were too. "Beorc—" He held his frantic horse. "They bid us go, fall back—Ruadhan, he held them, run all the way, he told us, and he stayed, him and ten of the bowmen—Lead them back, he told me; the old men and Ruadhan, they bid us go—"

"Let us get up there," Rhys said.

"There be all the Bradhaeth behind us," Blian said. Tears made tracks through blood and grime. "Lord Rhys, there was no holding that—" He twisted about in his saddle, casting a look backward, looked toward them yet again. "We be the first—break the way, Ruadhan

said, if need be; the farmer-lads come after, them as
could double up on horses; and Tuathal and his lot to
put a shield behind them; and since yesterday we've
been battered at—they've broken through, the Bradhaeth has, and four, five times we've had to fight them
since yestereve."

There was silence, only the blowing of exhausted
horses.

"Go," Beorc said heavily. "Get behind us. Move easier. From now the road is safer."

"Aye," Blian said. He drew his horse's head up. He
rode through their midst, he and the men with him,
slowly now; but then he stopped, and came back, and
all his men with him. "We are not cowards," Blian said.

"No," said Beorc. "You are not."

"My cousin was right," Rhys said, riding near, with
Owein and Madawc beside him. "Go back, all you Caer
Wiell folk. Part of us will scatter through these hills, part
of us go west and south; we can at least delay them."

"And what after?" Beorc said. "No. There is no hope
in that. We gather those we can save. Then we go
home—and quickly."

A cry sounded through the hills, a singing they had
heard before at Caerbourne. Horses shied. Men swore.

"Wail all you like!" Rhys shouted at it, lifting his
sword. "Here's iron for you!"

The wailing died away; the grass whispered.

"A horse," Blian said, looking to the right of them.

There was no horse there. The hoofbeats came and
vanished into distance, both unnaturally swiftly.

They gathered at the gate and outside it, a great confusion of horses and people with bundles; but Meadhbh
had none, like her mother, like her brother, like all of
them who had had most and now were leaving it. She
had lost too much to care for any part of it; only she
had brought her tiny box of treasures in her pocket, the
bright bird's feather, the river-smoothed stones, the
things that she had gathered in her walks and rides with
her father. Having lost him she had little longing even
for these things, but thought she might want them and
regret them too late, these small strange objects; the rest
she left uncaring, though she had silver pins and gold,

and fine clothes and a silver ring. She went empty
handed down the stairs, and so did Ceallach, with their
mother, with Muirne, with her bundle of clothes; but
they had their Sidhe gifts about their necks, and the
stones of Caer Wiell under their feet, and the memory
of the tower hall and all its days and nights in their
minds: that was what they took away that mattered.

There would be a guide, their mother had said: if it
had been their father come home, their mother would
have said that first, so they went without real interest in
questions. Their thoughts were all to what was behind
them, to feathers and stones and the thought of their
father sitting in his corner. Now that they were out of
the rooms it seemed to Meadhbh he might indeed come
home, a memory sitting in hall, the Cearbhallain's great
sword on his knees, his hands tending it, the light golden
and flickering on his face. The hall was his now, lost like
him, once the door was shut behind them.

They came down the last steps, where already the air
seemed to tingle with perhaps and might be. The Sidhe-
gifts burned. They looked up: they knew the small brown
creature that turned up in their way without being there
the moment before. "It's the Gruagach," Ceallach ex-
claimed; but it seemed their mother knew this: nothing
today seemed to daunt their mother, not even a Sidhe
before them.

"Gruagach," Meadhbh said; all at once the Sidhe-gift
at her throat ached the more, or her heart did. She
thought of her father and it was as if the world had
started moving again, or she had; as if she had come
alive again—her heart hurt, but she lifted her head and
knew that she had not truly lived between that night and
this, though the world had gone on. Suddenly she felt
surrounded by secrets, finding her mother—her
mother!—meshed with the Sidhe.

Her father had a hand in this. He must have. The
world was bending round them like water round a rock,
disasters flowing past them, and somehow *he* was in it.

"Come," the Gruagach said, motioning with long, lank
hands. "O hurry, hasten. The ponies will come, the fine
horses, all, all."

"Gruagach," their mother said, sharp as she spoke in

hall. "Gruagach, there are more of us—up on the road by Hlowebourne."

It stopped. It hugged itself and rocked, its dark eyes wrinkled up in pain. "O gold lady, the Gruagach cannot reach them. They come as they can. The big red Man, the small dark one: the Gruagach has known them, the Sidhe has touched them, no more, no more can help them. Come! Come! Come! The people, the fine, polite people—no, no delay, come, hurry. It comes, it comes, dark up the dale; I cannot say its name, but the river cannot stop it." It turned, hopped a few paces away, clambered long-armed up the side of a shaggy brown pony. "Haste. O haste!"

They heard Domhnull's voice above the others, shouting at folk to move; he came with Leannan and Cein and Cobhan, a whole troop of the boys leading their father's horse and their ponies and horses for themselves through the press. They stopped suddenly; all about them silence fell, and then cries, as if only then folk had seen the brown man and his pony.

"Come," the Gruagach said, beckoning, "o Man, the Gruagach knows you, far we rode together—come, come, come, the horses too, o hurry! From north and west they come, the dark things, the shadow. Ride, ride, all who can: the Gruagach will lead you!"

Some magic fell on them all: the air was full of it. Folk scrambled for unsaddled horses that did not shy, handed children up that stared wide-eyed, bewildered. Meadhbh took Floinn's mane, trying to get up, and Floinn never flinched when she clambered belly-down and awkward. Her brother was up on Flann. Domhnull helped their mother and Muirne up to a white nosed mare and gave her mother the halter-rope.

"My husband," a woman said; "my son," said another. "How will they find us? Where are we going?"

"To safety!" their mother said, all sharp. "Where they would want you."

"Give me leave," said Domhnull, delaying, holding Iolaire's halter. "I will find the rest of us."

"You have a duty," their mother said sharply. "You have a lord—still; come with us."

"Now!" The Gruagach cried—like some part of the brown pony itself he was, atop its back with knees drawn

up. He waved shaggy arms. The air wavered about them; the murky dawn became gray mist, and the gates were naught but shadow.

A forest lay before them. The Gruagach rode out with his pony and all at once they were moving: Domhnull walked, caught all unwilling and desperate, leading Iolaire beside them. Then he seized Iolaire's mane and swung up, settling himself. He rode a distance in front and then rode back past them, his face showing no sign of the grief that ached in the Sidhe-gift when he was near. "Keep together," they heard him call. "Come, come on, my lady gave her orders. The luck is on us; it always was. Keep sight of one another, call out if anyone should falter."

We have left Beorc, Meadhbh thought. *And Rhys and all the men. I might go to him.* She clutched the Sidhe-gift at her throat, and wondered if she could go so far as a border she had never seen. But *no,* she thought, oddly sure of something with so much pain in it; the way streamed ahead of them, and she was bound with Ceallach: it was no less dire a way, no less perilous than that their men took. It was their way, and she must never leave it.

Beyond the trees soon other creatures followed. Deer moved, ghostly through the mist and darkness; a fox trotted; there were other creatures, as if even Caer Wiell's wild things were going, as if all life were leaving the land. Meadhbh turned and looked back at the column they made, the end of it lost in mist, horses, riders, a few of the men walking, carrying children on their backs. The great oxen and even the cattle were with them, loose, moving with patient care; a flock of sheep walked along beside, quite un-sheeplike sure where they were going. There was the old spotted hound that was almost blind; there were foals and yearlings following after the mares. Domhnull rode back out of the mist, shepherding the line; he had taken a child up in front of him.

The Sidhe-gift burned. Meadhbh held it in her hand, and felt Ceallach near, knee to knee with her as she looked again to the forest ahead. The way grew dark. Trees towered up, and the mist threatened them; but always just in front of them rode her mother with Mu-

irne, and the swishing tail of the Gruagach's brown pony.
She shrugged her cloak about her, feeling cold and glad
that her mother had thought of warmer clothing.

Father, she thought. The thought kept growing in her,
not a hope, but a certainty. She looked back again: she
saw Leannan. The harper rode by Domhnull, and a doe
and fawn walked soberly beside him. A pony carried
Ruadhan's Seamaire, who had someone's baby in her
arms and a little girl behind her. There was Cook afoot,
still in her apron, with two of the scullery maids and a
cluster of the pages. The mist gave them up and took
them back again, and they were there and not there, all
of Caer Wiell. She looked about in fright, relieved to
find her mother still in front of her, with Muirne, the
mare padding along with soundless steps, tame like all
the others. The Gruagach sat backwards on his pony,
watching them all with dark and sober eyes.

The grove had suffered. More leaves had fallen; dark
things had crept close but there was still power here:
Cinniuint still lived, though his leaves were dimmed; so
did Miadhail, and the others. So Arafel came to it afoot
from Airgiod, where Fionnghuala waited. She gathered
what she wanted, took up the armor that was hers, her
weapons. She looked about her, touched Miadhail's
leaves. She wove protection then, a patient spell of different sort, with all her strength, for she was leaving, not
to see this place again: she whispered names, and drew
on all they held; she set the stones to singing, a bright
clashing in the breeze. It was exchange, strength pouring
into the earth, the air, consuming itself at last: its dura-
tion would be brief, after so long ages, a brightness soon
to fade. Flowers bloomed again. Cinniuint budded, blos-
somed; Miadhail put forth new leaves; Ciataich greened
again, and the air was fresh and good. The grove became
what it had been. She gazed on it, fit to break her heart,
and turned then and walked away. One backward look:
her kind had ever been flawed, and so elves had fallen
to fair voices whispering of what had been, what might
have been. But it was time to go.

She turned her face to Airgiod, to shadows Fionnghuala held at bay. "Begone," she said, powerful in this
place, a voice so still the breeze might have drowned it

and so sure it could be heard through thunder. Light
shone about her; it reflected in the waters, moon-cold
and having the sun about it: elvish armor, elvish
weapons.

Duilliath advanced, and summoned other allies. From
Dun Gol they came, streamed through the hills on
horses fleet as nightmares. But there was worse than
Duilliath; there was the Voice that moved them all, and
that was what she sought, to keep its attention on herself, to threaten with what fading might she had, so long
as it should last.

She swung up to Fionnghuala's back. The elf horse
trembled, threw her head.

Now the whisper reached her, as it reached the drow,
coming softly through ghostly trees. It sang battle-joy
and madness, tempted to glory and abandon—but that
too was temptation, calling her forward as the grove
called her to return, to wrap herself in safety, to fall
asleep with it when the end should come.

So they had erred once, to turn to the dragons in their
wars, the ancient, the long-remembering; and this one
was oldest, most persuasive, having spells within his
voice.

This one they had never tamed. This one had seduced
them. *Follow me,* it had said, *drive out Men, yield nothing. Remember pride. Take what is yours. I am power,
more than all my kind; listen to me. Listen.*

"Not I, old Worm," she answered it. "Come find me
if you can . . . if you can break my binding."

The dark rider was there again before them, as he had
been since Hlowebourne, in this day that was no day,
with the sun wrapped n cloud. They had gathered what
of their folk they could, and now they came southward,
daring no pause now, for the Bradhaeth came behind
them; Damh's horsemen scoured the land and columns
of smoke went up from steadings all about the hills.

But that rider was no man of Damh, no Man at all:
Beorc knew him for what he was; and doubtless Rhys
did. As for Owein and Madawc, they lay dead beyond
Hlowebourne ford, and Blian had fallen with them, with
no few others in that hail of Bradhaeth arrows. So it

was not surprising that this rider had joined them, went
with them, behind, before them.

My lady foreknew this, Beorc thought, not for the first
time; and now he dreaded worse, that all else she had
foreseen might have fallen on Caer Wiell, Donnchadh
moving up the dale with fire and slaughter.

Rhys said no word. The small man's lips were set and
hard; he had no curse for the enemy, no threat but his
look, which was black and baneful. From wildness he
had gone to a fey dark rage, and never spoke, not since
Owein fell beside him.

But now the rider paced close beside them, a shadow
on the day, darker than the southron banners.

"You!" Beorc cried, having had enough and caring
nothing whether others thought him mad. "Be off with
you! We have no more to give you!"

He could not see the face; but he saw others looking,
saw haggard southrons half-draw swords, letting them
fall back in uncertainty; but Rhys reined aside, his blade
full-drawn; and then he stopped cold, for other riders
waited in the shadow of the trees beside the road. His
face, went gray. The sword-point wavered.

"No," Beorc said. "Rhys, stay back."

"It's Madawc."

"Caer Wiell," Beorc said, "Rhys, *Caer Wiell.*
Remember."

The southron backed his horse. Its ears were flattened;
its eyes were white-edged, its nostrils wild: it fought the
rein and shied, stumbling in exhaustion. The column
broke in rout; the day dimmed; the rain broke on them
in heavy spatters as they ran.

Still Death stayed with them; and their horses that had
leaped forward in panic ran now with strange slowness.
Hounds coursed beside them, loping dark shapes; in the
hills the Bain Sidhe wailed. Death rode next to them,
the black horse showing bone dimly through its shadow
flesh: the rider turned his cowled head, almost, almost
facing them.

"Death," Beorc shouted at it, rash in desperation, "do
you make bargains?"

"Sometimes."

"Then give my lord back to us!"

"Would you find him?" The pace quickened, and

somehow their horses kept it. The way darkened still, into night and terror. "Then follow: my way, iron can pass. You should remember that, Scaga's-son."

"Beorc!" It was Rhys' voice behind him. "Beorc—gods—"

"Do not falter," the dark rider said beside him, and sped then before them like some eclipse of light and life. "Caer Wiell stands empty; your lady has gone before you to find your lord—Would you have battle? I shall give you that: blood and vengeance!"

Beorc followed; he kept the shadow before him, heard the baying hounds, and Blaze never faltered, dodging along a track of dead trees and desolation, under a moon red and leprous. No stars shone in this might. No wind blew but carried despair with it.

"*Beorc*—" Riders overtook him, his own folk, Rhys, riders shining with pale banners which were the black banners of the sons of Dryw, the darkest hue of the world above made pale by this night.

White things fluttered; something deerlike raced beside them, pursued by the likeness of hounds.

"Stay," voices whispered from the trees, the thickets. "Ahead is pain and wounds. This forest is less dire than the way ahead."

"Your lady will join you here," whispered others. "Your lord has thrown away his chance of worlds to come. Turn aside, follow no more. There is peace in darkness."

"No!" Beorc cried, a voice that had carried across battlefields, but here it seemed wan and weak. "Pay no heed to the voices!"

Then other riders joined them, pale-faced, on horses that moved with soundless stride.

"Madawc!" Rhys cried. "Owein!" A third came close.

"You see I did not leave," Blian Cein's-son said, riding by them.

And others were there, a shadowy band of riders; a plain-faced man rode at their head.

"Ruadhan," Beorc named him.

"You cannot pace us now," Ruadhan said. "We go ahead of you. Look for us at Aescford."

The riders passed them then, pouring ahead of them like shadows in the dark.

Lord Death stayed before them. From Caer Wiell folk rose a shout that shook the shadows. "Follow!" Beorc cried; "Follow!" Rhys shouted. They knew their way now; a madness had fallen on them, that they raced side by side, given a second chance, a hope, a tryst there was no failing.

Before them in the night were fences, sheds, a rambling house with its windows still alight, under a huge old tree. A heron watched them ride by, solemn sentinel along a streambank, water glinting in the starlight—for here were only scattered clouds. Ahead of them the Gruagach slid off his pony and the two ran side by side, the pony jogging, the small Sidhe capering and dancing as if walking were too ordinary for him.

The deer scampered off, with the moonlight on their backs; the fox left them; the sheep went straying, the great oxen too. Only the horses and the ponies kept on their steady pace, and folk began to murmur and to call out to one another as the spell unraveled.

Meadhbh and Ceallach rode up by their mother and Muirne; Leannan joined them with a drowsing rider at his back, one of the youngest pages. Domhnull came up beside them, on Iolaire, and the stallion snuffed the wind and called a greeting to the valley and the barns.

A greeting came back to them. And the doors of the steading opened, pouring out light and people.

"Where can we be?" asked Muirne. "Are they Caer Wiell folk?"

"No," Meadhbh said. There was a shiver in this place, like air before a rain. "It is Sidhe. O mother—"

"We are safe," their mother said, in a faint, faded voice. "I heard once of such a place—Scaga told me of it, when I was young—We are safe here. We must be."

All the people poured after them, up the hill between the fences; and folk met them there at the fence. The foremost of them was a huge man with hair and beard glowing ruddy as the torch he carried.

"I am Beorc," that one said. "And you are welcome."

SIXTEEN

LIGHT AND DARK

Something dire came near. Arafel lifted her head, hearing the difference in the wind, the stillness of the trees. Beneath her Fionnghuala fretted, anxious. "Hush," whispered Arafel.

A darkness drifted close to her in the mist, growling, threatening her a moment, then sinking down to wait. She ignored it. It was not what she had felt.

Other small things had stalked her along Caerbourne. Most of the ill went two-footed, humankind, Men the like of which she had long known, robbers, bandits. She wasted no time on the likes of An Beag. Their ambush, which they had set for Caer Wiell, caught them nothing but a sleepy shellycoat come rattling up out of Death's dark river into Caerbourne's willowed banks, and she had laughed to see them run. A tree had flourished at that laughter, put forth buds, tried life. As for the shellycoat, it dived back again, rattling and grumbling; and the Men had run for walls and safety.

But other men had worked their malice. When she looked into the mortal world she saw the north asmoke, and some of that smoke came from Caer Wiell. In that sight she had no joy at all, in the ruin of the land, the orchards, the place to which she had set her own hand, greening and loving it—less than her own woods, but greatly even so, respecting the Men who had poured love on that iron-sown earth. They had coaxed growth there, where forest had failed, in the land Dun Gol had ruined. Now it burned. Now its folk were homeless.

Those who still strayed, she guided where she could, with what thought she could spare: *West,* she whispered, *go westward through the hills;* and scattered fugitives kept running, abandoning everything but hope of Eald— Men from the border, hurt and lost; a steader's fleet-footed daughter . . . such found the paths, following will-o'-the-wisps and wishes, while things darker than they knew how to fear coursed over the hills and under. They were the drow's dark dogs, hastening to a summons too great for them to wait for such small prey, to a border that was forming.

"Come," she said to Fionnghuala, and they trod their careful way farther—far more slowly than Fionnghuala might have carried her, but no more quickly could she work—touching here a tree that still had strength, drawing constantly on what remained of Eald, deep-rooted in Cinniuint. They were not great magics. She had done as much for Caer Wiell once, in the greening of its fields; but they were deep magics, all the same. They had needed all the might of Don Gol to overcome them thus far and they were, with Cinniuint, the binding on Lioslinn's chill depths. She drew a tide of life in her wake, bringing her Eald with her. Sometimes her workings were fragile as a flower springing up where the elf horse had trod; or a seed's bursting its shell; or a failing tree's few leaves given strength to cling. Her work widened from that beginning, taking its own course east and west, flowed wide, dimming Duilliath's ghostly trees and giving place to a smaller, truer growth. Across the waters of Airgiod lilies bloomed; on Caerbourne's banks an old willow drank a bit and ventured all his fading strength in a few new leaves, and an old oak did the same, mistaking the touch for sunlight. Even beside Death's river unaccustomed flowers bloomed, ghostly white.

Drow could not cross this advancing tide. They fled before it. But now the ill came near, appearing just before her: drow, pale and slim and having shadow and fire about them, so that looking at them was like looking beyond the sunset. A wind obeyed them, chill and killing; it warred with life. Even so a small gold flower bloomed, and threatened all their magic. They yielded backward, wishing to regroup, but she fought them, step by step in her advance.

"Such struggle costs you," one said, whose name had been Suileach.

"There is Cinniuint," the other said. "His roots are deep, but even there things delve."

"Lord Death will perish soon," said the first. "He prospers now. But he will pass when Men do."

"You are corrupt, o Arafel, to cherish such allies as Men and Death. You are Sidhe. It is unnatural."

"Your magic fails. It has Death at its roots. Look on us; remember what you are. No more of war." Suileach drew close. "The green shade might come again to Dun Gol. We might call it again Airgiodach, of silver leaves and stars."

"Do you remember? We were friends."

Against that one she drew the sword; and it vanished, but Suileach remained.

"Like the leaves in the forest," said Suileach, "are our numbers. And this Man—Ciaran is his name. Do you seek him? We have not forgotten him. We can show you where he is."

"Be gone, Suileach!" She extended not her sword but her left hand toward him, with the magic that she wove. "Or yield to *me*—you know what I offer. Memory. Green shade, fair sun—"

It cried aloud, cold as it had grown; it could still feel torment, and the green magic burned it. "We will have these things. We are wiser than we were. Peace, Aoibheil! Who now makes strife, but you?"

"Cold jewels, lifeless wealth, the fall of Caer Righ—these things you wrought! You serve a dark thing that hates us—have you never seen that?"

"Hates us—do Men not hate us? You would have shared the world with them and look how they repaid you."

"Men the Worm corrupted—O Suileach, think! if thought is left you. The dragon used you; it never loved elves or Men. It set one against the other."

"O Aoibheil, does the stone of yours remember? Of Caer Righ you made Dun Gol." Malice came through the voice, so great a malice it almost overthrew her. *"Come closer."*

She had flung up her hand to shield herself; her sword was dimmed; the stone at her breast went cold.

Lioslinn, it whispered, and not Suileach, but another thing speaking through him, in the face of which she shivered. *Hail, Arafel. Come, Arafel; you must keep coming. Others will attend this Man. You and I must meet. The bindings—o weave them with all your strength— come, spend it. Mine will not diminish in the least and yours is fading.*

Even Suileach had faltered. The drow retreated in disorder, recovering then with distance. "Ciaran," it called back spitefully. "Ciaran, Ciaran, Cuilean."

She ventured no attack, no answer. She only stood still, and that itself was effort, in the dread that blew about her. "You cannot touch him," she cried to the empty air. "Try, Suileach. *Try.* When one of us goes *that* way, neither you nor I can hold him."

"Because he desires nothing—recalls nothing." Malice leaped and crackled like fire in the voice from among Duilliath's black trees. "But for you to use him he must keep something of himself—and by that something we can hold him, by that something bind him, in pain and torment, O Aoibheil, as long as yours will be—Revenge, Aoibheil—revenge and patience—these we know. We will give you to the dragon."

"Begone!"

"Shall we go to this Man of yours?"

It vanished. But the voice was slow to fade.

Something touched him, faint and far away. He remembered, then: sometimes he wandered, and even Aodhan lost the way, in the woods that were everywhere across the face of the world, in the maze of his thoughts, the tangle of his desires. Going anywhere was difficult; going the way that he must made his heart ache. But that voice spoke now in a tremor of the ground, in small shudderings as if the earth itself knew pain.

He looked over his shoulder, toward the darker trees, and there were elves.

"Brother," they hailed him kindly, "what do you here astray?"

He had seen them before. They had never come so close. He gazed on them, on faces fair and perilous, into the eyes of Sidhe. They were not Sidhe of the kind he knew. He read cold power there and lust for a thousand things to which elves might be tempted.

"Let go the stone," they whispered. "It hinders you."

Aodhan shied, breaking the spell. Then he could look away, desperately toward the west.

"Let it go, Ciaran Cuilean!"

He clutched the stone within his hands; they held his Name in theirs, and it was hard, hard, not to hear them. There had been a place, a hall, faces that he loved. They wished to show him these things, to bind him to the name that once had been enough for him; they offered these things, and his heart ached, somewhere in the stone.

"Ciaran," they called behind him. "Ciaran!"

Aodhan ran, ran toward the west, spurning the earth beneath him. Small darknesses leaped at him. The dark elves pursued. On and on he fled in his despair, seeming at last to gain a little.

But there was worse ahead. He felt it, like a rift in the world itself, a blight on all that was.

He broke from the woods on a hillcrest, and it was there, in the plain that stretched before him, a darkness the like of which he had never seen, not in the world and not in Death's domain. It lay from hill to hill, and reached toward the sea, casting a pall everywhere, from Caerbourne to the north. The likeness of horses moved in it; it glittered with spears and arms.

He had never felt so naked as on that hillside, where distance meant nothing and that darkness might see as well as be seen. The stone burned with icy cold, and Aodhan faltered, shivering, coming to a standstill. Love, duty, all these things seemed small and far and fleeting against such a thing. The hills lay broken, having given up the secrets at their roots; every tree was slain; every blade of grass had perished in that darkness.

"No, go on," he urged Aodhan, though all the fear that was gathered in him counseled otherwise. "They are at our heels—*go on!*"

You will perish, their doubts assailed him.

And an attention which he had felt but slightly until now turned full upon him.

There, it said, *he is there,* and the hills themselves quaked with it. He was shaken; his bones ached; he looked behind him for retreat and Aodhan broke stride and turned.

But: "No!" he cried then; and the elf horse veered back to westward. He kept going, into the darkening wind. His substance blew in tatters. He heard his name called behind him and before, but it was not all his Name. They thrust at him with weapons, but those nearest him were shadows to him: iron pained but could not touch him. Drow sought him with their cold power: they named Aodhan, and Arafel; and at every naming the stone burned, until there seemed nothing more desirable in that maelstrom than to cast it away, to have relief of pain.

There was another voice. He could not hear what it said, but it reminded him of life.

But, *Ciaran,* the wind sang, *Ciaran Cuilean—what do you here, astray?*

He went forward. Over all that distance, he heard the gulls.

"It is your brother coming," the Dark Man whispered calmly; and Donnchadh, the body that was Donnchadh's, lifted its face from the plain before them. There was little left that answered to that name. That which did remain remembered kinship, and a shiver passed through the flesh, a remnant of fear for vanished reasons, a remnant of jealousy and regret.

She still drives him, said Duilliath. *She moves other things, in other realms. But these are thin shields, King-of-Men, unlike ours. I speak of dragons. Come, let us deal with him.*

My nephew. Donnchadh remembered the reason of his fear recalling that this was not the direction that they had begun, not the thing the Dark Man had offered him when first he let him in. *O gods, what have you done?*

O, sweet self, it is late to ask, is it not? You must meet him. Think, think, how to name him—think of him, and show me that.

The host advanced. They moved slowly, being great in number, being in this world and others. They shed small groups which sped as things could which traveled in one realm only, one band toward the south, to the siege of Dryw in his mountain fastness; another by An

Beag toward Caer Wiell, but these were nothing to the numbers that remained. They had crossed the Caerbourne, and some had drowned in that flood, but advanced the more swiftly in Death's dark realm, yet another front, a portion of the whole.

A pair of youths climbed a hill outside Caer Donn, one fair, one dark, but the hill was hollow and full of promises.

You are not afraid now, the voice told him. *You are Sidhe the same as he, no more—old as the world and direr than Death.*

A pair of brothers embraced outside the King's tent at Dun na h-Eoin. But he was the King now; and his brother—out there beyond the lines.

An Beag has served you well, the dark Sidhe whispered, *even by being there. Caer Wiell has come to us; we had no need to seek it. They have found a place: Men could never take it—but we shall. Your brother's elvish ally . . . her name is Arafel. Remember it. She has favored this haven. But we shall have it. And the last of her will fade.*

Donnchadh's visions faded; he remembered such a valley as he began to remember darker things, prisoned beneath the hills, elvish dead . . . cold and heartless hate, smothered under bindings and hatred of Men and all their doings.

That which had been Donnchadh winked out, lost in that gale of wrath. Those about him had another aspect than they had had, having gone pale and strange; and the horses that bore them had brought their other aspect into this world. Some of his followers had sought to flee, but these were hunted, and no more tried after them. Most had ambition only to be the hunters, which was all they had ever wanted, to give pain and not to feel it. Breandan, one had been, seneschal of Donn; Geannan another; Wulf, new lord of Ban, murderer of the last. They had acquired the calm, cold grace of elves; they had become beautiful, but no Man met their eyes.

Duilliath looked out on the world unhindered now; he smiled with Donnchadh's lips as the black horse leapt forward, a fuath of shifting shape, speeding with speed no horse could match. He drew his tainted sword.

*   *   *

"I know why you have come," said Beorc, the stranger who was so like their own, as they shared his table in the yard beneath the tree, "and I know where you hope to go, lady. You will ask have I seen him; I will tell you no. And all of that is too simple. I will tell you you must not go, and I know you will never heed. You cannot. Your luck is on you. And on all your house. Against that I have no power. I fare as you do. No more will I say than that."

"Riddles," said their mother. She was not wont to raise her voice. It trembled now, so that Meadhbh clenched her hands and stared at this Beorc at whose tables they were guests.

"My mother deserves more than that, sir," Caellach said, who was never wont to say anything at all. He stood up from the table beside Meadhbh, tall as he could. "If you do know—"

"Young lord," said Domhnull.

"I am not any lord," Caellach returned, "My father is."

"You are King," said Beorc quite gravely, and Meadhbh's heart turned in her, for there was a great silence down the table, among the steaders and those of Caer Wiell who had found seats. Others moved about the yard, children shouted, horses called to each other down at stable, being in a strange place; Beorc's own folk went to and fro with baskets of bread and plates of cheese for their guests and they had broached a cider-keg on the porch of the rambling house where folk gathered, finding heart to laugh. But at the table no one stirred.

"Ceallach," their mother said, "sit down, please." And Ceacllach did that, quietly, but he was not quiet, not inside: Meadhbh knew. The elf-gift burned, and the master of the steading gazed at them in a way that made it worse. *He is Sidhe himself,* Meadhbh thought, *or something very like; but there is iron in this place, if not in getting to it. We would not be safe if this man were angry.*

But he was not angry. He gazed at them quietly, holding his secrets, his beard and hair stirring in the wind which came on them then. His wife beside him—Aelfraeda, he called her, who was crowned with gold braids that shone in the torchlight—she sat still and wise-looking. *Like some king,* Meadhbh thought, *and queen. One wants to call them lord and lady. And our father would like them—he always talked with our farmers, of horses and weather and grain*—She found herself remembering home all in one tumbling moment, and gathering up the pieces of everything that had shattered; but sadness came with it too, a different kind of sadness than she had ever felt, a sureness of loss, of change imminent that could not be called back.

He was looking straight at her, in that way the Sidhe had done, and that gaze passed on to all of them.

"Here is shelter," he said, "young King, lady of Caer Wiell, and all who come with you—but outside, all about us, there is evil gathered. Evil is truly what it is, not as Men measure it, Men who want this and that and name their enemies evil, who also have desires. *This* wants nothing. It *is*. What it does it does because of itself." He rose from his place, towering above them. "Once upon a time, my friends—is that not a fair beginning? —the Sidhe came into the world; they came, and loved it, and would not see it change.

"They had wars. They were not without ambition. There were older things in the world. With most of them they warred—but not the dragons. The dragons seemed fair and wise; they shone beneath the sun like gold and brass together. Their wings—ah, their wings, like sun through ice, their wings.

"But they hated change themselves and the Sidhe to them were change. The oldest of the dragons was fairest, but no Sidhe could master him—he was too great, he said. But he would give advice to any who would seek him out.

"After all, he said—the world might change again, and who knew what way his folk would go? Even then a folk arose who shifted from day to day, who brought iron and mortality. Perhaps the dragons would go and serve humankind instead.

"There was nothing fairer than Nathair Sgiathach, prince of dragons.

"There was a prince of the Daoine Sidhe; Duilliath was his name, and of all the Sidhe his was the proudest, quickest temper.

" 'Come,' said the winged Worm. 'I shall bear you on

my back and show you what Men and Death are.' Then
begins my tale. . . ."

The way grew darker, the chaos roiled, and still they
cried his name. Aodhan flew, spurning Aescbourne's
flood, striding long past mortal steeds. But those came
that were not mortal, that were nightmares and worse.

"Brother," he heard. "Ciaran, my brother—" shouted
across the tumult.

Then he looked. He must. A Man rode toward him;
and he knew this Man, through all the toll of years and
other changes too. "Donnchadh," he said. He faced this
rider, weaponless.

A darkness passed between, a sheet of darkness, a
torrent of horned things and hounds, a rider on a horse
that gleamed with bone.

"Lord Ciaran!" someone else cried. "Run! Do not
trust him!"

It was Ruadhan, from the border; it was Madawc and
Owein the southrons, and others came besides, a rush
of shadowed riders. There were border archers—a black
sleet of arrows fell into the press; they were figures that
moved like dream, arrows that fell with deceptive
swiftness.

"Lord!" cried other voices; it was Beorc and Rhys, not
dead—arrived on lathered horses, with haggard faces, and
their weapons solid iron. A troop of riders was with them,
coming from darkened air. "Lord wait for us!"

Aodhan turned beneath him, leaped forward, bearing
him away. Tears were on his face, blinding him; there
was pain again, of loss and grief. But: *"Go!"* he shouted,
consenting, and now the elf horse flew, faster, faster,
faster, till all the world blurred about them to a dim
gray light, till the air smelled of sea and they found the
sun. Water scattered from Aodhan's hooves, splashing
droplets that seemed to fall and fall.

The pain stopped then. "Liosliath!" he cried, flinging
out his hands. "Liosliath! *Liosliath! I have come as far
as I can! Come to me now—the rest is yours!"*

He ceased. That was all.

The elf horse threw its head, it danced and turned; its
rider, having bowed his head, straightened and lifted his

face again toward the shadowed east where riders clashed and died.

He had brought little with him; he touched the stone about his neck and shut his eyes and came more fully into this world. He had neither weapon nor armor; he had not even fully his own shape being in this Man's— Ciaran's—body: but one thing he drew with him by the power in the stone—a silver horn. *Daybreak* was its name: Camhanach. He had no strength as yet to sound it; he was still mazed in the change, mazed as battle swept the plain.

"—Duilliath," he said. And louder: *"Duilliath!" Gray strength* was his essence. He rode forward, as far as Aescbourne's banks. *Liosliath* was his name. Men were being pressed back and back toward him, behind their shield of ghosts; drow came at them, fuaths, every sort of ill amid the darkness. He felt the world different than he had known and dimmer; but from the stone a thousand memories came flooding, a Man's memories, his love, his life, his understanding of the world. He knew all of these Men, the allies of Lord Death. Love welled up in him, and pride, from somewhere in the stone. Hard-pressed, mortal men and ghosts made a wall about him, taking him for their lord: with iron and lives the living defended him; with courage, the human dead.

He lifted the horn and sounded it.

The earth quaked. The drow shrieked one awful cry. "No," one shouted, who lifted a venomed sword. "Fall back—O cousin, you do not defeat us! You only draw new battle lines. And she is there, our cousin, when you release the Worm—A world divided, Liosliath! That is what you win—but Aoibheil is ours!"

They retreated; the lesser evils flowed after them, less swift, leaving mortal allies in confusion and panic on Aescbourne's wooded shores.

"Lord!" Beorc cried. "O gods, my lord—"

A second time he set the horn to his lips and pealed out a note wilder and louder than the first.

The meal was done, the tale of dragons ended. Beorc turned down his cup and looked at them all. There was a scurrying beside him. The Gruagach scrambled up on the bench.

"A thing has happened," said Beorc, gazing at them all. Aelfraeda rose and took his hand. The wind increased. Leaves began to fly from the tree above them as if autumn had come in an instant. They fell onto the table, among the dishes. Meadhbh's heart was beating hard with a fear she could put no name to, but some spell had been on them all the while Beorc was speaking. And now the Gruagach was staring at them with round dark eyes, and her mother's hand sought hers on one side, and Ceallach's on the other. "Lady," Beorc said, "you brought your folk here for refuge. But no one can claim it who does not wish it, for whom it is not the last of hopes. And you cherish other hope than this. So good night to you. Farewell. A horn has blown in Eald; and that summons we may not deny."

Their mother rose; and they stood, dismayed to see the tall steader walk away from them, and all their folk withdrawing. He turned again toward them, lifted his hand as if he would bid them farewell.

Then everything ceased to be—the house, the fences— all the tumult of people. They stood alone, they, their mother, Domhnull—beneath a dead and leafless tree, on a hillside whispering with grass.

"Domhnull!" their mother cried, "O Muirne—!"

Meadhbh shivered. The elf-gift burned and dazed her. There was ill about them, except in one direction.

A horn sounded across the hills. Yet again the air thickened about them and they stood in twilight, on a riverside littered with the dead, where a rider on a white horse stood amid a knot of Caer Wiell and southron riders—

That one slid down from the horse and came to them as others dismounted there in this dreadful place. Their mother stood still, by them and Domhnull—*not our father,* Meadhbh thought, seeing the advancing figure with a new and more terrible ache within her heart. She felt Ceallach's hand clench hers.

He came to their mother, this tall elf so much like their father and so smooth-faced young: he took her hand and knelt and kissed it as if she were some queen. Then he rose again, and their mother's hand left his slowly, with such sorrow as she drew away. Domhnull moved at once to take her arm; Beorc was there glowering, and Rhys—but Meadhbh could never stir from where she stood, gone cold inside as the stranger turned to her.

"Meadhbh, Ceallach," said the elf prince—only that; but when he bent a look on them it felt—there was no word for what it was: the elf-gifts ached with it, which all the world was not and she wanted it to be again.

He walked away; the elf horse came to him. He swung up to its back and it leaped away with him, so swiftly only the heart could see it, away from them, across the river where there were things she never wanted to see. *He is in danger,* Meadhbh thought. Nothing was what it ought to be; there were men lying dead, blood everywhere and such a poison of iron—She wanted to run, run, run, to some refuge where none of this was true; she wanted to strike and make things what they were again, she wanted, wanted, wanted—

Lost, a voice wailed from the river. *O lost, lost—the kind children. I follow, I follow through the waters—I hear; o come! come! o help—"*

She went to that voice; it was so easy. Her brother came with her—or perhaps he had gone before. They were *there* on the banks deep within the trees. They heard their mother calling, "Meadhbh! Ceallach!—o gods—Beorc—"

"*Caolaidhe!*" Meadhbh called.

A horse snorted, close by their feet. They looked and it was a young man clad in nothing but the shadow, with red and dreadful eyes.

"*Seaghda* am I," said that one. "Caolaidhe is afraid. Camhanach has sounded and the world is in danger of it. It brings the day. Come! I will carry you. I have no master. But I will take you up."

The water stirred and sang: a fair face drifted in muddy water, in flood and rapid current. It was Caolaidhe, the each-uisge. "Where river runs, run I. O children, trust me, trust Seaghda—where river runs, run I. Seaghda is frightened too, but he will never say so. Come with us, kind children, come o come—keep us free, no slave to Sidhe or dragon."

"Help us," Ceallach said. "Help us if you can."

Water splashed; a branch snapped. The each-uisge was coming up, trailing weed and water; the pooka came to

Ceallach, moving through the brush. "Meadhbh!" came their mother's voice. "O Ceallach—"

Meadhbh seized the each-uisge's mane. Here was help and power, if she could only tame it. She climbed and it was easy; all at once she was up and the each-uisge was moving, not like a horse but like the river itself, smooth and dreadful; and Ceallach on Seaghda raced beside her.

They ran along the river south, so swiftly—"No!" Meadhbh cried; "Wait, turn back!" cried Ceallach; but the fuaths never heeded. Black and dreadful they ran the rivercourse, turning into another river, and a greater; and now toward the sea, where other horses came, white horses out of the foam, in the breaking of thunder.

Then ships came from nowhere, from the sunlight, wide-sailed, gliding swift as gulls before the wind; and light was all about them.

"They are the Sidhe!" Ceallach cried; and it was as sure in them as their own names. "O Meadhbh, the Sidhe have come to help us!"

A stormwind swept the weary men that held a hill at Aescbourne. That wind scoured their faces, cracked in the tattered banners, brought the smell of green things where was the stench of blood and death. Men swore. "Hush," said Domhnull, getting to his feet. And Branwyn lifted her head, hearing something—feeling it, who had lost too much to feel any hope at all: her heart beat faster—it was the wind, and thunder, and something passed them, skirled about them, raced off eastward, like storm. The sound of horns came pealing, pealing off the hills; and it set a faint cold tingling in her veins, like nothing else she had ever felt. It was Eald; it was brightness, and something of her own, sped safely—*O run*, she wished them, *O run, run, my children!*

"My lady—" Domhnull was by her, gathering her cloak about her. He had armed himself: there was no dearth of weapons on this littered ground. They stood in stormlight now, in thickening murk as sunset faded; perhaps he had seen what had passed him—there was that look within his eyes. "The Sidhe," she said in wild speculation. "Domhnull, did you hear them?"

"I heard it," said Beorc, who came up from the shoulder of the rise. "Something went past, at least. They know it out there too, and they'll move." He pointed into the dark, by the trees along the river. "The enemy is gathering. It's getting dark fast, and that wind on whatever side won't help our archers. I'd advise the horses be loosed. They'll only be confusion when the arrows come. And gods know we've nowhere to be riding to."

She looked at him. If there was any fear in Beorc, if there was grief or weariness or any other thing, he showed none of it. When they had not found the children he had set about ordering this and that calmly, choosing this place, this sandy hill halfway to the sea. He and Rhys and Domhnull—Hold here, he claimed his orders were; and none of them gave any hint in voice or look that they could not hold this place forever.

"Do that then," she said. She wrapped her cloak about her. She felt the earth tremble, heard the baying of hounds.

SEVENTEEN

NATHAIR SGIATHACH

The earth trembled beneath a darkened sky in this edge where magic met desolation. The chill air shook to the peal of a distant horn, and in that moment Arafel's heart leaped in startlement, in joy turned swiftly bittersweet—for this hope came at cost, and she knew that cost. It came at direst risk, wide and wild and shaking the world in its path. Liosliath! A friend had reached the sea and brought hope with the leaving of his life. That was Camhanach sounding, to the peril of the earth.

Eald waked from slumber. Every pact and vow the Sidhe had shaped in their parting from the world unsealed itself, for that was the undoing of it, that horn, sounding Daybreak after dark. An elf had crossed all the barriers with Camhanach in his hand and now the ships themselves might come, the great silver ships, and the herds from behind the wind. She might have wept for terror; she shouted instead for joy, at the threatening hills. "Ceud Failte!" she cried to her kindred as the elf horse danced beneath her. *"O Welcome! Welcome home!"*

The green magic surged. Fionnghuala leapt forward as the echoes of that horn still rang among the hills. The dark Sidhe fled in panic from the hooves, the small ones scuttled under stones and into any shadow they could find. Harpsong sounded. It was memory and magic, echoing across the land in every place that had ever held Harp and harper . . . from Dun na h-Eoin and the ruins

of Caer Wiell to the heart of Eald itself, to magic bound
in elvish jewels and the wind that stirred the trees.

But Dun Gol lay before her now, the way to Lioslinn.
She saw the drow massing like shadow on the hills before her eyes and that shadow grew, turning all her
power. "Turn," she urged Fionnghuala, "turn now! No
farther. We have delayed all we can."

The elf horse obeyed at once, whirling back in the
direction they had come, flying now, striking thunders
from the air, shaking lightning from her mane. There
was hope now in the return of the ships: they went to
find it. They sped along the path they themselves had
made, through the land she had shaped and healed.

But: *Ruin,* the dragon whispered, away to the east, in
the depths of Lioslinn. *Ruin, o Arafel—for* all *bindings
are undone now—and it was Cinniuint bound me. The
tree is dying, do you not feel it? Camhanach has slain it,
and I am free! Your magic fails. Stay and meet me,
Arafel.*

She put a hand to the stone, even while she rode; but
in nothing could she tell whether the dragon lied. Her
magic, Cinniuint's, they were both the same, woven deep
into the land and air and running rivers.

Despair, the dragon said. *Your magic is failing, failing, Arafel.*

Then a darkness swept before her in this land she had
reclaimed. Drow flooded the way before her to cut her
off, between her and Airgiod. They streamed down from
the hills, a host with elvish banners, among them the
standard of the King.

It is your cousin, the dragon said. *Duilliath has found
you. And Cinniuint is dead.*

Fionnghuala checked her pace, turned westward—but
on those hills too were shadows; and from north and
eastward—from the north came drow from Dun Gol;
from eastward the dragon began his slow advance, shap-
ing the land in his turn, binding what he had made until
his path was sure.

"Stay, stay," said Arafel, patting Fionnghuala's neck,
seeking some way yet of escape among the hills. The elf
horse turned this way, that way, striking thunder from
her hooves, shaking herself and throwing her head.
Nothing yet had dismayed Fionnghuala; but now they

were well ensnared, now the circle narrowed, and to the east they must by no means go. Arafel took her sword in hand. There was mist about them. The air grew chill and hushed.

O Arafel, the sweet Voice said, far nearer now, *Arafel, now do you believe? In this little valley neither of us may win—all that we would wish. But is that not the way of things in this wicked world? Turn from them and come to me. I will treat you well, with honor. I will give you place with me, among my servants. Only Duilliath will be greater.*

It did not deserve an answer. Fionnghuala turned as she looked about her. The east lay open, blank with mist, inviting her to try it: in the east Nathair Sgiathach hoped for that, in his ambush in the hills. On other sides the drow advanced, riders on fuaths and black beasts, with smaller evils trailing.

These Men of yours, the silken Voice went on, deep as thunder, soft as summer rain. *O Arafel, did you truly think yourself Men's warden? Bindings you laid on me, but I was not asleep. There was the lord of Damh, my neighbor—it took so little, a whisper in his dreams; then came the massacre at Aescbourne Ford, an end of one King of Men, the makings of another.*

She looked south, gazing on the hate that spoiled the land, on Duilliath and those beside him, who rode on horned beasts beneath their glowing banners.

Murder and murder, the dragon mocked her, still chuckling at her back. *Evald served me well. Yours the Cearbhallain, the harper, perhaps; surely Ciaran Cuilean; but mine were Laochailan, Donnchadh—and Evald's tainted line. The children, the fine fair children—of Evald's blood, of murderer and thief and king—O Arafel, what might I yet make of them?*

"Duilliath," she shouted, ignoring that silken voice. "I weary of you!"

"Put away your sword, cousin," the cry came back at her left. "There is no use in this."

Something must keep the magic, the dragon whispered. *Duilliath knows well that we have gained a prize in you. Any small Sidhe might we have bound—for our Cinniu-int; but you will serve far better, willing or unwilling. Tell me, what would the Daoine Sidhe not venture—knowing you within our hands?*

It was truth: of her a great binding could be made, as great as that which had flourished about the elvish tree, herself and the stone that was her heart, to bind the realms together and govern all their magic. She had made herself like the tree himself, rooted in all realms, and she stood within their reach.

Come, said Nathair Sgiathach, *cast down your weapons. Do you still hope for Liosliath—and the Daoine Sidhe? I have called him for you. And he has come this way—alone. If one of you will serve us, well, what might we make of two? Then let the others come. Dun Gol will be avenged.*

Still the circle narrowed. She saw the green land die, saw leaves blacken. Fionnghuala laid back her ears and paced and fretted, leaped forward as they came—but there was here no shifting, no escaping from realm to realm: they were deep in Eald already and there was nowhere left to run.

It was the harping that had guided Liosliath, the song within the stone. And now it was stilled. *"Arafel!"* he cried and Aodhan ran the harder, ran with all his heart for him, taking risks, finding ways even when trees sprang out of mist, when roots impeded and branches raked and clung. Magic failed and every trial of magic let some green thing die. It was Arafel all his efforts bled, Arafel whose strength now alone sustained Eald, as much of it as survived.

He rode with nothing, nothing but Camhanach and the stone; the Man had worn no armor, carried even less; and in extremity, the Man haunted him. Liosliath remembered the lady's careworn face, the bright eyes of the children—so rich this Man had been. He could never now forget them, this kindred he had despised. He had fought them once, no less than Duilliath; he had slain them, had warred against their iron and their changing of the land—fought for them at the end of his age, when he had no other choice. He had made Dun Gol of Airgiodach, after which no elf found joy in remembering. One by one the others of his kind had hung the stones on Cinniuint's boughs and passed from Eald, when they

could no longer love the world that Men would make
or endure the thing that they had done.

He had been last but Arafel, an age of the world ago:
for pride he stayed, for duty—that Cinniuint should
hold.

But what care we? he had asked her. *What matter, if
Cinniuint should perish, if this world should pass away?
There is no restoring it, Arafel, only waiting—We have
shut that door and sealed it. What gain is left?*

But a Man had shown him the worth in it, shown him
in brief bright fire, a life so blinding swift in days and
nights he had hardly understood it, who had never yet
grown old. An elf had learned something in this land of
seasons: an elf sped now with a Man's knowledge and a
Man's faithfulness and fear; he should never be free of
these things, would never wish to be.

"Arafel!" he cried. He went as wildly as Ciaran would
have done, hearing the dragon-whisper threatening all
that he had loved.

Aodhan leaped the lesser darknesses, dodged the
greater, evaded roots and branches in the flicker of an
eye. Drow loomed before him on beasts of glowing fire,
of water shifting shapes and every sort of horror. They
wished to hold him, but he would not be held: the elf
horse overrode them as they caught and clawed at him,
outraced them in wind and moon-green light.

Life struggled all about him. Now there was grass beneath, now barrenness and dead trees about them, now
clear air, now mist, and the rushing shapes of riders on
black beasts that constantly shifted aspect. Fear was the
venom of their swords, poisoning the Man with the
dread of death, poisoning the elf with doubt and hate—
if they *could* do so; but the Man was dead already and
the elf had no doubts to use. "Go!" he urged Aodhan,
and the elf horse flew beneath him, finding ways through
ambushes, through mist and shadows. He felt battle
through the stone, felt danger and desperation. "O Arafel, *hold fast!*"

A mass of shadows gave way before him. He saw a
clearing, a snarling horde that circled Arafel. Fionnghuala had fallen. Arafel was afoot and bleeding, her brightness dimmed with dark; Fionnghuala struggled to rise,

swayed up, dark-streaked with blood; and sent a horror flying, lightning-struck, while Arafel used her sword.

Aodhan never stopped: the dark Sidhe scattered from his hooves, scattered from his lightning bolts, and the elf horses circled, herding all the shadows, striking and harrying them in retreat until there was space within the grove. Arafel saw him in a moment when the air was still.

Then she sank down on one knee, her hand upon the ground, her head drooping, for her hurts were many and deep. There was pain within the stone, great pain and weariness; he took that pain such as he could, sliding down from Aodhan between her and the dark.

"Liosliath," said a voice from among the shadows. It touched Ciaran's self, deep within the stone.

Donnchadh, the memory said.

But his own: *Duilliath.*

The wind streamed past, but there was no chance of calling: that was the nature of what they rode, with neither rein nor saddle. There was no need of clinging as the fuaths ran, matching strides with the Sidhe host's elvish mounts, black amid their light.

They had left the shore behind, and Meadhbh wept for her mother, for Beorc and Domhnull, for Rhys and all the others—"Stop!" she cried at the elves; and Ceallach: "Help us!"

But nothing would stop the rush that swept them on, and nothing stopped the fuaths.

Now they came up beside the first, the elvish captain. Unarmored he was, like the rest a bowman, his arrows fletched with light. His white horse ran because it would, reinless as the fuaths. He seemed young: there was none of the Sidhe but looked both young and fair: there was no age among them. They were all cold light and dreadful and there was terror about them as they went.

"Turn back," Ceallach pleaded still. "At least leave someone behind to help them!"

"It is not our people," said the elf, "not our war."

"Then let us go back!" Meadhbh cried.

"It is what you bear that draws you," said the elf, "not what bears you."

Meadhbh touched the gift that she wore. *A virtue of finding,* she remembered.

They have no hearts, a whisper came to her. *They hung them all on trees, to forget this land, to forget all that they have done here.*

"That is the dragon speaking," said the captain staring straight ahead. "Do not heed it; shut your ears—"

That elf's name is Nearachd. He has no love of Men. He covets what you bear—would have it if he could. Beware him.

"Be still, old Worm!" Nearachd cried into the air.

What are you to them? What was your father? They killed him. Your mother left to die—

They rode suddenly into mist and trees, shifting and turning now; branches came between. "Keep with us!" Nearachd called. "Keep with us, young Sidhe! Do not listen to that voice!"

Young King without a kingdom, young queen born of thieves and murderers—o hear me, young ones: see what virtue brings—what it brought your father.

Be still, be still, Meadhbh told it. She clenched the elf-gift in her hand and thought of Ceallach beside her, only, only Ceallach. She grew calm and still inside: perhaps it was her doing; perhaps it was Caolaidhe's cold heart. Beside them the pooka ran, at home in this shadow. She saw her brother's face, that it had shed its grief, that it grew very cold, like the Sidhe. Dark things took shape before them: elvish arrows flew at them with light no less dreadful than the shadow.

It is not a place for us, she thought, despairing, and then cast despair away, remembering Liosliath, and the kindness in his eyes. She felt a strength within her hand, imagining a tree—young it was and few its leaves, and yet it lived, lending her something of warmth and life.

Find them, came a voice within her heart, bubbling like waters. *O hold, hold, hold, the precious thing I bear upon my back. Dark water, dark paths, no fuath fears them.*

She feared, feared for all the world, for what was left worth loving, for the east light and the last beauty and the small band standing against the dark somewhere behind them. *Home,* she kept thinking, remembering the faces of her kindred. *Home, home, home.*

Her brother rode beside her. There was a light about him, about her now, and the elf-gifts were that brightness.

The drow's sword was in his hand, tarnished silver, poisoned. His comrades made now a ring about the grove, a darkness cold with hate.

"I would not fight you," said Duilliath, "either one. There is nothing more to gain but wounds—on either side. Give up, cousins."

Liosliath stood watching, every shift of eye; and at their backs the two horses moved, circling, small mutters of thunder, pacing the ring that was all that remained of Eald on the earth. They were protecting Arafel . . . who gained her feet, such as she could.

But the circle diminished more, grass curling black. "Liosliath," he heard her call his name, felt a sword-hilt touch his hand. He closed his hand on it, lifted it; the blade shone bright against the dark.

"We have done this before," Duilliath reminded him.

"Not well enough," he said.

More grass perished. A flower died. The drow came nearer, and there was about him the gleam of sullen fires. The blades lifted, crossed, flickered with subtle passes, feigning ease, feigning movements that led to this side and that.

Faster, then and faster. The line of green drew inward, held. They battled back and forth on that line which he could cross and drow could not; and the wind was blowing, with chill that grew and grew. He heard his name called, heard the dragon-voice.

"Ware!" cried Arafel.

The border yielded all at once, a falling inward. Grass blackened, a flower died and went to dust: Duilliath thrust forward on the instant and Liosliath flung up a hand, took the point, unarmored as he was. The blade slid through his palm, venomed, cold and keen. His own moonbright point touched Donnchadh's armor, found a hold, went deep, and snapped within the wound.

"Brother!" wailed what had been Donnchadh.

It perished. The drow lingered longer, fading even so, a fair cold face, a wail, a passing chill. Horns were sound-

ing, riders were coming; the drow sped in retreat, racing
for Dun Gol.

The trees faded; the mist remained. The riders came
in sudden pallor, and two that rode on fuaths, two their
hair red as sunrise; two steeds black and sleek. Thunder
muttered; elf horses neighed and stamped. There was
light within the grove.

"Arafel!" cried Nearachd, leaping to the ground.
"Liosliath!"

Then Liosliath felt his wound, the cold within his arm,
felt the strength ebbing from him with a flow of blood
dark as the night about them. He wavered on his feet,
and there were friends about him; there was Arafel before him, after so many ages—face to face.

Stay, came a Voice through the earth itself, soothing
and seducing. *O stay, Daoine Sidhe. Do not think to
retreat from me.*

"Do not listen," said Nearachd. "The ships are waiting, Aoibheil. An old dragon will never take us. Come.
There is nothing more to gain."

"Nothing more," said Liosliath. He looked at her with
ages stored up of hope, of waiting, but something came
into the stone that dimmed it all at once. She looked
sadly faded, streaked with darkness that was blood; there
was sorrow in her eyes and heartbreak in the stone.

"You   understand,"   she   said.   "You   would
understand."

"Haste!" cried Nearachd.

"No," said Arafel.

"Would you still hold to this land?" Liosliath asked.
"O Aoibheil, no more."

"But there are Men," she said. "If we quit this world
to go to safety—we leave them to the Worm. We have
weapons. We are not defeated yet!—O cousins, have we
learned nothing? What happens here matters to the
balance."

"If we should fall to it," said Gliadrachan," o Aoibheil, the risk—"

"It matters," Liosliath said. "Aoibheil is right." He
still held the broken sword, heard the dragon coming,
felt cold steal up his arm. He touched the stone he wore,
the dreams that all the others lacked. "I remember. I

remember Caer Righ before it was Dun Gol. We made both. Myself—I stand with Aoibheil."

"Then you do not stand alone," said Gliadrachan, leaping from her horse.

"Not alone," said Nearachd, and others leaped down, setting arrows to their bows.

So they set themselves and waited, and now they heard its tread, felt the shiver in the air. Arafel stood with them, nocked the last arrow that she had. "Stay back from it," Liosliath said, standing by her. "It aims most at you."

She had nothing.

Foolish, said the Worm. *Why struggle? You have seen the world changed from all it was. Would you have it back again? We can remake it. It can be anything we will.*

Then was cold and a time that passed measureless, when nothing stirred at all. The dragon was with them, how they had not seen, came glittering like bronze and gold, moving slowly as in some dream, and as it came it seemed the sun had come into that darksome place and shone, glowing on its scales. Its wings blew away the mist and fire coursed the veins that webbed them. Most of all its eyes—its eyes were no color at all. They drew in the eye that tried to see what in truth that color was, and nothing was there at all.

No need of weapons, said Nathair Sgiathach. *No need of struggle. The leaves will grow again, the lakes be pure, all things that you desire.*   •

Bows unbent, strings eased, their arrows unsped. The Sidhe stood mazed and lost. In the grove the last green perished.

But one, Meadhbh held her elf-gift within her hand. This leaf, this point of light shielded in a mortal hand, it burned, it had warmth when all had failed, when the each-uisge's trembling stilled, as spellbound as the elves. It loomed, this dreadful thing—it wanted them; and the thing she had, that Ceallach had, it spied this now and drew them.

"No," she said, and louder yet: *"No!"* cried Ceallach.

One Sidhe moved. It was Arafel, who crashed to one knee, who suddenly bent her bow; it shook and faltered, the arrow leaped and settled on the bowstring.

The dragon lunged and the arrow sped into its numbing eye. It wailed, it reared, its wings beat in storm and whirlwind as it rose into the air.

It rose and rose, a shadow now, like a plume of smoke above them; it hovered, plunged—somewhere beyond the hills.

The earth shuddered. There was silence.

Then the world began dissolving, blown on winds that blew it all in shreds of light and dark.

There was quiet on Aescbourne's banks, on the sandy hill, quiet in the midst of battle—the enemy fell back, yet another time.

Death was there again. Branwyn had seen him. Rhys had told her who he was, the dark ally who was sometimes here and sometimes not—she saw ghosts; and horrors. There were things horned like stags, clawed like bears, with wolvish eyes, worse even than the enemy. She huddled there behind a wall of shields, of men she loved, of all the world left to her. Weapons flew; arrows struck shields—

And then the silence, as if the world had held its breath. She rose, gazing outward past a sudden gap, for shields had dropped. The air felt strange and cold, the very earth seemed wavering in shadow and in light like light through thickest cloud.

"Where are they?" someone asked. "Where have they gone?"

There were hoofbeats, drawing near. The dark rider had come among them; and suddenly there was nothing else—the hill, their little band, the rider who beckoned.

"Come," Death said. "Your battle now is ended. You must leave this place and quickly. Trust me now and come."

Branwyn held then. Her breaths seemed slowed or her life went quicker: she saw—everything, as if the day had come, when yet there was no color. The rider beckoned yet again.

"Traitor," said Beorc. Shields moved slowly; Domhnull brought his up: she saw this, saw Rhys on his feet again, the Boglach shaft still in his side; but he held his sword, left-handed, facing Lord Death. "There were bargains, and you failed."

"All the world is failing. You have no part in what

will be. Lady Branwyn: come to me. Come now. Come first and bring the others."

"No," she said to Death himself, said it softly, with all her heart; and cried out, for it seemed he tried to reach them. *"No!"* The world quaked. "Go away! Let my people be!"

"You are mine. These folk belong to me." He came closer; his sword was drawn. It shone with baleful fires. "Rhys, Beorc, and Domhnull—"

"Let be!" Branwyn cried. She felt bitter cold, but she descended toward the dark all the same. Men moved slowly about her, in the colorless, dreadful light. They wished to stop her, held out their hands, fading like the world. "Let them go, let them all go and I will come."

"Gods, no!" said Beorc. He thrust up his sword, met Death's.

The iron parted, left him weaponless. The world swirled about them all . . .

. . . And color came, pale at first, like mist on meadows, a touch of green and coolness. The mist gave way to sun, to trees about them, silver-leaved, hills folding about them.

"Beorc!" Domhnull cried. But of all of them, only Beorc was missing from their number. Branwyn was with them still and all the ghosts had gone. They stood few and tattered, bewildered in this place. There was silence, but for the wind. Then—

"Welcome," piped a voice. "O welcome gold lady. O come, come come!"

It was the Gruagach, perched upon a stone. Three ponies waited near him, and a tall piebald mare.

"Gruagach," said Branwyn, "o Gruagach—Come where?"

"You are there already. Follow, follow now. Some ride, some walk, not far, not far, o my Men, my gold lady, follow as you can."

Rhys thought to walk; he could not. His men caught him in their arms and set him on the horse. So they did for others that were hurt too grievously to walk, and the ponies bore them gently.

The Gruagach went before them, dancing as he went

up, up the vale while the hills unfolded. They went with all their strength, with hope in what they should find.

The steading lay before them, just as it had been before—if anything, more rambling and larger.

They came as quickly as they could, some even running at the last, for Caer Wiell folk were streaming down the hill to meet them, and foremost, two red-haired children.

"Meadhbh! Ceallach!" Branwyn cried, and ran to catch them in her arms. Muirne came, and Cein, Cook and Seamaire, Cobhan and Smith and Domhnull's kin—there was no lack of tears; and laughter mingled with them, for all that they had saved.

"The elves brought us," Meadhbh said. "They're here."

Last the steaders came, with the tall, red-haired master and his gold-braided wife.

"Come," said this Beorc, who was very like their own.

"Welcome here, three times welcome. Here is a place better than the last, a refuge from the world for as long as you want to stay."

EIGHTEEN

Farewells

Autumn came and winter, and the Sidhe who had passed near the steading in their riding appeared less frequently and not so near, appearing sometimes in the distance and sometimes passing by night in wind and rush of thunder like some wintry storm.

But with snow deep on steading fields, there still was warmth and crowded comfort, for somehow they had found a place and nook for everyone. The storage on the west of the house was warm and snug; and the ample barnloft held some residents: they nested everywhere, did Caer Wiell folk, like sheltering birds, and began to laugh again now that their dread was past and griefs were healing. Children of Caer Wiell began to play with steading children and make snowball ambushes, while farmers of both the steading and Caer Wiell talked of spring.

And spring came. The snow melted straightway under a pale fair sun, the nights seemed warmer with gentle winds and a strangely greenish moon.

"Planting time," the farmers said; and the plows turned up sharpened and the tools set on the porch.

"Who did that?" Caer Wiell folk asked.

And the Gruagach looked wise.

There was an evening the fuaths came, down by the little stream that wandered by the steading; they appeared as two black horses grazing on the margin; and on another evening a black horse bounded the fences just for sport and raced across the fields.

"That would be Seaghda," said Ceallach, and felt a longing in his heart that was cramped by fences.

Meadhbh felt a longing too, a restlessness beneath this open sky; at night she heard the forest singing, and she thought of the Daoine Sidhe—for they had never left her heart. Indeed a thing had happened with the elf-gifts, and they were never quiet, so she had never been much distressed at the absence of the Sidhe. *Not yet, not yet,* they said to her and to Ceallach within their hearts.

And there was much to do here, with Caer Wiell fok, with their mother, with Muirne and Domhnull, and Rhys as he healed. There was all the steading to find out about, and there was riding to be done, with Flann and Floinn to carry them again. The Gruagach kept them company on the piebald mare, or on the brown pony, and was sometimes there and sometimes not, according to his whims. They learned the heron's name from him, and what the owls were like, who hunted in the barn; they learned all the horses' true names, and where the brook came from, high up in the hills, and where the brook went, which was down to the sea if one followed it.

We shall go there someday, Meadhbh thought, as she planned other things. And always in her heart she knew the wider world was alive and all about them: she knew when the Sidhe were near that no one saw; and most of all she knew that there were two most dear to them who would come when hearts were healed.

Rhys for his part began to fret about, now that he was healed; one found him sitting on the steading porch and staring forestward. And one evening:

"I shall ride south," he said. "The Sidhe said all was well there, but my folk and I—we've all been too long from home. The road at least should be safer."

"I shall ride with you," said Domhnull. "To see these mountains of yours." So Muirne looked up from her spinning by the fire, saying nothing, but with anxiousness.

And Branwyn said nothing, thinking only that such partings were inevitable. That was what she had learned in life. She saw Meadhbh and Ceallach, how a silence came on them in winter and lingered into spring. She marked how grave they could become, how wise their eyes had grown. Ceallach, the folk called her son, quite simply, for he was still a boy; but *the young King* Beorc named him when he spoke of him. King he was, but of what she did not know; and what her daughter was she hardly dared to guess—Meadhbh, Beorc called her, just Meadhbh and nothing more, but with that tone he used on *King*. Meadhbh rode where she liked and nothing harmed her; the ponies came when she wanted and the owls answered when she called to them.

Branwyn did not hope to keep them, or anything else. But she cherished what she had, which was the warmth of friends about her, a hearth to sit by, fences that kept things generally where they belonged . . . but they could keep nothing in nor out that tried. And this was the way of things. Spring came. Her children strayed; Leannan went walking in the hills and sometimes they heard his harping where he played alone, harp-song drifting like magic down the hills, sweeter than ever were the songs he played for them.

And most of all the Sidhe came back with the greening of the land. They would pass on their white horses, usually in the morning, riding from the south.

So Branwyn sat on the porch this morning, while Rhys and Domhnull were about whatever preparations they made, and Smith was hammering away down beside the barn. She counted all her memories and wished—so many things.

"They are coming," said the Gruagach, sitting on the step where he had not been before, and then he was gone again.

So Branwyn stood up, glancing to the south; and her heart lifted with the sight of elvish riders by the stream.

And the whole steading stopped its business when a whole band of such riders turned up toward the yard.

"Bring food," Beorc called, "and drink! Visitors have come!"

Meadhbh and Ceallach arrived from wherever they had been; Domhnull came, all out of breath, and Rhys; and Muirne from the house. But Branwyn stood still, her heart beating hard, her hands clenched together, for it was Arafel with Liosliath.

The riders came up by the fence. All clad in green they were, with gray cloaks, and a light seemed to go about them, like the sun upon far hills. They carried bows and swords, rode reinless, and when they slid down by the gate the white horses vanished in the way those horses had.

Folk gathered, making a ring about them—it was always like that, that folk wanted to see, and somehow felt a silence on them and a dread.

"Rhys," said Liosliath, offering his hand. "Domhnull." It was a familiar gesture, like one they had known and lost. He embraced the children, touched their faces; and on his left hand was a mark like a pale smooth star. They kissed him on the cheek and he touched his lips to each brow.

Branwyn clenched her hands. But then he looked at her, and came to the porch step where she stood. His eyes were gray, not at all like Ciaran's; nothing about him now recalled the Man that she had loved—except a gentleness as he took her hand and touched it to his lips, that, and the look within his eyes: *I was his friend,* it said. *He loved you; loves you still.* "Branwyn," he said. So it was duty that he paid, this prince of the Daoine Sidhe, who was older than the hills about them and younger than the dawn. She was earth and knew it. But he had to love them. It was Ciaran's heart he had, buried deep within his own.

"Come," said Beorc, "come, sit and drink. Leannan, where is your harp? Be welcome, all who come."

So they went to the great table in the yard. The Gruagach had snatched a cake; he had a pot of ale and perched on the fence to watch. A fox rested near, his long eyes dark and wise. There was milk and honey, cakes and ale and cider and mounds of butter yellow as the flowers that bloomed down by the stream. Her children were there, her friends about her, all that mattered in the world; and she felt fortunate again.

"Is it well with you?" asked Liosliath.

"Well enough," she said, "lord elf."

"The fuaths are back," said Meadhbh at once.

"Oh, well," said Arafel, "that was certain." She sipped at the cider and a smile touched her face. "Tame trees," she said.

"We like them," said Beorc. "And tend them."

"Fences," said Arafel in gentle scorn.

"They have stood you in good stead, elf."

"That they have." A light was in her eye and dancing in the stone that hung upon her breast. "I shall bring you wild honey when next we come. The Gruagach likes his saucer and his cup of ale, but most of all he likes the fields, o Man. For that he labors. And still your fences stand; and shall. But there will be singing in your brook come moonrise. And that presence will take no saucers and respect no fences." She set the cup aside. "May your tame trees flourish, neighbor. And those who care for them. The luck is on this place and rests on all who find it."

"On our friends," said Liosliath, whose way it was to say little. "When you go south, I shall go, and show you wonders."

"Might we?" asked Meadhbh at once.

"Not yet," said Arafel. "But someday soon—The gifts I gave you: how do they fare?"

Meadhbh looked distressed then, looked at Branwyn, and Ceallach did, in a way that boded something that foretold secrets and Sidhe things long kept from her. Her heart ached without knowing why, at the look in her daughter's eyes. *I love you,* she thought at her children: she was doomed to love the Sidhe, at last, the green magic, the things that would not be held. "I love you," she shaped with her lips, and thought: *even if I lose you now.*

They brought out the gifts, but no longer leaves—they were stones, filled with light. "They changed," said Ceallach to the Sidhe. "They changed that day."

"So did Miadhail," said Arafel. "He was the only tree born within Man's age. They were his life you bore; no one else could have borne it but Sidhe born within his age. Nothing could have shielded them but mortal flesh. Your burden was more precious than even your father knew. Now they hold your hearts; be careful of them, to keep them what they are."

She looked at Branwyn, a long, gray glance in which the wind forgot to breath and nothing stirred. "This place will hold you while you will. Forever if you like. But take my counsel—go."

"Go where?" asked Branwyn. "Where should we go? Our enemies have Caer Wiell—do they not?"

"Do you not know by now,' asked Beorc beside her, "that you are beyond the sea—that the land has left the world?"

"Then my father—" said Rhys. "My home—"

"Oh, your mountains are here," said Liosliath. "The forest, the plain—all, wherever Camhanach sounded in Men's hearts—all of it came away from the mortal world, and lodged here, forever in faery. The world of Men goes on much as it was. It will not miss this little corner of it. Your mountains, Caer Wiell and Donn— Dun na h-Eoin of the Kings, they stand here—Men might till the fields, heal old scars, live in peace with Eald as it exists here—Have you not seen gulls fly here? They come from behind the wind."

"The realms are divided now," said Arafel. "The dark things and the brighter came into faery at Camhanach's call—we could not take the bright and leave the dark to Men. Caer Wiell might be; many things might be if one summoned them, Branwyn of Caer Wiell."

"Go there," said Liosliath. "Build your Caer Wiell."

Tears burned in Branwyn's eyes so that the Sidhe brightness wavered. "If *he* were here, lord elf—"

"Do what pleases you. He would say that if he were here."

She thought on it, on fields golden in the sun, on steadings far and wide, and something widened in her heart, forever.

They rode out into the morning and Arafel looked back as the Gruagach capered along the fence rail a little distance, as earthborn horses paced them and whinnied salutation to their own.

"Care for them!" Liosliath called. "Take care of them all!"

"The Gruagach is with them," the brown man called. "Fair, O fair in the morning, Daoine Sidhe, and the spring will be long, O long—fare well, fare back, light shine on you, Daoine Sidhe!"

The steading fields lay brown beneath the plow; the hills were turning green and Men had their work before them. Liosliath loved these human folk; there was no helping that.

And if Arafel searched her heart she found a certain joy in seeing the works of Men, neat fields, well cared for, folk keeping their boundaries and observing such swift change within them. They were scattered far, from Dryw in the south to these folk of the steading. At Dun Gol the drow slept fast. In Lioslinn, in those dark waters—no one knew what slept. But Men would wonder, They would be faring here and there through Eald, and dreaming dreams of things not yet done; but that was the way of Men.

Men were chance, and risk, and change.

And sometimes there was greatness about them. Liosliath could say so.

If one thing was certain, thought Arafel on this morning of the world, it was that change might happen; and the Daoine Sidhe rode through the land today in hope of things unfound.

ON NAMES

Ealdwood is a place in faery and has like all such places an indefinite geography. The nomenclature is Celtic and Welsh, with a touch of the Old English, so this particular corner of faery in language and in spirit sits at some juncture of lands where there has been much coming and going of various peoples, likeliest some corner just above Wales.

In this world the speakers of the English are farthest east; the Welsh to the south; and the speakers of the Celtic tongues have their homes farthest seaward; but they mix at Caer Wiell.

As for the elves, they have generally Celtic names, or the Celtic is very like elvish: or what it once was.

Certain of the names like Arafel and Evald which appear early and often, show a different orthography, being somewhat older in the story, and here retained in mercy to the reader. In further sympathy for the reader who may never have dealt with any of these tongues, the following table may provide some aid, and some delight as well, since the names of Eald are, if one knows how to look at them, our own.

There are many sounds to be passed over very lightly: the reader skilled in languages may come closest to the ancient way of saying them just by the hint of them passing over the tongue. But this was very long ago and accents change even over one hill and the other, let alone in and out of faery. For the sake of those readers who only wish to read without tripping on the words,

459

this table will give little hint of these almost silent sounds, paring them away until only the simplest version is left. C will denote the words that are Celtic; W the Welsh; OE the English.

In general, in the Celtic words, be it noted, mh and bh are the sound we call v; ch is breathed, if possible, as in the familiar lo*ch,* a word for lake (but k will do); -gach has often by our day gone to the sound of a hard -gy; and the profusion of vowels has generally a single simple sound at the heart.

In the Welsh most notably -dd- is -th-.

In the English, easiest to render ae- as simple e-.

Where a name has a more familiar form, it will be given in capitals.

And if for any reader this small list provokes further curiosity, Celtic, Welsh, and Old English reference works are not that difficult to find. A good place to begin is, after all, with names, the -nesses and -hams and -denes and -eys that come off modern tongues as if they had no meaning in themselves. Names do have power, after all, that of conjuring images of places we have not seen.

aelf (elf) OE an elf
Aelfraeda (elf red a) OE from aelf [elf] and raeda [counsel]
aesc (esh) OE ash
Aescbourne (esh burn) OE ash brook: ASHBURN
Aescford (esh ford) OE ash ford: ASHFORD
Aesclinn (esh linn) OE ash pool: ASHLIN
Airgiod (ar gi ud) C silver
Airgiodach (air gyud y) C silver leaves
Alhhard (al ard) OE sacred courage: ALLARD
An Beag (an beg) C small
Andochas (ahn-doch-as) C despair
Aodhan (a o dan) C rascal: AIDAN
Aogail (a ogel) C deathshead
Aoibheil (a o vel) C joy: ARAFEL
ap (ap) W son of
Arafel (ar a fel) C from AOIBHEIL, qv.
Ban (ban) C fair, pale.
Banain (ban en) C fair; Bannen
Bainbourne (ban burn) OE fair brook: BANBURN
Bain Sidhe (ban shee) C a Sidhe whose wail portends

death; usually appears near water, usually in the shape of a woman washing bloody clothes; lit. White Sidhe: BANSHEE

Bebhinn (beev in) C Bevin

Beorc (burk) OE birch: BURKE

Beorhthramm (burt ram) OE bright raven

Blian (blin) OE slender: BLINN; BLYNN

Boc (bok) OE deer: BUCK

Boda (boda) OE herald: BODE

Boglach (bog lach) C marsh

Bourne (burn) OE stream

brad (brad) OE broad

Bradhaeth (brad heath) OE broad heath

Branwyn (bran win) W from BRANGWEN (bron win) white breast

Breandan (brendan) C raven: BRENDAN

Brom (brom) OE broom plant: BROM

Cadawg (Ca doc) W warrior; CADDOCK

Cadhla (ca ly) C fighter; CALEY

caer (ker) W stronghold

Caer Damh (ker dav) C stag keep

Caer Glas (ker glas) C gray castle

Caer Luel (ker lel) OE castle keep: CARLISLE

Caer Wiell (ker well) OE spring keep

Caerbourne (ker burn) OE castle brook

Caerdale (ker dale) OE castle dale

Caith (kaith) C battleground: KEITH

Camhanach (kavanak) C daybreak

Caoimhin (ku EV in) C kindly: KEVIN

Caolaidhe (Keely) C thin: KEELY

Carraig (KAR rak) C standing stone

Ceallach (kelly) C warrior: KELLY

Cearbhallain (KER va len) C fr. Spearthrower, victor: CARROLLAN; CAROLYN

Cein (shawn) C old: SEAN: SHAWN

Ceud failte! (ked faly-tya) C a hundred welcomes!—hail!

Ciaran (kiran) C twilight: KIERAN

Ciataich (ketik) C delight

Cinhil (kin il)

Cinnfhail (Kin vel) C head

Cinniuint (kennent) C fate, luck

Cobhan (Kovan) C hill: COWAN

Coille (cully) C woodland: CULLY

Coinneach (Ko en nach) C moss: KENNETH
Conmhaighe (Kon vay) C hound: CONWAY
Cuilean (kul an) C cub: QUILLAN
Dalach (da lach) C advisers: DALEY
damh (dav) C stag; horned beast
Daoine Sidhe (thee na Shee) C the People of Peace; the folk of Faery. Often powers felt to be dangerous and perhaps ill-wishing are named by names felt to be quite contrary to their natures, to avoid calling them up accidentally or offending them by mentioning their true names; again, the feeling is that the true name is not for using. And of course the Daoine Sidhe are not likely to give the true name of all their kin for common use. Other names are the FAIR FOLK, for much the same reason. SIDHE applies to many kinds of creature: the Gruagach by some extension is one of the Sidhe and so are some things very much worse to look on. But the Daoine Sidhe are the highest of their kind.
Diarmaid (der mit) C free: DERMOT
Diomasach (dem say) C proud: DEMPSEY
Domhnull (donal) C ruler: DONAL; DONALD
Donn (don) C brown
Donnchadh (don chad) C brown tartan: DUNCAN
drow (drow) C fr. drough; dark elf
Dryw (drew) W sight: DREW
Dubh (du) C black
Dubhlachan (du la han) C dark: DOOLAHAN
Dubhlaoch (dooley) C dark fighter: DOOLEY
Duilliath (dul yeth) C shadowleaf
Duine Sidhe (dena shee) sing. of DAOINE SIDHE, qv.
Dun na h-Eoin (doon na hey win) C tower of birds
Dun Gol (doon goal) C hill of weeping
each (ek) C horse
each-uisge (ek wiskey) C water-horse; a type of fuath, which entices one to ride and then drowns the victim who is stuck to the each-uisge's back. See: fuath.
Eachthigern (ek ti arn) C lord of horses
ead (ed) OE noble
Eada (ed) OE noble: ED-
eald (eld) OE old
Evald (ev ald) OE fr. AECWEALD, oak wood
Fearghal (fir gal) C valorous man: FARREL
Feochadan (fo ka dan) C thistle

Fionn (fee an) C fair: FINN
Fionnbhar (fin var) C fairhair
Fionnghuala (fin el a) C white shoulder: FINELLA
Fitheach (fay ak) C raven
Flann (flan) C red: FLANN
Floinn (floin) C red: FLYNN
fuathas (fyath-as) C hate, spite; also, a water-dwelling Sidhe such as the each-uisge or pooka. Many baneful Sidhe appear as black animals.
Gaelbhan (gelven) C white
Geannan (gennon) C pale
Gearr (gear) C spear; also CEAR: GEAR-; GER-
Glas (glass) C gray
Gliadrachan (li-ad-ran) C lightsome
Gruagach (gru gy) fr. C: hairy. The word has scattered meanings. As one of the Sidhe, this is one of the working sort who performs homely tasks.
Gwernach (gwer nak) alder stream: GARNOCK
haeth (heath) OE heath: HEATH
Haesel (hay sel) OE hazel: HAZEL
Hagan (ha gen) C little: HAGEN
Haraleah (harley) OE haremeadow: HARLEY
Hlowebourne (lowburn) OE low water
Holen (ho len) OE holly: HOLLIN
Hrothhramm (roth ram) OE famous raven
Hugi (hu (g) i) OE wise: HUGH
Laochailan (la ok lan) C hero: LACHLANN
Leannan (lennon) C cloak: LENNON
linn (lin) OE pool: LYNN
lios (li-ess) C Sidhe fort
Liosliath (liess-lia) C Sidhe fortress; LESLEY
Lioslinn (liess-lin) C Sidhe fort lake
Lonn (lon) C strong: LONN
Madawc (maddock) W good: MADDOCK; MADOC
Meadhbh (mev) C: laughter: MAEVE; MAB
Meara (mer a) C wild laughter.
Meredydd (me re dith) W sea; MEREDITH
Miadhail (mithil) C precious
Muirne (murn a) C hospitality: MYRNA
Nathair Sgiathach (nayer skey-ak) C lit.: winged serpent; dragon
Nearachd (ńyerakt) C fortunate
Niall (ne al) C hero: NEAL

Odhran (odrin) C pale

Ogan (o gan) C youth

Owein (owen) W noble: OWEN

pooka (pooka) C a fuath which appears in the form of a black horse, and which entices one to ride it—to (as the legend runs) disaster: POOKA, also PHOOKA

Raghallach (rahkly) C brave: RIDDOCK; RIDLEY

Rhys (reese) W burning; glory: REECE; REESE

Riagan (regan) C little king: REGAN

righ (ree) C king

Ronan (ronan) C seal ring: RONAN

ruadh (ro ak) C red; red deer

Ruadhan (ro an) C red; rowan: ROWAN

Ruaidhrigh (ru a ree) C red king or deer king: RORY

Scaga (s(k)a(g)a) ()=soft; stand of trees: SHAW

Seaghda (shea) C kingly: SHEA

Seamaire (sha-mare) C shamrock

Sgeulaiche (skel ly) C storyteller: SKELLY; SKULLY

shellycoat a type of fuath which has no skin, but is covered with rocks and shells and debris from river and lake bottoms which rattle as it moves. It drowns its victims.

Sidhe (shee) See: Daoine Sidhe

Siobrach (sov rak) C primrose

Siodhachan (sheehan) C peace: SHEEHAN

Siolta (shel ta) C waterfowl

Sobhrach (sov rak; sovry) C primrose

Suileach (sullak) C darkeye

Taithleach (tul ly) C experienced: TULLY

Tiamhaidh (tiv ak) C drear

tighearn (ti arn) C lord

Tuathal (tu-aly) C northerner: TULLY

wiell (well) OE spring

Wulf (wolf) OE wolf